# Thirst

*To Sandy*

*Insanity or Evil?*
*Reality or Hallucination?*
*You decide!*

*Daria Deschamps*

Y0-BZK-572

# Thirst

*Dania Deschamps*

*White* *Bull*
*Publishing*

Copyright © 2006 by Dania Deschamps

All rights reserved. No part of this book may be reproduced in any form without the permission of the publisher, White Bull Publishing, P. O. Box 1698, Ada, Oklahoma 74821.

Printed in the United States of America

ISBN 0-9769085-0-6

To

My Mother, Olga

The Boys, Jordan and Sylwester

And

The Two Sweet Peas

# ACKNOWLEDGMENTS

Foremost among my supporters has been my husband, George Braly. With degrees in aeronautical engineering and law, as well as an enduring love of classical music, he is my true Renaissance Man. We began as law partners and evolved–I, into a writer of fiction–he, into a source of innovative ideas and a leadership role in the world of general aviation modifications. A wellspring of unending encouragement, "Braly" has my gratitude and my love.

Walter Atkinson, our steadfast friend, aviator, dentist to the LSU Tigers (Go Sooners!), possesses a wide scope of knowledge and a zest for living life to the fullest. He took time to advise, guide me and see this book to fruition. I am eternally grateful.

My heartfelt thank you goes to all who have made this book possible: Aren Howell, close friend and Science Fiction writer, spent hours reading and provided brutally honest criticism. Nancy Shew, Assistant District Attorney for Pontotoc County, Oklahoma, and former English teacher, read, re-read and critiqued the manuscript when she was not otherwise busy prosecuting criminals. Ray Quiett, LPD, LMFT, nationally certified counselor, internationally certified by the ITAA, furnished direction for research into the complex minds of serial killers. Patti Sanders, legal assistant, provides the humor that diminishes stress in our office, inspired the character of Dominique's legal assistant, did the free-hand lettering for the book title and otherwise spent hours reading, editing and spotting inconsistencies. Betty Maeder, another legal assistant in our office, did the final reading and editing. Finally, my beloved aunt, Nora Rojas, a writer in hiding, was there for me, always willing to give her time, advice and positive strokes.

# PROLOGUE

"It was stupid to make threats." There was no inflection, no stress or intonation in the pattern of his speech. "You should have known better." He hit the door hard with his briefcase, effectively slamming closed the room's only exit.

"Just calm yourself, and get out of that raincoat." She kept her voice even to mask the anxiety building deep in her chest.

"Calm down?" he screamed, his face flushing a deep red. "You tell me you're pregnant, demand I give up my life to marry you or you'll expose me, and you want me to calm down?" Neck veins bulged against his deeply tanned skin forming a throbbing road map of high blood pressure. "Don't think I don't know what you've been doing."

She felt outside of herself, a mere observer who wondered if he had remembered to take his medication. The thought dissipated, quickly erased by the harshness of his voice.

"I loved you, bitch!"

She flinched, taken aback by droplets of saliva hitting her face. No one had ever spit at her before. Any other time and place she would have laughed at such juvenile behavior.

"You were nothing more than a common whore. Now you're a filthy blackmailer." His face twisted into a grotesque mask of fury.

She had never seen him like this, and it frightened her. "That's not true. We loved each other." She pleaded, "Just listen to what I have to say. Let me talk to you. Please."

Without a word, he stepped toward her.

Her eyes perceived the glint of a light bulb reflecting on metal. She looked down, saw the knife he carried in his right hand and momentarily froze. "No. . . Please. . . Listen. . . . "

He took another slow and deliberate step, his features set and expressionless.

In desperation, she reached for the phone and never saw, nor heard, him take the final stride.

One arm quickly encircled her still small waist. A final movement and the blade slit her throat.

* * *

He turned her toward him, watching the crimson life force as it spurted from the carotids. His eyes glazed, and he began to salivate, a hungry hyena thirsting at the sight and smell of its kill. Her blood was warm, almost hot. It flowed down his face and hands, first caressing, then searing, sending electrical current coursing throughout his body. The instant he cut her, his cock had stiffened. Now, as her blood spewed and ran, the world throbbed between his legs. He felt the lubrication ooze, as torrid and scalding as her blood. He had to touch himself, to squeeze, to stop the feelings that threatened to erupt.

He lowered her to the floor, surprised and overwhelmed by his sexual response to the ruby red elixir on his lips, by the heat it had created in his dick, by the sudden need for release. No longer capable of reason, he felt only the mass of blazing nerve endings that made orgasm an urgent and inevitable culmination to the deed he had perpetrated. In life, she had never aroused him to such a fevered pitch. Never before had he experienced this exquisite agony. He fumbled with his zipper, thought he heard someone grappling with the door but couldn't stop. He shot his cum on the rug.

# 1

Dominique Olivet awoke as the first rays of morning sun gently brushed her cheeks and tickled her consciousness. She knew better than to resist the Key West sun. Such a soft, golden kiss could only mean it wasn't yet seven. Any later, and the solar caress on her face would be as hot as the breath of an over-anxious lover. She stretched and sneaked a glance at the clock. It read six thirty-five. She smiled. She was always right, unless a cloudy or rainy day confused the issue.

Hours earlier, the night's storm had passed into the Gulf of Mexico. The sun's rising signaled the day-long steam bath to come. She tried to turn her face toward the west and away from the sun for a few more moments of oblivion. It was wasted effort. Long, black hair caught under her shoulder as she attempted to maneuver, and her eyes popped open. "Damn." She was wide awake now, awake and able to recall a time when luxuriating in bed, reliving the events of a previous evening, or contemplating the future, was nothing short of delicious. At this point in her life, bed was for sleep and for sex when she couldn't avoid it.

She rubbed her temples, attempting to erase the veil of forgetfulness separating her from the nightmare she had left behind. She remembered an odor, a vaguely unpleasant smell, yet one with which she was familiar. Unable to bring the memory into focus, she forced herself out of bed and toward a busy day at the courthouse.

She was careful not to awaken Bill who was sound asleep and snoring lightly. She looked at her husband's face, softened by slumber, and wished she could feel more than irritation, and a mild affection, for the father of her two young children. She shrugged away the thought and circled their bed, headed for the shower. As she walked by, lifting her hair into a knot, she bumped Bill's arm. He reached under her gown and tugged on her bikini panties.

"I don't know why you've taken to wearing clothes to bed," he growled with morning desire.

"Sorry, babe. Not this morning. I need to be out of here early. Can I have a rain check?"

"You wouldn't need to leave so early if you didn't insist on going to that God-damned church every day," he grumbled under his breath.

She wanted to yell at him, to tell him that God didn't disappoint her like he did, but instead, she ignored his words. Children shouldn't have to hear their parents arguing. She teased him with undulating hips. "You didn't answer, husband. May I have a rain check?"

"Sure." He was smiling now. "Since you asked so nicely."

She could always placate him with the promise of sex. Bill burrowed back into the pillow. He was snoring again before she stepped into the shower. She loved a hot shower in the morning, the hotter, the better. It made the blood flow until her golden skin turned rosy and tingled. It made her feel alive.

She examined her reflection in the mirror. *Not bad for a thirty-seven-year-old mother of two.* She could easily pass for twenty-five if she cared to lie. She frowned. Maybe she could fool the mirror but not herself.

This tropical city, paradise as she thought of it, was the place of her birth. She had lived in Miami for many years and then in Washington State with Bill, but Key West was home. She had been pulled back as surely as iron is drawn to a magnet. *Once a Conch, always a Conch.*

Conch, pronounced *konk*, was the proper name for the large seashells with the iridescent, pearl-like interiors which, long ago, had been used by inhabitants of the South Seas and the Caribbean as oceanic horns, intended for warnings and welcomes alike. It was also the designation given to the modern natives, a status symbol which automatically entitled you to membership in a loosely defined dynasty that, as long as anyone could remember, reigned supreme in the island city. The best an outsider could hope for was to live in Key West long enough to be considered a fresh water Conch. Conchhood proper was a birthright.

Aside from her children, her happiest memories were of the adolescent years she had spent here. After graduating from law school and giving birth to their first child, she had convinced her husband that Key West was a good idea. The return hadn't disappointed her. The tropics flowed in her blood, and she easily melted into the sizzling days, balmy nights and smelting pot of diverse humanity. It was only here that she could hear the pumping of the earth's heart. Bill, on the other hand, soon came to hate everything about the southern-most city and tourist Mecca in the Continental United States.

She moved quickly, and by seven-fifteen, she had brushed her hair and tied it into a ponytail that would keep her neck bare in the humid heat of a late September day. She wore large hoop earrings and minimal make-up. Her subtle olive skin tone was such that a bit of color on full lips and mascara on already dark lashes was enough to make men look twice. She stared into the closet and pulled out a beige linen suit. Manolo Blahnik stilettos were a concession to the hereditary petiteness she hadn't been able to escape and to the poverty she had left behind. She sprayed herself with cologne and looked in the mirror. Satisfied with the reflection, she gave Bill a soft kiss on the cheek. "Time to get up, hon. You have a nine o'clock meeting."

The tall, lanky man under the covers thrust a pillow over his head and ignored her. Unfazed, she walked to the French patio doors, opened them to Boo, the ninety-five-pound German Shepherd waiting patiently outside, and laughed as the happy dog jumped on the bed, bouncing and barking. Whether he wanted to or not, her husband would soon be out of bed.

Her next stop was up the stairs to Jordan's room. Her son was seven, old enough to be concerned with the concept of privacy. She knocked before going in. "Good morning, sweet pea. Are you about ready for some breakfast?"

"Yeah, man. I'm hungry."

"Yes, not yeah. Ma'am, not man," she chided. "You're watching too much television and forgetting the rules of grammar, young man. Now, what would you like for breakfast?"

"Oreos and milk?"

"Try again, Jordan. You know those things are pure sugar," she said in a more serious tone. "It's either Honey Nut Cheerios or oatmeal. That's as sweet as you're going to get, so make up your mind."

"Oatmeal, I guess." Her son looked glum and mumbled under his breath.

"What did you say?" she quizzed, confident he wouldn't lie.

"I said, 'I wonder if all lawyers are mean?'"

"No, Jordan, just your mom. You know, the person who has to look out for your health and your teeth."

She laughed, closed the door and headed to Daniella's room. The three-year-old was a miniature of her mother. Bill's only contribution was the fairness of her skin. "Wake up, sweetie. It's time to get dressed."

Daniella crawled out from under the sheets, rubbed her eyes and without saying a word walked over, raising her arms to be picked up. Once settled in her mother's lap, she whispered, "Why do I have to get up, Mommy?"

"Because I love early morning hugs and kisses but mostly because Mimi is sick and can't come in. School is out today, and both you and your brother are going over to Linda's."

"Oh, goodie. Is she going to take us to the beach?"

"You bet." Dominique smiled. "Now, let's get you dressed."

***

"Are you sure you can take the day off to watch the kids?" Dominique asked.

"What's the matter? Are you having a guilt trip about this?" Linda gulped down a mouthful of coffee as she spoke.

"Yeah."

"Well, don't. We've been friends forever, and you'd do it for me if you could." She smiled pleasantly. "Besides, versatility and free time are some of the advantages of having a home-based business and being your own boss."

"I *am* my own boss," Dominique retorted, "and it doesn't do me much good. I take less time off, and I work harder than I did in Seattle."

"You really do look tired," Linda volunteered. "Maybe you should ease up a bit."

Dominique shrugged. "I had a nightmare last night. That's all. It wore me out. You know how I hate it when I have bad dreams."

"Don't I ever. So, tell your buddy, what was it all about?"

"Murder." Dominique wrinkled her forehead in thought and then added quickly, "The only thing I recall vividly is a peculiar odor. Whatever the smell was, it's something I'm familiar with. I just can't quite put my finger on it."

"If it wasn't indigestion and it's important, it'll eventually come to you. It always does. You have the gift."

"You mean the curse, don't you?"

"I wish you'd quit saying that." Linda's voice was laced with exasperation. "It's not a sin, you know. You don't initiate it; it just happens. Why do you always assume it's a bad thing?"

Dominique sighed, her face suddenly haggard. "Because I don't know why it happens or what I'm supposed to do with it. When I have one of those dreams, it scares the hell out of me. How would you feel?" She didn't wait for an answer. "Is God the source, the good genie from a magic lamp I rubbed the right way in Catholic school? Or is it something evil enticing me to play with the unknown, just waiting to devour my soul?"

Linda looked dumbfounded. "Whew. I didn't know we'd be getting so deep this early in the morning."

"Well, damn it. Next time, don't ask something you don't want the answer to."

Linda was quick to apologize and turn the conversation in a more light-hearted vein. "I'm sorry, sweetie. I just wasn't expecting that profound a response over decaf. Anyway, I should be the one to call it a curse. After all, your first whopper of a prophetic dream cost me a soul mate."

Dominique managed to laugh. "Right, and I suppose the wife he had waiting at home thought he was her soul mate too?"

"Maybe if you hadn't dreamed her, she wouldn't have existed." Before Dominique could reply, Linda added, "Just kidding."

The odor again filled Dominique's nostrils, and the hairs came up on her arms.

# 2

Dominique made a quick stop at her office and then drove to St. Mary's for morning Mass, a habit ingrained during her days as a student of the religious sisters at the Convent of Mary Immaculate. As a child, she had gone because the nuns made all the children attend. Nowadays, the short daily Mass brought her solace. Her morning ritual fulfilled, she drove down Truman Avenue and turned onto Whitehead Street in the direction of the courthouse.

She opened the car windows and inhaled the trade winds. Swaying palm fronds, the violins of nature's orchestra, played a barely audible melody. Bougainvilleas blazed in a kaleidoscopic array of colors: magenta, red, yellow, coral and lush purple. Elderly homes, long on years, short on paint, but flower-festooned with the brightest and palest hues in nature's palette, stood ready for an island visitor's lens. Almost as a reflex, she stared right, waiting for a view of the Ernest Hemingway house. She strained to see the mansion through the wrought iron gates, the only place where the home wasn't obscured by its red, brick wall and riotous tropical greenery. She had toured the old estate, had seen it from the street thousands of times, yet it never ceased to fascinate her, and she sometimes wondered about the disintegration of the famous family who had once lived there. For now, however, she wondered about nothing; she was at one with the loveliness of her surroundings, and she was content. If she had any regret, it was that she didn't have time to make a pit stop for *café con leche*, the Cuban coffee concoction heavier on cream and sugar than caffeine.

She walked into the courtroom with two minutes to spare. Her client, the daughter of a local, was there to enter a guilty plea to a first DUI. The deal was a good one as those things went. She whispered to the girl, stressing the importance of avoiding a second alcohol related offense.

"Good morning, Dominique," the judge said as he entered the courtroom. Juan Sanchez, Sr. sounded somber this particular morning, not his usual, jovial, Hispanic self.

"Good morning, Your Honor."

She hated being addressed by her first name in the courtroom. Informality diminished the awe one should feel in the halls of justice. In the presence of the court, she referred to colleagues as "Mr." or "Ms." no matter how well she knew them socially; the judge was always "Your Honor" or "Judge," and she never failed to wear a suit. In the beginning, she had been unmercifully teased about being big-city uppity. She had ignored the jibes, continued to act and dress in the manner with which she was comfortable, and after a time, when the novelty wore off, the jokes stopped.

"When was the last time you tried a criminal case, young lady?"

Anywhere else, such a form of address would be considered sexist. Here, it was different. Judge Sanchez thought of her as young, and so he conferred the dubious title. She had heard him on numerous occasions refer to a fellow attorney as "young man." The judge was from the old school, and no one thought it worthwhile to re-educate a man only a year-and-a-half from early retirement. Occasionally, she would respond in a teasing manner; however, something in the jurist's demeanor told her that today was a day to ignore his idiosyncrasies. "I think it was about four months ago, Your Honor." Dominique sighed quietly. The question did not bode well.

"You'll be happy to know you're doing it again. Did you hear about the incident at the Casa Marina last night?"

"No, sir. I listened to music on the way in." Her attempt at lightheartedness did nothing to soften the expression on his face.

"You should have had the news on," the judge said curtly. He glanced towards the court reporter and quickly went on. "Ben Hargrave has been charged with rape and first degree murder. He was represented, for purpose of First Appearance only, by Mr. Johnson of the Public Defender's office. That was held at seven o'clock this morning. The defendant has executed an affidavit of insolvency, and my inquiry into his financial status indicates he doesn't have fifty dollars to his name. The Public Defender's office has a conflict; the defendant otherwise qualifies for representation by the Public Defender, and as of now, I'm appointing Dominique Olivet as his attorney. The State has filed its Motion For Pretrial Detention." The Judge looked over at the court reporter again and noticeably slowed his speech. "This Court has found that proof of guilt is great and presumption of guilt is evident; therefore, Mr. Hargrave is to be detained pending trial. I've set the arraignment for one o'clock on October 18 to allow time for the Indictment to be returned. Is your calendar clear?"

"Yes, Your Honor, but—"

"No buts, Dominique. Not unless someone in your family is at death's door."

"Fortunately that's not the case, Judge, but you know I'm a sole practitioner. A capital case is going to be all-consuming. I won't have time for my regular clients. It's not fair to them, and I can't afford that kind of fall-off in my income."

"It's only going to take all of your time if you let it. This is not a complicated case."

"There's a man's life at stake. That—"

"You're not going to change my mind with that kind of argument. Every other attorney in town has the same problem, and this man needs a defense."

"But, Your Honor, I haven't attended the required ten hours of continuing legal education on capital murder case defense this past year. I think that disqualifies me from appointment."

"It won't work, Dominique. You know this city doesn't have enough capital murder cases for any of its attorneys to fulfill the lead counsel requirements of the Rules of Criminal Procedure.

These are exceptional circumstances and you are more than qualified. I will so find in my order. Now, is that all?"

"Yes, sir."

Dominique handled the DUI plea bargain and walked out of the courtroom, her heels miniature hammers harshly striking the terrazzo floor as she hurried to the elevator, looking neither left nor right. She jabbed at the button on the wall, crossed and uncrossed her arms, and punched the button again.

"Your Type A personality is showing, Ms. Olivet."

"Good morning to you, too," she snapped at the tall, dark-haired man who walked up beside her.

"What's *your* problem?"

"*I* don't have a problem. *You* do."

"What is *that* supposed to mean?"

"It means Judge Sanchez appointed me to represent Ben Hargrave."

"Well, don't get yourself all steamed up. I'm sure we can work something out. No one wants to take this case to trial."

Rolf del Castillo was the State's Attorney, an astute and tenacious prosecutor who would be a tough adversary. He was from a prominent and wealthy Key West family, and rumors floated that he had his eye on politics. She knew the man to be respectful of his position. He would never hesitate to ask for the death penalty, though, as a practicing Catholic, he was personally opposed to it, and he didn't enter into plea bargains, if at all, until the last minute. What on earth would bring the chief prosecutor to be conciliatory this early in the game?

Rolf was no stranger. As a child, she had been one of the needy scholarship girls at Mary Immaculate; yet Rolf, the rich kid, had always been nice to her. They had shared secrets high in a turret of the del Castillo mansion and been each other's best friend. After the morning's courtroom events, however, Dominique didn't like anyone, much less the man who would be her nemesis. Furthermore, she didn't much care for his flippant attitude about this case. "That's just great, Rolf. Why don't we plea bargain the man before I've even spoken to him? I can explain to Hargrave how much better it will be to take your deal rather than risk frying in the electric chair. He should bite on that one, and we can finish the case quickly. Hey, he might be innocent, but who cares, right?"

"I didn't deserve that, Counselor. The man is as guilty as they come. I'm trying to think of a way to spare you both—you, from your first big loss and Mr. Hargrave, from the very real possibility of being sentenced to death." He turned on his heels and was gone down the corridor.

"Rolf!"

If the prosecutor heard, he gave no indication as he disappeared around the corner.

"Shit." Her temper had to be a genetic thing, the result of a Hispanic mother and a French father. She sighed, vowing to herself to search out Rolf later in the day and apologize. In all likelihood, she would need the plea bargain he was waving in front of her, and it wouldn't do to prejudice him against her client because she had bitten his head off.

***

"What took you so long?" Patti inquired as Dominique walked in.

Patti Sanders was forty-something, divorced, with two grown children. She was friendly, cheerful to have around and possessed a kinky sense of humor that had earned her the nickname "Patti Pervert." The woman was also intelligent, had paralegal certification, and Dominique considered her an asset to the practice.

"You're not going to believe this. Judge Sanchez appointed me to represent Ben Hargrave."

"The Casa Marina guy?"

"That's the one."

"Shoot!" Patti screeched like a wounded owl.

"If we find out the victim was shot, that's a great pun," Dominique said dryly. *Good Lord, the law is warping my sense of humor.*

"Why isn't the Public Defender's office handling it?"

"Sanchez said they had some sort of conflict."

"They'll probably ask for the death penalty on this one," Patti went on, her tone a cross between urgency and annoyance.

"Uh huh. Judge Sanchez left no question about that when he appointed me. It's really weird though. Right off the bat del Castillo volunteered he would be amenable to a plea bargain."

Patti ignored Dominique's comment and went straight for the money. "What will we get paid? Did he say?"

"We?"

"Okay. So, how much will *you* get paid?"

"I'll be damned if I know. I can assure you it's not going to be what I would be able to charge a private client. To top it off, there's no chance of any up-front money. I didn't exactly have time to research the question."

"You know what, I wasn't thinking when I asked that. I don't care how much it pays. This is one case we don't want. Plea bargain the guy, and let's close this out."

"Whoa. Hold on a second. What the hell is going on here? I'm getting the impression I'm out of the loop, and I don't like it."

"My God, you don't know do you?" The legal assistant didn't wait for an answer. "Are you ready for this?" Patti's brown eyes danced, and it was obvious she thought she was guarding a juicy morsel.

"Oh, for heaven's sake, just spit it out," Dominique replied irritably.

Patti spoke in a semi-whisper, "Okay, but we need privacy." She tailed Dominique to her office, promptly pulled up a chair and leaned over the desk. "To begin with–"

"Would you please speak up? No one can hear you. *I* can't even hear you."

Patti frowned, but the volume went up a notch. "I'm trying to tell you that the girl who was raped and murdered was Regina DeWalt."

"You're kidding, right?"

"Nope. That's probably why her name's being kept quiet for now."

"Alicia's niece? Is this one of your not-so-great jokes?"

"No, I swear. Even I wouldn't joke about something like that."

Alicia Fernandez was Judge Sanchez' legal secretary and, for all practical purposes, his right arm. Work, a widowed mother, and visits from her niece, Regina, seemed to be Alicia's life. When Regina turned twenty-one, she had come to live with her aunt, and Alicia publicly doted on her. If the rumor was true, Alicia must be devastated.

"Are you sure?"

"My source is good. You didn't see Alicia at the courthouse this morning, did you?"

The nightmare's odor again filled Dominique's nostrils. "No. Now that I think about it, she wasn't at her desk. I was running late and didn't give it a second thought. I should have. She's never not there. No wonder Sanchez was in a bad mood. Good God." She shook her head and stared at nothing in particular.

"Hello, are you still with me?" Patti's voice broke into her thoughts. "I feel badly too," she was saying, "but I didn't think it would hit you so hard. How come I had no idea you were close to Alicia?"

"I'm not, but she's always been nice to me. I liked Regina too, and Alicia thought she hung the moon. Regina was the daughter she never had." Dominique rose and began pacing. "I can't even begin to grasp the loss of one of my children. Can you?" She wasn't really expecting the obvious answer. "There, but for the grace of God, go you or I. It's never crossed my mind that anything could happen to Jordan or Daniella—not here in Key West. We have drunken brawls, dammit. We don't have murders." She shook her head in disbelief. "Regina didn't do drugs. She didn't run with a wild crowd. If it could happen to her, it could happen to anyone."

"For those very reasons, Alicia's not going to feel very kindly towards you when she finds out you're representing the killer."

"*Alleged* killer," Dominique responded out of professional habit.

"Whatever. The point is, unless you can prove Ben Hargrave innocent, you're going to be on that woman's shit list for trying to get him off."

"You know what? I wouldn't blame her." Switching directions, she asked, "Does anyone know why Regina was killed? Does the guy have a criminal record?"

"From what I've heard, the assumption is that she tried to re-sist the rape, and it made him angry. But no, he doesn't have a record of any kind, not even a traffic ticket." Patti looked at her watch. "Not to cut the conversation short or anything, but don't you think you need to get over to the jail and interview the guy? You're tied up all afternoon, and you have the Rodriguez custody modification set for two hours starting at nine-thirty tomorrow."

"You're right. I'm gone." Dominique walked to the door and stopped. "I may not see you before five, so leave the Rodriguez file on my desk. Tell the mom to wear a plain dress, not too much make-up or fancy hair, and remind her to have the kids in their Sunday clothes. I don't want them showing up in tattered jeans or shorts.

"I don't suppose I need to tell you, but as soon as the official death announcement comes out,  see to it that flowers are deliv-ered to Alicia and to the funeral home."

"The usual?"

As a child, Dominique had been told by one of the religious sisters that the white rose was the flower of the Virgin Mary. It had become her favorite, and she sent them for almost every occasion. "You know I'm a creature of habit."

# 3

Dominique passed through the doors of the Stock Island Detention Center and was immediately greeted by Tiny, a man who was anything but. At seven feet two inches and four hundred or so pounds, most people were scared of the jailor and rarely looked him in the eye. There was history between Dominique and Tiny Bishop. It dated back to a time when she was new to the Key West legal scene, and Tiny held a firm, and very public, conviction that the legal profession was no place for a woman. Dominique had won Tiny's respect and his friendship.

"I need to see Ben Hargrave, Tiny."

"Oh, no. Did you get stuck with that one?"

"I'm afraid so."

"Believe me, you don't want that case."

"You're right, I don't, but there's nothing I can do about it. Judge Sanchez wouldn't let me get a word in edgewise. Do you have a room that's clear of vomit?"

It was their joke of the month, and Tiny's laugh boomed. "Yes, ma'am." Only weeks earlier an attorney had somehow managed to meet with his client before the guy was completely sober. According to the jailer, it had not been a pretty sight.

Tiny escorted her as if he were guarding a gossamer doll. Hand on the small of her back, he guided her in the all-too-familiar direction and glared at any trustee who, not knowing better, dared to whistle or make an out-of-line sexual comment. Recipients of his stare, she knew, would pay later.

"It's amazing how the really bad ones sometimes don't look mean at all," the big man commented. He opened the door to the room being used for private consultations. These days, it was a sure bet there would be a freshly opened can of deodorizer. "I'll bring him in and be close by if you need anything."

* * *

Ben Hargrave appeared to be in his late twenties, had a head of lush, wavy, light brown hair, blue eyes and the usual Key West tanned complexion. He was extremely clean. That, in and of itself, was unusual for the regular inhabitants of the Monroe County Detention Center.

She stood to shake his hand. "Mr. Hargrave, I'm Dominique Olivet. I've been appointed to represent you."

His response was direct. "Ma'am, I want to get something straight. Regina and I were to be married. I loved her. I wouldn't hurt her."

She wasn't surprised. Every criminal she had ever represented had sworn his innocence. She had quickly learned that people behind bars were ordinarily not to be taken at their word. The repeat offenders were the most flagrant liars. "All my clients tell me that, Mr. Hargrave. Why should I believe *you*?"

"I don't know. All I can tell you is that I didn't do it." He cleared his throat. "Listen, I need to be out of here so. . . ." He choked and swallowed hard. "I need to be at Regina's funeral."

Dominique felt an unexpected tug of sympathy but spoke harshly. "For starters, Mr. Hargrave, Regina's family isn't going to want you anywhere near them or her. Secondly, even if you're innocent, you're not leaving here any time soon."

Ben Hargrave frowned. "You mean there's no chance you'll be able to get the judge to reconsider and let me out on bail? Isn't it possible to ask for a rehearing?"

It was obvious Hargrave was well educated. He understood the possibility of having a second hearing on the same issue a judge had already decided, and that sometimes, the court would reverse its previous ruling.

"What I mean *is* that in a capital murder case where the proof of guilt is evident or the presumption is great, there is no such thing as bail, period. Frankly, I'd figure on being stuck here for a while."

"You're assuming I'm guilty before you even hear my story?"

She didn't answer the question, instead launching into a rote recitation of words programmed in her memory. "Judge Sanchez set your arraignment for one o'clock on October 18." Hargrave didn't stop her, and she continued the explanation. "An Arraignment is nothing more than an appearance before the court. The Indictment which contains the charges against you will be read out loud, and the judge will ask you how you plead. I presume, from what you've said, that you wish to enter a plea of not guilty?"

"Yes, ma'am," he answered adamantly. Then, looking directly at her, he added, "You don't believe me, do you?"

Her response was cryptic. "It doesn't matter whether I believe you or not, Mr. Hargrave. As your court appointed counsel, it's my job to provide you with the best possible defense. As a matter of fact, even if you told me you were guilty, it would be incumbent upon me to advise you to plead not guilty in order to give yourself time and some leverage to negotiate a plea bargain with the State's Attorney.

"By the way, if it's your intention to take the stand and testify on your own behalf, please do not admit to me that you're guilty. I can't ethically permit you to get on the stand and lie."

"Ma'am, I understand all that. I also understand that you're convinced I'm guilty. I need someone who's willing to help me prove I didn't kill Regina, and there's no way you can do that unless you believe what I'm telling you." Hargrave began pacing. "I'm not stupid, Ms. Olivet, and I have a friend in law school. I'm aware that the burden of proof is on the prosecution, but the fact is that it's the jury who'll make the decision, and unless I convince them I didn't do it, they'll convict, whether the prosecutor presents enough proof or not. I wouldn't have been arrested if I wasn't guilty; that's the mentality of a jury." He turned to stare at Dominique. "You don't want to go out of your way for me, and frankly, I don't want you as my counsel."

Dominique reddened. It was her duty to defend this man to the best of her ability, and she resented him thinking she would do otherwise. Her anger, however, was also partially driven by the truth of his words. He stood accused of murdering a friend, and she had no desire to do any more for him than was ethically necessary. "I'm sorry to disappoint you, Mr. Hargrave, but you have no money; the Public Defender's office has a conflict, and therefore, you're stuck with whomever the court chooses to represent you. That happens to be me. Perhaps if I weren't competent, you could ask the court to replace me, but it so happens I'm a very good lawyer. It looks to me like we're both stuck."

\*\*\*

Dominique's stomach growled, a sure sign it was time to consider what she wanted for lunch. Briefly, she thought about going to the house for a bite of leftovers, but then she remembered it was Wednesday. Bill would be home on his noon break. She settled on Jose's Cantina, a small, hole-in-the-wall Cuban restaurant on White Street. The food was good, and luckily, it hadn't yet been discovered by many of the thousands of tourists who roamed Old Town's narrow streets.

She glanced at an almost cloudless Key West sky, pulled out her cell phone and keyed in the airport number, talking as she drove. "Janie, this is Dominique." After exchanging the customary pleasantries, she said, "I'll be out there right after lunch. Have someone pull the Dragon Lady out of the hangar and leave her on the ramp, please. Tell the guys to be sure the tanks are topped off. I need to fly to Miami and back."

At the corner of Truman and White, she slammed on her brakes for a scooter running the red light. Traffic was always crazy. There were tourists in rented cars, on scooters, on converted golf carts, on bicycles, basically on anything that had wheels. They drove too fast, were drunk or were busy taking in the sights. Any way you looked at it, they created motorized mayhem for pedestrians and other drivers. She cursed under her breath and, for the umpteenth time, reminded herself not to compound the problem by driving and talking on the cell phone at the same time. Several blocks later, she spied a rare open parking place on Petronia and swung quickly around the corner.

She entered the restaurant and greeted the owner's wife, a rotund, jolly woman who always saw to it that the "lady lawyer," as she referred to Dominique, received larger portions than the other patrons. It was a favor Dominique wished she would forego.

She noticed Judge Sanchez and Rolf sharing a nearby table and nodded in acknowledgment.

"Dominique, could I speak to you for a minute," the judge called out.

The last thing she was in the mood to do was talk about Ben Hargrave, but there wasn't a choice. He was, after all, the judge. She walked over to their table.

"Would you care to join us? I'll pay," Sanchez offered.

She voiced the most polite brush-off she could muster. "Thank you, Judge, but I need to file papers in the District Court of Appeals in Miami this afternoon, and I want to double check them while I eat. I'll take a rain check, though. No smart woman would pass up a free meal."

"That'll be fine. You just let me know when," Sanchez said patting her on the arm. He smiled, but his voice took on a serious note. "I wanted to apologize for my abruptness this morning. I imagine you've heard the news by now."

"Yes, sir, I did. There's no need for an apology." They were the right words for the moment, and she meant them. "I understand how upset you must be." The judge sighed, and it registered on Dominique how haggard he looked. Sanchez wore the face of an older man who hadn't slept the night before. "How's Alicia doing?" she asked.

"You can imagine. She did not take the news well." He cleared his throat before going on. "Her mother called the family doctor, and he sedated her." Sanchez shook his head. "I should have been the one to tell her, but the police contacted Rolf first. It fell on him to break the news."

"It must have been hard for you," she said, turning to the prosecutor. "That's a tough job."

"It was."

The tension was intense, and Dominique swallowed hard. "I owe you an apology. If it helps, I'm willing to make it in front of His Honor."

"What happened?" the judge asked, his face reflecting puzzlement.

"I was in a foul mood this morning, sir. I'm afraid I took it out on our esteemed state's attorney. You know how it is when you're born with Hispanic blood. It's not always easy to control the temper." She tried to look humble.

Rolf smiled, and the tension disappeared. "Was that your way of saying you're sorry?" he teased.

"Yes," Dominique answered seriously. "I was completely out of line. You know I have nothing but the greatest admiration for you."

"Don't worry about it. Apology accepted. This morning's forgotten."

"Great," she responded with relief. "Now I'm really famished, so I'm going to leave you gentlemen and do some reading before my table is covered with food."

She retreated to her usual spot near the front glass door where she could keep tabs on the clouds. She had no sooner opened her briefcase than the food appeared: a platter of black beans, yellow rice, roast pork and green plantains fried so crisp they crunched between your teeth and disintegrated into delicious bits of flavor. When she was sure she couldn't consume another mouthful, the waitress laid down a plate of *flan*, a caramelized custard that was Dominique's favorite dessert. She ate every bite, out of habit keeping her ears attuned to conversations at nearby tables. Eavesdropping was a harmless source of amusement.

"I guess you have her vote if you should decide to run," Sanchez commented to his luncheon companion.

"She's a good one to have on your side."

"Are you going to be able to deal with her on this one?"

"We'll just have to wait and see."

The Perfume of Roses,
and the Stench of Death.

# 4

She glanced at the welcoming sign, *Key West International Airport,* and smiled, remembering the first time she had seen it and thought it a joke. She learned soon enough that the sign was correct. Years earlier, Pan American Airlines had launched its first flight from Key West to the foreign soil of Havana, Cuba, forever qualifying the tropical airstrip as an international airport.

All that really mattered to Dominique was that it housed "Dragon Lady," her 1967 V-Tail Bonanza. She had dubbed the aircraft after a defendant against whom she had obtained a civil judgment, the collection of which had made the plane's purchase possible. It was Dominique's toy and after the children, her pride and joy. In the air, she left all cares behind until time constraints or weather forced her to land.

"Key West Ground Control, One One Romeo Tango on the ramp with information Echo. VFR to Kendall-Tamiami."

"Roger, Romeo Tango. Taxi to Runway Nine."

"Roger. Romeo Tango."

She stopped short of the runway, nose into the wind, performed the last minute check and then, "Key West Tower, One One Romeo Tango ready for take-off."

"Romeo Tango, hold short for landing traffic on short final."

"Roger. Holding short, Joey."

She spotted the junior Juan "Chez" Sanchez' Piper Cheyenne coming in. It was hard to miss those brown and orange painted stripes. The combination made for an ugly airplane. She much preferred the burgundy, red and white trim on her bird.

"One One Romeo Tango, taxi into position and hold."

"Roger."

She taxied to the end of the runway and watched for the Piper to exit the runway. Waiting brought back the night's disquieting dream, and she was anxious to be up and gone. With the skill of a military pilot, Chez was quickly out of her way.

"Romeo Tango, you're clear for take-off." Joey paused, then came back, "Romeo Tango, we had a problem with your hangar door. We'll try and get it fixed this afternoon."

                              * * *

"Stop worrying about it, Dominique," Bill said irritably. "Alicia will understand you had no choice." He swerved toward the sidewalk to avoid an oncoming scooter crossing the center line. "Shit!" His fist came down heavy on the horn. "Those things should be outlawed."

Dominique kept silent. When Bill was on his high horse about scooters and tourists was no time to make a point. Instead, she retreated into her thoughts. Once she had been appointed to represent Ben Hargrave, she was ethically bound to use all legal means, including technicalities, to secure his acquittal. She could not permit a man to be convicted, much less executed, without requiring the State of Florida to prove him guilty beyond a reasonable doubt. She hadn't been able to make Bill understand that there was a greater problem than insuring the prosecution met its standard of proof. She needed to clearly demonstrate Hargrave's innocence, or Alicia would never forgive her if she obtained the man's freedom.

As they drove up to the Dean-Lopez Funeral Home, Bill pointed toward the side of the building. Regina's parents, supporting a weak-kneed Alicia, were leaving. Dominique breathed a sigh of relief. She wasn't ready to face the bereaved aunt.

Dominique entered the viewing room followed by a reluctant Bill who was of the vocal opinion that all caskets should be closed. Sitting with a corpse, he said, was only degrees less morose than staring at one.

She approached Regina's body filled with an acute awareness that the spirit of the girl who lay in the ornately carved, mahogany casket had found its eternal home elsewhere. It was disconcerting to be sad at the untimely end of life and yet to feel nothing for the empty shell that remained. Fascinated, she studied the frozen features. She touched Regina's cheek, lightly running her fingers over the exposed skin, hunting for anything that might elicit emotion for the lovely, embalmed cadaver. The young woman's face was cold and rubbery, much like that of a treasured doll from Christmas long-ago. Dominique was about to withdraw her hand, when her fingers, gingerly caressing skin in the manner a blind person reads Braille, transmitted a flaw running from one side of the girl's neck to the other. Regina DeWalt's throat had been slashed.

Instantaneously, all other thoughts were forgotten, and she focused on the laceration. It appeared to be about eight or nine inches in length and had been well concealed by the mortician's makeup. If her fingers hadn't reached Regina's throat, she would have missed it entirely. She was gawking at the wound when Bill touched her shoulder. She jumped, once again surrounded by the nightmarish odor.

"Are you ready to go?"

Identifying the smell seemed particularly important, but each time she reached for the answer, it moved just beyond her grasp. She had to stop thinking about it. If she let go, didn't try so hard, it would come to her. "Yes, I'm ready."

"Good God. I can't believe you touched her."

She didn't bother to answer. It was obvious to her now that this death had not been an unfortunate striking out by a lover in the heat of passion. Whoever knifed Regina intended to kill.

\* \* \*

Later that evening, the aftermath of dinner cleared, Dominique bathed Daniella and made sure Jordan was ready for bed. She telephoned Rolf at home and asked if she could come to his office the following afternoon. Allowable investigative expenses under Florida law were meager; her first step in representing Ben Hargrave would have to consist of asking questions and learning as much as she could from listening. They scheduled a three o'clock appointment.

"Bill, would you read to the kids, please? I need to see about Mimi."

"Sorry, hon. I have papers to go over."

"Just for a few minutes? It's been a long day, and I could really use some help. I've got to get ready for a nine-thirty custody hearing, and I haven't cleaned up the kitchen yet."

"Go check on Mimi," he responded, his face still buried in the newspaper. "Jordan and Daniella can skip their stories for one night. It's not going to kill them. You've got them spoiled, you know."

The heat rushed to her face. "I just don't understand you. We talked about this before we got married. You agreed it was important, yet I'll bet I can count on the fingers of one hand the number of times you've read to those kids."

"You read to them every night so it doesn't really matter, now does it?"

He was irritated. She could hear it in his voice, but she was in no mood to watch her tongue. "That's not the point. The point *is*, I wouldn't have to do it every night if you would do your share. Don't you understand? It's not just their educational development we're talking about. When I read to them a lot of cuddling goes on. They need that same emotional connection to their father."

"Don't be so dramatic, Dominique. My parents didn't read to me, and I've managed to obtain a post graduate degree. I haven't developed any bizarre psychological problems as a result of their failure. Don't you think you're blowing this out of proportion?"

"Right, and you're so close to your parents that if I didn't buy the cards and the presents and remind you to call them on special occasions, they wouldn't hear from their only son at all."

"Look," he said harshly, "if you're tired of doing it, we have well-paid help. Tell Mimi to read to them every other night."

"You just don't get it, do you?" She didn't wait for his answer. "Never mind, I'll do it myself." Her response was caustic, but her eyes filled with tears, and she turned away.

Bill wasn't abusive to the children. Money was no object either. He was a wealthy man by virtue of his paternal grandparents and was generous with Jordan and Daniella so long as they required only money or presents. He simply had no interest in spending time with them, nor did he wish to participate in the details of raising them to adulthood. The marriage was a fiasco. She had admitted that to herself long ago, but it was her fault, not his. He had never pretended to be something he wasn't. After Jordan's birth, she had come to the realization that she had projected her image of the ideal man onto a charming date and married him under that delusion. She reached for the story books.

Once the children were asleep, she crossed the back yard to the housekeeper's quarters. She was hopeful Mimi was well and would return to work the next day. She could practice law, cook, care for the children, run the house and keep a not-very-helpful husband pacified for a short time, but she couldn't do all those things well for very long.

By the time she slipped between the sheets, Bill appeared contrite and promised to take the children flying. It was nothing new. Anytime he wanted in her pants, he was cooperative and sweet.

The Monroe County Courthouse, 502 Whitehead
Street, was constructed in 1890, by William
Kerr who also built the Convent of Mary
Immaculate.

The clock tower, one-hundred feet tall
and boasting an observation deck, was
once the highest point on the island.

# 5

"*In The Name, And By The Authority Of The State of Florida. . . .*" The bailiff read the language of the Indictment.

Judge Sanchez solemnly addressed the defendant. "Do you understand the nature of the charges against you, sir?"

"Yes, Your Honor, I do."

Judge Sanchez had been extremely fond of Regina. Moreover, anything that hurt Alicia deeply had to pain him as well. If not hatred, he had to be feeling anger toward the defendant. Nevertheless, true to his judicial oath of office, he betrayed no hint of personal feelings. He showed Ben Hargrave the same respect Dominique had seen him accord every other citizen appearing in his courtroom. She was impressed by the demeanor of the stone-faced man who sat on the bench. Still, he was personally involved, and he should have immediately made arrangements to step down from the case.

"How do you plead, Mr. Hargrave?"

"Not guilty."

"Very well. Your plea is duly noted. Defendant having waived a speedy trial, this matter is set for trial on January third. Counsel, are your calendars clear?"

Neither attorney indicated a scheduling conflict and the judge rose to leave the courtroom. He was stopped by Ben Hargraves' voice. "Excuse me, Your Honor. I have something to say."

Dominique wasn't surprised, had even anticipated what her client might do. The judge turned to face the young man who stood at her side, and she wondered whether the experienced jurist noticed the slight quiver in Hargrave's voice.

"Yes, Mr. Hargrave?"

"Sir, this lady believes I'm guilty. Under the circumstances, I don't think she's capable of providing me with the defense I need. It's nothing personal against her. I'm sure every other attorney in town feels the same. What I'm asking is for Your Honor to appoint an out-of-town lawyer to represent me."

The judge registered no visible reaction. Instead, he turned to Dominique. "Did you communicate to your client that you thought he was guilty?"

"I did not, Your Honor. Mr. Hargrave stated to me that he thought I believed him to be guilty; therefore, I could not adequately represent him. My reply was that his innocence or guilt was irrelevant, that it was my ethical obligation to defend him to the best of my ability."

"There you have it, sir. Ms. Olivet's word has always been–"

Hargrave interrupted. "Your Honor, what she's saying is true. She never came right out and said she thought I was guilty. It was the gist of what she said and how she said it. If you'd heard her, you would know how she feels."

"Mr. Hargrave, Ms. Olivet has explained to you the nature of her ethical obligation. I'm sure she will live up to that obligation no matter how she might personally feel. I would add that you should consider yourself fortunate to have her as your attorney. She is very good at what she does." The judge nodded to the court reporter. "This court has heard defendant's oral motion for removal of counsel and appointment of an out-of-town attorney. The court has questioned defense counsel regarding the allegation that she is biased against her client. It is the court's opinion that defense counsel comprehends her duty and has always been ready, willing and able to fulfill that obligation. It is, therefore, this court's decision that Ms. Olivet will remain as appointed defense counsel." Judge Sanchez turned to Hargrave. "I will not listen to anything further regarding this particular matter. Now, is that all?"

"Yes, sir."

* * *

Ben Hargrave followed Tiny Bishop into the meeting room, his eyes downcast. Though Dominique spoke to her client, he would not look her in the eye. She knew exactly what he had to be thinking. He was out of his league here on this island of close-knit, cliquish natives. He needed an out-of-town lawyer, one who understood how to work the system and who had enough clout not to be home-towned. He had blown his opportunity in the courtroom. Now, he was at her mercy, and there was nothing he could do about it. She almost felt sorry for him.

"Mr. Hargrave, I've got a three o'clock appointment at the prosecutor's office. By law, he has to provide me with all the information he has regarding your case, particularly anything in his possession that might tend to exculpate you. I believe Mr. del Castillo will do that without requiring me to obtain a court order. I'll be in his office for an hour-and-a-half or so. I suggest that after I'm finished there, you and I sit down and go over the details of what happened. Is that satisfactory?"

He raised his head and eyed her suspiciously. "I don't have a choice, do I?"

"No, Mr. Hargrave, you don't, but you do have a choice whether to make my job easier or more difficult. The harder you make it, the harder it will be for me to defend you. If I were you, I wouldn't cut off my nose to spite my face; however, that particular choice is yours."

For now, there was no more to say. She walked to the door and knocked to get Tiny's attention. As the door opened, she turned back toward Hargrave and, seemingly of their own accord, words flew out of her mouth, "Furthermore, just so we're clear on this, I don't believe you did it."

* * *

Rolf sat at his desk, wading through documents that needed his signature and waiting for Dominique. It did not surprise him that she had come a long way from the impoverished young child who had worn outgrown school uniforms recycled by the nuns. Even as a little girl, she had been as tenacious as she was bright. She had matured into a beauty, worked hard and made a success of her life, yet as far as he could tell, she wasn't any different in personality and temperament than when they had played together as children. He'd had a little boy's secret crush on her then; he had great admiration for her now.

Through the panels that created an oak and glass checkerboard on the front wall of his office, he saw her walk in and stand, talking to the receptionist who guarded the gates to this inner sanctum of the people's protector. "Come in," he called into the intercom before rising to meet her.

Dominique graced him with a smile that lit her face and made him heady. Unnerved by the sensation, he locked his eyes to hers, only then remembering that as an impressionable boy he had almost drowned in those dark pools.

She touched his arm in greeting. "I appreciate your taking the time to go over this with me." She frowned slightly. "You know, I've been back for almost five years, and I think this is the first time you've been able to sit and talk with an old friend."

Her words jarred him back to reality. How much he had wanted to spend time with her he would never let on. Only he could know that his childhood crush had grown up right along with the rest of him. "I don't know what to say. You've shamed me. It's true that leisure has been at a premium since I took office, but there's no excuse for not making time for friends."

He heard his own words as if from a distance. Why, after all these many years, was he so uptight about demonstrating friendship toward her? They had been childhood buddies. Now, she was a woman, and he found himself unbelievably attracted to her. Surely he could handle that. He had never cheated on his wife and wasn't about to begin now. Even if he were tempted to betray his marriage vows, he doubted Dominique would be unfaithful to hers. And, Good Lord, how presumptuous of him to even contemplate that she might be attracted to him as other than a friend.

The frown on her face had again been replaced by a smile. "It doesn't matter, Rolf. I shouldn't have said that. We're all busy. Besides, I've heard you're considering politics. Your plate is full."

His future, as the eldest son of one of Key West's most affluent families, had been assured from birth. He came from wealth and had brains to back up the money. He graduated number one in his class at Notre Dame, went to law school on a merit scholarship he didn't need but justly deserved and then returned to his hometown. He claimed Sarah, the most beautiful and popular girl in town, as his mate. They moved into a wing of the del Castillo home on the Atlantic, and there they were raising three daughters on whom he doted.

While in law school, he made himself personally wealthy by investing in Oklahoma oil and gas leases during the boom and then getting out at the right time. The money he made, he invested wisely. He hadn't wanted the family mercantile business nor had he wanted a solo practice. From the very beginning, he dreamed of becoming a prosecutor, and he pursued that goal with determination. As Assistant State's Attorney, his conviction record was an impressive one. He was indebted to no one, and it was his personal money that funded a well-thought-out, strategic campaign. Within five years he had become *the* prosecutor. Though his family name certainly hadn't hurt him, he had earned the job. No one could deny that. He reminded himself that most people would consider his life close to perfect. He couldn't ask for more.

He didn't want to discuss politics, so he ignored her implied question and brought the conversation back to business. "So, now that you're here, what can I do for you?"

"You know what I'm looking for," she responded, easing herself into the chair closest to his desk. "I want to know everything you do about Regina's murder and why you arrested my client."

Rolf sank into his own chair, leaned his head back and stared at her. "I'm not going to stall and make you create paper, princess. Everything I have access to is yours." Without a thought, he had used the nickname he'd given her years earlier when they played on the sands outside his parents' home. He realized his mistake immediately but thought it less obvious to ignore the slip. "None of it is going to help your client," he explained. "There's absolutely nothing I've come across that in any way serves to exculpate Hargrave. In fact, everything we have only goes to show how and why he did it."

"Well then, fill me in." She pulled a legal pad from her briefcase.

Up until now, he had made it a point not to involve himself in any cases in which Dominique was defense counsel. Criminal cases often demanded cooperation and close contact between the State and the defendant's attorney, and there was no sense in putting himself squarely in the face of temptation. Now, he had no choice. The murder of Regina DeWalt demanded nothing less than the lead prosecutor.

In a monotone, he began reading and paraphrasing from the slim file on his desk. "Sometime after midnight on the morning of Monday, September 21, the police dispatcher received a call from a lady in room 333 of the Casa Marina. The caller said she could hear a man screaming in the room next door. According to the report, she also heard the voice of a woman who, she thought, sounded frightened. The caller was talking pretty fast and hung up without identifying herself, but we have since learned from the hotel register that it was Mary Elizabeth Adams, a tourist from Massachusetts. When we looked her up at the hotel, Ms. Adams told us that after she hung up from talking to the dispatcher, the volume of the man's voice decreased. Although she thought maybe he had calmed down, she went ahead and put her ear to the wall. The tone of his voice still sounded menacing to her. She heard the woman say something about calling the police and then she couldn't hear anything else. That worried her." Rolf hesitated. "I'm sorry to say our police department didn't respond as quickly as they should have. I don't know why but–"

Dominique stopped writing. Her voice dripping with indignation, she broke in. "Oh, come on, Rolf. You *do* know why. They thought it was a domestic dispute, and they didn't want to be bothered. The cops figured if they took long enough, it would blow over, and they wouldn't have to mess with it."

He couldn't argue with her; she was right. "Whatever the reason, according to this report, it took them thirty minutes. When they did get there, they knocked, and no one answered. The day manager opened the door, and Officers Rodriguez and Smithson went in. Your client was kneeling next to the body, knife in hand. Regina was dead from a slash wound to the neck."

"Did Hargrave say anything?" Dominique asked, again making notations as she spoke.

"No. In fact, there is a specific mention by Smithson that the guy seemed to be in shock. He was ordered at gunpoint to drop the knife and didn't do as he was told. Officer Rodriguez says in his report that Hargrave appeared to be in a daze. Rodriguez wasn't sure whether Hargrave would attack him when he approached to take the knife, so he had Smithson keep his weapon aimed, just in case. It wasn't necessary. Your guy remained frozen. Rodriguez literally had to pry his fingers off the knife and then lift him to his feet. He never said a word."

"Just because he had the knife in his hand doesn't mean he did it. It could be—"

Smiling, Rolf interrupted her. "You haven't changed. Always looking for the best in everyone."

"As I was about to say before you butted in," she said, smiling in response, "it's possible Hargrave came into the room, found her dead and picked up the knife."

"Yes, it's possible. It's also theoretically possible the sun won't rise on the world tomorrow, but it isn't very probable, is it?"

"That's also true. But, for the purpose of investigation," Dominique persisted, "it's possible Ben Hargrave came in, found Regina dead and then made the mistake of picking up the knife."

Rolf sighed. She never gave up. "Oh, it's possible. The problem with your theory is that there are too many other factors pointing to his guilt."

She wrinkled her brow and stopped writing to look at him again. "Like what?"

"Don't worry. I'm going to tell you, but first, may I have my secretary get you a cup of coffee? I need one myself."

"I would love a Coke, if that's possible. The real thing, please. Not one of those diet monstrosities."

He chuckled. "That hasn't changed much either."

She had always loved Cokes. To her mother's dismay, she would wake up with a Coke and go to bed with another one in hand.

He buzzed his receptionist, who quickly appeared at the door. "Sally, would you please bring me a cup of coffee. Ms. Olivet will have a Coke, in a glass, with lots of ice."

"Yes, sir."

"You remembered?" Dominique sounded surprised.

"How could I forget? Mama always made sure you never had less than four ice cubes. She knew you liked it really cold, so she would serve it in one of those bright-colored, retro, aluminum tumblers that frost up on the outside. Sorry I can't conjure one of those up."

"Those were the most wonderful Cokes I've ever had," Dominique said, smiling softly. Suddenly serious, she asked, "How is Mama Reina doing?"

"We think, and pray, that she's doing great. She just had her one year checkup. The doctors didn't find any evidence of recurrence. They have her on Tamoxifen, and we're very hopeful at this point."

"I'm so glad. Would you please tell her I asked about her? Tell her she's in my prayers every night."

"I most certainly will. She'll be glad to hear that you asked." He leaned forward across his desk. "She misses you, you know."

"I miss her, too." Dominique choked and cleared her throat. "So, what are these other factors that tell you Hargrave is guilty?"

He forced himself to return to the business at hand. "For starters, although few people in town even knew that Regina had been dating, or seeing, or whatever it was she was doing with Hargrave, it was serious enough that the guy was determined to marry her. We have witnesses at the Casa Marina who will testify to that."

"Who, and so what?" she said quickly. "You don't usually kill someone you want to marry."

"Slow down there. You know not to ask compound questions."

Dominique laughed. "Sorry. Point well taken." She enunciated her next words precisely and slowly. "Okay, so who will testify?"

"You don't have to overdo it." It was the old, familiar childhood game of one-ups-manship. "The janitor for one. I'll get you names before you leave."

"All right, part two. If he loved her, why would he want to slice her throat?"

Rolf went on. "After he came out of his catatonic state, and after being properly Mirandized I might add, your client admitted that a week or so before the murder, Regina wrote him a note and explained she was pregnant. He confronted her in her office. Three witnesses were in the hall and heard some of what was said. One of them was the same janitor I referred to before. He seems to be in on everything that goes on out there. Anyway, all three say they heard your client screaming, and they all agree he said something to the effect of 'You will do what I say, or else.' Apparently, Hargrave has a temper. There's still an unrepaired closet door where he slammed his fist through the wood during that visit."

"Be that as it may, Hargrave wouldn't have admitted anything to you if he was guilty. He's too well educated to have implicated himself."

"You know better than that. Intelligent people do stupid stuff all the time. Besides, he knew there were witnesses to most of what he told us."

She ignored the comments. "Who was the occupant of the room she was murdered in?"

"No one was registered to 335. Supposedly, it was empty."

Dominique was staring at the credenza under the window, and he wondered if she noticed the vase of white roses he had purchased on his way to the office.

* * *

An hour later, tired and disappointed, Dominique left Rolf's office. She had notes outlining what he had gleaned from the police and his investigators. She had copies of statements and names and addresses of witnesses she needed to interview. There was no doubt in her mind that Rolf had told her everything he knew. She had hoped to hear some shred of evidence that would bolster a defense. To the contrary, everything made her client appear guilty as hell. Still, intuition nagged her.

She was exhausted and not quite sure which had worn her out the most, trying to scrutinize every bit of information for possible leads or having to deal with someone to whom she had been close as if he were now no more than a casual acquaintance. She couldn't get through to the man. He would warm to her for a moment, but then, like the local sea turtles, he would retreat into his shell. She had hoped that after today's meeting, their friendship could resume where it had left off all those years ago. The thought had been childish. They hadn't communicated for years and though their professional destinations hadn't differed greatly, their paths had been radically dissimilar. Today's effort at some sort of intimacy was her last.

# 6

It was late when Dominique again appeared at the jail.

Tiny was there to open the door. "Hey, little lady. How'd it go in court today? Any luck in getting out of this mess?"

"No. Not that your newest resident didn't try. He asked the judge to appoint him an out-of-town attorney, but His Honor wouldn't have anything to do with that." Dominique shrugged. "I guess I'm in it for the long haul."

"I don't know why the guy wouldn't want you to represent him. He must not know very much about what goes on in this town or he'd realize how lucky he is to get you."

"Thanks, Tiny. I appreciate that."

"It's you who would be been better off without the likes of him." Tiny's face twisted into something that resembled a snarl.

"Well, there's nothing to do now but try and find a way to prove his innocence."

"You think he didn't do it?"

"All I can tell you is that he says he didn't, and I have a gut feeling he's telling me the truth."

"I sure hope you're right. I don't like to see you wearing the black hat. It looks bad for him, though." Tiny walked Dominique to the softest chair in the office. "You wait here, and I'll take him to the conference room. I'll come back and get you."

Dominique smiled at Tiny's words. It was obvious he was bidding for a few minutes to spruce things up.

* * *

When she entered the room, Hargrave actually smiled at her. "How did it go at the prosecutor's office?" he asked, walking out of her line of vision. She was caught off guard by his relaxed manner and almost missed the seat as he pulled the chair out for her.

"Not very well, I'm afraid. Mr. del Castillo let me see everything he had, but none of it's helpful. If anything, it adds to the already bad problem we have because you happened to be in the room with the knife in your hand. Let's face it, if we were playing *Clue*, everyone would hazard a guess that it was you, in the hotel room, with a knife." As soon as she said it, she could have swallowed her tongue.

"It sounds really bad." He shook his head and his face again took on the familiar tense expression. "I don't know what to tell you except that I didn't do it." He clasped his hands in front of him, wringing his fingers. "I can say that over and over again until I'm blue in the face, but it doesn't do any good."

"I apologize. It was a sick joke. Let's go through this thing and get on top of how we're going to show it wasn't you." She had yet to hear Ben Hargrave's story; Rolf's disclosures only pointed to the man's guilt, and yet, once again, she was voicing a belief in his innocence. She considered herself a creature of logic. That trait had helped her excel on the undergraduate level and later, in law school. She hated the intrusion of emotion into a picture that should be viewed with rationality, and still, in recent years, it had occurred more times than she cared to remember. Stymied by logic leading her in one direction and intuition in another, she had followed common sense at the expense of a knot in her stomach. This time it was different.

Hargrave seemed to relax on hearing her words. "Would you mind calling me Ben? I don't have any friends here, and it would make me feel better just to hear someone refer to me by my given name."

Dominique smiled. "I'll tell you what. I'll call you Ben, if you'll call me Dominique."

"Yes, ma'am."

"And don't call me ma'am." Dominique laughed. "It makes me feel ancient."

"Oh, no, ma'am, I mean Dominique. I was taught to address all women that way. Actually, what I was thinking is that you seem to be awfully young for a lawyer. No offense intended, but you do have some experience, don't you? I mean, the judge said you were good."

"Don't panic, Ben. I've been doing this for fourteen years."

"Thank you, Lord."

Dominique laughed and Ben joined in.

"All right," she said, "Getting down to business, I need to hear from you exactly what happened and not just on the day of the murder. I want the whole story, all the way back to the time you first met Regina. If you don't mind, I'll ask you questions. When we're finished, if you don't think your answers give the whole picture, I'll let you fill in the gaps. Okay?"

"Sure. I'll tell you anything you want to know."

Dominique pulled out her pad. "For starters, when and how did you meet Regina?"

"Well, I don't remember the exact date, but it was in March. Two buddies—George and Sam—and I came down to party and fish." He smiled ruefully. "You know, for the tarpon. The game fish are great here, and there are plenty of pretty girls to have a good time with. It was just a long weekend type thing. Med school doesn't give you a whole lot of time off."

Ben appeared nervous and babbled inconsequential details, but she didn't want to stop him. "Go on."

"We were staying at the Casa Marina. Friday night, they had free eats and drinks around the pool. We were going out night fishing on a charter boat and thought we'd take advantage of the freebies. It might be a while before the captain had time to rustle up something for chow, and we didn't know exactly what his idea of feeding us would be. At any rate—"

"Let me stop you for a minute, Ben."

"Yes, ma'am."

"I told you. Don't call me ma'am. Now, let me see—you have money to stay at a very expensive hotel, to charter a fishing boat and to party all over town. Explain to me exactly why I'm representing you as if you were indigent."

A look of embarrassment came over his face. "I'm sorry, I thought you knew. My parents are rich. I'm not. I just go to school, or at least, I did. I have to depend on a trust fund controlled by my folks until I graduate from medical school. Actually, that's part of the story. They cut me off when they found out about Regina."

"All right. Let's get back to the freebies by the pool."

Ben began to talk and as he did, a haze came over the vivid blue of his eyes. Dominique knew he had slipped into the past.

* * *

It was Friday night, and quite a few of the Casa Marina guests had already had one too many complimentary drinks. Ben and his pals sat around a table enjoying relief from the tension-filled atmosphere of medical school. They were on their fourth or fifth drinks, and their plates were loaded with free food they hadn't yet eaten, but would, just in case the pickings were slim on the fishing boat.

Ben's eyes lit on a willowy, sarong-clad brunette. She was lovely, had Hispanic flair and was definitely walking his way.

"What can I do for you, gentlemen?"

By now, George was drunkenly obnoxious and brazen. "You can do me, baby. How 'bout a little nookie?" he slurred.

The young woman ignored the alcohol talking. "I'm sorry, sir. The Casa Marina Bar has no such drink."

George persisted. "Come on, sweetheart. You know what I want." He slammed his glass on the table for emphasis. The effect was to shatter the table top, sending shards flying in all directions.

The waitress seemed stunned. She didn't say anything, just stared at her hand as blood oozed and began to drip. George laughed uncontrollably.

Ben grabbed a cloth napkin off the table, jumped up and immediately applied pressure to the laceration. "I'm so sorry, miss. George is really a pretty good guy. He's just had way too much to drink before putting any food in his stomach."

"I'll have to report this."

"What's your name?"

"Regina."

"Regina." Ben turned on his most charming smile. "That's a beautiful name. Regina, please don't do that. If you do, we'll be kicked out of the hotel. We're here for a long weekend, just trying to have a good time. I promise nothing like this will happen again. You're much too pretty to be hardhearted." At his last statement, Regina smiled back. Ben felt he was making headway.

"My hand," She looked down again. "It's cut. I probably need to have someone look at it." She grimaced. "Maybe I need stitches."

Ben applied gentle pressure. "Look, see? Your hand's stopped bleeding. It's just a little cut. I'm a third year med student, and I can tell you it's nothing. It just needs a bandage. I happen to have one in my pocket." He dug around and came up with a medicated strip which he applied with the proper drama. "If you don't turn us in, I'll personally make it up to you. I promise."

"The table top's broken. How do I explain that?"

"I'll go in and talk to the manager and tell him that I accidentally broke it. I'll pay whatever it is. And here's a little something for you, for all your trouble." He placed a  hundred dollar bill in her hand.

"I can't accept this."

"Sure you can. If you don't, I'll drop it on the ground, and a lucky someone else will pick it up."

She grabbed for the money even before he finished the idle threat. "What's your name?" she asked tentatively but with a smile.

"Ben. Ben Hargrave."

"Well, Ben Hargrave, just how are you going to make it up to me? I think something a little more personal than money is in order."

"You don't want the money?"  He did his best to look surprised and reached to take back the cash.

"I didn't say that." She had a tight hold on the bill and quickly stuffed it into her pocket.

"I'll tell you what. You keep the money. We're getting ready to go out on a charter fishing boat. How about if we leave George here to sleep it off and Sam and I take you instead?"

"I don't get off work till midnight," she said, regret evident in her voice.

"All right then. We're supposed to be back in by one. How about if I take you out for a very expensive late dinner?"

"There aren't any decent eating places open that late."

"Fine. How about tomorrow night? Dinner, dancing and anything else your heart desires."

\*\*\*

A question from Dominique brought Ben back to the present. Regina, he said, had accepted the offer, and they'd had a wonderful time. After that, when studies permitted, Ben had returned to Key West to see her. It wasn't long before she was in his bed.

A month down the road, Regina had been promoted to night manager of the hotel. Ben was in love and so, he thought, was Regina. He had taken her home to meet his parents in Bal Harbour, a ritzy suburb of Miami Beach.

His mother asked Regina all sorts of questions. Where had she gone to college? Who was her family? What did her parents do for a living? Regina stared at the marble floors, at the circular stairway with the gold-framed family portraits on the wall, and Ben knew she wanted to disappear. Later, when Regina went to bed, Sondra Hargrave told Ben, in no uncertain terms, that the young lady was simply not acceptable. By morning, her husband lending support, she informed her son that Regina was not to visit again. If Ben wished his generous allowance to continue, he was to give up trips to Key West, and he wasn't to see Regina DeWalt.

Ben, however, hadn't stopped seeing Regina and had continued his trips to the Keys.

\*\*\*

"About a month and a half ago, my parents retaliated by cutting off the money."

"So, what did you do?"

"I took an emergency leave from school, borrowed a hundred bucks from Sam and headed here."

"Key West is an expensive place to hang out." She was only pointing out the obvious. "A hundred dollars doesn't go far. How did you live when you got to town?"

"I found a job at Margaritaville, and Regina let me live at the Casa Marina."

"You were paying for a room?" Dominique asked incredulously.

"No way." He looked askance at her. "I didn't pay. She would just move me from room to room, depending on where she needed to put guests."

"Did anybody else know about this arrangement?"

"Well, the janitors and some of the maids knew I was living there. I can't say if they were aware of the financial arrangements, but they had to have been suspicious because Regina was moving me every couple of days. You wouldn't do that with a regular paying customer." He stopped, then added, "And I presume the day manager, who was a friend of hers, must have been in on it. Otherwise, I don't know how we could have gotten away with it for very long."

"What happened after that?" Dominique prompted.

"I wanted to get married right away. I figured we could live on Regina's salary and save mine so I could go back to school next semester. I figured it would be rough for a few years, but we could make it. By the time I turned thirty, I would be practicing medicine, the trust would terminate, and the bulk of it would be turned over to me. We'd fly high."

"So, why didn't you get married?" Dominique was intensely interested in the answer.

"Regina said she loved me, but she couldn't marry me."

"That doesn't make sense. Did she say why she couldn't marry you?"

"Oh, yeah, she told me, all right," Ben said in a caustic tone. "She thought she was pregnant by somebody else."

This wasn't sounding good. "You must have been furious," she prompted again.

"That's an understatement," he said, looking straight at her. "I'm not proud of what happened, but I was angry. What man wouldn't be? I screamed obscenities at Regina. The whole place must have heard." He looked at her suspiciously. "Hasn't anyone said anything to you about that day?"

Dominique smiled wanly. "As a matter of fact, at least three people heard it and told the detectives. According to those witnesses, you yelled that she better do what you said 'or else'."

Ben fell silent for a moment, his forehead scrunched in thought. "Oh, Good Lord. I had forgotten that part. I just wanted to know what was going on. I was mad as hell. The 'or else' only meant I was ready to walk out and never come back." He hung his head. "Regina finally broke down and told me that when she met me, she was having an affair with a married man. She said she had been involved with him for years. Even before she met me, she had wanted to break it off, but he wouldn't let her; he threatened to tell her aunt what had been going on if she didn't continue."

"That doesn't seem like much of a threat, particularly when he was a married man who probably didn't want anyone to know. Sounds like pure bluff to me."

Ben nodded his head in agreement. "I don't think Regina was thinking logically at that point. She was Catholic. Her whole family is. She loved her aunt dearly and was afraid if Alicia found out, she would disown her. She kept on sleeping with the guy."

"Did it stop or was she having sex with both of you?" She didn't wait for an answer. "By the way, who was this guy?" It was another one of those compound questions she would never ask in the courtroom but slipped in otherwise.

Ben shrugged. "Don't know who the guy was. She would never tell me, but shortly after we met, she found out she was pregnant. She told the bastard, and he dropped her like a hot potato."

"And all you did was scream at her? Didn't you want to hurt her when you found out about all of this?" Dominique asked, staring into her client's eyes.

Ben's face reddened. "I don't hit a woman for any reason. I called her a whore and some other not very pretty names." He looked sheepish. "For a second, I did want to lash out at her. Instead, I slammed my fist through a closet door and took off."

"Where did you go? What did you do?" Dominique was weighing every word against what Rolf had told her.

"I went to Sam's place and stayed there for a couple of days. I was trying to get my head on straight."

"What then?"

"You have to understand that I had fallen head-over-heels in love the very night I met Regina. I didn't want to lose her." An unchecked tear rolled down his face. "I decided that if she had been sleeping with him for years and nothing happened, and then she comes up pregnant right after we start having sex, the baby was probably mine. She had her reasons for getting involved with that guy, but they were in the past. She was finished with him. I decided we could make a good life together. I went back and told her that—over and over—until it finally sank into her head that I loved her and was going to marry her, no matter what."

"Did you ask for a paternity test?"

"No. She offered, but I didn't want it. I had made up my mind the baby was mine, and that's the way things were going to be." His cheeks were now wet, but Ben paid no heed.

"Did she agree to marry you then?"

"Oh, God, yes. She was so happy. I wish you could have seen her face. We were both happy and planning the rest of our lives, trying to decide what the baby's name would be, depending on whether it was a boy or a girl. We planned to be married three weeks from tomorrow." Ben lost his composure and broke down in sobs.

Dominique rose and without hesitation, put an arm around his shoulders. "Take your time, Ben." She handed him a glass of water and waited a minute. "Can you go on?"

He took a drink, inhaled deeply and nodded.

"What you've told me sounds wonderful and more than generous on your part," she said, "but I've got to know how the hell you came to be in that room, standing over her body with a knife."

Ben took a deep breath, exhaled and began. "Okay, on that night—the night she was killed—Regina had just moved me into room 335. The hotel was about full to capacity, and it was the only room left. She wanted to talk to this guy, to tell him someone else was going to take responsibility for the child. I didn't want her to have anything more to do with him, but she said he had been good to her for a long time, and she owed it to him to take the weight off his shoulders. She told me she was going to have him come to the room while I was gone so they could have some privacy and none of her co-workers would hear what was going on.

"She gave me the key, and I didn't see her again. I left right after that to run a few errands. I didn't want to run into the bastard. Him, I would have punched out." Her client had a faraway look, and Dominique didn't stop his narration. "I was working two jobs, and when I got off my day grind at the Lower Keys Animal Clinic, I barely had enough time to grab a sandwich before checking in for my night bartending gig at Margaritaville. After I got off work, I stopped by a late night grocery on Duval to pick up something to eat in the room."

"What time did you get off work?"

"It was just about midnight. Ordinarily I would work until one thirty when they close, but I got off early that night."

"What time did you make it back to the hotel?"

"About a quarter till one. I remember because I looked at my watch, wondering whether I had time to see Regina before she left for home."

"Was the door locked when you got there?"

"I think those doors lock automatically. I just assumed it would be and used my key." Hargrave stopped talking and stared at the floor.

"I know this is hard, Ben, but you need to go on and tell me the rest of it."

"Regina was on the floor." Hargrave hugged himself and bent over in the chair. "Just from the amount of blood all over the place, I should have known she was dead, but she was still warm, so I checked to see if she was breathing. She wasn't. I remember trying to feel the baby kicking, but I couldn't. I knew then that they were both gone." He broke down sobbing.

Again Dominique waited for him to regain his composure.

When he did, he told her that he didn't remember picking up the knife. He didn't remember anything until some time after he arrived at the police station. He had cooperated with the police, answering whatever questions they asked, except for one. "I didn't tell them it could be someone else's baby. I didn't want her reputation ruined."

The Key West Cemetery was moved to its present location at the "dead" center of Old Town in 1847 after a major hurricane floated bodies out of its more coastal location.

The main entry gates are at the corner of Margaret and Angela Streets. The main boulevard is lined with box tombs common for the 20th century.

# 7

Dominique rose early on the day of Regina DeWalt's funeral. As usual, she hadn't slept well, but there was nothing demanding alertness on this particular morning. Bill was out of town; the children were at the home of friends, and Mimi was off. She fixed herself a cup of *café con leche* and walked to the pool. Outside, Boo waited anxiously. Dominique obliged by ruffling the dog's ears with one hand while she sipped the hot liquid. Soon, the heat permeated her body, and beads of sweat began to pop out. She let her robe drop, raised her arms above her head and feeling the morning breeze on her unclothed skin, dove into the water, leaving only a tiny ripple at the surface to mark her entry.

After twenty laps, she fell back to float. She watched the pale blue sky infused with meringue-wispy clouds and found it disconcerting to see heavenly gaiety on a day when earth-bound humans would, with pomp and circumstance, perform the somber ritual of burying the dead. Unexpectedly, she shivered with apprehension. She searched for footing at the shallow end of the pool and quickly climbed the steps out of the water, in one fluid motion sweeping up the green robe and hastily covering her naked body. She looked around, saw nothing but felt the piercing eyes that focused on her. Hurriedly, she retreated into the house.

She was stepping into the shower when the phone rang.

"Little lady, your client is about to climb the walls of his cell," Tiny announced with exasperation. "He says he needs to talk to you, something bad."

"Okay. Put him on."

"Dominique?" Ben's voice was shaky, and he sounded upset.

"What's the matter, Ben?"

"I have to be at Regina's funeral."

"You know I can't help you with that," she replied, talking to him in the soft tone she would use with a distressed child.

"I love her. I have to be there to say goodbye. She's got to know I was there." His words carried an undercurrent of desperation.

"This is hard for you. I know it has to be, but try to understand."

"Yes, ma'am, I know, but. . . ." Ben stopped trying to talk and began to cry softly.

Dominique stood silently for a moment longer, listening. She took a deep breath. "Ben? Ben?" There was no response. "Ben, put the jailer on the phone."

Again, there was no sound from her client, but a moment later she heard Tiny's voice. "See what I mean?" the big man said, not unkindly this time.

"Tiny, please have Hargrave dress in the court clothes I left with you. Bring him to St. Mary's at nine thirty-five."

"Ms. Olivet, you know there's nothing in the world I wouldn't do for you, but I can't do that. It would cost me my job."

"Listen to me, Tiny. Get Hargrave dressed, and lend him your sun glasses. Drive him to the church. A friend of mine—light brown hair, wearing a navy blue dress—will meet you outside." Tiny grunted. Before he could interrupt, she hurried on, "She'll bring him back to your car before everyone starts filing out of church. No one will recognize him, and he won't run. I can assure you of that." Her voice had a confidence she didn't feel. "If something should go wrong, which I'm sure it won't, you're to say I represented to you that I had an order signed by Judge Sanchez instructing you to transport Hargrave. I told you I didn't have time to bring the order to the jail, and I would deliver a copy for your records after the funeral. You, of course, accepted my word as an officer of the court. I'll take the heat. You'll be off the hook. I give you my word."

"Are you sure? If anything goes wrong, you could be disbarred."

"I understand that. It'll be fine. Don't worry."

"All right, little lady." Tiny's sigh was loud. "This goes against my better judgment, but I'll have him there at precisely nine thirty-five. Tell your friend not to be late."

"Thanks, Tiny."

"I just hope this doesn't backfire on you, that's all."

Dominique sat on the edge of the bed, her eyes closed. Perhaps what she had done wasn't legal, and maybe not ethical on the face of it, but her instincts had pushed hard, urging her to acknowledge Ben's innocence. As a victim himself, the young man deserved to attend the funeral of the woman he loved and had planned to marry. If he wasn't there, the right to say goodbye to Regina, and to a child that would have been his, could never be restored to him. She wasn't about to let that happen.

\* \* \*

"Are you ready?" Dominique asked as soon as Linda answered the phone.

"Yeah, but it's early."

"I know, but Bill had a meeting in Miami, and he's gone. Come on over. By the way, what are you wearing?"

"My usual. You know, that navy blue thing I always wear for depressing occasions."

Over coffee, Dominique took a deep breath and explained what was about to happen.

"Oh, shit," was Linda's only response.

\* \* \*

When they arrived at the church, Dominique lost count of the number of people who approached her wanting to know if it was really true that she had been appointed to represent the killer. She was relieved to be recognized by one of the ushers and escorted to the area reserved for members of the bar. She found herself seated next to Rolf and a somber-faced Juan Sanchez, Sr.

Rolf momentarily laid his hand on hers as she sat down. "After this is over, I'd like to talk to you. Do you have time?"

"Yes, of course." Shivers ran the length of her spine. For the next hour, she didn't hear a word the priest said; her ears, for the next hour, were attuned only to any sound that might indicate something had gone wrong.

"Excuse me. My pager's vibrating," Rolf whispered as he stood and inched in front of her.

Dominique watched him walk to the back of the church, and her heart sank. Hands clenched tightly, she waited for the commotion indicating she would soon be reported to the Ethics Committee of the Florida Bar. Nothing happened, and Rolf didn't return to his seat.

As soon as Mass was over, she rushed to find Linda who was waiting directly outside the door, a look of extreme relief, and some annoyance, written on her face. "Your guy is back with his jailer. I swear, Dominique, if you ever do anything like this to me again, I'm going to disown you. My nerves can't handle stuff like that. Do you realize I felt like a criminal? I was scared to death I was going to be arrested at any moment. They would read me my rights and cart me off to jail. My son would have to go live with his deadbeat father. God, that was awful." Linda shook her head in apparent disbelief of the morning's events.

"I'm sorry. I truly am. I promise I'll never impose on you like that again, at least not to that magnitude." Dominique smiled ruefully. "I had to make a quick call on this, and I didn't know how else to handle it. Am I forgiven?"

Linda said something that sounded vaguely like a yes and continued to talk a mile a minute. "I could never, ever, be a police person or private eye or anything like that. I'd pee in my pants at the first sign of a crisis. Toward the end of the Mass, del Castillo walked right past us. I thought, for sure, my goose was cooked.

Dominique, I'm not kidding you; I almost passed out. Thank God he didn't blink an eye."

Dominique ignored the monologue. "I should go out to the cemetery. Do you want to come?" she asked calmly.

"Nope. I'm headed home. This is all I can take for one day. I need a good stiff drink, and I don't care what time day it is."

"Okay, sweetie. I'll see you later. Bill probably won't be home till tomorrow, so we can have a drink and maybe watch a movie. The kids are spending the weekend with friends."

"Okay. Whatever."

"And, thank you. A lot."

"Yeah, sure. Don't think twice." Linda walked off, mumbling to herself.

* * *

The grave-side words were brief. Dominique relaxed and con-centrated on what was going on around her. Other than exhaustion, there was no expression on Alicia's face. It was as if all life had been drained from her as it had ebbed from her niece.

Dominique approached her, looked into her eyes and seeing no anger there, put her arms around her. "I know nothing anyone can say will help, but I want you to know you're in my prayers. I'm so sorry about having to–"

"Don't worry. I'm not angry with you," Alicia said softly. "I know an accused has to have a lawyer, and Juan explained to me that he didn't give you a choice."

"Thank you. You don't know how much that means to me. I wouldn't hurt you for the world."

Dominique took one last look at the casket and then moved out from under the canopy. She scanned the area for Rolf. Not seeing him, she walked to her car, stopping every now and again to gaze at the various gravestones.

She had played in the historic cemetery as a child, never fear-ful of the spirits who might roam its nineteen acres. The original cemetery had been located near the southernmost point of the island. It was moved after the hurricane of 1847 disinterred bodies and washed them inland or out to sea. It was now bounded by Angela, Margaret, Passover Lane—appropriately named, Dominique thought—Frances and Olivia Streets. The local joke was that after 1847, the cemetery had been re-located to the "dead center" of Old Town. The rocky soil had made digging six feet under difficult. As time went by, many of the deceased were stacked several high, condominium style. It was a picturesque place with headstones that were sometimes as humorous, irreverent and quirky as the residents themselves. "I Told You I Was Sick,"and "At least I Know Where He's Sleeping Tonight," were two of Dominique's favorites. Today, she wondered how many funerals those who lay under a blanket of earth, or who were housed in whitewashed aboveground tombs, had attended before it was their own turn. Had they been fearful or accepting of the grim reaper?

She opened the car door and sat down, in retrospect wishing she had brought the MG. Regina had always drooled over the 1951 classic black roadster. It would have been a fitting sendoff to drive it in the funeral procession.

"God damn you! What the fuck did you think you were doing?"

Dominique's body felt as if it were levitating off the seat. She had been distracted and had no idea anyone else was in the car. "Damn *you*, Rolf! You about gave me a heart attack!" she yelled at the stone-faced man who leaned over from the back seat.

Rolf didn't immediately answer, and it seemed to her that an eternity passed before he spoke again. "You know that if I open my mouth about what you did today, your career is over."

She gripped the steering wheel tightly. What could she possibly say to explain her actions? At least he'd had the decency not to make a scene at the church.

"I can't believe you lied to Tiny. Don't you realize Hargrave could have run? You would have been responsible for the escape of an alleged murderer."

She turned to face him, and Rolf stared at her hard, his eyes black as night.

"Yes, I know that."

"Why then? Just explain it to me," he hissed.

Dominique fixed her gaze on him. "Do you remember when we were children and my cat, Mooki, died? My parents buried him while I was at school. I cried and cried because I hadn't had a chance to say goodbye. You tried so hard, but you couldn't make me feel better. You went home, came back with a shovel and dug him up. You washed him off and dried him. I got to pet him, tell him I loved him, and then you buried him again."

"I remember," he answered, his voice now soft.

"That's why I did it."

"Princess, someday that heart of yours will get you into big trouble."

Relief registered, and the tightness in her chest relaxed. "Does that mean you're not going to report this?"

"Report what? I don't know what you're talking about."

"Thank you, Rolf."

"Please, don't ever do anything that foolish again. Next time, I may not be the only one to discover it." He brushed her cheek with his hand, opened the door and walked away from the car.

It was over.

*A more elaborate tomb*

# 8

Alicia Fernandez and her mother sat in the living room of the lanai-style home purchased twenty-five years earlier. They were finally alone. Alicia's sister, Jenna, had been given a tranquilizer. Her husband sat with her in the back bedroom that had belonged to their daughter. The only sound in the house was that of the chair where the elder matriarch, silently crocheting, rocked to and fro in a slow, steady rhythm. Outside, birds sang.

Alicia, puffy-eyed and wan, sat hunched over on the divan. She clutched a photograph of Regina to her chest as tears ran unheeded down still youthful cheeks.

"It was God's will, daughter. There's no use in crying."

Alicia neither looked up nor answered.

"The Lord always demands atonement for sins," the older woman continued.

Alicia turned on her mother, a venomous look on her face. She spit her words out toward the gray-haired woman who hadn't once taken her eyes from the task in which her hands were engaged. "Mama, do you really believe God would cause the death of a mother and her unborn child as the price of reconciliation?"

"I don't question God, Alicia." Mrs. Fernandez didn't drop a stitch.

"I don't question God either. I question you and how you look at God. Jesus paid our price for us, Mama. God doesn't demand sacrifices anymore. You're still back in the days of 'an eye for an eye.' I prefer to believe in the loving, caring Lord we see in Christ. God didn't demand Regina's death. She died because God gave us free will, and there are evil people in the world. One of them took her life. That's all. I'll cry until I can't cry any more. I'll cry for Jenna, for me and for what we've lost. I'll cry for Regina and for the baby who didn't have a chance to be born. Don't you dare tell me not to cry. There's a lot to cry about in this house, Mama."

The women returned to their silence.

* * *

Linda had been soused when Dominique arrived home, was now even more so. The two women sat by the pool sipping Key Lime daiquiris.

"I hope you don't think the booze makes up for what you put me through today," Linda laughingly slurred.

"Hey, it wasn't just you, you know. I went through hell, too."

"Yeah, but you deserved it. It was all your idea. I was just the sucker you pulled in. Anyway, let's forget it. I don't want to think about that nightmare for a long while."

"One day you'll look upon it as an adventure."

Linda glared.

Dominique smiled. She wouldn't tell her friend that Rolf had caught on. She wouldn't tell anyone. If what she had done ever came to light, she didn't want his political future to suffer because he had chosen to keep silent and shelter her. Instead, she secretly cherished his gift, a feeling of protection she hadn't enjoyed since childhood.

"Regina looked really beautiful at the funeral home," Linda said, "almost as if she were alive and just sleeping."

Dominique wasn't in the mood to talk about the emotions she had experienced viewing Regina's body. She led the discussion in another direction by talking about something that was puzzling her. At first it had been a nagging, unconscious feeling at the funeral home. At the grave-side service it had filtered through to her consciousness. "Did you notice the coffin by any chance?" she asked.

"You bet." Linda inappropriately giggled. "It was absolutely gorgeous. Looked like hand-carved mahogany. It must've cost a bundle."

"That's exactly what I was thinking. None of Regina's family has the money to pay for something like that, not even if they took up a collection among all the relatives. I'm really curious as to who paid."

"Maybe Judge Sanchez forked out for it." Linda pulled a bill from her bra and threw it on the table, laughing. "Think this would do it?"

Linda was too drunk to be of help, but it didn't matter. Dominique was primarily talking to herself. Sometimes she thought better if she said things out loud. "That crossed my mind, but I don't think so. It had to have been outrageously expensive. I calculated somewhere in the neighborhood of seven to ten thousand dollars. Sanchez wouldn't spend that kind of money, not even for Alicia's niece; he's too tight. It's a pretty safe bet it wasn't him."

"Are you just curious, or is this important to your case?" Linda peered out from half-closed eyes but surprisingly, her question made sense.

"Both, I guess. I'm not really sure what relevance it has to the criminal case, but it wouldn't hurt either the case, or my curiosity, to know."

"You need a private eye." Linda laughed, finishing off the last sip in her glass.

"That's not as comical as you might think. If we had the funds, I'd hire a detective on the spot. Obviously, if Ben's not guilty, then someone else murdered Regina. Who did it, and why did they want her dead? If I hope to get an acquittal, I've got to give the jurors something to hang their hats on."

There was no response, and Dominique looked over at her friend. Linda's eyes were closed, and her head hung down awkwardly. Dominique grinned like the Cheshire cat. Linda wouldn't care to see herself in this inebriated condition. She poked her with an index finger, trying to awaken her. The only response was a grunt. She lightly shook her arm. There was still no response. "Linda?" Nothing. She was out like a light. "Hello, are you in there?" Dominique yelled straight into her ear.

Linda jumped, dumping her stemmed glass to the concrete floor where it shattered into slivers. "Geez, you scared me!"

"How much have you had to drink today?"

"I don't know, and furthermore, I don't really care." She slurred the words.

"That's fine, but you don't have any shoes on, so stay put till I sweep up your mess."

"It was your fault. You didn't need to scream at me." Linda giggled.

"I didn't scream. I merely spoke in a loud tone of voice," Dominique said, an impish grin on her face. "Just hang tight for a minute while I get a broom."

The cleanup completed, she smiled and said in a much softer voice, "You're going to have one hell of a hangover tomorrow, and I don't intend to go to Mass alone, so you'd better head home, take a bunch of aspirin, and go to bed."

"Yes, ma'am."

After Linda made two unsuccessful, and shaky, attempts to rise, Dominique took hold of her arm and helped her friend home. Returning to the house, she settled back in a patio chair. Everyone was gone; it was two o'clock in the morning, and she was in no hurry for bed. She still hadn't unwound from the events of the day. She served herself another daiquiri and breathed deeply. The only sound was the incessant song of crickets, and every once in a while, floating on the breeze, the faint sound of a mournful horn being played, probably somewhere on Duval Street.

\*\*\*

"Why are you up so late, Counselor?"

Dominique jumped for the second time in twenty-four hours. She looked around but couldn't make out where Rolf's voice was coming from. "You've got to stop sneaking around like that. My heart can't take it."

Rolf laughed. "I wasn't sneaking around. I was walking on the sidewalk side of your hedge. That's not mysterious or illegal that I know of. So, what are you doing outside this late at night or, should I say, this early in the morning?"

"Well, if you'll come around to the gate, I'll let you in and tell you all about it."

"You sure it's all right? I don't want to wake anyone."

"It's fine. There's no one around to wake up. Bill's in Miami. The kids are spending the weekend with friends, and the housekeeper is off. Yours truly is alone."

There was no response, and she felt his hesitation. "Oh, good grief, Rolf, just get over to the gate. I can't see you. I'm talking to a bush for heaven's sake."

Rolf had never visited before, and she was happy to show off the garden. She took pride in having chosen the trees that had been added to the existing landscape when she and Bill had purchased the house—palms, of course; bananas; mango; guava; and papaya, probably because of her childhood enchantment with the tiny, slick, ebony seeds that slipped through your fingers like liquid mercury from a broken thermometer. Potted plants, shrubs and ferns co-existed in harmonious disarray, and flickering white lights, discretely hidden in the trees, brought the dark-bottomed pool to sparkling life.

"This is beautiful," he said as he walked through the gate. "Do you sit out here often?"

"Thank you, and yes, I do, mosquitoes notwithstanding. Insect spray is a wonderful thing, though I do wonder what it's doing to my insides." She shrugged, "It's preferable to a case of West Nile Virus." She smiled ruefully. "Now, it's my turn to ask. What are you doing out walking the streets of our fair city at two o'clock in the morning?"

"I couldn't sleep."

"Sit down," she offered.

Rolf did as she asked, eyeing Boo with suspicion. "I didn't hear your dog bark. Does it bite?"

"*She* does both, but, if she senses you're friendly, she doesn't bother herself. I think what counts, is whether you smell hostile. I wouldn't worry about her."

Rolf seemed relieved.

"Have a daiquiri. It'll help you relax," she said, walking to the teacart and pouring the last of the pitcher's contents into a large goblet. Her hand shook faintly as she held the slightly melted drink out toward him, and some of the contents trickled onto her fingers. She licked away the sticky sweetness and smiled at him, quickly looking away when his gaze tried to hold hers. She searched for something to say that would break the tension. "I'm sorry. I know I'm responsible for the stress you had to contend with today."

The attempt was successful. He immediately assumed his professional demeanor. "Let's not discuss that." He took a sip from his drink. "Actually, I needed to speak with you this morning, but after all that happened, I forgot about it until I was in bed," he said.

"Oh?" Dominique's curiosity was aroused, but she waited, somewhat impatiently, while he took several more sips.

"I'm not sure if you understand that I'm willing to hand you a good bargain, one that will have Judge Sanchez' seal of approval," he volunteered.

Now her adrenaline was pumping. "What's going on, Rolf? On the day I was appointed you indicated your willingness to take a plea. That's not like you at all. Now, here we go with the same subject again. Why? What's going on that I'm not privy to?"

He hesitated momentarily. "I don't think I'm breaking any confidence by telling you that, almost immediately after the family was informed of the murder and the fact that Regina was pregnant when she died, there was a conversation with the judge. Neither Alicia nor the girl's parents are desirous of having Regina's private life exposed. They want to protect her reputation. Sanchez has indicated he will go along with their wishes."

"Was Alicia aware that Regina was seeing Ben Hargrave?"

"She was. I think she actually liked him."

"Did she have any idea Regina was pregnant?"

"No, she didn't. Regina was tall; I guess that enabled her to hide her condition. I felt bad having to tell Alicia at such a painful time."

Dominique frowned. "My client informs me that when he was arrested, he told you Regina was pregnant–"

"That's right. Of course, he wasn't telling us anything we wouldn't have learned from the autopsy. Looks like he knocked her up and then didn't want the child."

"I wasn't finished." She made an effort not to sound exasperated. "Hargrave said he knew you assumed the child was his. He didn't tell you anything different because, at the time, just like her family, the only thing he could think of was to protect Regina's reputation. I'm telling you right now that Regina wasn't sure the baby was Hargrave's. She had been seeing a married man and the baby could have been his."

Rolf fell back in his chair. "Damn. If Hargrave was in love with her and felt betrayed, that's all the more motive."

She rose from her chair, walked over to him and as he opened his mouth to make another comment, she jammed her napkin between his teeth. "I'll try again to finish," she said.

Rolf spit out the paper, smiled and kept his mouth shut.

"When she informed the married guy she was pregnant, he was quick to tell her to get lost. So, you see, it's possible this man, whoever he is, might have been so angry or frightened of exposure that he wanted her and the child dead," she offered.

"You didn't have to draw the conclusion for me. I was going to list that as one of the options before you so cruelly gagged me." The prosecutor smiled. "Hey, remember, I went to college and law school, too. I took logic."

Dominique laughed. "That's why I'm talking to you about it, you dolt. Two heads are better than one, especially when yours is so big."

It was Rolf's turn to laugh and then his face turned serious. "Dominique, I've never had the opportunity to tell you how proud I am of what you've done with your life. As a kid, it never crossed my mind that one day we would both be attorneys on opposing sides of a capital murder case."

"Just what did you think would become of me?"

"I don't know. I remember thinking you didn't fit the standard mold for a girl." Rolf hesitated before going on. "I mean it as a compliment. You never played games. You always said exactly what you were thinking."

"Thank you." She had missed his friendship and his companionship. She just hadn't realized how much. She brought her mind back to the law and took a sip of her drink. "You give some thought to what I told you about the pregnancy. Now, exactly what kind of deal is it that you're offering?"

Rolf's response was quick. "First Degree Manslaughter, fifteen years in Raiford. With good behavior, he can be out in three."

"All right," she said. "For my part, I've listened to you, and I'm honor-bound to pass the offer on to my client. Let's face it; it's the kind of generous deal that a guilty man with the deck stacked against him couldn't afford to pass up." She finished her drink. "You need to understand that Ben Hargrave swears to me he didn't do this. I have a feeling he's not going to take any plea bargain, no matter how juicy."

"Understood. Now let's just hope this works out the best it can under the circumstances." His face was somber.

She tried to lighten the mood. "You know, if he refuses your offer, it's going to tell me one of two things."

"What?"

"That he either believes I'm so damn good at what I do that I can convince a jury to acquit in the face of everything you have pointing to his guilt or, the more likely scenario, that he truly is innocent, and he wants to stand on principle."

Rolf laughed and then fell silent, his gaze locked on Dominique. "I suppose I'd better go." His eyes never left her.

"I suppose."

Suddenly, it was hard for her to breathe. She walked him toward the garden entrance, afraid to talk or even look at him.

At the iron-latticed gate, she stopped. Neither spoke, then Rolf stepped forward and gave her a gentle hug. "Good night, princess. Sleep well."

"Somehow, I don't think I will." It would not be the law keeping her awake tonight.

He made no effort to leave. Instead, he kissed her hand, all the while keeping his eyes locked on hers. "One thing I did know," he said softly. "I was sure you'd grow up to be a beautiful woman. I wasn't wrong."

Her cheeks burned, and she hoped the darkness prevented him from seeing the flush that must be there.

He walked out the gate, hesitated and then turned back. "I should tell you that I saw you swimming naked this morning."

Dominique's mouth dropped open.

Rolf went on quickly. "You need to be careful. There's a gap in your hedge, and if someone happens to look through at just the right angle, you're very much exposed. I happened to look…," he stammered, "and then I couldn't stop looking." His eyes would no longer meet hers.

She was stunned by what he had said, even more so by her response. "Did you like what you saw?"

"What do you think?" he asked, smiling.

Dominique stood at the gate, watching while Rolf disappeared into the early morning darkness. She felt a shiver run through her body and hugged herself as she walked back to the patio. She grabbed a hand spade out of the garden basket, dropped to the ground and began feverishly digging. Presently, she heard the sound of Mimi's whistling, faint at first then louder.

"Good God, child, what are you doing?"

"Digging holes for flowers."

"I can see that. Do you mind explaining just why you're doing it in the dark, at four o'clock in the morning?"

Dominique stared up into the housekeeper's face. "I'm not quite sure. It just seemed the thing to do."

A Catholic Confessional

# 9

"Bless me, Father, for I have sinned."

"Welcome to the house of God, my child. May the Lord be in your heart and on your lips so that you may properly confess your sins," began Father Madera's intonation. "In the name of the Father and of the Son and of the Holy Spirit."

Dominique crossed herself. "Thank you, Father. It's been a year since my last confession."

"And what have you been up to that I haven't read about in the newspaper?" the gentle priest asked, chuckling. "I know you've been dutiful about attending church and seeing that the children are here." Father Madera hadn't seen her enter the confessional, but it was a small town, after all; as soon as a parishioner opened his or her mouth, the priest would recognize the voice.

"I confess to Almighty God, and to you, Father, mostly the not-so-terrible, venial sins. I try, but it seems the harder I try, the more little things I do that I know wouldn't be pleasing to God."

"It happens to all of us, Dominique. We're only imperfect human beings, even we priests, although our parishioners tend to forget that at times. The fact that you give thought to what you do, that you try to do the right thing and that you're sorry when you don't, that's what counts. I'd say you're not doing too badly. Tell me what gives you the most trouble."

"Goodness, Father, you should know by now. It's always the same things. I lose my patience and my temper too easily. Sometimes, when the children aren't around, my speech includes a few choice words you wouldn't approve of. I tell fibs. You know, a little embellishment here and there, telling friends they look good when they really don't, a fake excuse when I'm late, that sort of thing. I just plain forgot to attend Mass on one holy day of obligation this year, which meant Daniella and Jordan also missed it, and I know I'm as guilty as the next person of gossiping. I've probably seen more than a couple of movies the Church disapproves of. It really sounds terrible when I list them one after another. Believe me, there're a lot more if you want to take the time to listen."

"You're being too hard on yourself. Now, let's get to the concerning part. Are there any mortal sins that need forgiving?"

Dominique hesitated. "I don't think so. I mean, I can't recall realizing that something is considered a sin so serious that it imperils your soul and then making a conscious decision to do it anyway." She took a deep breath and finally spit out what was really eating at her, "But, there is one thing that nags at my conscience, and I'm not sure how bad it is."

"Tell me about it."

"Well, Father, I have a friend, a man I've known practically all my life. We're trying to work together. Not actually together. He's prosecuting, and I'm defending, but I don't think of him as an opponent. I really believe he's looking for the truth, too. It just so happens, that we see it differently at the moment. I'm rambling, aren't I?" She didn't wait for the priest's response. "Anyway, I tell myself I only consider him a friend, but Father, there's enough of something there to make me feel guilty. I think about him, and enjoy his company, too much. I want him around too much." Dominique sighed and fell silent.

"Do you lust after this man, child?"

She reddened and found herself glad to be on the other side of a darkened confessional. "I don't think so. I try not to think about that in relation to him."

"Have you done anything physical with Rolf?"

Dominique had understood that the priest would immediately know to whom she referred. Still, she would have preferred for him to keep his knowledge internal. Hearing Rolf's name come out of her pastor's mouth removed her feelings from the realm of the abstract and made them real. "Father," she said indignantly, "you didn't have to say his name out loud. And no, I haven't even kissed him." Again, she hesitated. She would have to worry about it later if she kept silent; that meant it needed to be said. "He did give me a hug, and he kissed my hand." It had been such a special moment, yet sounded banal as she told it now. She wanted to get this over with, and her words knocked against each other, becoming almost unintelligible as she picked up speed. "And he told me he accidentally saw me naked through the hedge, and Father, I can't believe it, but I asked him if he liked what he saw. I didn't mean to say that; truly I didn't. It just came out; like projectile vomiting when I was a child." She swallowed hard and waited. She knew the words of forgiveness would come. They always did, from any priest, if you repented of what you had done wrong. Still, she felt guilty and needed those magic words to be said.

The priest's voice soothed her. "Don't spend time worrying about it, Dominique. There's nothing sinful about most of the emotions you've described to me. You could feel that for a good friend. You must be very careful, however, not to let them get out of hand and not to act on them in a way you shouldn't." The priest chuckled. "I'm not surprised at your response to Rolf. You are always quick with the comeback." In a more serious tone, he went on, "What you need to do is to keep your meetings with Rolf as public as possible. Don't provide opportunities for something to happen that shouldn't. Think more about your husband and concentrate on building a closer, more spiritual bond between the two of you. If you do that, your feelings for Rolf won't be a problem."

Dominique didn't know how, and didn't try, to explain to the priest that attempting closeness with Bill was useless. They were polite and civil to each other; sometimes there was even an element of affection between them, but it was all superficial. If there had ever been any emotional depth to their relationship, it had disappeared so long ago she could no longer remember it. She was desperately lonely. "I'll try Father. I promise." Dominique concluded, "For these and for all the sins of my past life that I might have forgotten to confess, I am truly repentant."

"Very well. Let me hear your Act of Contrition."

She began reciting the words she had learned all those years ago. "O my God, I am heartily sorry for having offended Thee. I detest all of my sins because of Thy just punishments, but most of all because they offend Thee, my God, who art all good and deserving of all my love. I firmly resolve, with the help of Thy grace, to confess my sins, to do penance and to amend my life. Amen."

"As penance, I want you to go to the library and select two books on how to improve husband wife relationships. Give me a book report when you're finished, and I want to hear several examples of how you've tried to put the advice into practice."

Dominique bit her lip and squelched an urge to say what she was thinking. It seemed to her a priest could give more helpful advice on marital relations if he had some practical notion of what it was all about.

"I absolve you from your sins, Dominique, in the name of the Father and of the Son and of the Holy Spirit."

* * *

Dominique was cooking dinner when the telephone rang, and Mimi hollered for her to pick up the extension.

"Ms. Olivet, this is Harrison Hargrave. We just read about our son's arrest in the *Miami Herald.* The article said you've been appointed to represent him. We can be ready to leave Miami in a couple of hours if you can see us first thing in the morning."

Dominique hurriedly scanned the duplicate appointment book she kept next to the phone. "I can see you at nine-thirty, Mr. Hargrave. You must understand, however, that I cannot tell you anything Ben and I have discussed. I will listen to what you have to say and then relay it to Ben. It will be up to him to decide whether I should speak to you, and if so, how much I'm free to pass on. Is that agreeable?"

"Yes ma'am. We'll be at your office at exactly nine-thirty."

# *10*

"Where did you go last night?"

"What?"

"I heard you get up in the middle of the night. You got dressed and left the house. Where did you go?"

"I couldn't sleep. I just went for a walk, that's all." Rolf didn't want to talk about it. It was only six-thirty in the morning. He needed to try and get an hour or so of sleep before going to work. His walk hadn't done him any good. He had come home after being with Dominique, and sleep had eluded him for the remainder of the night.

"Where did you go?" Sarah's voice now had a nagging, insistent quality to it that was unlike her usual polished manner of speaking.

"I told you. I went for a walk. I didn't go any place in particular."

Sarah got up, walked to his side of the bed and stared down at him. Her voice went up several notches. "I want to know where you went."

He wasn't sure where the conversation was headed, and he felt guilty. "Is this an inquisition? What's bothering you, Sarah?"

"I was awake when you came home. If you were smart, you would have showered before you came back to bed. You reeked of perfume, and there was liquor on your breath. I want to know who she is." Sarah glared at him, her hands clenched into tight fists.

Rolf had smelled Dominique's cologne on his walk home. He had thought it was simply his imagination, the result of wishful thinking. Now, he needed to pacify his wife. He stood and put his arms around her. "There's nobody, Sarah. I stopped for a drink. When I got home, I put on the first pajamas I could find in the dark. It must be stale aftershave or maybe even some of that stuff you wear." He put his hands on his wife's shoulders and looked into her face. "You know I've never cheated on you. I'm either at work or else I'm here with you and the family. Why are you turning suspicious on me all of a sudden?"

An angry tear ran down Sarah's cheek, and Rolf pulled his wife close, burying her head under his chin and hugging her tightly in an effort to calm her emotions. He felt strangely detached, as if not a part of the scene but watching an ancient drama from some place outside himself. When he could tell she was no longer crying, he sat her on the bed. "Now, what is this all about?"

"Something's wrong, Rolf. I can tell. You've never been one to share what you're feeling. That's usually okay with me because I'm not either, but lately, you've completely closed up. I talk, and you don't listen. You don't seem to care whether we have sex or not. You don't sleep much, and when you do, you toss and turn."

There wasn't much he could say. "You're making something out of nothing, sweetheart. Let's just talk about this."

She looked up at him. "You've never left the house in the middle of the night like that before and then perfume and booze. What am I supposed to think? I don't care what you say; it didn't smell like anything I know." Her voice grew harsh. "If you're having an affair, I want it kept discreet. I'm not to be embarrassed, so whatever you have to do, do it away from Key West. Above all, keep in mind that there'll be no divorce. Not under any circumstances."

Her words hung cold in the air, and he moved away from her. "Look, Sarah. Right now I'm involved in the biggest case to hit Key West in years. It's a delicate situation. I want justice done, but

I don't want to risk my chances at election either. Trying to take care of both isn't easy. I worry, and I don't sleep well. It has nothing to do with you, and I assure you, I'm not having an affair. I did have a drink. You, of all people, should know I don't have time left over to be fooling around. My conscience is clear, and you shouldn't be worried. Just try to be patient with me, okay?"

Sarah's face came alive with relief. "I'm sorry, baby. I didn't know you were having a difficult time at work. I'm sorry."

"It's okay." It wasn't really. She had said the words, and she couldn't take them back. If it wasn't so personal, it would be amusing. "Let's try and get some sleep."

In bed, Sarah curled up against him, her head on his shoulder. He felt like a stone, cold and unwarmed by the body entwined with his own. Why hadn't he told Sarah the truth? He hadn't planned to end up at Dominique's house. Why would he? He hadn't known she would be alone; had no way of knowing she would be up in the middle of the night. The meeting had been one of those quirks of fate. Nothing had happened between them except an innocent hug, a kiss on the hand, and he could have left that part out. Why had he hesitated? It was too late to say anything about it now. The only thing that didn't confound him was to hear Sarah say that she was more worried about her reputation and maintaining the marriage than she was about losing his love to someone else. He wasn't surprised. He had probably known it all along.

Exhausted, he tried to sleep. Visions of Dominique's dark eyes, of her lush naked body, filled his thoughts. Vaguely, he felt Sarah move to her side of the double bed.

She put on her robe and left the room.

\* \* \*

"Good Morning." Dominique barely looked at Patti. "A big cup of coffee, please."

The legal assistant glanced up. "You look like shit."

"Thanks."

"I'm sorry, but you could pass for a walking zombie. Was it a horrible weekend?"

"There was Regina's funeral, and I didn't sleep. Does that answer your question? Whatever you do, don't cross me today. I feel like biting someone's head off, and you're awfully close."

"I'll just hibernate in my little cubby and stay out of the way."

"No luck, kiddo. We have things that have to be done. Now, get me some coffee, please. I need something to get the blood pumping. And get yourself a legal pad."

Patti returned quickly with a mug of coffee and several premenstrual pills.

"Thanks for the caffeine. Don't need the pills. I just got over my period last week." She took a big swallow. "First off, Ben Hargraves' parents will be here at nine-thirty."

"Wow. Did he have you get in touch with them?"

"Nope. They found me." She gave no further explanation and kept on talking. "In the meantime, start on the skeleton of a Motion for Change of Venue. I'll revamp whatever you can come up with. I think the grounds are obvious: small town, deceased was a native; everybody knew and liked her. Defendant is from out of town, victim is the niece of court personnel and acquainted with the judge. No possibility of fairness, etc. etc."

"Slow down. I can't write that fast."

"Sorry. Second thing," Here, Dominique swallowed hard. "Draw up a rough draft of a Motion to Disqualify. Judge Sanchez had affection for Regina; she was the niece of his long-time secretary; he has to be biased against the defendant."

"Are you sure you want to do that? Trying to disqualify the judge is an awfully big deal." Patti eyed her incredulously.

Dominique ignored her and continued to talk. "Check the Rules of Judicial Administration and the Code of Judicial Conduct and cite to them. Don't waste any time, hon. If I recall, this has to be done within ten days of the time we realize there's a problem. Obviously, we've known from minute one."

"Dominique, I'm trying to get you to think twice."

Dominique ignored her. "I just don't understand why Sanchez hasn't removed himself. The canons of judicial conduct require a judge to disqualify himself if his impartiality might reasonably be questioned. He has to be aware of that." She frowned. "Make sure you have the date on your calendar; we can't miss this ten-day deadline. If he rules the motion is legally insufficient, I'll have to take a Writ of Prohibition to the District Court of Appeal."

"Hell, you're going to piss him off royally."

"If he's rational about it, it shouldn't bother him. He'll realize the appropriate thing to do is ship it off to another judge in Dade County and let someone else carry the burden. He would be doing the right thing and avoiding a major headache to boot. If he doesn't take it in the proper spirit, that's his problem. I have to file these motions. If I don't, I'll be guilty of malpractice in the event Hargrave is convicted. I don't see that I have a choice."

"Whatever you say. You're the boss."

"Well, hallelujah. Sometimes I think you forget that minor fact." Dominique managed a weak smile. "After things calm down this afternoon, we need to discuss a witness list and strategy for a re-hearing on the bail issue."

"And, with all of this, just when am I supposed to do the work you've given me for our other clients?"

"I don't know, hon. I may have to hire a legal temp to help you out. Meanwhile, you might have to work late for a few days." Dominique bit her lower lip in frustration. "Not only is the State of Florida going to inadequately compensate me, it'll probably end up costing me money to represent this guy."

"You could deduct it from your income tax as a charitable contribution," Patti suggested.

"Unfortunately, the IRS says lawyers can't do that. We have to swallow the loss."

\* \* \*

Five minutes early, the Hargraves walked through the front door of Olivet & Associates. There were no associates, and Dominique had no intention of ever having any. As a new attorney in town, she had simply liked the sound of it, and that had been that.

"Mr. and Mrs. Hargrave, I'm Dominique Olivet. Won't you have a seat, please?"

Sondra Hargrave didn't bother with niceties. "Let's not beat about the bush, Miss Olivet. We want Ben to have the very highest caliber of legal representation money can buy. Can you tell us who's considered the best on the island?"

The words rankled. In Dominique's opinion, this meeting was not getting off to a good start. Her answer was curt and to the point. "Aside from the eminent attorney who's prosecuting your son, madam, you're looking at her. Now, what can I do for you today?"

Harrison Hargrave intervened. "Sondra, be quiet. I'll handle this."

Fire blazed from Sondra Hargrave's eyes, but she remained silent.

"I must apologize for my wife, Ms. Olivet. She's very worried about our son, and the situation has her on edge. Both of us are upset, as you might expect."

"I understand." Dominique spoke the appropriate words; however, her gut—together with the story Ben had related—told her there was more to Sondra Hargrave than worry over a son's serious legal problems. She was an overbearing parent and a classic bitch. Dominique had no doubt that if Ben's mother pictured you as a threat, the slim, sinewy woman with high cheekbones and beauty-parlor-blonde hair would quickly move to eliminate you from her life.

Mr. Hargrave continued, "The paper said Ben had been forced to accept a court appointed attorney because he had no money. Our son is not a pauper, Ms. Olivet. He has a very generous trust fund available to him." He glanced at his wife before going on. "We cut down, and finally eliminated, distributions to him in order to discourage his relationship with the young lady who was killed. It was only a temporary thing, until he came to his senses. Of course, he will have access to it now for purposes of paying any necessary legal expenses."

Dominique turned away from Mrs. Hargrave and spoke directly to Ben's Father. "I'll be speaking to your son later this morning. I will be sure to pass that information along to him."

"When can we see Ben?" The concern was evident on the elder Hargrave's face.

"Your son is in one of the dorms in Unit A. They're more restrictive there. I think visitation on Mondays starts at eight in the evening." She buzzed Patti to make sure of the times. "Because you're from north of Marathon, you'll be entitled to forty-five minutes, and because you're his parents, both of you will be allowed to visit with him at the same time. I'll forewarn you that the surroundings are not very pleasant."

Dominique turned back to Sondra Hargrave. "May I ask why you didn't approve of Regina?"

"The fact is, Ms. Olivet, I didn't have anything against Regina personally. She simply didn't come from the same social strata as our son. You can overcome or camouflage the genetic pool for a while, but in the end, DNA will prevail. Regina could never have been comfortable with our social peers, nor would she ever have been accepted. She would have been a hindrance to Ben's career and social standing. We simply could not permit that."

"I see." Intentionally, Dominique moved her left hand, flashing the three carat diamond solitaire Bill had given her when they became engaged.

The effect was instantaneous. Sondra Hargrave dripped honeyed saliva as she precisely enunciated her next words. "I'm sure you understand how it is. We cannot mix with just anyone."

"Oh, believe me, Mrs. Hargrave, I understand perfectly," Dominique purred maliciously. If she had been a cat, she would have arched her back and extended her claws.

\* \* \*

"Dominique, I've been waiting to see you. It's not enough, I know, but thank you for what you did for me." There was none of the mother's arrogance in Ben's face. "You could have easily lost your license if something had gone wrong, and yet you stuck your neck out and made it possible for me to go to Regina's funeral. I'll be forever grateful. I wanted you to know that."

"I'm glad I could help," she managed to stammer. A simple thank you was fine, but more elaborate expressions of gratitude were difficult for her to handle. She wasn't sure why. Perhaps it was because, as an underprivileged child at St. Mary's, she had said thank you many times for necessities provided by the kindness of others. She had been grateful, of course, but also embarrassed by the need to accept. She did not want to see that self-conscious gratitude on the face of someone else. "How's it going otherwise?"

Ben's response was quick. "Do you know I'm not permitted to use a regular razor? I have to wait my turn for a communal electric. They're afraid the prisoners will create some sort of weapon, I suppose." He looked down, running the fingers of both hands through his hair. "Good Lord, a week ago Regina and I were planning a life together. Now, she and the baby are gone, and I'm locked up. I keep hoping it's all a bad dream, that I'll wake up, and everything will be the way it was before, but it doesn't go away."

"I'm truly sorry, Ben. I'd like to move quickly so you can get the heck out of here. The problem is, I can't do that. I need time to figure out what happened and why. We don't have an investigator, and snooping around isn't exactly my area of expertise. It'll take me longer than it would somebody who knows what she's doing." Momentarily, she had mentally focused on the plan she was formulating, almost forgetting Ben's parents. "As a matter of fact, all of this is irrelevant. Your–"

Ben interrupted her. "You would go beyond the call of duty for me even though they won't pay you what its worth?"

Dominique frowned. "I know you don't mean it that way, but the question's offensive. When I take a case, I give it all I've got. So, I think, would any other ethical attorney. You've got a lot riding on it, as do most people who need a criminal lawyer." She smiled at the young doctor-wannabe. "I'd much rather be paid what I'm worth, but if it doesn't work out that way, I still do the best job I know how. I'd be willing to bet you'll be the same way when you start practicing medicine."

Ben looked contrite. "You're right. I didn't mean the question the way it sounded. I'm sorry. And, will you please accept my apology for the way I acted when we first met? I know I got lucky when they appointed you."

"That's all right," Dominique replied. "Believe me, I didn't particularly want to represent you either. I knew Regina. I know and like her aunt. For that matter, it's not an easy situation for anyone who lives in Key West. We all pretty much know each other. That's one of the reasons this case doesn't belong here. First thing I'm doing is to ask the court to ship this case to Dade County. I'll bring you a copy of the finalized motion."

"Thank God. I was going to ask you about that."

"It should work. If the judge is thinking straight, he'll be anxious to be rid of us. If he doesn't grant the motion and you're convicted, it will be good grounds for an appeal. Also, in case he refuses to move the case out of Monroe County, I'm preparing a motion asking him to recuse."

This time, Ben looked at her as if he didn't understand.

"In plain English, that means I'll ask him to step down and have another judge assigned to the case. A refusal would give us another ground for appeal in the event you're found guilty."

"Whatever. You're the boss."

Again, she remembered the Hargraves. "As I was going to say before we got sidetracked, it looks as if you will have new counsel in the near future. He or she can take over where I leave off."

Ben's head snapped up. "No!" Then, seemingly bringing himself under control, he spoke in a normal tone of voice. "What the hell are you talking about? I don't want anyone else. I was fortunate to get you. I won't be that lucky again." There was a look of panic on his face.

"You don't need to worry, Ben. You will probably be more than able to pick among the best legal minds in the country."

"No way. I want what I've got. Why are you trying to back out on me?"

"I'm not backing out on you. It's just that your parents are here. They called last night and came to see me first thing today," she explained. "They're waiting at my office for me to let them know if you'll talk to them this evening."

Ben looked suspicious. "You haven't told them what we've talked about, have you?"

"I haven't told them anything," she reassured him. "I didn't have to. It's all over the Florida papers. The agreement was that I would listen to what they had to say and pass any message on to you. It would be up to you how much, if anything, I was free to tell them."

"What did the old parental unit mouth off about?" he asked sarcastically.

"Your father did most of the talking."

"That's surprising. He's usually pretty well run over by mother dearest."

"Apparently that's not the case when your welfare's at stake." She couldn't help herself, "He literally told her to shut up."

A smile crossed Ben's features. "What did the old man have to say?"

"He told me you have access to a substantial trust fund. He admitted they had cut you off in hopes of terminating the relationship with Regina, but now you will have full access to it for legal expenses. At that point it was obvious, but he also stressed that you have no need for a court appointed lawyer. Of course, he wanted to know if they could see you."

Ben heaved a big sigh. "I'm angry with them, big time," he said, "but they're still my parents. I do want to see them. I have no one else. Besides, I'm in dire need of money. The only condition I'll impose is that I want you in the room during the meeting."

"Ben, this is a personal matter. Don't you think it would be better if it was just family?"

"No."

She frowned, wondering how she was going to work it out. "Okay," she finally said. "I'll see what I can do. Your parents may be rich, Ben, but they're still bound by the same rules as everyone else. Normally, they would see you in one of the visitation booths. Since I'm your lawyer and we will probably be discussing legal maneuvering, let me do some talking and see if I can't arrange for us to use the booking room."

"I'm serious. Either you're there with me, or there's no meeting."

\* \* \*

Sondra Hargrave, tears streaming from her eyes, embraced her grown child.

Mr. Hargrave managed, "Are you all right, son?" before wrapping Ben in a warm embrace.

Dominique was glad the young man had family. He needed someone desperately, and an attorney did not come close to providing the emotional support he would require to see him through this ordeal. She pushed her dislike of his mother to the back of her mind.

Ben's father cleared his throat. "Now son, there's more than enough money for legal expenses. Have they said how much bond will be?"

Dominique answered for him. "Bail has been denied. I'm afraid Ben will have to sit in jail until we are able to obtain a rehearing and present what evidence we can to change the Judge's mind."

Harrison Hargrave gave her a harsh look. "It doesn't appear to me, Ms. Olivet, that you did a very good job. I don't understand what happened. Bail is always set. It may be high, but it's set."

"Dad!" Ben's voice was loud and sharp.

"It's all right, Ben. Let me try and explain to your father." Dominique turned to the older man whose looks were reflected in her client's features. "Mr. Hargrave, under Florida State law, every person charged with a crime is entitled to a pretrial release on reasonable conditions" and she stressed the next word, "*except* in certain specific cases. One of those exceptions is in a capital murder case where the proof of guilt is evident or the presumption is great. Those defendants don't get bail, period. What usually happens in this state is that the court automatically makes what is called a probable cause determination at the First Appearance and the person arrested stays in custody. The burden then shifts to the defendant to change the court's mind. Now, as you probably know from reading the newspapers, your son was found with the body of the victim, knife in hand. Until some evidence can be found to rebut the overwhelming presumption of his guilt, the chances of the court releasing him on bail are nil and none."

Ben's father looked chagrinned. "I understand. Yet again, I have to apologize. Stress sometimes brings out the worst in a person, and apparently, I'm no exception."

Dominique was gracious. "Don't worry about it. If I were you, I'd probably be in the same frame of mind." It was fortunate for Ben that he took after his father, Dominique thought. She could warm to the sincerity of the senior Hargrave.

"All right, dad. You say I have access to the trust fund for legal expenses. Well, I need money right now. Maybe we can get the judge to change his mind, but to do that, we need an investigator, and that takes money. It's going to take money to try and prove that I didn't do this, and it's going to take money to pay my lawyer."

"Don't you think the first thing we need to do is to decide on a lawyer?" Hargrave, Sr., asked his son.

"I have an attorney, dad. The only difference is that I can now afford to pay her." Ben turned to Dominique and smiled. "That is, if she's still willing to go the distance with me now that the court won't be coercing her."

"Ben, are you sure?" she stammered. "You've got the money to hire someone in the big leagues."

Ben's jaw set. "You showed faith in me when you had absolutely no basis for believing my story. You've made me feel you actually care what happens to me. I need someone like you if this fiasco isn't going to do me in. Will you please stay with me through this?"

Sondra Hargrave's prolonged silence ended. "Ben, have you gone out of your mind? This woman," she said, glancing at Dominique. "—No offense intended, Ms. Olivet—is a little fish in a big pond, and it's your life that's at stake here."

"You're right. It is *my life*, and I'm the one who's going to decide who represents me."

"Ben, we're not about to let you draw out money to–"

Ben didn't let her finish. "Mother, you can either provide me with money to pay Ms. Olivet well and to hire an investigator, or she'll continue to represent me as an indigent, which I am every time you close the flow of money from the trust fund. You can help her give me the best possible defense or you can let her go at it on her own and hope I don't receive the death penalty."

It was Ben's father who responded. "Son, as far as I'm concerned, you call the shots. I wouldn't make the same decision, but then I'm not in your shoes. If this woman is the lawyer who can help you sleep easier at night, then so be it." He turned to Dominique. "I presume you have a trust account for the safekeeping of clients' funds?"

"Of course."

"Well then, please provide me with the name of the bank and the account number. I'll wire a quarter of a million tomorrow. I'll expect an accounting of your time and the manner in which the money is spent. If those funds run out, call and let me know. I'll wire additional monies. Is that satisfactory?"

"Of course, but you must realize that Ben is the captain of this ship. I make decisions with him. I don't discuss the case, or strategy, with you unless I'm directed to do so by your son. Understood?"

"Yes. It most certainly is." Harrison Hargrave shook her hand.

## "Beware"

Eve image by Picasso Gaglione, Stampland, Chicago, Illinois; Snake image from Amy Kinsch, Beeswax Rubber Stamps, Ione, California.

# *11*

Dominique came up through a fog bank of sleep to the insistent ringing of the telephone. A quick look at the bedside clock showed two-seventeen in the morning. Instantly, she was fully awake. Telephone calls in the middle of the night, if they weren't pranks or wrong numbers, were always bad news.

"Dominique?" The caller didn't need to identify himself. It was a somber-voiced Rolf.

She walked out of the bedroom, portable phone in hand, so as not too disturb Bill, who hadn't stirred. "What's wrong?"

"I'm on a cell phone, so I can't talk freely. Do you remember what we used to refer to as Merry Christmas Park?"

"Of course."

"Meet me there in ten minutes."

Her stomach lurched. What could possibly be so important that it required her to leave the house at a time when most of the town was asleep? Certainly their middle-of-the-night talk in her garden couldn't have caused Rolf any marital problems. After all, it hadn't been planned, and nothing major had happened. She hadn't bothered to tell Bill about it. She had no idea whether Rolf had mentioned it to his wife.

She tried to awaken Bill to tell him she was leaving. He barely grunted. Moving about the room in the eerie light provided by the full moon, she pulled on a pair of jeans, threw on a tee  and raced out the door, stopping only to let the housekeeper know she would be back as soon as possible.

* * *

Merry Christmas Park, so named because, as kids, she and Rolf had come to this deserted stretch of beach to play on Christmas day afternoons, was not far, and she arrived within minutes of the call. She spotted Rolf's white Cadillac before she actually saw him. The instant she killed the engine, he was out of the car and waiting for her.

"What's wrong?" she asked anxiously.

"You never know who's listening in on a scanner. I couldn't afford to tell you where I was.  That's the reason for meeting here. Get in the car, and I'll drive you."

"Drive me where? What's going on?"  She was becoming more apprehensive by the minute.

"We're on our way to the Sanchez house. He's dead, Dominique."

"The Judge? You can't be serious?" The look on his face told her this was no sick joke; he was completely serious. "What happened?"

"The only things certain right now are that he was murdered and that he's been dead long enough for rigor mortis to set in."

"Good Lord," she said in a whisper.

"You were apparently the last person to speak to him. At least, your name was the last on  Caller ID."

"What? I'm sorry; I was thinking how awful this all is. First Regina, now the Judge. It doesn't make sense. And what about Alicia? How's she going to be able to handle it?"

"*I said,* you were the last person known to have spoken to him."

His words sank in, and she couldn't believe the implication. "You mean, I'm being taken in for questioning in the middle of the night? This is stupid." None of this made any sense, and she was becoming angry. "You know I called both of you at about the same time last night to let you know I was staying on as paid counsel."

"Look, Dominique, we have to question you. We need to know how the judge sounded when you spoke to him, what exactly was said—that sort of thing."

"For that you get me out of bed in the middle of the night? This couldn't wait until morning?"

He reached to touch her arm, but she pulled away.

"Don't get yourself all worked up," he said taking a deep breath and speaking calmly, "The real reason you're here is because the judge was killed in the same manner as Regina. I thought you would want to see the scene. I'm doing it under guise of trying to obtain pertinent information. Otherwise, I would have no excuse at all to take you there. As it is, I'm skating on thin ice by having you anywhere near the place. Do you understand what I'm trying to tell you?"

"Yes." Rolf was going out of his way for her, and she didn't know what else to say. They remained silent until they arrived at the Whitehead Street house.

The large, two-story home was cordoned off by crime scene tape, and most, if not all, of the police cruisers in Key West were parked in front. The lights blazed in the residence, giving the appearance of a late-night gala in progress. A lone, law enforcement officer stood on the sidewalk, holding Rolf's parking place.

As they passed through the living room, Dominique spotted Juan Sanchez, Jr., on the couch. His face was buried in his hands and his body shook with sobs. A female police officer was attempting to offer consolation.

"It was Chez who found his father," Rolf explained. "He said he had been trying to reach his dad all evening. When it got to be one fifteen in the morning, and the judge still wasn't answering the phone, Chez became worried and drove over to check on him."

"Where is Mrs. Sanchez?"

"She's in Miami, visiting her sister. Chez wants to be the one to call her, and I intend to honor that request, but he needs to calm down first. He's barely been able to speak since he found his father. The police dispatcher had a difficult time understanding him when he called in."

"Have you been able to question him at any length?"

"Right now, you know all I do. He saw his father; immediately knew he was dead and called the police. He hadn't touched anything except the doorknob as he came into the house and then into the bedroom. Oh, and he touched the telephone."

"Is that where he found his father, in the bedroom?"

"Yeah. Come on. Follow me." Rolf led the way up the white carpeted steps to the second floor.

She found herself wondering why Mrs. Sanchez had covered the reddish-brown, glossy, wood floors with carpeting; noticing that the chandelier over the stairway landing was too modern for the time period of the house; thinking anything, it seemed, that might keep her mind off the scene to which she was about to be exposed.

Two police officers in a military at-ease position, stood at the door to one of the upstairs bedrooms. Without a word, they stood aside.

"This isn't going to be a pretty sight," Rolf said under his breath as they walked into the room.

She merely nodded. The stench was heavy, and several seconds passed before she was able to will her eyes to focus downward. A naked Judge Juan Sanchez lay on the floor in front of a woman's antique dressing table. In this all-too-feminine room, obviously decorated to suit the taste of his wife, the pearly white carpet had striking patches of blood. Some of it was congealed, giving the appearance that a careless child had dropped small globs of cherry Jell-O on the luxurious shag. Amber urine marred the rug, as well as human feces expelled by the relaxing muscles of death. The dying man had fallen on his right side, and despite a feeling of detached surrealism, Dominique was curious as to how the head could have fallen at such a peculiar angle to the rest of the body.

Two more steps and the answer was obvious. The judge's neck had been slashed, so savagely, it appeared to be hanging by only a grotesque thread of human tissue. His head had dropped back, the fall unnaturally wedging it behind the right shoulder and a robe he had apparently intended to don. The face looked toward the door, macabre eyes and mouth open wide, a frozen look of desperation and an unspoken cry for help on the now bloodless, albino-white features.

A sour taste rose in her throat. She took a step back and turned, grabbing at Rolf to steady herself. A protective arm went around her waist. Momentarily, she let her head rest against his chest and then, almost immediately, she straightened. Trying not to breathe deeply, she said, "I need a closer look."

"Are you sure? This isn't easy, even for the seasoned professionals."

"Yes, I'm sure. I just wasn't prepared, I guess. I'll be all right." She cupped her hand over her nose.

Rolf guided her toward the cadaver, keeping his arm tightly around her waist.

She gently pushed him away and squatted next to the body. Being careful not to touch anything, she carefully scrutinized the severed throat then turned and looked up at him. "What kind of blade makes such a ragged cut?"

"I haven't discussed it with the M.E. yet, but probably some sort of serrated edge. I've been told it's not the same sort of cut that was on Regina's neck. Hers was smooth. They're similar, however, in the sense that they're both quite deep and go from side to side."

"I'm ready to leave this place. I think I've seen all I need to."

"One of the cops called Jose's Cantina and they opening up the place for us. Do you want to go over there? We can grab some coffee and talk about this for a while."

"Sure. Just get me the hell out of here." She experienced a sick feeling and a sudden knowing. Despite the reek of human waste, she at last identified the odor of her nightmare—the odor to which women of childbearing age are accustomed on a monthly basis. It was the smell of blood.

\* \* \*

Minutes later, they stood outside, inhaling deeply and drinking in the early morning air that carried the sweetness of flowers on its breath. Here there was no hint of the odor of death. Rolf listened to the ebb and flow of the town as it stretched and flexed its muscles in preparation for a new day.

"This isn't the end of it," Dominique said, sighing softly.

He hadn't been prepared for her words. "What makes you say that?"

"I can feel it. I can feel the hate," she said in a flat voice. "Whoever it is, isn't finished yet."

Her words locked him into a memory long-buried, and suddenly he was pinning her against the vine-tangled fence. "Dominique, don't do this. Don't talk like that. Not to me of all people. Please."

She tried to push his arms away. "Don't be so serious; I was just mouthing off." She gave him a forced smile. "If someone sees us like this, they're going to get the wrong idea. It's a small town, and we don't need problems."

Rolf released his hold, embarrassed and very aware that she was now trying to pacify him. "Damn. I'm the one who's sorry, princess. You frightened me. You weren't mouthing off at all. You and I both know that. You had one of those premonitions again, didn't you?"

She didn't answer.

"Don't you think I remember that day on the beach, the morning you told me there was a body around the bend, partially hidden by sea weed. You wouldn't go look, but you wouldn't budge until I did. You were right. It was there, pasty, bloated and partially eaten by sharks and barracudas. I got sick and barfed all over the poor bastard." His voice was full of intense emotion he couldn't hide.

Dominique looked at him with something akin to relief. "Your mother was furious at first. Sat me down in that big chair in the kitchen and told me I shouldn't be playing around with evil spirits. I tried to explain I wasn't doing anything; it had just come into my mind, like a scene from a movie. She kissed me and told me we were going to church to pray for God's help."

"You were gone a long time. She thought I was sleeping when you two got back, but I wasn't. She put you to bed, and then, for hours, I heard her praying. She was still at it when I finally fell asleep. She was so worried for you."

"Now it's you who worries for me, huh?"

"Guess it's a habit left over from childhood. I always had to rescue you from some escapade or other." He managed to grin, and the seriousness of the moment eased.

"I beg your pardon. I only called for you as a last resort, and besides, I seem to remember having to come to your assistance a time or two."

"That's funny. I don't recall that."

"Probably because it offends your sense of masculinity. Well, let me refresh your memory, Mr. Prosecutor. How about the time you climbed up the avocado tree in the neighbor's yard and then couldn't get back down? You weren't supposed to be up there, and if your parents found out, you were going to be in big-time trouble. Who was it that had to sneak into your garage, drag out a ladder that was way bigger than I was and then lug it three-quarters of a block to get you down?"

"Okay. Okay. So we helped each other out." He was amused and relaxed, again not prepared for the next words that came out of her mouth.

"He's going to try for me next, Rolf, and I don't want to leave my children."

\* \* \*

She sat, hands folded, staring out the side window of the car. The nudging, gut feeling that had convinced her Ben was innocent now warned that her own life was in danger, that she was surrounded by profound hatred. The island no longer seemed beautiful, and the sounds of humanity resonated in her ears like a soprano's sour note. It wasn't for herself she feared. It was for Daniella and Jordan. They needed her. She blinked away tears of frustration that threatened to spill over. Tears did no one any good. Whatever happened, she would not permit herself to be victimized. She shook her head, trying to concentrate on the scene they had left behind at the judge's home.

For several minutes, nothing was said, and then Rolf's hand reached over and covered her own. He spoke reassuringly. "I won't let anything happen to you."

She cleared her throat, giving herself time to find the right words. "It means the world to know that you care after all these years. It really does." She breathed deeply and let out a sigh. "I've missed you, Rolf. I really have." There, she'd said it. Maybe there wouldn't be another chance, and she wanted him to know. "But, the fact of the matter is that you can't be with me, twenty-four hours a day, seven days a week, and you can't order police protection just because I have a hunch my life is in danger. It sounds ludicrous to even say it out loud."

"I'll hire private protection for you."

She was emphatic. "No, you won't. I can handle it."

"Do you carry a firearm?"

She reached into her pulse and pulled out a small gun, a .25 caliber Beretta semiautomatic. "I trained with it on the police range in Miami. My aim was damn good, too; I shot the heads off most of the targets. I don't relish the thought, but I won't hesitate to shoot anyone who threatens me."

"Not good enough," he said, frowning. "It's one thing to shoot a stationary target on the range. It's another to shoot at a moving human being. You would have to have eagle-eye accuracy to bring anyone down with a .25. You need something like a .38 Walther PPK, something with enough force to knock a man down even if the shot doesn't inflict a mortal wound."

She must have frowned because he quickly added, "A James Bond gun."

"All right, I'll get one."

"Where's your concealed weapons license?"

She smiled sheepishly. "I'm sure it's at the office somewhere. I'll find it and go buy what you said."

"No. Please. At least let me do that much for you. I own an extra, and I don't want you contending with the three day cooling off period. Agreed?"

"Agreed," she answered gratefully.

"You need to find that license and carry it with you.

"Yes, sir." She smiled. "And thank you."

"I don't want anything to happen to you." Rolf's face was drawn and serious.

\* \* \*

Later, seated at her regular table at Jose's, they talked with the police officers who had been at the scene and drank Cuban Espresso laden with sufficient caffeine to keep them going through the day that lay ahead. After a time, the on-duty officers left and only Rolf, Dominique and a sleepy-eyed owner remained.

"I don't know about you, but I'm confused," Dominique offered.

"In what sense?"

"Well, I was working from a premise that if Hargrave's story was true—and I now firmly believe it is—then the killer was Regina's ex-lover. It made perfect sense to me. As soon as she told him she was pregnant, he dropped her. Maybe when she called, he thought she was going to blackmail or expose him. What better motive? Unfortunately, the judge's murder puts a damper on my theory. Why would the ex-lover want to go after Sanchez?"

"It's possible we're dealing with two different people."

"Come on now. You're kidding, right?" The owner brought the last of the espresso, and Dominique added sugar to both their cups. Might as well add a sugar high to the caffeine one. "Both MOs were identical except for the type of blade used. This is Key West, Rolf. What are the statistical odds of two throat slashers in town?"

"There's always the possibility of a copy cat," he responded, gulping down the thick, black java in one swallow.

"You know, you've just basically admitted that my client didn't kill Regina, and you wouldn't have called me in the middle of the night if you hadn't thought so then." She went for broke. "You ought to drop the charges against him."

"You're right, of course," he said quickly.

She thought she detected amusement in the way he smiled at her, almost as if he had been expecting the words and was surprised she had waited so long to say them.

"Sanchez' murder did make me doubt Hargrave's guilt, but I can't dismiss. Not yet. Technically, there's too much incriminating evidence against your client. You've still got your work cut out for you."

"It was worth a try. Any defense attorney would have asked. Would you like some donuts to go with the caffeine?"

"Why not? What's a little more sugar. Are you still into glazed?"

She nodded, and Rolf signaled for the owner. Then, he turned serious. "One thing to keep in mind is that the killer is strong. It wouldn't have been difficult to handle Regina, to keep her pinned with one arm and slash with the other, but the judge would have been a different story. Sanchez was getting up there in years, but he was big-boned and muscular, and he worked out regularly. He was strong for his age. I know because we used the same gym. In fact, we worked out together yesterday afternoon. It would have been difficult for any man to bring him down."

"I agree," Dominique commented, wrinkling her brow before biting into a donut.

"I need to mention the workout to the M.E. Sanchez probably had lactic acid in his muscles and that might distort the time of death estimate based on the rigor mortis." He made a note on the napkin in front of him and stuck it in his pocket. "A penny for your thoughts, princess."

"I was thinking that it's obvious the judge didn't put up much of a fight. It could have been somebody he knew, somebody he tried to talk to and reason with." She glanced out the window to check the weather, a habit she had acquired soon after learning to fly, and noted the soft, diffused light that comes when the sun is just below the horizon. "It's almost morning. You'd better take me back to my car. I hate to think of the talk if the State's Attorney were to be seen in the wee hours of the morning dropping off a woman who's not his wife."

He drove to where they had left her car and walked around to open the door. "If you don't have a hearing first thing in the morning, stop by the police department. They need a written statement from you."

* * *

An hour later, Dominique ran hot water and scrubbed hard, using first a wash cloth and then a pumice mitt, trying to make her skin feel clean again. Two people she knew, two people Alicia had loved, were dead. They had died brutal, ugly deaths. No matter how much she washed, how much soap she used, she felt dirty, somehow sullied by what she had seen. Tears joined the water running down her face. Ultimately, she gave up, wrapped herself in a terrycloth robe and walked to the guest bedroom on the other side of the house. She told herself it was because she didn't want to awaken Bill.

Without removing her robe, she climbed under the covers and curled into the fetal position. Sleep, as it turned out, was a state worse than the tired wakefulness she had sought to escape. She dozed, then woke with a start, sweat on her brow, shocked into consciousness by a nightmare in which the Dragon Lady and her pilot were engulfed in flames.

St. Mary Star of the Sea, is the oldest Catholic
parish in South Florida. The first church,
erected in 1852 at another location,
was destroyed by fire.

The present church, designed in High Victorian
Gothic style, was dedicated August 20, 1905
and is located at 1010 Windsor Lane.

# 12

Dominique's first stop was the police station where she was formally questioned and a statement was taken. She managed to learn that investigative efforts hadn't turned up anyone who had seen anything at the jurist's home. The only exception was the next door neighbor to the east who had been in the kitchen eating a late-night snack and had noticed the junior Sanchez when he arrived. No foreign fingerprints had been found. There were no signs of a break-in; however, that wasn't unexpected. It was generally known that the Sanchez family, like many Conchs, did not lock their doors.

The investigating sergeant agreed that the case against Hargrave was now in doubt. He indicated he would re-interview the few witnesses they had from the Casa Marina. After that, he would talk to his chief and see where they wanted to go from there.

* * *

She drove to the southern end of Old Town and knocked on a door she knew well. Presently, through the etched, glass panel, she spotted a familiar and beloved face. The door quickly opened to let her in.

"Dominique, at last you come to see me. I thought you'd forgotten this old woman."

"I could never forget you, Mama."

Dominique threw herself into the older woman's open arms. Besides her daughter, there were two females in this world she loved deeply: her judgmental mother who now lived far away and was busy with her own life and, more particularly and passionately, Mama Reina.

Reina had been loving and eccentric for as long as anyone could remember. She wore long skirts composed of sewn-together bands of fabric, all in bright, primary colors. She had once told Dominique that a Calusa Indian friend made them for her. Dominique didn't know whether the story was true. Personally, she thought the skirts resembled Seminole attire; however, there were a few descendants of the original Indians still in Key West, and she preferred to humor Rolf's mother. Reina's blouses were sometimes long-sleeved, at times short-sleeved, rarely high-necked, often low cut, but they were always consistently purple. It was her favorite color. Her black, gray-dappled hair hung to her waist in long pigtails, and she eternally sported a twisted bandana wrapped around a heavily lined forehead. Her neck supported numerous and assorted chains of gold and silver. She was short, plump and jovial. She didn't have a drop of gypsy blood, but she had the looks and the temperament and an odd ability to see what others could not. Dominique and Rolf had always known that.

She followed Reina into the massive old kitchen with its black and white tile floor, butcher-block island and stainless steel counters. The big cozy armchairs were still there, flanking the open fireplace which, when the home was first built, had served as a cook stove. Surely the fabric on those chairs, the most utilized furniture in the entire house, must have worn out during the intervening years; however, if they had been re-upholstered, Reina del Castillo had managed to find the same fabric Dominique remembered from long ago.

"I don't understand," Reina said, eyeing Dominique and addressing her in melodic Spanish, "Why didn't you come to see me when you returned to Key West?"

"I'm sorry." Dominique lowered her head in shame and responded in the tongue Reina had used. "I could lie and make up something about how busy I've been with children and profession, but it wouldn't be the truth. I think it had more to do with how much I loved you as a child, Mama. Rolf was married when I came home. He avoided me like the plague for some reason, and I knew his wife and children would be here with you. Maybe I was afraid I had been replaced in your heart, that nothing would be the same. I wanted to remember things the way they were—how much love you gave me during all those years when you were my second mother and I practically lived in this wonderful, old house."

"Dominique, don't you know no one could ever replace you? You were the only little girl I ever had."

They embraced again, laughing and talking, their words tripping over each other.

"Good morning, Reina." Sarah del Castillo strolled into the kitchen, a statuesque blonde beauty attired in a cream-colored, satin housecoat. She smiled and lightly kissed her mother-in-law on the cheek.

"Good morning, Sarita. I want you to meet Dominique Olivet, a young lady who is very dear to me. Dominque, this is Rodolfo's wife."

"Hello, Dominique." Sarah turned to Reina, "We've met on several occasions, Reina. She's married now, and her last name is Daniels."

Dominique corrected her. "I don't use my husband's last name."

"I'm sorry, I didn't know," Sarah graciously responded. "I've tried to break my mother-in-law of calling me Sarita, but she doesn't seem to listen, so I understand how you might not appreciate being addressed by the wrong name."

It was obvious Sarah didn't particularly like her husband's mother, and Dominique instinctively came to Reina's defense. "Sarita is a lovely nickname Hispanics have for Sarah. You're a beautiful woman. I'm sure that's why Mama thinks of you as Sarita. It's good to see you, Sarah." Dominique marveled at the flawless, peaches-and-cream complexion. The woman had obviously just gotten out of bed, didn't have on a bit of make-up and looked stunning. No wonder Rolf had picked her for a wife.

Sarah poured herself a cup of black coffee and lit a cigarette. She sat down at the kitchen table, took a sip and looked at Dominique with curiosity. "What brings you here so early in the morning?"

"No special reason. I just wanted to talk to Mama, and I knew at this hour of the morning I would find her in the kitchen with plenty of *café con leche*." Dominique didn't know what else to say. She wanted to talk with Reina, but what she had to say wasn't any of Sarah's business, even if this did happen to be her home now.

Sarah made no reply; instead, she turned to her mother-in-law, "The girls are getting dressed. They will be down for breakfast in a few minutes. Why don't you fix them some bacon and eggs?"

Reina responded casually. "Dominique and I have much to catch up on. I think *you* need to serve the children while we go out on the porch."

"Reina, I've got a beauty parlor appointment at nine," Sarah whined. "That would make me late, and this is color day. Why don't you take care of it like you always do?"

Reina was adamant. "No. Not today. The food's already cooked. It just needs to be re-warmed in the microwave. If that won't work for you, tell the girls to do it themselves. They know how to work that new-fangled oven better than I do."

Reina took Dominique by the hand and led her to the back porch. Dominique noticed that Reina was careful not to extend the hand on the side from which her breast had been removed. When Reina had Dominique settled, she wandered off in the direction of the kitchen and returned with two mugs of *café con leche*. She made herself comfortable in a rocker next to Dominique and took her hand. "Now, *hija*," Reina used the Spanish word for daughter. "I understand, wrong though you were why you haven't come to see me for all this time. So, why are you here now?"

Dominique saw no way but the truth. "Mama, do you remember when I knew there was going to be a body on the beach?"

"Of course. That's not the kind of thing you forget."

"Well, I had another of those premonitions yesterday. I know whoever killed Regina DeWalt and Judge Sanchez is going to come after me next. Just in case, I need to get my affairs in order. I want to make sure you know how much I loved you–still love you–and how much I've missed you. That's as simple as I can make it."

"My poor baby, come here to me." Reina rose and again extended her hand to Dominique. The older woman led the way to the top of the steps that descended to the sandy beach below. She seated herself and Dominique on the top step and cradled Dominique's head on her shoulder. Gently she stroked her hair. Dominique's eyes closed in grateful relaxation. "Did you see your own death, baby?"

"No, Mama. I only sensed he would come after me. Then, early this morning, I dreamed my plane was in flames, and I rose out of the fire like the Phoenix."

"You know that's not bad, *hija*; the Phoenix lives. It's a good sign. Remember, dreams speak symbolically. I think God is telling you some bad times are coming, but He also wants you to know you'll be all right in the end. You need to be very careful, and you must tell Rodolfo. He'll believe you."

"He already knows."

"Have you seen my boy, little one?"

Dominique smiled. "I've seen more of Rolf this last week than I have the entire time since I returned to Key West." She continued, feeling an explanation was necessary, "We're on opposite sides of Regina DeWalt's murder case. That means we have to talk a lot."

"You and Rodolfo do better working together than you do fighting." Reina smiled.

"Well, we're both looking for the truth. In that sense, we're on the same side."

"Good." Reina tilted Dominique's head to look directly into her eyes. "Everything is going to be okay. I just know it. Rodolfo will take care of you."

"I can take care of myself, thank you," Dominique answered hotly.

Reina laughed. "I know you can, but it never hurts to have help. You used to come to the aid of my stubborn son all the time, didn't you?"

"Yes, and I'm glad you remembered, but–"

"And, you didn't think he was weak just because he asked you for help, or because you offered and he didn't refuse, now did you?"

"No."

"Okay. I know you're grown up, a professional and all that, but don't be hardheaded. If my boy can help you, you let him. Do you understand?"

"Yes, ma'am." She couldn't help smiling. It felt right to be here. "I love you, Mama."

"I love you, too, h*ija*, very much."

Reina began again to stroke her hair, and Dominique marveled that she was being treated as if she were still a young child. She relaxed, letting herself enjoy the pet names, the reassurances and the caresses. Verbally sparing for a living wasn't much fun. It definitely was not the formal debate with rules of politeness that she had naively anticipated in high school. To receive from Mama the love and attention usually reserved for a child was soothing and nourishing to the hungry soul.

It was almost noon by the time she forced herself to break away. She didn't see Sarah again and left, still fearful of the troubles her dreams were predicting but solemnly swearing to Mama that she would never again stay away for long.

\* \* \*

It was lunch time when Dominique walked into the reception room of her office. She was surprised to find Patti still there.

Her secretary looked up and frowned. "I imagine you're dog tired; I heard you didn't get much sleep last night. Do you want me to order something for you to eat?"

"Yes, please," Dominique responded gratefully. "By the way, I went by the jail on the way here, trying to find Tiny Bishop. He wasn't there. Track him down for me, and ask if it would be possible for him to come by the office this afternoon. If not, ask him what time tomorrow would be good."

"What do you want with him?"

"I'll tell you after he and I talk. Oh, and call the employment agency. Ask them to send over some prospective legal temps. You can do the interviewing. I'm not in the mood. Hire the one who suits you. You're the one who's going to have to work with her, or him, as the case may be, so it might as well be somebody you think can do the work and can get along with your quirky personality." Dominique waited for her assistant's response and wasn't disappointed.

"Well, screw you."

"Sorry. I'm completely and solely heterosexual." Dominique laughed.

Patti called out to have lunch delivered and made several short phone calls. She turned to her boss, cupping her hand over the receiver, "Tiny is so excited at the thought of coming to see you I think he wet his pants. If it's okay, he'll be here in about fifteen or twenty minutes."

\* \* \*

"Little lady, I don't think I'd better sit in one of those." Tiny Bishop was looking at the wing-back chairs. "I'm too heavy." He backed away. "You'd have one expensive chair to repair."

"Don't worry about it. They're stronger than they look."

Tiny smiled. "Like you?"

"Yeah, just like me."

"What can I do for you?" he inquired.

It was the first time he had ever had contact with Dominique outside of the jailhouse, and she knew he must be curious. "I heard you have your private investigator's license. Is that right?"

"Yes ma'am. Never have made use of it, but I have it. You just don't know when the occasion might arise."

"If you're willing, Tiny, I think this is the time."

Intense interest showed on his face. "What is it you need, ma'am?"

"Well, I know that because of your seniority, you work only the day shift at the jail, and you're off on weekends. I need an investigator and a bodyguard. I was hoping you might want the job."

"Why do you need a bodyguard?" Sounding puzzled, he added, "And why me?"

"I need a bodyguard because I believe my life is in danger. I don't really want to say anything beyond that just yet. I want you because I know you and trust you. I'm aware that you were close to Judge Sanchez and that he relied on you to take care of him when his life was threatened several years ago. Let's see what else? Oh yeah, if someone doesn't know you personally, your size scares the hell out of them. On top of that, you're intelligent and reliable. I guess that about sums it up."

The big man turned a bright, tomato red. "I'll take the job. When do I start?"

He wouldn't look Dominique in the eye, and she sensed his embarrassment at her compliments. "You haven't even asked how much it'll pay or what the hours will be," she reminded him.

"It doesn't matter, little lady."

"I'll tell you anyway. You might change your mind."

"No way," Tiny quickly interjected.

"I need someone who can spend nights at my house seven days a week and be available to me twenty-four hours a day on the weekends. The job doesn't pay much initially, five hundred dollars a week, but there will be a hefty bonus at the end if you help me prove Ben Hargrave is innocent. Are you still willing?"

"When do I start?"

"How about tomorrow?"

"I'll be here at five o'clock today to escort you home. If your life's in danger, I'm not waiting around twenty-four hours."

"Thank you, Tiny. I appreciate that." Dominique smiled with relief. Knowing the gentle giant would cover her back made the picture less bleak.

"No. I want to thank *you*, Ms. Olivet. I consider it an honor that you asked. I'll see you this afternoon."

She walked Tiny to the office entry and, out of the corner of her eye, noticed a package sitting on Patti's desk. She dropped down in one of the chairs facing her legal assistant. "What's that?" She pointed at the brown-wrapped box.

"Mr. del Castillo brought this by while you were in with Tiny. He said you would know what it was about and to tell you there's a note inside." Patti wolf-whistled. "That man is one hunk of beautiful manhood." The secretary pretended to swoon in her chair. "I batted my eyelashes at him, leaned over to expose some boob, and he didn't blink an eye. What's a girl supposed to do anyway?"

"For starters, remember that he's married." Dominique glared mockingly.

"Well, don't tell me you don't think he's good looking."

Dominique smiled despite her melancholy mood. "I have to admit he's easy to look at. He wasn't bad in the sixth grade either, but I've noticed age has added a certain new element to his appearance."

"You knew him way back then?"

"Yes, ma'am. By the way, you would really fall all over yourself if you heard him play the piano. I've been told that's improved with age as well." Dominique suppressed a yawn. Last night was fast catching up to her.

"Well, so what is it? What's in the package?"

"A .38 Walther PPK."

"A what?"

"A James Bond gun." Dominique sighed.

"Yipes. What do you need that for?"

"Protection," Dominique responded as she, package in hand, rounded the corner towards her office.

Patti was immediately on her tail. "Why do you need protection? What's going on you haven't told me about?"

* * *

Late in the afternoon, Dominique sat at pool-side, sipping an iced soft drink with the children.

Bill emerged from the house. "Dominique," he said quietly. "I need to speak to you. In private, please."

She knew from the expression on his face that this wouldn't be a pleasant conversation. "Sure thing, hubby. Jordan, Daniella, you two go play. Your father and I need some time to do grown-up things." She smiled at them.

"Are you going to try and make more babies?" Jordan asked with an impish grin.

"Jordan! No, we're not. And if we were, we wouldn't tell you." She laughed. "That's big people business."

The children happily trotted off.

"Okay, hon. What's up?" she asked.

"What's up? I see a giant sitting in my living room who tells me he's staying with us for a while, and you have the nerve to ask me what's up? Don't you think this is something you and I should have discussed first?"

Dominique was shocked, mainly because Bill was right. She should have talked it over with him. It surprised her to realize how little they truly communicated. This was, however, not the time to get into a discussion about their deteriorating relationship. For the most part, her husband was perfectly happy with the way things were. As far as he was concerned, today's *faux pas* on her part wasn't a major event in their lives. It would soon blow over and be forgotten. "I'm sorry, Bill. I truly am. You're right, of course. I should have called you and talked this over. Everything happened so quickly, I just didn't think to do it. I took steps I thought necessary to protect myself for the children's sake, and I guess I just blew it as far as you were concerned. Can you get over being upset with me?"

"What the hell are you talking about? Protect yourself from what?" Bill looked puzzled now, anger forgotten.

Dominique tried to think quickly. She couldn't tell him about her premonition. That would anger him. He was completely left-brained and hated that part of who she was. She decided to tell the truth, without elaboration. "There's been a threat to my life, and I felt I needed immediate protection. I hired Tiny Bishop to come home with me when I close the office in the afternoons, to stay with us overnight and on weekends, and to do some investigative work on the criminal case I was appointed to handle."

Bill seated himself next to her. "Who threatened you?"

"I don't know. I think it's the same person who killed Judge Sanchez. He didn't identify himself."

"Were they able to put a tracer on the call?"

"It has to be a long phone call, I think, and you have to have forewarning before you can put something like that into effect." Perhaps her statements was misleading, but they weren't really out and out lies. She looked toward the pool where the children were playing, "Could we talk about this later?

Bill ignored her question. "Did the guy say what he wanted from you?"

"No. Not exactly. I think it all stems from my appointment to represent Ben Hargrave."

"Well, then, that's easily solved. You just go to whoever it is that's been assigned in place of Judge Sanchez, explain what's happened and ask to be removed from the case."

Dominique glanced at her husband, aghast. "In the first place, I'm no longer court appointed. My client has been given access to an ample trust fund, and I'm being well paid. In the second place, what you're suggesting would make me a coward."

"You're worrying about the impression you might give the people around you? You are one stupid woman." Bill raised his voice, an unusual occurrence for him. "You should be worried about the children, about me, about the impact on us if something happens to you. What about us? What happens if we accidentally get caught in the middle?" He lowered his voice. "There's not going to be any further discussion. I want you off that case. Let some man take care of it."

Dominique's face reddened. She had always made most of the decisions in the family because Bill didn't want to be bothered. Now, he was actually ordering her. She really didn't know him at all, and sadly, much of what she did know, she didn't like. "Bill Daniels, don't you ever tell me what I can and cannot do. Am I making myself perfectly clear?" She went on, not waiting for an answer. "It was wrong of me to bring a stranger into this house without consulting you. For that, I've apologized. The rest is nonnegotiable, and we're not going to talk about it again. I may be scared—as a matter of fact, I am scared—but I am not a coward, and I won't have my children thinking I am. I intend to take all feasible precautions and continue to do the best job I can for my client. Case closed."

"You're a damn hard-headed bitch!" Bill responded hotly. He turned his back and returned to the house.

Their civility and superficial gestures of affection, she now realized, held back much that was festering under the surface. "And you're not at all the man I thought I married," she responded sadly.

*  *  *

Here they were again, crammed into St. Mary's for yet another funeral. Once more, the local attorneys occupied their places of honor at the front of the church as was customary at the death of one of their own. Who would attend her requiem she wondered casually, and what would they think of her after she was gone?

This time her husband was grudgingly in attendance. Bill hated funerals, but Dominique had convinced him, once the harsh words between them were glossed over by sexual overtures on her part, that it would look bad if he didn't attend. At the registry book, they spoke briefly to Rolf and Sarah. Unseen, Rolf squeezed Dominique's hand in a gesture of support. She grasped at the emotional lifesaver.

The priest did not say much about the life of the man who all present knew well. It wasn't customary in the Catholic Church to eulogize a person during Mass. The church ritual was intended to aid the spirit of the deceased make the transition from the physical world to that of the spiritual. Words of praise which might console friends and family were reserved for the grave site. During the homily, the Catholic version of the Protestant sermon, the priest voiced his hope that the recent killings were an aberration, that it would be a long time before such things happened again in the island city.

Dominique breathed deeply. There it was again, the odor of blood—now inexplicably  commingled with the scent of white roses. Her skin crawled.

# *13*

Why did she have to ruin everything? He had loved her, he really had, more than he'd ever thought he was capable of loving anyone. Well, that wasn't precisely true, he thought, doing the utmost to be honest with himself. There was, in fact, one person he loved more. Himself. He was God's creation, and as such, he owed it to the Supreme Being to protect that masterpiece of human genesis. If you were content with yourself, and he was, then you knew God was happy with you, that you were one of His success stories. In that case, your own life was of primary importance. Over and above everything else, you had to protect the sanctity of what it was that made you who you were, that made you what God had intended. He should have realized Regina was flawed from the first moment she indicated to him she wasn't happy with her life. But no, he thought he could salvage her, make of her what the Lord had willed. He was so wrong.

Regina had eventually rebuffed his efforts. She weighed morality by human standards and stupidly, found him lacking. She used her own human ruler as a measuring stick, and she threatened him. She dared to menace a glorious opus of God. She had no conception that she was putting the entirety of his person in jeopardy. That, he could not tolerate, no matter how much he cared for her. Poor fool. She had decimated their love. She put herself and her unborn child above him, and it was a fatal mistake. He hated her for destroying the love they had felt for each other. He hated her even more for obliterating the image he held of her. It was now almost incomprehensible to him that he had imagined her to be mature and intelligent. Oh, she was pretty, and she spoke well enough, but she had been no more intellectual than all the rest of them. Not at all worthy of him and his devotion.

Still, physically she had thrilled him until the very end, could still do so each time his mind replayed the magnificent jolt that permeated his body when the warmth of spurting blood made contact with his skin. Each drop of her blood had carried with it a life force of its own, an electrical current that instantaneously traveled to, and culminated, between his legs. Never before had he experienced anything so erotic, so invigorating, so excruciatingly unbearable. He had swelled and throbbed. The sound of a key in the door had not stopped the explosion as he unzipped his pants. Even now, thinking about it, he grew hard.

Compelling himself to ignore the present response of his body, he sat in his room of mementos, strategically planning the next move. He needed to concentrate on the task at hand. All of this was her fault. He hadn't wanted to kill her, but she had forced his hand.

He hadn't planned to kill the elder Sanchez either; he had just wanted to talk to him, to explain what had happened and why; to get it through the man's head that Hargrave had to be found guilty. He wanted to fuel Sanchez' fire. There must be no room for mercy, no legal loopholes permitted through which the incarcerated man might wriggle. That Hargrave wasn't the killer was irrelevant; the man defiled Regina and confused the issue of the unborn child's parentage. His punishment would be just and would serve to close the case in the eyes of the authorities.

He no longer wanted to maintain the affair, he had explained to Sanchez, but Regina was never to be touched by another. She should have faded into the background, raised the bastard and graciously accepted whatever assistance he sent her way. Instead, she whored herself and threatened him with a child that might not even be his.

The longer he talked, the more the judge had looked at him aghast, as if he were crazy, insinuating that he needed to be committed to the state mental institution. "You killed her, didn't you?" Those were the old man's last words. Juan Sanchez was another fool who couldn't be suffered.

The judge's death was not in vain, however. Standing there, bathed in the old man's life blood, mouth open to savor and swallow from the carotids' fountains, he had finally understood. There was no male or female, no heterosexual or homosexual; there was only life and the scarlet fluid that sustained it. Taking into himself the energy that gave life to another added to the majesty of his own being. It was the ultimate climax.

A new judge, an outsider, would soon be brought in. He couldn't chance an intervention with a stranger who was not a Conch and had no ties to the island. Hell, Sanchez should have understood the power of a man who drank another's blood. He should have accepted the knowledge he had been handed and insured that his rulings during trial led the jury down a one-way street to a guilty verdict. Instead, the stupid man had sealed his own fate.

In all probability, her scumbag lover would be found guilty anyway, he reasoned; they had found him with the murder weapon in hand. There had been a moment of panic when he realized the knife must have fallen from his briefcase, but in the end, it had been a good thing. Medical students were supposed to be intelligent, but this imbecile had picked it up, providing the only prints the authorities would find. He could no longer assure that the man would receive death, but surely, the jury would return a guilty verdict. Unless, and he tensed at the thought, Dominique Olivet got in the way. Damn that woman. Females had no business being in the legal profession. They thought with their hearts and not their heads. Logically, she should have accepted that all the facts pointed to her client's guilt and tried to work out a plea bargain. But no, she was bound and determined to prove Hargrave innocent to further her own career, and she was good. Too good. She might get Hargrave off, and then they would search for someone else. He couldn't let that happen.

That fucking misfit of a lawyer must be eliminated. Unfortunately, he'd miscalculated when he killed Sanchez. Because he had not gone there with the intention to murder, he'd used what he could find, a knife from a cheeseboard Sanchez had carried to the bedroom with a nighttime snack. Though both murder weapons had been disposed of miles out in the Gulf, there were now two people killed with the same type weapon, one of those murders committed with Hargrave behind bars. That fact would help the bitch in formulating her defense. He would not let her imminent death follow the same pattern.

Fuck. What was the world coming to? He was trained to kill in war. Now, he was killing civilians, and it was all the fault of two fucking women. Carefully, he cleaned the rifle he treasured, the one that had brought him out of Vietnam alive. Soon, Dominique Olivet would belong to him. That magnificent life force would become a part of his body.

# 14

In the first row of the courtroom sat Mr. and Mrs. Hargrave with Ben's older brother and the friends who had accompanied Ben to Key West months earlier. Today's proceeding was a rehearing on the issue of bail, and they were waiting, watching and hoping that Dominique could change the new judge's mind.

Regina's parents were also in attendance, along with the girl's maternal grandmother and Alicia, who was now thin, haggard and all but impossible for any, except close friends and relatives, to recognize. The death of her niece, together with the murder of her employer and friend, coming so close together, had aged her. Regina's family sat distant from the Hargraves.

The remaining open space overflowed with news media jostling for the best positions.

At the prosecution table, Rolf was assisted by Scott Reynolds, a junior attorney fresh out of law school. He was there, Dominique presumed, to learn and to get his feet wet in a big case.

Ben Hargrave sat with Dominique at the defense table. On this day, he looked a member of the class into which he had been born, wearing a navy blue suit, white shirt and a maroon silk tie supplied by his parents.

On the bench was Norman Rothman, a Dade County retired jurist with many years of courtroom experience. Rothman had been assigned by the Court Administrator for the Sixteenth Judicial Circuit to cover Monroe County until the Governor could appoint a new judge to fill Sanchez' unexpired term. Judge Rothman was a no-nonsense jurist, accustomed to decorum in the courtroom. There would be no small town informality today, and Dominique felt herself slip into familiar territory.

Judge Rothman had reviewed the file, listened to argument of counsel and taken Dominique's Motion for Change of Venue under advisement. His decision not to rule immediately on that particular issue meant that he wanted time to research the most recent applicable case law before making up his mind. The ruling might come tomorrow or it might come weeks down the road. There was no way to tell; nevertheless, it seemed apparent to Dominique that Judge Rothman would move the case to Miami.

Today, however, it was his job to determine whether Hargrave would be released on bail pending trial. He began by telling the attorneys that he would hear the matter in the order in which it had been originally filed—the prosecution would go first on its Motion For Detainment Pending Trial, and the burden would then shift to the defense to show why the prosecution's motion should not be granted.

The hearing was scheduled to begin at three o'clock. If Rothman thought this would be over in two hours, he was sadly mistaken. Dominique's hopes of prevailing on the bail issue were not high, but she intended to use this time as a fishing expedition for any evidence that might be helpful to Hargrave's defense.

It was shortly after three when Officer Jack Smithson took the stand. He testified pretty much as Rolf had reported to Dominique that he would.

There were several points she wished to clarify, and she rose for cross-examination. "Officer Smithson, did you see any signs of the key to the room?"

"Yes ma'am. It was on the floor, just inside the door."

"It is accurate to say that my client showed no signs of anger when you approached him, isn't that correct?"

"Oh, yes, ma'am; that's exactly right. The guy didn't show signs of anything. He was a zombie. That's why I read him his rights twice. I wanted to make sure he heard and understood."

Next on the stand was Officer Joe Rodriguez, a young rookie. This was his first time on the stand. His hands trembled, and his voice shook. On questioning by the prosecution he testified that it was only after they had returned to the station that Hargrave became responsive and communicative. He had refused an attorney saying he had nothing to hide. All in all, direct-examination was pretty much as Dominique had anticipated. She was about to announce she had no cross-examination when her gut nudged her. She remembered Rodriguez stating that he had gone through Regina's purse, but she couldn't recall the mention of any specific contents. "Officer Rodriguez, what did you find when you went through Ms. DeWalt's purse?"

"Objection, Your Honor. This is outside the scope of direct."

"Overruled, Mr. Reynolds. The officer previously testified on direct that he went through the contents of the victim's purse. Ms. Olivet is entitled to follow up. Please answer the question, Officer."

Rodriguez looked at the judge and then at Dominique. "I found all the usual things one would expect in a woman's purse and then some. You know, comb, lipstick, compact, a bottle of Motrin." He paused momentarily, closing his eyes in an apparent effort to remember. "A roll of Lifesavers, some pens, keys, perfume, a small notebook and her wallet. I think that was about it."

"Was there anything written in the notebook?"

"No, ma'am. It was just blank pages."

"What about the wallet," Dominique began. She stopped and rephrased the question. "Was there anything in the wallet you thought was out of the ordinary?"

"Yes, ma'am."

"Please describe what that was."

"Well, Regina—I mean the victim—had more than two thousand dollars in cash. It was about three hundred dollars over that. The two thousand was in starchy, fresh, one hundred dollar bills."

"Why did you find that out of the ordinary, Officer?"

"Because I knew Regina personally, ma'am. She didn't make that much money. I was surprised when I saw all those bills."

"Was there anything else you thought unusual?"

"Yes, ma'am."

"What was that?"

"Her checkbook was, you know, actually part of the wallet. When I looked through it, I found she had been depositing two thousand dollars every month into a savings account. At the same time, she was making regular biweekly deposits into her checking account. As I said, I knew her personally, ma'am. She was paid every two weeks, so I assumed the deposits into the checking account were her pay checks. I was puzzled as to where she was getting the additional money she was putting into savings."

"Did you ever discover where that money came from?"

"No, ma'am. Still have no idea."

If Rolf knew about this, why hadn't he told her? She didn't yet understand the significance of the money, but it could very well be related to the murder. "Did you tell the State's Attorney about the money?" Dominique glanced at Rolf. His face was serious, but she couldn't read his expression.

"I did not, ma'am." He quickly added, "It wasn't my place. It's the duty of the detectives to notify the State's Attorney of any details they feel are important."

"Do you know if any of the detectives did that?"

"No, I don't, ma'am."

She was wondering just how many times in a row she would be addressed as "ma'am", when she saw Tiny come in to the courtroom, wiggle his finger at her and stand by the small gate separating the attorneys from the public areas of the courtroom. "Your Honor, with the court's permission, may I take two minutes to approach the defense investigator who's just entered the courtroom? I believe he has an urgent message for me."

"Permission granted, Ms. Olivet. As a matter of fact, this appears to be a good time for a fifteen minute break. We can all stretch our legs and get a drink of water. Court will resume at four-ten, promptly." The gavel sounded, and all stood as the judge left the courtroom, his bailiff in tow.

Dominique hurried toward Tiny, walking past the prosecution table where Rolf remained standing behind his chair. "I didn't know," he said in a low tone of voice.

Tiny's face was beet red; it was obvious he had been rushing in the afternoon heat. "You're not going to believe this," he whispered handing her a folded sheet of paper. "I've had it checked for prints, and there aren't any, so don't worry about handling it."

Seven simple words, written in flowery cursive: "Check Regina's blood type against her parents." There was no signature.

"Where did you get this?"

"I went by your house after lunch. Your housekeeper was out somewhere, and I don't know what time she left, so I have no idea when the note was put there. Somebody stuck it between the screen and the wood door." He was breathing hard and stopped to take a deep breath. "I checked the door for prints, but no luck. Listen, I've got to get back to the jail. I'll see you at five, either here or at the house."

Dominique walked over to Rolf. "Smile for the cameras, and act as if we're checking our appointments." Rolf pulled a small leather book from the inside pocket of his jacket and began to flip through the pages. "I need to talk to you," Dominique said as she pointed to a spot of no particular importance. "Is it okay if I come by your house tonight, ostensibly to check on Mama?"

"Make it around ten," he responded, a puzzled look on his face. "The children will be in bed then, and we won't have to contend with them. They like to monopolize my time when there're up and I'm home. Meanwhile, I'll make it a point to find out why the money wasn't mentioned to me."

Court resumed at exactly four-ten. Judge Rothman was, if nothing else, punctual. He made it clear that when a time was announced, it would be strictly adhered to. At the start of the proceedings, he'd had everyone in the courtroom synchronize their watches. Four-ten did not mean four-nine or four-eleven; it meant four-ten precisely.

Officer Rodriguez again took the stand. Dominique was quick to rise. "I have no further questions of this witness, Your Honor."

"Do you have any re-direct, Mr. Reynolds?"

"No, Your Honor. As far as the prosecution is concerned, this witness may be excused."

"Very well, Officer Rodriguez, you may step down. You're finished here for today."

Next to take the stand was the Monroe County Medical Examiner, Dr. Benjamin Silvas. Dr. Silvas had been in Key West for as long as Dominique could remember and had to be bumping seventy. He was brilliant, however, and his mind remained agile. She respected him and was anxious to hear his testimony.

The assistant prosecutor again rose. "Dr. Silvas," he began, "you performed an autopsy on the body of Regina DeWalt?"

"Yes, sir, I did."

"Were you able to determine the time of death?"

"Yes. Life ceased at approximately forty minutes after midnight on the morning of September 20."

"Please tell this court your finding as to the cause of death."

"The cause of death was a knife wound to the neck which sliced through the carotid arteries, severed the spinal cord and caused exsanguination." The witness slid a thumb across his throat in a slicing motion.

Instantly, Dominique was on her feet. "Objection, Your Honor. The witness' movement of the hand was irrelevant and prejudicial."

"Overruled."

"Doctor, do you have an opinion as to whether death was instantaneous?"

Dominique once more jumped up. "Objection, Your Honor. Irrelevant. We are here today only to determine—"

"I understand the law, Ms. Olivet," the judge replied curtly, "however, I see no harm. There's no jury here to be prejudiced. Objection overruled. Continue, Dr. Silvas."

Dr. Silvas went on as if there had been no interruption in the exchange, "No, it wasn't. In my view, there is no such thing as instant cessation of brain activity—unless, of course, the brain is destroyed by some cataclysmic event. We don't have that situation here. It is my opinion that Regina DeWalt's brain continued to function and comprehend what was taking place until—"

Again, Dominique rose. "Same objection, Your Honor." Why was an imminent jurist permitting this kind of testimony? Was he merely intrigued with the gruesome details?

"Overruled, Ms. Olivet. Proceed, Doctor."

"As I was saying, I think her brain continued to function, and she knew what was happening to her until the disruption of circulation caused loss of consciousness and then death."

"On what do you base your opinion?"

"The medical literature has numerous references to that sort of phenomena. For example, there are the anecdotal reports regarding Europeans executed by guillotine during the Middle Ages. The executioners would find every tenth head or so moving its eyes, perhaps in a desperate effort to communicate."

This time, Dominique didn't bother to object. The judge was right, of course. Irrelevant and poisonous though it might be, this wasn't a jury trial, and there was no real harm. In front of a jury, permitting such prejudicial testimony would be reversible error. Judge Rothman and Dr. Silvas both knew that. The medical examiner had to be toying with the new man on the block, having a little fun with Scott Reynolds. She doubted the doctor would ever make such comments in front of a jury. Rolf definitely needed to bring his unseasoned assistant up to par.

By the time Reynolds finished his questioning, it was four forty-five, and the judge announced it was a good time to adjourn for the day.

Dominique was repulsed; that the brain could comprehend its separation from the body that gave it life sent chills of horror down her spine.

The interior of St. Mary, Star of the Sea,
is in the Byzantine style.

# 15

"So much for pretending to visit my mother," Rolf said as soon as he opened the door.

"What do you mean?"

"I called to let Mama know what was going on, and she immediately made plans to be away from the house with Sarah and the children."

"Why?"

"She felt we wouldn't be able to discuss business with the family here. She took them on an overnight to Miami to shop for clothes." He shrugged. "I had no say in the matter. There's nothing Sarah likes more than shopping."

"So, do you expect me to be as coy as you were when you discovered there was no one at home with me?"

"I wasn't being coy. I was uncomfortable about the situation, that's all," he said dryly.

"Well, if it makes you feel any better, I'm the one who's uncomfortable now."

He stepped aside. "We can't just stand here, so come on in."

Dominique entered the formal living room. As far as she could tell, nothing had changed. If Sarah had put her mark on anything, it didn't show here. She fell into a large over-stuffed chair and curled her legs under her.

"Okay, counselor, what did you need to see me about?" His tone was formal.

"Not even the offer of a cold drink? Just right down to business, huh?"

"I'm sorry. To tell you the truth, I feel guilty as hell."

Dominique laughed. "That's what comes from being Catholic. We're always feeling guilty about something or other. It's part of the religious upbringing."

Rolf didn't join her in laughter. "And I'm trying to make sure that there's nothing to feel that way about."

She gave up trying to be humorous. "I'm sorry, too. I knew that, and I should have just let it be. Here, this is what I wanted you to see." Out of the pocket of her jeans she pulled a photocopy of the note Tiny had found earlier in the day. "By the way, if it gives you some sense of righteousness, we have a chaperon parked outside.

"What are you talking about?"

"I hired Tiny Bishop as my bodyguard and investigator."

Rolf glanced out the window. "You weren't kidding." He turned back to look at her. "Where's your car?"

"I rode my bike."

Rolf raised his voice. "Dominique, that's not safe. What the hell kind of bodyguard is Bishop if he lets you pull something that stupid?"

"It's not his fault. I insisted. I suppose he could have quit on me to make a point, but then, I wouldn't have had anyone to follow me here."

"I don't know what to do about you." His voice held the tone of exasperation she had heard often when, as a child, she had done something that got them both in trouble.

"There's nothing for you to do about me. I'm not your responsibility, now am I?" Before he could respond, she added. "Sorry. I didn't mean that. I'm a bit on edge."

"Don't worry about it. Let's just start all over again. Now, where did you find this note?"

Dominique quickly explained Tiny's discovery.

Rolf thought for a moment, let out a breath and watched her carefully. "Do you have any idea what it means?" he asked.

"As a matter of fact, I think I do, but why am I getting the impression you're way ahead of me?"

He was insistent. "First, tell me what you think."

"My initial thought was that there would be no sense in saying such a thing unless the parents' blood types would show the impossibility of either one being Regina's biological parent. So?" When he didn't respond quickly enough, she added, a little irritably, "Your turn."

"I tend to agree with you. I'm not sure what's going on, but I do know that during the years you were away, rumor had it that Regina was actually Alicia's child, given up for adoption to her sister and brother-in-law."

Instantly, Dominique was excited about the possibilities. "Who's the supposed father?"

"If the rumor's even true, and it appears from this note that it just might be, it was probably Sergio Sanchez, the guy she dated for a couple of years during high school." He frowned. "I'd sure as hell like to know who sent the note and why."

"Sergio Sanchez? The judge's brother?"

"His younger brother. He always wanted to be a priest; everyone, including Alicia, knew that. If she did get pregnant by him, I imagine she wouldn't have wanted to tell him. She doesn't seem like the type who would coerce a man into marrying her. Sergio is the pastor at some Miami parish now. He was the priest assisting at the judge's funeral Mass."

Dominique made a mental note to sic Tiny on this new angle.

"By the way, I now know why I wasn't informed about the money in Regina's wallet," Rolf added.

"You haven't broken all your old bad habits, either." She remembered that he would jump from one subject to another without warning and thought it fun to entice with a hint of news to come, then stop so that you had to ask for it. She smiled and complied, "And?"

He ignored her jibe. "Those idiots were positive they had the killer. Thought it was an open and shut case, so there wasn't any need to mention it. That was stupid, very stupid. I can assure you that nothing like that will happen again."

She had no problem envisioning the nervous detectives and the dressing-down that must have followed today's court session.

Shop talk seemed to relax Rolf. "Come on," he said. "This room's too formal. Let's sit on the back porch. We'll make a pit stop in the kitchen. I'm be willing to bet Mama made sure there were Cokes for you."

Dominique joined in good-natured banter. She was at home. If houses had spirits, this one was the essence of love, and she was transported to the happier days of childhood.

Rolf poured Coke over ice. "How about a shot of rum and a slice of lime?"

"No *Cuba Libre*, thanks. Straight Coke is fine. I'm suddenly in a good mood. No liquor required."

Drinks in hand, they walked to the back porch where, only days earlier, Dominique had visited with Mama Reina. They sat now, listening to the sea quietly lapping on the shore and watched the moon glisten on night water.

"Why can't things be the way they were, Rolf?" She turned to look at him, trying to read his face by the light coming through the kitchen window.

He didn't immediately respond. Instead, he reached for her hand and held it between his own. Slowly, without returning her gaze, he lifted her hand to his lips. "This is why not," he whispered.

She held her breath and time stood still—until seconds, or maybe it was minutes later, she found herself being pulled from the rocker.

"Come on. I'll race you down the beach," he teased, dragging her along.

"You're such a sucker. You never could beat me." She laughed.

"My legs were shorter then," he retorted, releasing her hand and pulling away at the water's edge.

"But I'm smarter now." She shot after him. Twenty yards down the beach, she took a deep breath, gave it all she had and momentarily pulled alongside him. As she did, she shifted her weight to the right and slammed him hard with her hip. Thrown off balance, he stumbled into the clumped-up seaweed. "I told you that you couldn't beat me," she gasped, running toward the imaginary finish line.

Inches before she reached sweet triumph, he swept her into the air and carried her ahead of him, a nautical figurehead with flowing dark hair that whipped his face. "Who beat whom?" He asked, laughing as he set her down.

"I crossed the line first," she argued playfully. She looked at his face, illuminated by the light of the full moon and her eyes no longer laughed. "Why? Why can't everything be the way it was?"

"It just can't. We're not kids any more, Dominique. What we had between us then, isn't acceptable now." He hesitated. "Nor is it possible for me. We're not the same people."

"I'm the same person you've always known. You've changed. Not me." Tears she couldn't stop ran down her face, and she dropped to the sand, sobbing.

Slowly, he lowered himself to his knees in front of her, reaching out to wipe away the tears. "What's wrong, princess? Why are you crying?" He brushed the hair from her face. "What do you want from me?"

Dominique confronted his gaze. "I don't know." Her emotions were too close to the surface. She truly didn't know, and she sensed that facing this now could throw them into a rift from which there might be no return. "I'm not crying because of you, dope. I think I stepped on a piece of glass or something." She lifted her foot and pointed to where blood oozed from the arch. She tried to laugh but barely managed a choked giggle. The pain in her chest hurt far more than the laceration.

Rolf examined her foot in the moonlight. "You have a piece of glass wedged in there. I don't want to pull it out until we have something to stem the bleeding. Come on."

"I don't think I can walk."

"You're not going to walk. Here, lean on me, and I'll help you."

Together they rose from the sand, and he lifted her into his arms. He carried her easily, and she relaxed, wrapping her arms around his neck and laying her head on his shoulder, grateful for the momentary feeling of peace and security.

"Don't think I'm not aware of what we're skirting around. Glass in your foot isn't enough to make you cry. You're too tough for that," Rolf whispered, looking down at her. "Your parents should never have taken you away from Key West. This was your home, the place where you belonged."

There was no more to be said. She closed her eyes and buried her face in the collar of his shirt.

* * *

Rolf still carried her as they entered the house. Dominique heard his whispered, "Shit," and raised her head. A scowl was painted on Sarah's face.

"I thought you were going to Miami. What happened?" Rolf asked.

"I'm the one who should be asking questions. It's obvious you weren't expecting me to be here," Sarah responded dryly. "You didn't tell us you were having company."

Reina quickly intervened. "That's not true, Sarita. Rodolfo told me earlier today that Dominique would be stopping by to discuss some business. He didn't hide anything from you. I didn't think it was important, so it slipped my mind to mention it."

"Well, it doesn't look like business to me."

Rolf ignored the chatter, gently setting Dominique down in one of the big chairs. He addressed his wife, "Sarah, you and I will discuss this later. In the meantime, a guest in our home is injured. Stop carrying on and find a towel for her foot. I'll get the emergency medical kit from the pantry."

Sarah didn't move, but Reina wasted no time grabbing a clean kitchen towel from a nearby drawer. "Let me see, child." Dominique bit her lower lip as Rolf's mother lifted the injured foot and examined the cut. "You have a piece of a beer bottle embedded in your foot. Rodolfo should drive you to the emergency room. This might take a couple of stitches and a tetanus shot."

Dominique balked. "I'm current on my tetanus shot, and I don't want to go to the hospital, Mama. It's been a long day, and we have court tomorrow morning. I'll be fine with some disinfectant and a bandage."

"She's bleeding on the floor." Sarah's voice was cold.

"Oh, I'm sorry." Dominique glanced down at the small pool created by the droplets of blood accumulating on the white tile. "I'm staining the grout."

"Don't worry about it, *hija*."

Sarah glared at both women. "You know, Dominique, you've been back in Key West for years now, and we hardly ever see you, even in this small town. Now, all of a sudden, you're in my life daily, my mother-in-law refers to you as her daughter, and my husband is carrying you around in his arms. Doesn't that seem a bit unnatural to you?"

Reina put her arm around Sarah's shoulders. "Please don't be upset, Sarita. Dominique has always been my little girl. She always will be, but that doesn't mean I don't care about you. That's not so hard to understand, is it?"

Sarah didn't answer and moved away from her mother-in-law.

Reina persisted. "How could you expect her to walk with a piece of glass in her foot?" she asked in a voice that was soft and conciliatory.

"She wouldn't have glass in her foot if she hadn't been out on the beach with my husband."

"I'm sorry you're upset, Sarah," Dominique was quick to interject. "It looks bad, I know, but I assure you nothing happened except for this cut on my foot. Maybe it will put you at ease to know that my husband isn't happy in Key West, and when the case Rolf and I are working on is over, we're moving back to Seattle." Once the words were spoken, Dominique was stunned, disbelieving they had actually come out of her own mouth. She loved Key West and hadn't considered leaving ever again. It was just that being close to Rolf brought quiet contentment one moment and devastating pain the next. She wanted to run to him and away from him. How could she honor her marriage vows when what she wanted, and couldn't have, stared her in the face? She had to get away.

Rolf stopped in the doorway, his face ashen.

"Isn't it a shame, honey?" Sarah smiled at her husband as she spoke, "We were just becoming friendly with your mother's surrogate daughter, and she'll be leaving town soon."

Rolf didn't respond. He walked to the chair where Dominique sat and knelt on the floor in front of her. "I'm going to pull this out on the count of three."

As he did so, the blood flowed freely. Reina applied ice cubes wrapped in a towel. Once the blood flow ceased, Rolf covered the cut with antibiotic ointment, gauze and a bandage. "I'll carry you out to Tiny's car," he said. "He can drive you home, and you can pick up your bike another day."

"I can walk." Dominique began to rise.

"You're not walking." Without waiting for a possible argument, Rolf lifted her from the chair and carried her toward the front door.

This time she didn't relax in his arms. Once on the front porch, she spoke calmly. "Put me down, Rolf. I'm perfectly capable of doing this myself."

"Very well. If that's what you want." Without another word, he walked back into the house, slamming the door behind him.

* * *

Dominique hobbled down the steps and reached behind her bike for the backpack she had stashed. As she bent over, looking for house keys while favoring her injured foot, she lost her balance and fell. It was then she heard an engine backfire and, simultaneously, perceived an eerie, almost silent whine. She had never heard anything quite like it before, but the feeling it elicited was unmistakable. It was the same palpable hatred she had sensed the night Sanchez died. Survival instinct took over, and she reached for the .38.

Understanding that she had narrowly escaped being hit by a bullet, Dominique stretched out flat on the ground. She peered through the shrubs, saw a moving shadow and shot off four rounds in rapid succession. Thinking with the swiftness of pumping adrenaline, she reserved bullets on the off chance her assailant might backtrack. In was only in hindsight that she blanched at the thought she might have fired at an innocent passerby.

*Where the shit is Tiny?* she thought just before the weight of the world landed on her body and everything went black. Through a haze, she distinguished voices. For the third time that night, she was being cradled in Rolf's arms.

"Dominique! Dominique, can you hear me?"

"I'm all right," she managed to gasp. "Tiny just landed on me like a ton of bricks. I'm not hit." She tried to get up, but the pain was excruciating. She feared that in his attempt to shield her, Tiny might have fractured one or more of her ribs. Again, she tried to raise herself. It was painful, and she groaned against her will.

"Mama, call Dr. Ortiz!" Rolf shouted to his mother.

Reina ran for the telephone. Sarah, still as an alabaster statue, stood in the doorway and stared silently at Dominique. Rolf and Tiny helped Dominique to her feet.

"I'm sorry, little lady," Tiny said, in a scared whisper.

"It's all right, Tiny. It really is." Dominique attempted to reassure him. "If there had been more shots, you would have taken them for me. I can't complain about someone who's willing to put his life on the line for me, now can I?" Tiny's face relaxed. "I need to get inside," Dominique uttered between painful breaths. "Could you help me up the steps?"

The two men did as she asked, Rolf hovering over her, a look of total and complete shock on his face. "Are you sure you're okay? You're positive you weren't hit?" he asked anxiously.

"I'm fine. I really am. I just had the wind knocked out of me. I need to catch my breath."

Police sirens screamed in the distance, and soon, police cruisers pulled up in front of the house. The doctor arrived within minutes and examined Dominique while Rolf paced the wooden floor. Finally, he said, "She's going to be fine. She'll probably be sore, but I'll give her some pills to take care of that and to help her sleep."

"I don't need sleeping pills," Dominique countered.

"They're not sleeping pills, Ms. Olivet. They're muscle relaxers. You don't need to take them if you don't wish, but if you don't, you're going to hurt in places you weren't aware were part of your body before today. It's your choice. If you take them, they'll get rid of the pain, but they'll make you sleepy in the process."

She swallowed the pills.

Officer Smithson poked his head through the door. "Is it okay to come in, sir?" he respectfully asked the prosecutor.

"Yes. It's fine. The doctor's finished."

The young policeman looked down at Dominique and, smiling, spoke softly, "You got off at least one lucky shot. There are drops of fresh blood on the sidewalk. It looks as if you hit your assailant."

Dominique glared, and in a now-strong voice, stated firmly, "I don't believe luck had much to do with it, Officer. You might find it interesting to know that I aimed."

Rolf smiled.

"Tiny, I think it's about time to head home." She wasn't successful in disguising a groan.

"No, child. I'm not letting you out of this house tonight," Reina declared.

"But Mama—"

"No buts. I'll call your husband and explain what's happened. He can come see you here, even spend the night if he wishes, but you're not going anywhere."

"Rolf, do something, please. Your mother is strong-arming me."

Rolf walked over to the couch and gingerly sat next to Dominique. "Mama's right, Dominique. You need to be here where she can take care of you until we're sure the medication has worn off. Besides, you don't want your kids to wake up in the middle of the night and see you looking like this. It would scare the hell out of them. I'll have whatever you need for tonight, and for court in the morning, brought over. Tiny can go back to your house and look after the family." He paused, then added, "I'm even willing to promise that what happened tonight will be kept under wraps for a while but, and it's a big but, only if you cooperate and don't give Mama a hard time. Deal?"

Dominique frowned but nodded in agreement. An hour later, barely able to keep her eyes open, she showered, cleaning off bloody scrapes as well as bits of dirt and grass and was tucked into bed by Reina.

"*Hija*, I thank God nothing serious happened to you." She kissed Dominique on the forehead. "You aren't really going to leave us again, are you?"

"Oh, Mama, I don't know." She took Reina's hand. "When I said that, I was upset. It's true that Bill isn't happy here. He hates the heat, the humidity, the mosquitoes; actually, I can't think of anything he doesn't hate about Key West, but we haven't talked about leaving."

Reina sat on the bed and stroked her arm. "You listen to me, Dominique, and listen carefully. I know you and Rodolfo have a problem. My son talks to me, and I read between the lines. I don't know if either of you, as well educated as you are, truly understands the nature of your problem, but I do know you can't run away from it. You need to resolve it between the two of you, and you need to do that here. Key West is your home. In your heart you know you don't belong anywhere else."

Dominique turned her face to the wall, but Reina didn't retreat. "You're in love with my boy, aren't you?"

Tears ran down Dominique's face and into the pillow. She didn't answer.

"I'm so sorry, *hija*." The older woman ran her hand gently along Dominique's arm. "I don't know whether this will help you or make matters more difficult, but he loves you too, very much. Maybe too much. It's so sad things didn't work out between you as I had hoped they would. On my knees, I'll pray for you both."

"Thank you, Mama," Dominique whispered, closing her eyes. Minutes later she was fast asleep.

\*\*\*

Shortly after one in the morning, Reina awakened to the sound of the bedroom door opening. She wasn't surprised. "*Que pasa, hijo*?" she asked, knowing the answer before he spoke it.

"I couldn't sleep." Rolf kissed her, but his eyes looked toward the bed. "I need to be here." He nodded in Dominique's direction.

"You know how much I love her, Rodolfo, but what you *need* is to go back to your own bed. Dominique isn't your wife." Reina was adamant. "Your woman is upstairs. This is crazy, *hijo.*" It wasn't for her daughter-in-law that Reina was concerned. She was cold, that one. Sarita had never loved her Rodolfo enough to be jealous. Of that, Reina had been certain from the start. That's why it had taken her so long to accept the woman into her household and why she had never been able to love her son's blonde wife. It was status Sarita relished and didn't want disturbed. Rodolfo had matured into a brilliant and good man. He deserved better than the stone-hearted beauty he had foolishly selected, but it was too late for that, and it was the daughters of the marriage for whom Reina was troubled. They were little angels who shouldn't suffer because the adults made mistakes.

"I'm aware of that, Mama," he persisted, "but I have to know that Dominique is safe in our home. If Sarah gets upset, I'll deal with it as best I can."

"Do what you must," Reina said in a voice that left no room for challenge, "but I'm staying right here. A man and a woman who aren't married shouldn't be alone in a bedroom. If Sarita came down and found you with Dominique there would be another scene, rightly so this time. The children might hear, and that's no good."

"You're right, of course. You should be here." Rolf put his arm around her shoulders and squeezed hard.

Reina heard Sarita's voice in her head, telling her again, as she had many times in the past, that it wasn't natural for a grown man to be so close to his mother. Reina had tried to explain that children, whether sons or daughters, in Hispanic culture, remain attached to, and affectionate with, both their parents. She hadn't been successful; her daughter-in-law couldn't comprehend that kind of family life.

Rolf walked to the side of the bed, placing himself between Dominique and the open window beyond which Officer Smithson patrolled. Rolf laid down next to her.

Reina sat in her rocking chair, watching two young people, both of whom she considered to be her own, now peacefully lying together as they had done many times during childhood naps. In her sleep, Dominique soon snuggled into Rolf's chest. He held her tenderly, as Reina had seen him cradle his own babies. Reina couldn't sleep. She stood, walked to the door and locked it. Sarita would have to knock.

An aura of evil and sadness enshrouded people she loved. She could envision no solution to the problems and dangers that had surfaced in past weeks. She sensed someone would be hurt, and she prayed for God's protection.

* * *

Like a swimmer ascending from the darkest blue of the ocean depths, Dominique rose through shadowed levels of unconsciousness, slowly floating toward the gilded, pale-blue of a Key West morning. In that delicious state, somewhere between sleep and wakefulness, she stretched, moaning audibly as she flexed aching muscles.

Still drifting in sleepy twilight, she became aware of sensuous human warmth against her own. Her nostrils flared with the scent of familiar skin and the rising tide of animal hunger. She sighed and burrowed deeper into the luscious cocoon of sexual desire. In response, a warm hand moved to possessively cup and massage her breast, sending shock waves of electric current coursing through her body. Her nipples hardened and begged to be touched. Between her legs, in that place her hand sometimes secretly caressed in the night, she was swollen, wet and hot. Whether she was on fire, or whether it was the body next to her that seared her with its own intense fever, she didn't know and didn't care.

Her hand slipped into her panties, seeking the core of heat, fingers sliding on the lubrication that gushed from deep inside. There was a sharp intake of breath, and a spasm shook her. Unsatisfied, her body demanded more. She was out of control, aware only of her desire, of the need of a female in frenzied heat. Frantically she turned, burying her face in the curve of his neck, her tongue licking, sucking, feeding off the salty taste of maleness— silently entreating him to love her. His skin was hot under her lips, and powerful arms pulled her closer still. She could feel his hardness through the thin layers of fabric that separated them. Her hand reached under the elastic of his pajama bottoms, searching for him, stroking him, exciting her further as he began to throb and a low moan emanated from the back of his throat.

It was at that moment she realized this idyllic scene couldn't be reality. She didn't snuggle with her husband, much less desire morning interludes with him. She didn't relish the smell of his skin and sometimes shrank from his touch. She didn't make love with Bill. She had sex with her husband when she couldn't avoid it, and she detested the act. What was happening now was obviously a beautiful and powerful dream. But she was awake. Her eyes opened, and she saw the matching reflection of surprise on Rolf's face as he also became aware of where he was, who he was with and what they had been about to do.

"Why are you in my bed?" she asked anxiously, her voice still throaty and rasping with emotion. She was unsure now of what might have transpired since she had fallen asleep, of how much had been a dream and how much was real. She felt deeply ashamed of her body's betrayal and desperately tried to ignore the heat that made her feel as though she would explode, melt or burst into flame. Never, even in the best of times, had she been so aroused by her husband, so lost in sensuousness.

Rolf was making matters worse, gazing with burning passion into her eyes, refusing to let her extinguish the fire that smoldered inside. "I just wanted to watch over you." He stumbled over his words. "To insure you were safe. I must have fallen asleep."

She looked away, trying not to acknowledge the still very visible physical response of his body. He reached over gently and brushed the hair away from her face.

"Don't touch me." Dominique's face took on a look of panic.

"Don't be like this." Rolf clenched his jaw and his voice hardened. "You have nothing to fear from me. Mama sat with us all night."

They both looked to the rocking chair, but there was no sign of Reina.

Rolf's hand turned her face, forcing her to look at him. "Nothing happened except what we both apparently remember from just a few moments ago. I would never knowingly betray your trust. Don't you know that?" he asked.

"I'd trust you with my life. It's not that."

"What then?" he asked, more gently now.

"Don't you understand? I can't bear to have you touch me and then be forbidden anything more." This time she didn't avoid his eyes. "I feel for you what I've always imagined a woman would feel for the man she marries, but you're not my husband."

"I should be. I want to be," he replied softly, tracing the outline of her lips with his finger. "I love you, Dominique. I always have. Even in elementary school, when boys hated girls and thought they were all stupid, I loved you. That's why I've tried so hard to stay away."

Tears ran, unchecked, down her face. She drew him to her and held him close, savoring the desire, love and peace with which he enveloped her. Long moments later, she forced herself to pull away. "Listen to me, Rolf. I'm only going to say this once." She took his hands and held on as one would cling to a life preserver. "I love you so much it hurts." She felt his hands tenderly squeeze hers. "We've been brought up in the same faith. We were taught that married love is a sacrament that joins two beings into one—the closest thing on earth to being united with God. I've never had that. I never even understood what that meant, until these past few weeks. I want to make love with you, but more than anything, I want to be a part of you. Can you understand that?"

"*Si, mi amor.*" He lifted her hands to his lips. "You know now what I've known since you returned to town and I set eyes on you. We need to talk, Dominique. When there's more time, when this murder case is over–"

"No." She said it with calm finality. "There's nothing to talk about. You were the smart one. I was foolish. You made the decision to stay away. You knew what would happen. I fought you on it every step of the way. I won't do that again. When this case is over, things have to go back to the way they were."

"I don't know if I can do that."

"We have no choice. You know that as well as I do. We took vows, Rolf, with two other people. We're bound for life. It's what our church demands. It's what we promised before God."

"But, you don't love Bill, and I don't love Sarah, not like this." He paused. "There's the possibility of annulment. We could–"

"Rolf." She interrupted him, by calling his name focusing his attention on her words. "We have children. Annulment, even if it's possible, isn't going to hurt them any less than a divorce." She took a deep breath and went on. "I can't make myself love Bill. I know that. I've tried for years, and it doesn't work. What I can do is to be faithful to my vows, whether I like it or not. That's what I've done, and that's what I'll continue to do. That's what you need to do. Please help me, Rolf. Don't tempt me. If you'll help me do what I must, then I'll stay in Key West. If not, I'll leave. I swear I will. I'm not strong enough to fight my feelings alone." She looked down at their intertwined hands.

He lifted her head and brushed the hair from her face. "We'll do the right thing, princess. I won't make it hard. I promise. I couldn't bear it if you left. If you're here, I can at least see you, even if only at the courthouse." He made an attempt to smile. She couldn't.

# 16

"Ms. Olivet, are you ready to continue with your cross?"

"I am, Your Honor."

"Very well. Dr. Silvas, I'll remind you that you're still under oath."

Dominique walked briskly to the podium. No bandage showed, and she wore the customary spike heels. Foundation covered areas of facial bruising. A scrape on her arm was hidden by the sleeve of her suit jacket. She occasionally favored her left foot, but only someone extremely observant would notice. A large, nasty cut on her right leg caused from hitting the jagged edge of the porch step when she dropped to the ground, was the only injury she had been unable to conceal.

There was no build-up, no setting of the stage in preparation for ascertaining the information she was after. "Dr. Silvas, what was the victim's blood type?"

Scott Reynolds immediately stood. "Objection, Your Honor. That's outside the scope of direct."

"Ms. Olivet, I believe Mr. Reynolds is correct. The prosecution didn't come close to that subject during direct-examination. Do you have any response to the objection?"

Before Dominique could answer, Rolf stood. "Your Honor, the State withdraws its objection. We have no problem with the witness answering the question." Scott Reynolds, looking puzzled, meekly sat down.

"Let the record reflect that the State has withdrawn its objection. Very well, Dr. Silvas, you may answer the question."

"A Negative, ma'am."

"Thank you, Doctor." Immediately, Dominique changed course. "I show you what has been admitted into evidence as State's Exhibit Number Three." Dominique handed the witness the ivory-handled knife that had been the instrument of Regina DeWalt's death.

"Yes, ma'am."

"You previously testified, that the width of the blade and its sharpness were consistent with the deceased's wound. Is that correct?"

"Yes, it is."

"How far posteriorly did the blade penetrate into the victim's throat?"

"As I recall, it stopped at the fourth cervical vertebra. The vertebrae encase the spinal cord; however, in this case it wasn't completely perforated. The spinal cord was intact."

"For clarification, the cervical vertebrae are that part of the spine that we commonly think of as the back of the neck?"

"Yes, that's right."

"I now hand to you what has been admitted into evidence as State's Exhibit Number Two. That is the autopsy report, correct?"

"Yes, ma'am."

"What does it list as the cause of death?"

"There were numerous injuries which, in and of themselves, would have been sufficient to kill the young lady; however, the primary cause of death, and what I listed in my report, was exsanguination."

"That is a medical term for excessive loss of blood?"

"Yes ma'am."

"How long, Doctor, would it have taken for the victim to bleed to death?"

"Both of the jugulars and the two carotids were severed, so I'd say it would have been rapid, somewhere between seconds and minutes, depending on whether you want to determine death by the stopping of the heart or cessation of brain function."

She made a mental note to rein in this nonsense. She would file a Motion in Limine asking the court, in advance of trial, to admonish the prosecution and its witnesses that such irrelevant and prejudicial remarks would not be tolerated in front of a jury. For now, she would ignore whatever game it was that the good doctor was playing.

"Can you tell us the sequence of medical events from the time Ms. DeWalt's throat was slashed until the time she actually died?"

"Yes, ma'am. The first thing is, she would have lost consciousness from the lack of circulation to the brain. Technically, at that point, she would have still been alive but with no hope of survival. I might also mention that her windpipe had been severed, but again, the primary cause of her death was that she rapidly bled to death."

"Dr. Silvas, was the entrance wound left or right of median, or as non-medical people would say, left or right of center?"

"It was right of median, or center, whichever way you prefer to state it."

"And the exit wound, I would then presume, was left of median. Is that correct?"

"Yes."

"Would it be correct to say that whoever slashed her cut from right to left?"

"Yes, ma'am, it would."

"If, as you stated on direct, Dr. Silvas, the killer was standing behind Regina DeWalt when he cut her, do you have an opinion, within a reasonable degree of medical certainty, whether the killer was right or left-handed?"

"Yes, ma'am, I do."

"And what is that opinion?"

"The killer was left-handed."

"What is the basis of your opinion?"

"We are taught in forensic pathology, and it's been my own personal observation after having performed hundreds of autopsies on knifing victims whose killers were subsequently found and convicted, that the natural motion is for a right-handed person to cut from left to right. A left-handed person will cut from right to left."

"Now, Doctor, you've said the knife stopped at the fourth cervical vertebra, correct?"

"Yes."

"Can you tell me the level at which the knife entered?"

"I'm not sure I understand your question, Counselor."

"Let me re-state it for you. Did the wound begin at the level of the fourth cervical vertebra and cut straight back?"

"No, it did not."

"Where did the knife enter?"

"The knife actually entered on the right side of the neck at about the level where you would find the center of the thyroid gland."

"Again, for purposes of clarification, where on the neck or throat area is the thyroid located?"

"Right about here." Dr. Silvas used his finger to point just about halfway up the center of the neck.

"Excuse me, Doctor, but the court reporter needs a verbal answer. She isn't able to take down your hand motion."

"I'm sorry. I've been through this many times. I should know that by now. The thyroid gland is located midway between what is commonly thought of as the top and bottom of your neck."

"Thank you. And which cervical vertebra would that correspond to?"

"That would be about the level of the fifth cervical vertebra."

"The fifth cervical is lower on the neck than the fourth?"

"Yes, ma'am. There are seven cervical vertebrae. The seventh is the last one down before the vertebrae become known as the thoracic spine."

"So, is it correct to say that the wound was at an upward angle from the middle of the thyroid gland to the fourth cervical vertebra?"

"Yes, that would be right."

"What, if anything, does that tell you about the killer?"

"That the killer was somewhat taller than his victim."

She had elicited powerful evidence. The State's own expert witness had told the court that the killer was taller than Regina and left-handed. Ben Hargrave was neither.

"Excuse me, Ms. Olivet," the judge said, interrupting Dominique's cross-examination of the doctor, "my bailiff needs a word with me."

Judge Rothman read the note handed to him by the bailiff and frowned. "Mr. del Castillo, may I see you in my chambers, please?"

\* \* \*

Rolf followed the judge into his private office.

"Close the door."

Seldom would a judge speak to the attorney for one side without the presence of opposing counsel. All communications between the attorneys and the judge were to include representatives of everyone involved in the litigation. Otherwise, it might appear that there was favoritism. Even if no actual lack of integrity was involved, such communications presented what legal ethics termed the 'appearance of impropriety.' For that reason, it just wasn't done. Rolf was both puzzled and curious.

"Mr. del Castillo, a plane has exploded. The aircraft involved apparently belongs to Ms. Olivet. There's a fatality, but because of the nature of the damage done by the bomb, the authorities haven't yet been able to clear away enough debris to identify the victim, or victims, as the case may be."

The unexpected words shattered Rolf's polished veneer. For several seconds he was unable to formulate a question or utter an appropriate remark.

The judge went on, "I understand Ms. Olivet is a personal friend of yours. You can tell her what's happened and ask the necessary questions to ascertain who the occupants might have been, or I can do it. I'll leave the decision to you."

"I'll take care of it, Your Honor."

"Very well. I'll adjourn these proceedings. We'll re-schedule as soon as appropriate. Please bring Ms. Olivet to my chambers.

You'll have some privacy here. When the time is right, please express my condolences."

* * *

"Mr. Hargrave, ladies and gentlemen, there has been an unexpected happening which necessitates the continuation of these proceedings. We will re-schedule as soon as possible." The gavel sounded, and Judge Rothman swept out of the courtroom, his black robe flying behind him.

"Ben, I have no idea what's happened," Dominique whispered to her client. "As soon as I do, I'll come by the jail or send word to you." Even as she spoke, Dominique's stomach churned uncontrollably, and her skin turned cold. Something was horribly wrong. Her senses knew it, and her body responded with physical symptoms.

Rolf approached and gently put his hand on her shoulder, letting it rest there until everyone, except the two of them, had left the courtroom. It was a completely inappropriate public demonstration of affection, and her anxiety level rose.

"I need to talk to you in the judge's chambers."

"What's wrong? What's happened?" She could hear her own panic.

"Come on. Let's go where it's private."

Numbly, Dominique followed him into Rothman's office.

"Dominique, do you know who would have been flying the Dragon Lady or the T34 this morning?"

"Has there been an accident?"

"Princess, please. Just answer my question."

"No," she almost hissed at him. "I don't know. I mean, I don't normally let Bill touch the Dragon Lady, but he flies the T34 all the time. Please," she begged, "please tell me what's going on. I know something's wrong." She heard her heart beating loudly in her ears.

Rolf exhaled before responding, "One of your planes has blown up. Judge Rothman didn't know which one. I'm sorry, Dominique, but there's been a death, and they don't know yet who was killed."

Horror, disbelief and shock, all combined—transforming her from the hard-hitting professional who had existed only minutes earlier into the living portrait of a woman in hell. "My children! Oh, my God! Where are my children?" She grabbed at Rolf's shirt. "I've been begging Bill to take them flying. Do you know where my children are?" This was a mother's worst nightmare, and she couldn't wake herself up.

"They're not sure," he responded sadly. "There's no one home. They have officers there right now, waiting to see who arrives."

Dominique pounded Rolf with her fists, irrationally castigating him for the abyss of anguish into which his words had flung her.

Gently, he took her by the shoulders and spoke softly and slowly, "I have children. I understand how you feel—how I'd feel—but try to be calm. We don't know that anything's happened to them, princess. They may be all right."

"Oh, God, no. Please, no." She pulled away and frantically paced back and forth, one hand over her mouth, the other holding her stomach. She circled behind the judge's desk and reached underneath to pull out the wastepaper basket.

Rolf grabbed a box of tissues off the desk. With two strides, he was at her side, holding her as she retched into the makeshift basin. When her stomach was empty, he wiped her mouth clean and lowered her into the judge's over-sized, leather chair.

"What's the best thing to do? Stay here and wait for word? Go to the hospital and see? Go home?" She looked to Rolf for a decision. She was beyond rational functioning, and no matter which road she took, her destination would be the pit of Hades.

"There's nothing to be accomplished at the hospital."

"Nothing? There's nothing left?" Her voice was a whisper of horror.

"The first thing we need to do is call the school and see if Jordan is there. Then we'll head to your house. I've got my pager, and there's a phone in the car. If word comes through, I'll be the first contacted."

"I can't remember the number," she said, her voice tinged with panic.

"What?"

"The number—the school phone number—I can't remember it." With those words, she finally began to cry.

"It's all right, princess. I'll make the call." Ordinarily, the school would not divulge to anyone, except parents, or a custodial parent if there was a divorce, whether the child was present, but this was Key West, and he was, after all, the State's Attorney. They would tell him.

Dominique held out her hand. She could feel nothing except the cold of the damned, and instinctively, she reached for his warmth.

Rolf placed the call and, foregoing the usual courtesies, asked the important question. He quickly turned to Dominique. "He's there, right in the middle of a spelling bee."

"Thank God." She let out the breath she had been holding and made the sign of the cross. Immediately, her thoughts turned to her other child. Where was Daniella? *Dear God, please let her be okay.*

"All right, let's drive over to your house." Rolf took her by the hand and led her out the door. As they walked down the long corridor, her legs gave way, and she sagged against him. He encircled her waist, half-guiding, half-carrying her to the car.

All Dominique could do was silently pray, *Dearest Lord, please don't let Daniella be dead. Please.* She repeated the words over and over, pleading to the Heavenly Father on whom she had always relied. Her mind was in disjointed and heated turmoil, yet her body felt only an unwarmable cold. She had heard of people in shock; a part of her wondered whether this strange and terrible state was what it was like. She couldn't reason, couldn't formulate contingency plans. She was thinking logically only to the extent that she comprehended her family was no longer intact. *If Daniella is dead, I. . . .* She couldn't finish the thought, couldn't face the possibility.

They traveled the short distance to her house in absolute silence. Rolf held her hand as he drove, squeezing firmly every so often. She was no longer irrationally angry, only grateful for his strength and kindness of heart. She clung to him for stability.

\* \* \*

Police cars were parked in front of the house, but Dominique instantly focused on the sight of a tiny figure riding a tricycle nonchalantly up and down the driveway. She jumped out of the car while it was still moving and lifted Daniella off the bike. Tears of relief poured down her face as she hugged her child.

"What's the matter, mommy? Why are you crying?"

"There was an accident, baby, and I thought you might have been hurt. I'm crying because I'm so happy you're okay."

"Don't cry, mommy. You look sad, not happy." Daniella patted her mother's cheek in childish consolation. "You know, even if I had a boo boo, Mimi would fix it."

"You're right, darling. I should have known that." Dominique smiled between her tears.

Police officers were questioning Mimi outside the front door. Once she could bring herself to look away from Daniella, she noticed that Rolf had joined them and was talking to one of the officers. The T34 was just coming off its annual, she thought. Perhaps it was one of the mechanics who had been killed. Rolf turned and walked slowly toward her, an unreadable, flat expression on his face. She knew her family hadn't been spared.

"Rolf, this is my daughter, Daniella. Daniella, this is Mr. del Castillo. You two have seen each other at the airport."

"Yes, I remember. Hello, Daniella," he said bending down to her level. "You're a beautiful young lady. You look very much like your mommy."

"Thank you," Daniella responded politely. "I'm glad to meet you, Mr. Dasteeyo." Her tongue tripped on the unusual name.

Rolf smiled. "Why don't you just call me Rolf?"

Dominique wanted to scream at him, but she understood that he was trying to keep a semblance of normalcy for Daniella.

"Oh, goodie." Daniella giggled. "That's lots easier. Do you have a plane too?"

"Sure do. I'll show it to you sometime. Right now, though, I think you should go over and play with Mimi. Your mother and I need to talk lawyer talk. That is, if it's okay with your mommy?"

Dominique hugged Daniella. "You need to do what Rolf says, baby."

Daniella scrambled out of her mother's arms, happily back toward the houses.

"I'm sorry, Dominique. It was Bill."

Dominique didn't respond.

Rolf continued, outlining the information he had just been given. "Your housekeeper said Bill was going to take the kids flying this afternoon and wanted to check the plane out first. Apparently it was in for its annual?" he asked.

Dominique nodded numbly, looking at him with empty eyes. "I feel like a bad person," she said flatly. "My husband's been killed in some sort of freak accident, and I can't think of anything except how fortunate I am that the children are okay."

"Don't be too hard on yourself. You've been through a lot today, more than one person should have to experience. It'll take a while for the shock to wear off." He squeezed her hand. "I've made arrangements for round-the-clock protection for you and the children, until this guy is caught."

"I don't understand."

"It was a bomb, Dominique."

"What are you talking about?" She bit her lip to keep from screaming, and once again the nauseating smell of blood and roses filled her nostrils.

"I don't want to burden you with any more of this right now. Are you sure you don't want to wait till later?"

"Hell, no. Spit it out." Anger sifted through her numbness.

"Here's what they know so far: When the T34 came off its annual, they couldn't put it back in its hangar because the hangar was locked, and they couldn't find their key. You had flown to Miami and left your hangar door open; apparently it wasn't working right. They just towed the T34 into Dragon Lady's hangar. By the time you came back, they had found the key to the T34 hangar, and they put Dragon Lady in there, intending to switch the planes the next day. When Bill came for the T34, the airport manager told him about the switch. Bill opened your hanger door, and the bomb blew."

Realization hit. "My God. I should be the one who's dead. It was meant for me." She bit her tongue until she tasted blood, but nothing changed. This was no nightmare. She heard Rolf's voice and concentrated on what he was telling her.

"Plainclothesmen will attend school with Jordan, just to make sure. Tiny can't be everywhere, every minute. We're not going to take any chances. If this guy wants to hurt you, getting to your children might be something he would try."

Numbly, she said, "Thank you, Rolf. Thank you for everything. I don't know what I would have done without you." She motioned toward the house. "I need to go. I should talk to the police, and I've got to call Bill's parents. I'd better start making some sort of funeral arrangements. I have to tell the children as soon as Jordan comes home from school."

She was talking to herself more than she was to him. She started to walk off and then turned.

"What about the body?"

"I don't think there is any reason to hold the body. It's not possible to conduct an autopsy. I'll make sure they release the remains to you within the next forty eight hours." He paused and then continued, "Dominique, you will either need to have a cremation or make arrangements for a closed casket service."

"I understand."

\* \* \*

Dominique walked toward her front door. One of the officers was waiting.

"I'm so sorry, Ms. Olivet."

"Thank you, Sergeant. Mr. del Castillo has filled me in." Her voice trembled, "Where do we go from here?"

"Our plans right now are run some checks and see who with a criminal record in this town might have either work-related or military experience that would enable him—and I'm presuming that we're dealing with a man here—to build that powerful a device. Aside from that, it was the hangar you normally use that was booby trapped. Unless someone knew about the plane switch, the killer expected it to be you who was blown up, especially in light of the attempt on your life last night."

"Oh, he was after me all right." Her voice trailed off.

"Do you have any idea why anyone would want you dead?"

She took a deep breath and steadied herself against a porch column. "My first instinct would be that whoever killed Regina DeWalt doesn't want me representing Ben Hargrave. As you know," Dominique smiled sadly before continuing, "I have a reputation for fighting hard and winning most of my cases. Perhaps the killer thinks the odds of Hargrave being convicted are better if he has a less aggressive lawyer." She rubbed her temples. "I don't know why I threw that out. After Judge Sanchez' murder, and the similarities between the two killings, any decent criminal attorney would stand a good chance of getting Hargrave off. I guess I really have no idea why anyone would want me dead.

"If you don't mind, Sgt. Ferguson, I'm not thinking straight, and I'm not of much use to you right now. I have a lot to do, and I'd like to spend some time alone with what's left of my family."

"Of course. I'm sorry, Ms. Olivet. We'll be sending off bits and pieces of what remains of the bomb. We might be able to determine where some of the components were purchased and maybe learn something that way."

* * *

At last it was over. She had spoken with Bill's parents, and jointly, they had decided to cremate. A memorial service had been held in Key West, and the Daniels were on their way back to Washington State with their son's ashes. It was the proper thing to do. Bill hated Key West; he would have detested the thought of his remains being buried with the heat, the humidity and the sometimes pesky mosquitoes.

Dominique was pretty sure her in-laws, who had never been extremely fond of her, held her responsible for Bill's death. They were solicitous because Jordan and Daniella were their only grandchildren, and their mother was someone they couldn't afford to antagonize. She didn't blame them. Bill had wanted her off the case, had even asked what would happen if her family got caught in the middle. The answer was now obvious, and Bill was dead. Pangs of guilt pricked her from all sides. She was unable to cry for the man to whom she had been married for twelve years; she didn't miss him. She wished there had been the opportunity to say goodbye, to thank him for two beautiful children who would not have otherwise existed, but then, if there had been time, she doubted either of them could have truthfully said "I love you."

She found atonement in the black attire of mourning, determined to show the children, and perhaps herself, that she had the utmost respect for Bill Daniels. She avoided Rolf by asking Reina to come to the house to visit. She did not set foot in the home on Duval Street again, and she begged Rolf's mother to make sure he didn't try to see her. Rolf honored the request, and she sometimes managed to stay busy enough to keep him out of her thoughts.

She considered sending Daniella and Jordan to stay with her parents until the killer was caught; both of them, however, clung to her. She consulted a child psychologist who convinced her the children were afraid she, too, might disappear from their lives. She elected to keep them with her, inconspicuously guarded twenty-four hours a day by Tiny and the assorted police officers Rolf managed to have assigned.

The killer would strike again. She just didn't know where or when.

* * *

Fuck it! He had made two attempts on the slut, and he had blown them both. He had been trained better than that. Hadn't he survived the war when there was no margin for error? Now, here he was, stalking a civilian female target, and he had bungled things twice.

Of course, the plane wasn't his fault. There was no way he could have known that nondescript wimp she was married to would open the door to the hanger where she kept her precious Dragon Lady. He couldn't have foreseen the switch in hangars. Eventually, he decided the botched bombing effort hadn't been his failure, and he felt better.

She was actually no better than a paid whore. He had watched her for years, ever since her return to the island. She had been so innocent when she left Key West. Now a mother of two young children, he had seen her in public, flaunting everything she had in a lemon yellow bikini that barely covered her nipples and the dark patch between her legs. The thought caused him to strain against the confines of his jockey shorts. A drop of moisture oozed out and wet his pants. He reached down and squeezed himself, trying to stop the pressure of desire building in his dick. He needed to forget those kind of thoughts so he could concentrate on formulating a new plan.

She had no virtue, had attended a deeply religious Catholic school and hadn't an iota of righteousness about her. She had let the prosecutor into her bed. He had seen it all through his night vision glasses. On top of that, the woman was a very real threat to him, to God's perfect creation and his life as he knew it. She had to be eliminated. Nevertheless, she had his profound admiration. Never for a moment had he expected her to drop and return fire. She had actually hit him; that was the most impressive fact. She had made it possible for him to taste his own blood, co-mingled now with that of Regina and Juan Sanchez, Sr. There weren't many women who could tantalize you like that, a brilliant, beautiful female with the guts of a man. He touched his right shoulder and relished the deep pain. It brought to mind the perfection of her features and the incredible inner strength that enabled her to fight for survival. He felt himself throbbing now. She had to die, but oh, how he wanted to bury himself to the hilt, to watch her death throes, to feast on the most majestic blood, all while impaled in the soft warmth of her crotch.

He couldn't concentrate, couldn't breathe. He needed to jack off, and then he would be able to plan his next move. His hand no longer squeezed. It began to move fast, and his hips thrust forward, imagining the depths of her pussy. Never had Regina creamed him this good.

Exhausted, he fell into a deep and peaceful sleep.

* * *

"Sarah wants to have a family picnic this Sunday. We can do it here and rent some tents and chairs. Would you like that?"

"Sure," Rolf answered his mother listlessly. He was staring into a cup of *café con leche,* every once in a while taking a sip. "I need something a little stronger than this today. Do you have some espresso?"

"*Si, pero que pasa, hijo?*"

"Nothing's wrong. I'm just not sleeping well, that's all. All I need are some powerful coffee beans. My assistant is on vacation, and I'm covering his cases. They're not particularly complicated, but there are lots of them."

"Why aren't you sleeping?"

"I don't have time to talk about it, and there's really nothing to talk about."

"Rodolfo, what's happened can't be helped. Dominique's husband is dead, and she's wise to stay away from you right now. What you need to do is pay more attention to the woman you married, and try to stop thinking about what you can't have."

Rolf glanced up at his mother; opened his mouth to speak, then thought better of it. As much as he loved Reina, and was close to her, this was something he didn't want to discuss. He couldn't possibly explain last night, couldn't tell his mother what had happened or, more correctly, what hadn't happened with his wife.

He could still see Sarah coming out of the bathroom in her black, see-through gown, the one she seemed to reserve for those times when, for inexplicable reasons, she felt it was about time to "do the deed." She hated fucking him, and he knew it. Two days this week she had worn the black signal. It had made him sick to his stomach to see the damn thing.

This frequency, he knew, was all about Dominique, though neither of them had spoken her name since the memorial service for Bill Daniels. Sarah had insisted on attending, ostensibly to pay her respects, clinging constantly to Rolf's arm, every so often resting her head against his shoulder. The woman was an actress. You had to give it to her. Anyone would think she actually cared.

In times past, Sarah had irritated him, but she had her good points after all, and he had tried to dwell on those. She was a good hostess. She didn't really take care of the children; that was Reina's department, but Sarah did see to it that they minded their manners, took piano and dance lessons, attended cotillion and did all the appropriate things that would insure a good social life and marriage for his girls. He appreciated her body's willowy perfection sufficiently to excite himself and utilize her to satisfy his sexual frustrations, though for neither of them had it ever been an act of love. Last night was the first time he looked at Sarah and felt revulsion. Last night was the first time he couldn't get it up.

"This is all about her, isn't it?" she had asked angrily.

"No, Sarah, this is about you and me and the fact that I'm tired," he had replied, wanting to drop the subject, to sleep and forget.

Sarah wouldn't let him. "Well, she may be free now, but you're not getting a divorce, so don't even think about it." She rolled over in bed and turned her back to him.

Trying to return to a sense of normalcy, he laid his hand on her shoulder and spoke in a softer voice, "Sarah, I'm never going to divorce you. You're my wife in the eyes of God, and that's how it's going to stay. We'll make it through this, and everything's going to be just fine. As soon as this case is over, we'll take the girls and go to Europe for a long vacation."

Suddenly cheerful, she turned to him again. "Oh, Rolf, that's wonderful. I can't wait to tell the girls." With each moment that passed, her mood improved and her speech quickened. "First thing tomorrow I'll start planning an itinerary. You have four weeks coming, and that would be just about right." She kissed him on the cheek. "I don't know why I let myself be jealous of that woman. I should feel sorry for her. She has no class, and she's just lost her husband. I guess she'll have to work really hard for a living now. I imagine she won't be going to Europe." Sarah laid her head on his shoulder and wrapped her leg around his. "I know it's your job that's causing so much pressure, honey, and I'm sure you'll be able to perform again. If not, you don't need to worry. It's not that important to me."

He felt like either screaming at her or vomiting. Instead, in a smooth voice, he said, "Why don't we just get some sleep. I've got to be up early in the morning."

Happily, she dropped little kisses all over his face, curled under the covers and was soon fast asleep.

He rose before daybreak, wanting neither to see his wife nor to speak to her.

Now, he gulped a cup of espresso, picked up his briefcase and after planting a kiss on his mother's forehead, pushed the screen door open and walked to his car. For a moment he sat behind the wheel thinking he caught the scent of Dominique's subtle perfume. It disappeared, and he knew it was his imagination.

He must not think of her. He was a devout Catholic. He believed in his faith, in its principles and its values. He loved Dominique more than he loved himself, and he thought of himself as a courageous man. He would take on the world for the love of that woman—but he could not, would not, challenge his God. It was his own mistake that had brought him to this point. He had married Sarah, knowing full well that his affection for her was not all-encompassing. He hadn't waited, hadn't searched for Dominique. If it was his fate to suffer because of youthful hormones and equally youthful mistakes, then so be it. Dominique was right to remind him of his beliefs—his responsibilities and obligations. She had proven herself to be all that he loved and admired.

He touched his forehead to the steering wheel. Then, letting out a deep sigh, he started the motor and drove away.

The front of Dominique Olivet's home.

# *17*

"Hey, Gertie. How's it going?"

Tiny peered over the counter at the gray-haired, somewhat-hefty, older lady who sat behind a desk in the Medical Records Department of the Lower Keys Medical Center. He smiled at her with genuine affection, and she returned it in kind. Gertrude Underwood was a close friend of the family, his mother's best friend and a surrogate aunt to him. Gertie had rocked him on her lap before he quickly grew much too big for that kind of childish pleasure.

"It's going great, but to what do I owe the honor?" she asked jovially.

"I came to take you to Mom's for dinner." Tiny smiled and bent down to give her a quick peck. "She's fixing some fried red snapper, and I'm starved. Don't have to be back on the job till ten, and I plan on packing it in before then."

"What's the matter? Isn't Miss Olivet the great cook she's cracked up to be?" She looked puzzled. "Is it proper to call her Miss?"

Tiny didn't know the answer to the second question, so he side-stepped it. "The little lady's a super cook. The problem is she has no concept of how much it takes to keep someone as big as me going. She gives me two helpings and thinks I'm full. I have to sneak around and have the guys drop off some late-night food.."

Gertie laughed. "I'll bet if you just talk to her, it'll work out. It's not like she doesn't have the money to feed you, however much it takes."

"Oh, I know that. It's just that I hate to embarrass her. She's so nice."

"Now, back to my original question. What's really on your mind? This is one place you've never visited before."

"Aw, Gertie, you know I hate hospitals. I get sick just walking in. I wouldn't be here if I didn't need a favor. A big one."

"I'll do what I can, sweetheart. What is it you need?"

"I've got to have the blood types of three people born here in Key West about forty years ago at the old hospital."

"Tiny, you of all people know that information is private. We're not allowed to give it out."

"Yeah, I know, but I've got to have it anyway. It's real urgent, Gertie. I wouldn't ask you if it wasn't. I'll never tell where I got the information. I give you my word on that. You know my word is good."

It took Gertie ten minutes to check the records and tell him what he wanted to know.

\* \* \*

Dominique was trying to be a good mother, reserving whatever smiles were left inside her for the children, but it was a tiring effort. She no longer had to sleep alongside a man she didn't love, no longer had to accept the insensitive groping of her body. Instead, she had to accept the guilt for his death, and that was much worse.

It was after three o'clock in the morning. She was exhausted but still couldn't fall asleep. She got up and paced the floor in frustration, played a game on the computer and finally wound up on the patio, sipping a glass of orange juice and vodka. It was a starlit, breezy evening, and the garden only served to remind her of Rolf's middle-of-the-night visit. She smiled to herself, remembering their exchange through the hedge. The smile disappeared as a shadow appeared around the corner. Her muscles tensed.

"Little lady, you shouldn't be sitting out here."

It was Tiny. If she wasn't so on edge, she would have known; no one else had that large a shadow.

"Someone could easily shoot through the bushes," he admonished.

"Oh, for heaven's sake. I'm sure there are officers prowling back and forth out there somewhere. If a person wanted to shoot me, they'd need to have a high powered rifle to do it from a distance. If that's the case, I'm a dead duck anyway, so it doesn't really matter."

"I didn't mean to upset you."

"I know that," she responded, sincerely apologetic. "You didn't do anything other than what you were hired to do. Listen to me Tiny. If we're going to be in close quarters for any length of time, you might as well understand that when I get overly tired, I become bitchy. Just shoot me yourself if I become obnoxious."

"Since this is a night for honesty. . . ." Tiny choked and hesitated.

"Yes?"

He took a deep breath and blurted, "You're starving me to death, little lady. I've got to have more food." That said, he stood quiet, staring at his feet.

"I've been leaving you hungry? Why didn't you say something sooner?" She clenched her teeth hard, trying to stifle her first urge to giggle since Bill's death.

Tiny shrugged his shoulders and grimaced. "Because I didn't want to make you feel bad," he muttered.

"Oh, good grief. That was sweet, but you should have spoken up. I'll tell you what, big man,  I'll just make more of everything and let you serve yourself."

Tiny smiled. "Mom says she just cooks as if there were four extra people in the house. Would it be too much trouble to do that?"

"You got it."

"Now that that's out of the way, I want you to know I've taken a leave of absence," Tiny added.  "I want to be able to guard you twenty-four hours a day, and that's the only way I can really do it right."

"Are you sure this isn't going to be a set-back in your job? It won't affect your retirement in any way?" She didn't want him jeopardizing his regular employment.

"Don't you worry. I'm the best jailor they have. They'll take good care of me and will be glad when I come back on board. It's no sweat."

"As a matter of fact, it is." She smiled. "It's hot, and it's awfully late. Why don't you hit the sack. I'll come in shortly." Before he could object, Dominique reassured him, "Remember, there are police patrolling right on the other side of that hedge."

Tiny snorted but smiled, apparently pleased with himself. "Sounds like a good idea to me. By the way, I saved my best piece of information for last."

"I'm all ears."

"Whoever wrote that note knew what they were talking about. Jenna and her husband can't be Regina's biological parents."

"Why not? What did you find out?"

"They're both O Positive. That combination can't produce an A Negative child."

"Next thing you need to do is—"

Tiny didn't let her finish. "Find out Alicia's blood type. I did that. It's A Negative."

"Bingo!"

* * *

Far too early, Dominique was awakened by the thunderous roar of a riding lawnmower outside the bedroom window. Still groggy, she threw a pillow over her head. It was useless. Other, and different clatter joined in. Soon, her ears sorted out a cacophony of garden equipment: lawnmower, weed eater, electric hedge clippers, the crackling of plastic bags being filled and tied.

Groaning, she rose and stumbled to the French doors. She might still be half asleep, but she knew this wasn't the day for the yard man. Besides, it sounded more like an entire work crew. Surely, her Cuban refugee gardener and his talkative wife couldn't make that much racket.

She threw open the doors to the second, unexpected greeting of the morning. Up-close, black-and-tan fur was all the warning she had before Boo's paws landed squarely on her shoulders, knocking her to the floor. A wet, warm tongue covered her face, and she was fully awakened in much the same fashion a cold shower sobers a drunk. "Boo! Sit!" she hollered at the animal. "Ugh!" *What a way to start the day.*

Still lying on the floor with her eyes closed against the saliva, she groped for an end table, felt for the box of tissues she kept there, grabbed one and wiped her face dry. She heard a deep, familiar laugh and hesitantly opened her eyes. Rolf stood in the doorway, staring down at her. From her angle, he appeared larger than life, and he sported a big grin. Instantaneously, the cloud of sadness that had enveloped her vanished. "What are you doing here? What's going on out there?" she blurted.

"I got a call from Chez. He suggested the male members of the Monroe County Bar Association come over here and take care of getting your yard in shape. We did his mom's last weekend. You two have concerns other than lawns and hedges."

"That's really sweet. It truly is. But you know, it's not like Bill or I ever did the yard work. I have a lawn man who comes every week. My gardening chores consist of planting flowers, feeding the Koi and, occasionally, dumping chemicals in the pool."

Rolf grinned even bigger. "It's the thought that counts, and besides, it gave me a legitimate excuse to see you." He continued hurriedly, "By the way, don't you think maybe you ought to get off the floor and put on some clothes before you come face-to-face with those lechers out there?"

"What?" Dominique looked down and checked the length of her tee shirt. "Oh, good grief. I wear a lot less than this on the beach." She hesitated and then decided on the truth. "I'm happy to see you."

"I'm happy to see you too, princess. It seems like forever. I've missed you." His voice dropped an octave, and the intimacy sent chills down her spine. "I was afraid you might be angry I came since you told Mama you didn't want to see me."

"That wasn't precisely the message. I wanted very much to see you, too much. That was the problem. I wasn't strong enough to be able to handle you along with everything else going on in my life. I'm not at all angry."

Rolf smiled and held out his hands to lift her from the floor. Dominique knew better than to touch him. If she dared to take his hands, she might not let go. She pushed herself up, and with a smile on her face, almost scampered to the bathroom in childish delight. There was nothing sinful about this; it was pure joy.

In a few minutes, she emerged in jeans and a tee shirt, face radiant and free of make-up, her long hair pulled into a simple ponytail. She intended to tell Rolf about the latest developments regarding Regina's parentage, but as soon as he caught sight of her again, his hungry gaze followed her every movement, no matter how slight. She felt his eyes as if they were his hands roaming her body.

"You're so beautiful," he said huskily. Clearing his throat, he added in a kidding tone, "even if you do look more like a seventeen-year-old than a sexually mature woman."

Dominique approached him slowly. Had Linda not arrived and rescued her from her own weakness, she would have freely walked into the arms of a very willing, and very married, man.

"Good morning," Linda's cheerful voice announced. "Are you guys just planning to stand here and chat while we do all the work, or are you going to come out and help make some sense of this jungle?" Linda looked at her as if to say, "Be careful, my friend."

There was, indeed, a large work crew. Joe Rodriguez was on the riding lawnmower. Chez, perched precariously on a ladder, was manning the electric hedge clippers. Dominique was impressed; it was probably the best hair cut those bushes had ever known. The Wilson brothers were in charge of raking Chez' droppings and bagging them for disposal. They saw Dominique and stopped what they were doing.

"Thank you, guys," she said, waving. "I appreciate all the hard work, but most of all, I appreciate your friendship. Chez, Rolf told me what you did. Thank you for organizing all of this." She tried to be jovial and not choke up. "For my part, I'm going back inside to fix the biggest brunch you'll ever eat. I'll let you know when it's ready."

* * *

Linda wasn't much of a cook, but she was good help and even better company.

Dominique hugged her friend in gratitude. "Thanks for the save."

Linda's face turned serious. "You've got to be careful, Dominique. If you can't keep your hands off Rolf and you're not strong enough to make him keep his hands off you, then you'd better stay the heck away from the man."

"I'm trying, Linda. It's just really hard."

She wiped her hands off on a kitchen towel and avoided her friend's eyes. Linda knew her far too well.

"You just remember, you're free now, but he's not. He's very much a married man, and he wants to run for political office He's not about to let a divorce ruin his chances for election."

"You're right. He won't get a divorce. I know that, but it's not what you think."

"Yeah, right."

"Stop being such a smart ass. Whether you believe it or not, it's not his political ambition that stops him. It's his faith."

"You're fooling yourself, Dominique."

"He's a good man, hon. He truly is." She had to clear her throat. "We've talked about it. The Catholic Church says he needs to stay right where he is, and he knows it's the right thing to do. I know it, too. I don't want him to get a divorce because of me."

"Oh, come on now. Maybe fifty years ago people stayed married because of their religion. That excuse for misery doesn't cut it any more."

Dominique glared at her. "Don't be so damn judgmental. I'm single only because Bill died. Otherwise, I'd still be unhappily married. As a matter of fact, so would you if Steve hadn't been beating you all the time."

Linda ignored the reference to her marriage. "What about annulment? I didn't look into it for myself because I wanted out fast, but it might be a possibility for him if he really wants to be free."

"I know as little about it as you do. I've heard of married couples with children having their marriages annulled. Never anybody I knew, but it wouldn't work anyway."

"He could always become Episcopalian. They permit divorce."

"It doesn't matter whether it's divorce or annulment. It hurts children the same. You know that. Besides, breaking with our faith isn't an option." She pointed the knife she was holding at Linda to make her point. "That's why you haven't remarried. You can't stand the thought of not being able to receive Holy Communion. If anyone needs an annulment it's you." She leaned over the sink and concentrated on the onion she was peeling. "He can't hurt his girls nor can he be on the outs with the Church, and I don't want him to. I've just got to accept the fact that my happiness can't be with him."

Linda kissed her on the cheek. "You're right, I guess. I'm sorry. I just want you to be happy. You're not, and it frustrates me."

"I know, and I appreciate how much you worry about me. For us, it just happens to be a no-win situation." As she spoke, a solitary tear rolled down her cheek. She wiped her face with the back of her hand and noticed Linda's forehead begin to wrinkle. Her friend's forehead always wrinkled when she was about to be caring and compassionate. "I'm forewarning you. Don't you dare start a pity party, or I'll cry for real. Right now, it's the dumb onion, that's all." Dominique held up a half-peeled onion.

"Are you sure you're okay?"

"Positive. Now, let's get busy with the meal I promised a bunch of hungry men."

"Dominique," Linda paused, a thoughtful expression on her face, "what if he didn't have children?"

"That's when an annulment would help."

* * *

The sun was beginning to lose its intense heat, and as they sat by the pool relaxing and enjoying the newly-manicured garden, Dominique filled Rolf in on the blood typing Tiny had obtained. Rolf didn't ask how Tiny had gotten his hands on the information. Not that it would have mattered. She didn't know. She hadn't inquired, feeling it was better to be left in the dark about this particular bit of sleuthing.

"When are you going to talk to Alicia?" he asked.

"Tonight. I invited her to come for dinner."

Dominique looked over at Linda, amused and oddly grateful. Her friend reclined on a lounge she had situated some distance away from the pool. She kept her face buried in a book and didn't participate in the conversation. Nevertheless, she was present and would occasionally sneak a disapproving glance. Dominique understood full well what Linda was doing.

"Do you think she'll tell you anything?" Rolf asked, putting down the glass of frozen Margarita he had just emptied.

"I don't know. I suppose it depends on whether she feels that divulging the identity of Regina's father will help us to apprehend the killer."

"You're sure Hargrave didn't do it, aren't you?"

"Aren't *you*?"

"We're having a staff meeting next month before the continuation of the bail hearing. I'll be giving serious consideration to dismissing the case at that time—if that answers your question."

She couldn't help smiling. "I won't mention it to Ben yet. Not until you've made your decision." Her smile broadened. "I think I know what the outcome will be, but I don't want his expectations too high, at least not yet." She refilled his glass. "Maybe I can pry some information from Alicia that will make your decision easier."

The words had no sooner left her lips than she was seized with a bone-chilling cold. It was a feeling of an evil so intense as to be touchable. Her arms instinctively wound themselves around her.

Rolf watched her and frowned. "Are you all right?"

"I'm fine," she lied.

\* \* \*

"Son of a bitch." That woman had the idiot wrapped around her little finger. If defense counsel had been anyone other than the cunt the head honcho sniffed and salivated after, del Castillo would never dream of dismissing. The stupid fool was thinking with the wrong head. No sooner had the thought crossed his mind than his own tool began to ooze and harden and his mind to wander to breasts and nipples, to pubic hair and the molten hole created only to pleasure a man. Each day his military equipment enabled him to secretly watch and listen served only to fuel his hatred of Dominique Olivet, to heighten and escalate his own detestable, but ungovernable, desire to penetrate her hot, creamy pussy.

He reminded himself to think logically. It was no longer a matter of assuring Hargrave's conviction. That possibility was lost. Now, he must protect himself and castigate the whore. He had to insure that she didn't nose into details of the other deaths. She must pay dearly for the interference that had derailed his plans.

He closed his eyes, picturing her writhing in agony, pleading with him to spare her life. His dick grew hard, and he felt the familiar lubrication as it emerged, one warm drop after another, tantalizing the sensitive, blood-congested head with its fiery moisture. Awake, he dreamed of the wonderful agony of the feminine mouth sucking his dick, tongue flicking and licking, all control gone as he became nothing but a giant, feeling, pulsating cock. He was throbbing now, and the world centered between his legs. He could think of nothing else, feel nothing else. He cursed the bitch whose odor of female heat permeated his nostrils. He cursed himself as he reached down and pumped.

* * *

Shortly after nightfall, Dominique greeted the grief-stricken woman whose job it was now to teach the practicalities of the Monroe County legal system to Juan Sanchez' successor. "How are you doing, Alicia?"

"I don't really know," the secretary responded flatly. "It doesn't seem there's much to live for, but then I haven't seriously considered suicide, and I'm back to work. I suppose those are positive signs. How about you?"

"I'm all right. I have to be for the sake of the children." Her words implied a grief that didn't exist. Uncomfortable with the deceit, Dominique cut the conversation short and excused herself to retrieve appetizers from the oven. She returned with a plate of stuffed mushrooms in one hand and a bottle of wine in the other. She poured some for her guest and then helped herself. "This Merlot is quite nice. It has depth without being snooty." She almost choked on the absurdity of the words. There was no easy way to launch into a subject that would bring further pain to Alicia, and she didn't know how to do it gracefully. "That sounded like a commercial, didn't it? In reality, I went through undergrad and law school on cheap Chianti and Blue Nun. I know next to nothing about wine. I'm trying to use up what Bill had on hand and quoting what he always said. I've no idea what on earth could make a wine snooty, unless it's the price."

Alicia was direct. "The wine is fine, I'm sure, and this is all very nice, but why did you invite me here tonight? We've never socialized before."

Dominique took a deep breath. "I could say that it's because I enjoy your company, which I do, or because I thought it would be comforting for us to have a meal and share some conversation." She couldn't dodge the issue any longer. "Neither would be the real reason though, and I owe you the truth."

"And, exactly what is that?"

"I've been doing some checking, Alicia, and I know you're Regina's biological mother. I need you to tell me who her real father is."

Alicia's face, though it paled, remained impassive. She didn't bother denying the truth. "Why do you need to know that? Regina is dead. Isn't that enough? Do you have to hurt more people?"

Dominique's chest tightened. "I'm sorry. I truly am. I don't want to cause you any further pain."

"Then drop it."

"I can't. As much as I want to protect your reputation, and that of your daughter, I can't permit an innocent man to be convicted. What you've kept hidden might well be what sets Ben Hargrave free without need of a trial." She went on quickly. "You made a mistake when you were young. You've obviously suffered for it, but no true friend is going to think any less of you because of the past."

Alicia's voice was harsh, "What about Regina's father? He made a life. There's a wife and a family now. This could destroy everything he managed to build."

Dominique wouldn't back down. "I'm sorry for him, too, who-ever he is, but the mistake was as much his as it was yours. He's going to have to own up to it."

"Why? What possible good can exposing all of this do now? What possible relevance can it have?"

Dominique looked squarely across the table. "For one thing, your daughter was making extra deposits of two thousands dollars a month into a savings account. That's a lot of money for a young working woman. Where did it come from? If it was being paid by her biological father, then it's possible Regina was blackmailing him. That would be an obvious motive for murder."

Alicia's face reflected sadness, but she appeared to relax. "My daughter wasn't that kind of person, Dominique. Her father wasn't in a position to acknowledge her, but he had no reason to murder her. He loved Regina dearly. If it helps to clarify things, I'll tell you that I'm the one who actually gave her the money you're so curious about. The payments were her father's idea, something he wanted very much to do for her." Tears streamed down the face of the woman who had lost a daughter as well as a friend, but she didn't break eye contact.

"Look, Alicia, I don't want to hurt anyone. I became a lawyer to help, not to harm. What I want is to make sure Ben Hargrave doesn't pay for a crime he didn't commit. I intend to find out who murdered your daughter, your boss and my husband. Tell me the truth. If it's not relevant to my client's case, you have my solemn promise that it won't become public knowledge."

Alicia nodded and sighed deeply. "You're very smart, you know, but you're completely off the beaten path on this one." She hesitated only momentarily. "Do you remember the whispers when I left town right after high school graduation?"

"I've heard about them."

Alicia sighed again. "I guess everyone who was around then remembers. I'm not stupid. I know the rumor; I was pregnant by Sergio Sanchez, the guy I had been dating for two years."

"And?"

"The truth is Sergio was never my boyfriend. He was a good friend, that's all. Sergio wasn't going with anyone, wasn't even interested in any particular girl. He became a priest, you know. At any rate, Sergio was just covering for his brother."

"The Judge?" Dominique was incredulous.

"Yes." Alicia's voice took on an air of strength and confidence.

"I don't understand."

Alicia smiled for the first time. "Juan and I fell in love when I was sixteen, and he was thirty-one. He had been practicing law for five years and was engaged to be married. My parents were initially upset because of the age difference; his parents, on the other hand, were furious. As far as they were concerned, I didn't come from the proper social circles to be an acceptable wife for their firstborn son. So, for two years, Sergio helped us sneak around, and Juan kept putting off his fiancée, waiting for me to turn twenty-one so I could make my own legal decisions. We loved each other very much."

"So, what happened? Why didn't you marry?"

"Right before graduation, I found out I was pregnant. I went to Juan, and he insisted we get married right away. Together, we told our parents. All hell broke loose. Juan's father said if he married me, he would be disinherited and no longer recognized as a son. Juan didn't care. In a way, it was one of the happiest days of my life. I was so sure of his love then."

"How did your parents feel about it?"

"They weren't thrilled, of course, but they were grateful that he was willing to marry me. For a Catholic family to have a daughter pregnant out of wedlock was shameful."

"So what happened? Why didn't you marry?" Dominique asked again.

There was no smile now. "It didn't turn out as we expected. Juan's father talked to mine, told him if he could get me out of

town and make the baby disappear, the Sanchez family was prepared to pay handsomely. I don't know exactly how much, but it
was enough to buy the house we live in now. I didn't know anything about it until after my father's death. I don't know why, but
Mother told me then. There was greed in my father's heart, and
that's a powerful emotion." Alicia wrung her hands as she went
on. "At the time, I didn't understand what was happening. They
had been so glad Juan was willing to marry me, and all of a sudden, my parents were thinking about what to do with the unborn
child. Mind you, my very Catholic father explained that an abortion was the wisest and most humane thing to do for a child who
would never know its father. I argued that Juan wanted to marry
me. Juan had changed his mind, my father said, and he didn't ever
want to see me again. I was heartbroken, but I wouldn't agree to an
abortion. I was adamant about that. I was whisked away to Miami
where it was decided my sister and her husband would adopt the
baby. Juan and his parents were told I'd had an abortion. I guess
that's when the money changed hands."

"Oh, my God."

"Almost immediately, Juan married his fiancée. They had a
son and a daughter, one right after the other. Sergio later told me
Juan never spoke of me again. When I returned to town, we avoided
each other."

"When did he find out the truth?"

"About seven years later." Alicia's eyes closed. "I was on the
verge of a nervous breakdown. I couldn't eat; I couldn't sleep. I
wasn't getting over losing Juan and having to pretend Regina wasn't
mine. My parents had me admitted to the hospital; our family doctor was quite accommodating. They told their acquaintances that I
was anemic and needed a transfusion and rest. Can you imagine
anyone believing such a feeble excuse? At any rate, Sergio told his
brother, and Juan came to see me."

Alicia's gaze became distant. Perhaps locked in her tragic past,
she no longer appeared to be speaking directly to Dominique or
anyone else in particular.

* * *

"Juan?" She couldn't believe her eyes. Could she be insane, living her life in hallucinations?

The image standing in front of her, however, spoke in a clear voice, "Hello, Alicia. Sergio told me you'd had to come to the hospital. I wanted to make sure you were all right."

"You're real? I'm not imagining this?" Her eyes flood with tears.

Juan approached her tentatively, laying a trembling hand on her shoulder. "Sergio said you were seriously anemic." He handed her a tissue from the bedside table.

After a time, her tears abated. "I'm not anemic. My parents put me in here because they think I'm going crazy. I probably am, but this place isn't going to help," she said between sobs that started anew. Her emotions ran away with her, and there was nothing she could do about it.

"I won't stay long."

She could see his jaw muscles twitch, and the vein on his forehead popped out—signs always there when he was tense.

He continued, "If it helps you to straighten yourself out, I want you to know I've forgiven you for what you did to our child. I think it's time you forgave yourself and got on with your life."

She was furious. "Don't you dare be condescending to me. I did the best I could. Our daughter is being raised by my sister and her husband. I hurt myself, not her. What did you expect me to do when you abandoned us, Juan? Bring her up on my own so she would forever be known in this town as your bastard daughter?"

Juan's face blanched, and he steadied himself against the wall before slumping into a chair. "A daughter, we have a daughter? She's alive? You didn't have an abortion?"

"What are you talking about? You may have stopped loving me; for all I know, maybe you never loved me, but you should have known me well enough to know I would never kill our baby."

"My parents told me you didn't want to marry me. They said you had gone away to have an abortion." He spoke hesitantly, a look of confusion, mingled with angry understanding, on his face.

Alicia stared at him. "My parents told me you had changed your mind, that you didn't want to marry me or ever see me again."

She voiced the statement as if it were a question. "I didn't know what else to do."

Juan looked at her, tears in his eyes. "I never stopped loving you, Alicia, not even when I hated you for leaving me and killing our child. I was packed, ready to take you out-of-state when my parents told me you'd gone." He clamped white-knuckled hands on the arms of the chair. "God, I'm sorry." He came to her side, took her gently by the shoulders and drew her close. "Oh, my darling, I'm so sorry for what I let myself believe, for what you've been through."

They held each other and wept.

* * *

"What happened next?" Dominique asked, knowing full well they had never married.

"He had seen me with Regina one summer. Somebody had told him she was my niece and now, all of a sudden, he'd come to the realization that she was his child. He wanted to see pictures, to hear every detail no matter how small."

"And?"

"As you know, there was no happy ending. How could there be? He was married with two other children he loved. What had happened wasn't their fault. He gave me a job and extra money every month to send to Miami for Regina's support. When Regina came to live with me, Juan increased the monthly payments, and just this last year, I began giving the money directly to her."

"Wasn't it hard to work with the man you loved and couldn't have?" Immediately, she caught herself. "I'm sorry, Alicia. That's none of my business. It has nothing to do with the case. It just slipped out."

"It's all right. I know it won't go any further. So, to answer your question, I might not have married him all those years ago when I should have, but he was mine—mine alone—and no one else's. Do you understand what I'm telling you?"

"Yes. Yes, I do."

"Our plan was that as soon as Juan retired, he would get a divorce, and we would marry. His children would be grown. He would have fulfilled his civic obligation, and his wife was tired of a loveless marriage. She thought he was impotent. . . ."

"I'm so sorry. Your loss was greater than I could have possibly imagined."

Nothing further was said for quite some time and little food was eaten. At the end of the evening, two bottles of wine stood empty on the table.

"You do know there's talk, don't you?" Alicia spoke softly as she stood, ready to leave.

Dominique's heart skipped a beat, and immediately the mask of the lawyer fell across her features. "People are always talking. What kind of gossip are you referring to?"

"About you and Rolf."

"And just what are they saying?"

"That you have a thing going."

"Not that it's anyone's business, but we don't have a thing going. We're close friends, that's all."

"I understand. I just thought you should know."

As soon as she closed the door, Dominique dropped into a chair, and tried to decide what to do. She felt an urgent need to physically distance herself from Rolf and everything that reminded her of him. She had some time before the continuation of the bail hearing. Perhaps if she took the children on vacation, if she was out of sight for a while, talk would die down.

\* \* \*

What the shit? Juan Sanchez, Sr., Regina's father? Damn hypocrite. That self-righteous, church-going, family man had dared to judge others while he broke the laws of God and man by humping someone other than his wife—by screwing a woman young enough to be his daughter. He should rot in hell.

Not one iota of remorse remained. The bastard deserved to die. If he had known then what he knew now, the old man would have suffered long and hard before he died. He spat, trying to rid himself of the blood he had co-mingled with his own. Death had come too easy to him. Too fast, too kind. The God-damned-fucking bastard.

You're not leaving town, cunt. No way. You'll stay right here, right here on a leash where I, and I alone, can determine when and how to punish your meddling Godlessness. Who the hell did she think she was, Miss High and Mighty of the too short, too tight, skirts? Immediately his thoughts wandered to what lay hidden and nestled under those skirts, of the dark, silky, damp curls that announced the entrance to her warmest recesses. He was clutching at himself now, bringing forth hot juicy droplets from the tip of his hardened shaft. He leaned against the bedpost, his hand moving faster, envisioning Dominique's tongue of fire circling his cock, licking the nectar of the gods, sucking hard for the hot cream he would give her. Dazzling fireworks heralded his climax, and he collapsed, gasping, on the bed. Fresh semen warmed his belly, lulling him into peaceful sleep.

The next morning he awoke, refreshed and armed with a failsafe plan. He knew beyond a shadow of a doubt how to keep Dominique Olivet from leaving Key West.

* * *

It was shortly after midnight on a late October night. Islanders and tourists alike prepared for ten days of Fantasy Fest—tourists drinking and partying in anticipation, the majority of Conchs stocking fridge and pantry to hibernate  and avoid the inevitable chaos that hit this time every year.

Tiffany Haller and Jimbo Griffin were at a friend's jump-start festivities.  Earlier in the day, they had danced in the nude at the Garden of Eden, a clothing optional rooftop bar above the Bull & Whistle. Later, more than a little drunk, and fully clothed, they had toured the Goombay Celebration in Bahama Village, savoring the food, sights and sounds of the Caribbean. They had come to Key West to taste the island experience some said was Mardi Gras, Carnival and New Year's Eve, all rolled into one. If the place passed muster, it would be the site of their upcoming spring wedding. Tiffany was especially looking forward to Pretenders in Paradise, supposedly the most notorious of the costume contests.

She had seen people in elaborate garb, obviously starting their celebrations early and been fascinated by seemingly ordinary women walking down the middle of the street bare-breasted except for body paint adorning big and button-sized boobs alike. Her ears picked up tourist talk, a cacophony of languages and dialects that made no sense to her ears. As the days passed and they waited for the main events of Fantasy Fest, she and her man laid in the sun and partied. Boy, had they ever partied. They listened to great music, danced and drank more than their fair share of the liquor that flowed everywhere like water. They walked Duval Street— the mile-long "longest street in the world," so dubbed because it began on the Atlantic and ended at the Gulf of Mexico—and did the "Duval Crawl," traveling from one end of Duval to the other, hitting a different bar every few feet, only afterward fully understanding the reason for the word "crawl."

One drink too many tonight, and she found herself needing to empty her bladder and breathe some fresh air so she could stay awake. The night was young, way too early for the evening's festivities to be over. "I'm going down to the beach to clear my head. I'll be back after awhile," she whispered in her fiancé's ear.

"Sure, babe," Jimbo slurred. He had been drinking, was now smoking a joint. He patted Tiffany's muscular, tight rear and twirled her eyebrow ring with his tongue. "Hurry back, doll. I'm aching for you." He took her hand and laid it on his groin. He was hard and rubbed himself against her hand, his eyes glazed from the high quality marijuana.

Tiffany laughed. She was still smiling when she walked out the door. She strolled forty yards down the beach, managing not to vomit. The clean, ocean air was indeed bringing her back to her senses. She smiled to herself, thinking of what lay ahead when she returned to Jimbo's waiting arms.

A man suddenly stepped out from a stand of pine trees, startling her. He stood in the shadows cast by the moon. "I'm sorry, miss. I didn't mean to scare you."

"That's okay," she responded, leery, and a bit frightened, but not wishing to seem impolite in a city where no one was a stranger.

"I didn't know there'd be anybody else walking the beach this late at night," the stranger commented, casually strolling toward her.

"I partied a little too much and needed some fresh air." She smiled and began to relax.

He responded with a friendly laugh. "I've lost track of time. Are you wearing a watch by any chance?" He was closer now.

Tiffany looked down at her wrist, trying to see the numbers by the light of the moon. "It's ten minutes after–"

One strong arm wound round her waist and held her tight, while the other expertly looped the garrote about her neck and twisted the handle. Her head partially separated from her body and fell to the side. He lowered his head in a ghoulish kiss, swallowing blood, letting it cover his face, his hands, and his hair. He gasped his climax. Her blood was all it took.

He had nothing against her, was glad her death had been quick. In Vietnam, he had been taught that it didn't hurt if you did it right, and he had become very good at doing it right. He lifted her limp body, head dangling, and carried it to the edge of the water. He quickly covered her with seaweed, removed his clothes and buried them. He walked into the sea—as he swam, washing away any blood he hadn't been able to retain. She was helping him accomplish his goal by nourishing his body and fueling his lust. She must have been a good woman.

Satisfied and relaxed, he walked, naked, to his car and a clean change of clothing.

# *18*

The bitch's schedule, since the death of her husband, had been hectic. She was preparing to leave the island on vacation and was at the office early most days. She had a case pending in Dade County Circuit Court in Miami, and several times a week, he would see the V-tail Bonanza head north. When she wasn't practicing law, she was doing something or other with the children. He watched her regularly for several weeks, and although her days were erratic, her nighttime habits were fairly predictable. She didn't sleep well and would wander into the garden late at night to sit and stare at nothing at all. This night, he knew, would be no different.

Over a period of time, he had learned that if she didn't take the portable phone with her to the pool area, she wasn't able to hear it ring in the main house. He waited, cell phone in hand, for her middle-of-the-night appearance. She didn't disappoint him. It was forty minutes after one when she emerged from the house carrying a drink. There was no sign of the portable phone. He stalled several minutes, wanting to be sure she was settled into her chair by the pool, that she wouldn't change her mind and return to the house.

He then quickly entered a telephone number.

\* \* \*

Rolf slept fitfully, Sarah at his side. Several times he had awakened from his tossing and turning and found her staring at him, cold and silent. Maybe, after Europe, she would return to her normal, self-indulgent nature; maybe she would leave him alone.

It was one fifty-seven when the telephone rang. As a prosecutor, he was accustomed to middle-of-the-night phone calls and answered on the second ring. "Del Castillo. What's up?"

"I've got your slut."

The voice was robotic, disguised by some sort of device, but the words were spoken in an oddly soft, sing-song, childish cadence. Rolf was suddenly fully awake and nauseous. "Who is this?"

"You know who it is. Don't play games with me, del Castillo. Such an important *hombre*, and you couldn't protect your delicious cunt. You should have known this would happen."

Rolf calmed himself, and shook his mind clear. He had ample men surrounding Dominique's house, more than even she realized. No way the killer could have gotten to her. The caller was bluffing. "What do you want?" he asked, playing the game, wanting to draw out the voice on the telephone.

"It's simple. If you don't get here and stop me, I'm going to kill her and leave her body for the birds of prey, or maybe, she'll wash out to sea, and the fish will get her. It will be your fault. For the rest of your life you will live with the knowledge that you were ultimately responsible for her death."

"Why are you doing this? What has she ever done to you?"

"You're stalling, macho man. You don't think I have her, huh? Well, let me tell you what—she's a great fuck, and I really love that butterfly at the base of her spine. It flutters its wings if you hump her hard enough."

*God, no.* Rolf froze. He had seen the tattoo the night of Juan Sanchez' murder, just barely visible over her low-slung jeans. "Where are you?"

"That doesn't matter. Be on the stretch of beach where the kids play on Christmas day in eight minutes flat. You don't want to be late, so synchronize your watch. It's now one fifty-nine."

"I'll be there." There was no response, only a click followed by the dial tone.

Immediately he dialed Dominique's number. *Come on, princess. Answer the phone.* After a dozen rings, there was no answer. On the chance he had misdialed, he hung up and entered the number again. Once more, the phone went unanswered. Where the hell was Tiny? Why hadn't he at least gotten her voice mail? Did she even have voice mail? He was firmly convinced the caller was for real. No one was answering, and how else would the killer know about the tattoo? The lunatic, whoever he was, had her, was hurting her. He pulled on the clothes he had thrown on the floor before going to bed and grabbed the .357 magnum out of the night stand drawer.

As he headed for the door, he was stopped by the sound of Sarah's voice. "This is about her again, isn't it?" She crawled spider-like across the bed toward him. "So help me, if you go to her, I'll make you pay." Her voice was guttural and filled with anger.

"Don't go there, Sarah." He slammed the door behind him.

Climbing into his car, he backed out of the garage and quickly punched in the number for the police station. He had to make sure.

"I'm sorry, Mr. del Castillo," the soft-spoken, night dispatcher responded, "this is Millie. Tina's on break, and I'm just covering. The off-duty officer guarding Ms. Olivet tonight is not in a patrol car. He has a cell phone, I guess, but I don't know his personal number or where that information is kept. Can I have Tina call you?"

"Son of a bitch!" He heard the woman's shocked inhale. "Sorry, Millie. It's urgent I know for sure if Ms. Olivet is at home. Have somebody call me on my cell, ASAP. You do have *that* number, don't you?" he asked, sarcasm creeping into his voice.

"Yes, sir."

*Shit!* There should have been three men guarding her. Why hadn't he been told of the  change in plans? He didn't have time to drive to Dominique's house. If he tried, he wouldn't make it to the beach in time, and she would be dead. He had to assume the bastard had gotten to her and was holding her as bait. He raced the Cadillac down Key West's side streets, squealing tires as he rounded the last corner.

He slammed on the car brakes with two minutes to spare and ran hard down the beach, his long legs pushing into the sand, moving faster than he thought humanly possible. He raced a hundred yards along the water's edge, shouting Dominique's name and suddenly stopped, afraid to take another step. In the distance, by the light of the moon, he could make out a human form amid the ocean's washed-up debris. "God damn you! Dominique!"

He forced himself on, falling to his knees when he reached the perfectly still figure. He distinguished long, dark hair splaying out from the seaweed-covered body. *Dear God, no. Please. Not Dominique.* Gently he brushed the ocean weeds from her face; his fingers–his entire body–shook.

His hands understood before his mind that the face he caressed was that of a total stranger. This woman of the grisly frozen features had some sort of body piercing at the end of her eyebrow. He looked into the face of a young girl, perhaps in her early twenties, her head almost separated from her body, her bloodless face white in the light of the full moon. He found himself deliriously happy. It wasn't Dominique. For the moment, that was all that mattered.

He grappled with his emotions and the confusion swirling in his brain. From a distance, he heard the sound of laughter. Not precisely human, it reminded him of the eerie cackle of the coyotes, the wolf-like wild dogs he had encountered on hunting trips to northern Texas and Oklahoma. Initially muffled, it grew in volume and intensity, and he recognized the heightening amusement of a madman who had played his joke and relished the result. Rolf stood, turning in the direction of the bizarre noise. "You God-damned, son-of-a-bitch!" he roared at the invisible tormentor.

Again, laughter—then gun fire. The bullet found its target, and Rolf gazed down in amazement, slowly bringing his hands to the center of his chest. Legs he couldn't control gave way, and he collapsed in the sand beside the girl with the eyebrow ring. He felt no pain, only a strange calm. Eyes open wide, he stared at the starlit sky and wondered how long it would be before Dominique joined him in eternity. It didn't matter. He would wait. The feeling was oddly pleasant. He smiled and slowly drifted into blackness.

\* \* \*

Dominique dozed restlessly. Her dream was a dark and ominous one. In the realm of the unconscious, Rolf ran alongside the waters of Merry Christmas Park carrying a bouquet of white roses, his silhouette illuminated only by shafts of moonlight. She ran ahead of him, looking back, calling to him, unable to comprehend why he didn't respond, why his expression was a tortured one. She called to him again, and he stopped but paid her no heed. The flowers dropped from his hands, and he fell at the water's edge. In the moonlight, she saw the blood seep from his chest and stain the sand red. "No!" She awoke, drenched in perspiration and breathing heavily.

"What's wrong, child? Are you okay?"

She rubbed her eyes and, with Mimi helping her, rose from the chair. She tried to speak, but there was a blinding flash in her head, and she found herself watching Reina del Castillo. Mama wore mourning black and sobbed bitterly. Dominique didn't stop to think. "Mimi, call 911. Tell them there's been a shooting at the beach where the kids play on Christmas afternoons." She ran for the garage.

Tiny had asked for this particular evening off to attend his brother's wedding in Miami. He expected to be late getting back or to spend the night on the mainland and return early the next morning. Just before leaving, he learned that, because of scheduling problems, there would only be one off-duty officer, instead of the usual three, covering the house. He wanted to skip the wedding, but Dominique insisted he go. Finally, he'd agreed, but only after she promised to stay inside and not go anywhere after dark. "If you leave, the officer is under orders to tail you. That'll leave no one guarding Mimi and the children. I'm not comfortable with that, and I don't think you would be."

There was no way to keep her promise to Tiny; she had to go. There was also no way she would leave Jordan and Daniella without protection. The solitary guard stopped her as she backed her car out of the driveway. "I have to go with you, Miss."

"Ordinarily, you would be right, Officer. I know you're under orders, but I'm on my way to see Mr. del Castillo, so there's no need."

"It's the middle of the night. Is Mr. del Castillo expecting you?"

"He's waiting on me right now."

"Can you tell me approximately when to expect you back?"

Damn it all. This was wasted time. "I'll be back when I'm back, Officer," she answered icily. "We have an emergency on our hands, or I wouldn't be out at this hour. You're holding me up."

The sternness of her voice intimidated the young man, and he backed off. "Be careful, ma'am."

* * *

Dominique spotted Rolf's Cadillac parked by the West Martello Towers. There was no one inside, and her heart sank. She grabbed her semi-automatic from under the seat, sprang from the car and raced toward the beach. Behind her, the lights of her Jag shone bright; the key remained in the ignition, and the driver's door stood open. She was barefoot, but her feet knew nothing of the sandspurs she crossed before reaching the soft, clean sand of the beach.

She looked down the shoreline in both directions and saw nothing. Immediately, and instinctively, she turned right, running toward the more isolated area of the beach where they had played as children. She stopped, hands on both knees, to catch her breath. When she could again breathe, she checked to make sure the gun's safety was on. She ran the belt of her robe through the trigger guard and cinched it close to her waist.

"Rolf! Rolf!" She cupped her hands around her mouth, giving more power to her voice as it strained against the evening breeze. She ran on, screaming his name until she was hoarse. There was no answer, except the squawking of the sea birds she awakened. Again, she stopped momentarily to catch her breath.

As she straightened, an image flashed painfully in her head. She visualized herself a young girl, once more seeing the seaweed-covered male body at the water's edge. She shook her head, attempting to dislodge the grotesque picture. Twice more she was stopped by the flashes of blinding light and the ghastly visions that followed. And then, she understood. She was seeing two bodies; this wasn't the past. The blazing fire in her head ceased.

She knew now where he was. Adrenaline pumping, she bolted toward the bend in the shoreline. She stopped—horrified—five feet or so from the still forms. Ignoring the woman, she stared at Rolf. He lay on his back, his eyes closed. White roses floated in and out on the lapping waves, forming a freakish halo at the top of his head. Blood oozed from his chest, staining the sand maroon in the light of the moon. The incoming water erased it like chalk from a blackboard.

She took one slow step after another and knelt at his side. "Rolf," she mouthed quietly. There was no response. Gingerly, she reached to touch his face. It was warm, but he wasn't breathing. There was no trace of a heart beat. "Oh, God." Fear stabbed at her. "Rolf! Wake up!" she screamed, slapping him hard. His head swayed back and forth in reaction to the blows, but there was no voluntary movement of his body. "Don't you dare die on me!"

Unreasonable anger fueled her words, and she slapped him again and again. There was no response. She came to her senses and slowed her breathing, trying to think, to assess the situation. She knew CPR, but Rolf was bleeding from the chest. If she performed the compressions and the blood was coming from a major vessel, he might bleed out and die right there on the beach. If she did nothing but wait on the ambulance, he would either be beyond help or, worse yet, might survive as a bed-bound vegetable. He wouldn't want that.

There was no way to get him on a hard surface, but she made sure his throat was clear, positioned herself at his side, placed the heel of one hand over the other on the lower half of his sternum and fingers raised, elbows straight, began the count. One, two, three, four—five compressions of the chest and pinch the nostrils. With the other hand, hold the head tilted back to open the airway. Breathe air into his mouth twice. Begin again—one steady sequence after another.

Rolf was muscular, his size in no way proportionate to her petiteness. Soon, she was covered in sweat, each and every muscle in her upper body screaming with pain from the force she exerted to compress his chest. She perceived the physical sensation of ribs cracking, reassured herself she wasn't strong enough to break bones and ignored the tears that streamed down her face.

What seemed like an eternity later, the wail of sirens reached her ears. She continued her efforts, and with what energy remained, screamed for help after every cycle. Two men raced toward her carrying supplies and equipment. When they reached Rolf, she rolled away from him, sobbing. "Help him. Oh God, please help him."

"Good Lord, it's del Castillo. Ms. Olivet, what happened?" asked the younger of the two, an EMT she had met on several occasions.

"Someone shot him," she responded in the factual voice of shock.

"How long has he been like this?"

"I don't know. When I found him, he was still warm, but he wasn't breathing, and I couldn't find a heartbeat. I started CPR."

"How long have you been at it?" he asked more gently.

Numbly, she replied, "I'm sorry . . . I just . . . I don't know."

"Open the airway and let's do some breathing for him." The older man spoke in a calm and commanding voice.

Everything in her world seemed to move in slow motion. She heard the paramedics as if from a distance: "Asystole confirmed in two leads." "Intubate." "Peripheral intravenous line, normal saline at KVO." "Seal the chest." "Starting EPI." "Atropine." "No bilateral breath sounds."

She was afraid to look at the portable cardiac monitor. "Please, God, please," she murmured over and over again. Rising to her knees, she softly began the prayer she had learned as a child. "*Hail Mary, full of grace, the Lord is with thee. Blessed art thou amongst women, and blessed is the fruit of thy womb, Jesus. Holy Mary, mother of God, pray for us sinners, now, and at the hour of our death. Amen.*"

"That's it," the older paramedic said, communicating with the emergency department, "We're out of here."

Dominique made the sign of the cross. "Is he going to be all right?" she dared to ask.

"I don't know," the older EMT said. "We've got him out of asystole, but he's not breathing on his own. All we can do is get him to the hospital and let the trauma people take over."

They transferred Rolf to a long spine board and immobilized him. Dominique sat at the edge of the road as they loaded him into the ambulance, her arms wound tightly around her knees, hugging them to her chest.

"Ms. Olivet," the younger of the two paramedics addressed her softly, and like an animal caught in the glare of on-coming headlights, she froze. "He has at least a fighting chance." Assimilating the words, she began to breathe again. "If he makes it, it'll be because of you. You need to ride with us." He held out his hand. "Let's go."

She climbed into the back of the ambulance and tried to stay out of the way. The emergency vehicle, siren blaring, sped through the streets of the city, rushing the critically injured prosecutor to the hospital on Stock Island. Minutes later, she saw medical personnel in white gowns waiting outside the emergency room entrance. The ambulance screeched to a halt, and Rolf's immobile body was transferred to a gurney. A sea of white gowns sped him through the late-night, empty hallways. She ran alongside. At the entrance to the operating room, she was stopped and asked to step away. Someone would show her where to wait.

She leaned over and whispered, "I love you." She thought she felt him squeeze her fingers in response.

\* \* \*

A woman wearing hospital identification walked up as Dominique paced the hallway. "Ms. Olivet?"

Dominique nodded but did not break stride.

"The police are waiting for you in the reception area," the stranger said, trying to keep in step. "They want to ask you some questions."

"I'll be right over there." She pointed toward the waiting room. "If they want to talk to me, they can come up here. I'm not going anywhere." She made her way toward the waiting area, counting the tiles on the floor as she walked. She staggered and felt someone take her arm and guide her to a sofa.

She had no idea how long she sat staring into space and praying. An eternity later, she saw Reina, Rolf's father, Sarah and Tiny rushing toward her. She ran down the hall into the older woman's outstretched arms. "He's alive, Mama."

"*Gracias a Dios,*" Rolf's parents murmured simultaneously.

Tiny led them back to the waiting area. Dominique paced the small space; it was easier than sitting still. She stared at the television screen, seeing nothing but a replay of the portable cardiac monitor's flat line.

"Are you all right, little lady?"

She didn't answer. Tiny gently forced her to sit in one of the upholstered chairs. "I asked if you were okay."

"It doesn't matter how I am." Cupping her head in her hands, she asked, "How did you manage to get here so quickly?"

"I just didn't feel right leaving you overnight, so I came back as soon as the wedding was over. When I got to your place, the housekeeper told me she had been listening to the scanner; she said something awful had happened, and I needed to pick up Mr. del Castillo's parents and wife and bring them to the hospital. On the way, I got a radio call from one of the guys at the station. He told me as much as he knew." Tiny blushed. "There's already talk, little lady. Lots of people in this town have nothing better to do than to listen to the scanner. By morning all of Key West is going to know about the shooting." He hesitated. "They'll be blathering about you and Mr. del Castillo being together and how you were wearing . . . what you're wearing." He pushed a sack at her. "Your housekeeper sent some clothes. I think you should change."

"Rolf could be dying, and I'm supposed to worry about filthy-minded people who have nothing better to do with their lives than gossip?" She bit her lower lip as she inevitably did in times of stress. Doing that didn't cause much pain; it was more like minor discomfort, but it was always just enough to focus a wandering mind on the problem at hand. If Rolf survived, his political career shouldn't be derailed by ugly rumors she might have prevented. "I'm sorry. I wasn't thinking; in a few minutes the police will be asking questions." For the first time, she became conscious of her appearance, of her eyes swollen from crying and of the silk robe stained with Rolf's blood.

It was Sarah who spoke in a firm voice, glaring as she did so. "We'll handle the private aspects of this later. Right now, we need to project a united front. We do whatever needs to be done to protect the family image."

Dominique was glad for Sarah's abrasiveness. It brought her to life. "Tiny, stall the cops." She was in lawyer mode, speaking decisively. "Go after Father Madera. Tell him I'm up to my eyeballs in quicksand, and I need to see him right away."

"Yes, ma'am."

"Hurry as fast as you can. And when you come back, bring Father in the side entry."

"You got it," Tiny responded. He took a step toward her. "In the meantime, give me the weapon you've got hanging there." He indicated the forgotten pistol hanging from her waistband.

She shrugged, untied the damn thing and gave it to him. "Don't worry. I have a permit for this one," she said in a monotone.

\* \* \*

Tiny quickly covered the distance from the waiting room to the lobby. He grabbed on to the first story his imagination conjured. Dominique, he told the officers, was preparing to clean up, after which she would be examined by a staff doctor. The police would then be allowed to speak with her. He was well acquainted with the detective and the two law enforcement guys working the graveyard shift, and they seemed satisfied with his explanation. They indicated they would grab some early morning coffee in the cafeteria and wait there for word that Dominique was available. As they walked away, a *Key West Citizen* reporter and assorted other media people trailed them.

Tiny broke several speed limits driving to the rectory. Father Madera's elderly housekeeper answered the early-morning incessant ringing of the doorbell wearing a frown and a robe far too heavy for the season. She announced that Father was still sleeping, and she was not about to wake him up. Tiny ignored her, scoped the layout of the rectory and, without permission, entered what looked to be the master bedroom. He tugged Father Madera out of bed and coaxed him to consciousness with caffeine. Thirty minutes later, Tiny was back at the hospital, Roman Catholic priest in tow.

Tiny found Dominique still pacing the floor. He noticed she had showered, combed her hair and was wearing the stuff Mimi had sent. He breathed a sign of relief that she wouldn't be photographed in the flimsy, bloody robe.

The del Castillos were holding hands and softly saying some words in Spanish which, Tiny assumed, were prayers. Sarah, stone-faced, leafed through a magazine.

"Dominique, my child, are you all right?" The priest took her into his arms for a brief hug.

"I don't know, Father, but the police are waiting to talk and take a statement. I need advice before I answer questions."

"Tiny told me about the shooting, but why do you want advice from me?" the priest asked, looking puzzled.

"I'll be outside," Tiny volunteered. "Let me know when you're ready for the cops." He grimaced. "Be prepared. The media are here too."

"No need to leave," Dominique said quickly." Please, just sit and listen. You should be in on what's going on."

All heads turned as a doctor, still in blood-stained scrubs, surgical mask hanging from his neck, entered the room. "Mrs. del Castillo?" He looked around, and his eyes settled on Dominique. She started to say something,  glanced at Sarah and, closing her eyes, looked down.

Sarah quickly stood.

Without missing a beat, the doctor shook Sarah's hand. "Ma'am, we've been able to repair the damage. Thankfully, the bullet didn't touch the heart. He sustained a good deal of blood loss, and we had to give him three units of blood. Right now, his condition is critical but stable. Anything can happen, of course, but his heart is in a steady rhythm, and he's breathing on his own. We'll inform you when he regains consciousness, and you'll be allowed to see him briefly at that time." The physician's voice was factual but kind. "It was fortunate that he got help almost immediately after the shooting. We don't believe there's going to be any neurological impairment."

Tiny watched as Dominique let out a breath and, like a drowning person given her first taste of life-giving oxygen, inhaled deeply.

"Thank you," Sarah said sharply. She asked no questions, sat down and went straight back to her magazine. *She's a strange bird,* Tiny thought. *I wouldn't want to be married to her if she was the last female on earth.*

The surgeon turned to Rolf's father. "Mr. del Castillo, I didn't see you when I came in," he apologized. "If there's anything I can do for you, please let me know."

"Thank you, Doctor." Francisco del Castillo extended his hand. "We're scheduled to meet with the police and the media shortly. I'm sure they will have some questions about our son's medical condition. If it's not an imposition, I would like for you to be present."

"I'll be more than glad to do that, sir."

The elder del Castillo was well-known by a large majority of Key West residents. Tiny breathed a sigh of relief that the old man would be there for damage control.

\* \* \*

Dominique began with her dream, and as best she could remember, related the sequence of events to her pastor and to Rolf's family. She left out little. When there was silence and no one immediately said anything, she added, "So you see, if I tell the truth, they'll either think I'm a lunatic, or they'll assume I'm lying. If I refuse to talk about what happened, they'll quickly conclude that Rolf and I were having an affair. I'm caught between a rock and a hard place." She wore a mask of calm.

Father Madera stood and looked around the room. "Unless there's a reasonable objection, I propose to be the primary spokesperson. The rest of you should take your lead from what I say. I don't think it's appropriate for Dominique to be cross-examined by the waiting vultures. She's been through enough."

There was silent agreement, and Dominique breathed a sigh of relief.

* * *

Cameras had been set up in a hastily created media room, and Dominique, along with Rolf's family and Dr. Ahern, sat in a semicircle of chairs surrounding the microphones.

Father Madera stood, cassock flowing in the breeze of oscillating fans that had been brought in to help the stressed air conditioning system, and quickly adjusted the height on one of the microphones. "Ladies and gentlemen," he began, "as you're aware, our esteemed State's Attorney was gunned down on the beach near the West Martello Towers early this morning. I am able to tell you that he has made it through surgery and is in critical, but stable, condition. I am also happy to report that he *is* expected to recover." There was applause from the crowd. "One of the paramedics who was on the scene has informed us that Mr. del Castillo's heart had stopped, and he wasn't breathing. He most certainly would have died had it not been that, almost immediately after the attack, he was found by one of our Key West attorneys, Dominique Olivet. She acted quickly, administering CPR until the emergency unit arrived. They were able to re-start Mr. del Castillo's heart and rushed him to the hospital where he was assisted by the trauma unit."

"Father," one of the reporters called out trying to catch his attention, "Father, I have a question."

The priest was polite but firm. "You may all ask questions, but first I want to finish this statement on behalf of the family and Ms. Olivet. As I was about to say, Ms. Olivet explained to us that she had fallen asleep when, at approximately two o'clock this morning, she was awakened by what she perceived to be a nightmare. In that dream, she visualized Mr. del Castillo's shooting. The crime location was familiar to her, a place where many of our island's children play on Christmas afternoons. Immediately upon awakening, she was confronted by a vision of Mr. del Castillo's mother sobbing and wearing black, mourning clothes. Ms. Olivet was momentarily confused—not sure if she was awake or whether the vision was just part of her nightmare. Fortunately, she followed her instincts. She instructed her housekeeper to call 911 while she rushed off to the location in her dream. There, she found Mr. del Castillo. He had been shot and was unconscious. As I've said, she performed CPR until the rescue people arrived. Ms. Olivet will receive a thorough physical exam–"

"Father–"

Father Madera ignored the interruption, continuing on with what he had to say, "After that, the doctors have advised me, the law enforcement people may interview her. Talking with Mr. del Castillo will, of course, have to await his further recovery. There is nothing more I can tell you at this time. Thank you very much. Now, is there anything that I need to clarify?"

"Father," the same voice, now filled with cynicism, came from the back of the packed room, "do you think this story's for real?"

With undisguised sternness, St. Mary's pastor responded, "There is no question in my mind. I have been acquainted with Dominique Olivet since she was a toddler. I know her to be an ethical and truthful person who happens to have psychic abilities which most of the rest of us do not possess."

"But Father," the reporter insisted, "isn't that sort of thing considered witchcraft by the Catholic Church?"

"No, it is not," the priest responded without hesitation. "I'm afraid there is a considerable amount of misunderstanding about the Church's stance on psychic abilities. This is neither the time, nor place, for a protracted thesis on the matter; however, I hope a short explanation will suffice." He looked out at the crowd as if daring anyone to interrupt him again.

"The Catholic Church recognizes that certain individuals have what we commonly refer to as supernatural powers: ESP, prophecy, the ability to talk with the dead. The list goes on. The Church believes such abilities can be gifts from God—charismas to be used for His purposes. The Catholic Church, however, views psychic claims with skepticism, especially if there is an effort by the individual to make money in connection with those assertions. That said, the Church does not recognize a distinction between black and white witchcraft. Any attempt on the part of the living to gain, to enhance, or to use, any such powers for one's own purposes is considered a sin. There is an important reason for banning initiation and manipulation of the paranormal and that is that if the supernatural event is not controlled by God, it is potentially evil. If, however, the communication or vision—or whatever it happens to be—isn't instigated by the recipient, doesn't call upon the person to do anything harmful and, as in this case, a warning given, and heeded, saves someone's life, then the church in no way disapproves. In that situation, it would be considered that God has acted beneficently through one of His faithful children."

"Do we know what Mr. del Castillo was doing on the beach at that time of the night?"

Sarah del Castillo rose from her chair. "I can answer that question." Walking to stand directly in front of the microphones, she continued, "My husband received a telephone call sometime after one-thirty this morning. The call woke me, and though I could only hear one side of the conversation, it was obvious to me that whoever was on the other end of the line was the person responsible for the killings that have been taking place in our city. The caller led my husband to believe that he had kidnapped Ms. Olivet and would kill her if my husband didn't stop him. I presume the beach is where Rolf was told to be. My husband is a courageous man. He would have done whatever was necessary to save a hostage. As it turned out, Ms. Olivet was safe at home, and it was she who rescued Rolf."

Sarah paused and smiled. "Father, ladies and gentlemen, I would like to take this very public opportunity to thank Dominique Olivet from the bottom of my heart. If it were not for her, I would have lost a beloved husband, my children would be fatherless, and Key West would have lost one of its greatest assets. I owe her a debt of gratitude I can never repay."

Father Madera nodded; isolated clapping began and soon became a standing ovation. Still smiling, Sarah walked over to Dominique, bent down and kissed her on the cheek. "Slut," she whispered.

Rolf's father rose and walked to the microphones. He briskly shook hands with Father Madera, then turned to the crowd and began to speak, "Most of the people in this room are known to me and are friends of my family. I want to thank all of you for your interest in the well-being of our son. I also want to person- ally thank Dr. Tom Ahern, both for his skill as a surgeon and for his human compassion towards his patients and their families." He paused for polite applause.

"As many of you know, although not biologically or legally ours, Dominique Olivet has been a daughter to my wife and to me since the day of her birth. During the time Mr. and Mrs. Olivet lived in Key West, they were kind enough to share their child with us, and we will always be grateful to them for their generos- ity. To know that this woman, who we love as our own, was the person who saved Rolf's life is indeed a gift from God. I do not say thank you to her only because those words are shabbily in- sufficient." He turned and faced Dominique. "God bless you, *hija.*"

Thunderous applause filled the room. Once more, Francisco del Castillo turned to the microphone as Mama Reina wrapped Dominique in her embrace. Sarah sat as still as stone. Rolf's fa- ther continued. "If I may now be excused, I will take our daugh- ter-in-law home. She should be with the children. My wife will remain here to spend the night with our son. I ask you to keep Rolf in your prayers. Hopefully, dawn will bring continued good news on his condition. Good night to all, and again, thank you to each and every one."

The end of the short speech brought further applause, and the lights from flashing news cameras filled the room. Francisco embraced Dominique, then took Sarah by the arm and led her off.

* * *

Once outside, Sarah smiled at her father-in-law and spoke in glowing terms. "That was quite a performance, Francisco. It wouldn't have been possible for Rolf to buy that kind of public relations."

Francisco del Castillo looked at his son's wife with disdain. "Sarita, it wasn't a performance; I meant every word. I want you to know that I heard what you said to Dominique, and I also mean this: If I ever hear you speak to her in such a manner again, it will be very difficult for me to treat you with civility in my home. I have no doubt I speak for your mother-in-law as well. Have I made myself clear?"

Sarah glared at her father-in-law. "Yes, you have."

They did not speak again and, once through the front door of the house, went their separate ways.

* * *

At the hospital, Reina kept her arm around Dominique as they left the media room.

"Mama, he almost died because he wanted to protect me." Tears ran down Dominique's face. "I know I can't stay with him, but would you call my room the instant he regains consciousness?"

"Listen to me, child. Francisco arranged with Dr. Ahern for you to have a private room across the hall from Rodolfo. As soon as all these curious people leave the hospital, I will call you. You'll come and sit with me."

Dominique's face lit up. "Thank you." The smile left her face as quickly as it had appeared. "I can't do that. I'm sure they will have a guard outside my room, and he'll see everything. Father Madera and Papa glossed everything over beautifully at the news conference. I don't want to fuel gossip."

"Papa is no idiot. You should know that," Reina responded gently. "He took care of everything. The men posted to protect Rodolfo will be on the elevators and in the stairwell to stop anyone from coming to this floor. Tiny will sit outside your rooms as the last line of defense, and his will be the only eyes that see. He thinks the world of you, and his family is indebted to us for times we have helped them out of financial difficulty. You come to the room when I call you. Tiny will never say a word to anyone, not even to you." Reina hugged her again. "Thank you for saving our boy, little one."

Several officers approached the women.

One of them spoke to Dominique. "Ms. Olivet, I'll make this short if we can just do it now."

"What do you want to know?"

"Is there anything you can tell us over and above what we heard at the press conference? Do you have any idea why the prosecutor was shot?"

Dominique's temper was short. "I have absolutely no idea. I thought that was your job." Her voice increased in volume. "I'm a lawyer. I'm supposed to do my fighting in the courtroom. You people are the ones charged with stopping this maniac!" She was yelling, could feel rationality flying out the window. "And it doesn't seem to me that you've done much." She took a deep breath and asked herself what she doing. It wasn't their fault. The killer was vicious and devious. The Key West Police Department wasn't experienced in this sort of investigation. There had never been such a murder spree in the city's history. She lowered her voice. "I'm sorry. It's been a very bad night. I know you're doing the best you can in a difficult situation."

"It's all right, ma'am. You've been through some terrible times; we know that." His smile was kind and his voice soft. "Can you tell me if you saw anyone at the beach when you got there?"

"No, I saw only Mr. del Castillo and the dead girl."

"Did you hear any unusual noises?"

"No." She shrugged. "The birds I woke up with my screaming. Other than my voice and the birds, it was a quiet night."

"Why were you screaming?"

"It was before I found them. I was screaming for Mr. del Castillo." *What a stupid question.*

"Did you sense anything?" The detective almost choked on his words, and Dominique couldn't help but smile. He was on unfamiliar territory, asking about something most non-Conchs found absurd and considered total nonsense.

What she had experienced on the beach would be of no help in the investigation; there was no sense in talking about it. "No, I didn't. I was too focused, first on finding Mr. del Castillo and then on trying to keep him alive. Sorry."

* * *

Reina lay in a portable bed brought in for family while Dominique sat curled up in a chair at the side of Rolf's bed. She dozed off and on, every once in a while reaching over to touch him and reassure herself that he was still warm and breathing. Shortly after daybreak, she heard him stir and moan.

"Dominique?"

"I'm right here." She took his hand and stood so he could see her face.

"Did he hurt you?" he rasped out anxiously.

"I'm fine. He never had me, Rolf. It was a ruse to get you on the beach. I was home—until I went looking for you."

He squeezed her hand. "I'm thankful you're not hurt," he slurred in a voice heavy with drugs. "It hurts like hell when I try to get air into my lungs." He was breathing rapidly, the vein on his brow throbbing, a sure sign he was in a great deal of pain. "Am I dying? Tell me the truth. If I'm not going to make it, I need to see my kids." He stopped speaking, worn out from the effort of putting several sentences together.

Dominique sat on the arm of the recliner and leaned over the bed, still holding his hand. Reina, a smile on her face, walked to the foot of the bed but let Dominique do the talking.

"Look me in the eyes, Rodolfo del Castillo. You know I've never been able to lie to you, at least not about anything important." A smile flickered across his face, and Dominique went on, "You are definitely not dying. The girl on the beach is dead. You came close, but you're going to be fine. You hurt because the bastard shot you in the chest, and I broke two ribs doing CPR."

"You saved my life?"

"No. The paramedics did that. I just kept your blood circulating until they got there." Sure now that Rolf would be okay, she grew anxious to leave. "I've got to go, Rolf. I was able to spend the night only because your dad pulled strings, but Papa and Sarah will be here shortly, and I don't want to cause any more trouble. Your parents can tell you anything you want to know." Rolf's hold on her hand tightened. "I'll be back this afternoon," she reassured him. "You just promise me you'll be out of here as quickly as possible. This wouldn't have happened if you weren't always trying to save me," she added softly.

"I love you, princess."

"I know." She swallowed hard. "I love you, too, but you need to stop talking." He released her hand, and she turned before he could see her tears. "Take good care of this hard-headed son of yours, mama."

"Thank you, *hija*. Come back soon."

\* \* \*

Tiny, arms folded across his chest, sat in a hallway chair. When his replacement arrived, he escorted Dominique out of the hospital.

She breathed in the salty air, unable to fathom what she would be feeling if Rolf hadn't survived. "Tiny, can you take me back to the beach and jump the Jag for me? I think I left the lights on, and I'm sure the battery's dead."

"No need, little lady." Tiny pointed to the blue, S-Type Jaguar in front of her.

No longer bothering to hide how utterly exhausted she was, she gave him a small smile. "Thanks. I appreciate your driving it over."

Tiny laughed. "I was here all night, watching your back. Get real. I could no more fit in that car than an elephant. The police did that for you after the news conference. You're a real hero, you know."

She didn't bother to respond. Rolf had lived, but nothing had changed; nothing was over. Thoughts churned in her head. The madman was still out there, wreaking havoc on the island city. What was the motive in his sick mind? Who would be his next victim?"

* * *

"Mommy, they're talking about you on television. Mimi and I heard it." Daniella hopped up and down. "You're just like Xena, Mommy."

"And I think you're making too much of it, little girl. Pretty soon everyone will forget about your mother, but *Xena, Princess Warrior*, will still be re-runs on the boob tube." She tried hard to laugh for her daughter's sake.

"Mommy, you said Mr. Dasteeyo was an important man, and he could keep us safe, so how come he got hurt?"

Dominique sat Daniella on her lap. "First, baby, his name is pronounced *del kas tee yo*. Can you say that?"

Daniella repeated it correctly on her first try.

"That's very good. I'm impressed." She hugged her daughter, enjoying the love that offered a respite from the evil outside.

"He said I could call him Rolf. Is that okay? It's a lot easier."

"He gave you permission. That makes it all right. Now, to answer your first question, Rolf took very good care of us, is still taking care of us. He has police all around to make sure nothing bad happens. Rolf just didn't know he should have someone taking care of him, too. He went out alone at night, and that's how the bad guy managed to hurt him. It won't happen again. He knows better now."

"Really?"

"Yes, really."

"Okay." Daniella wiggled out of Dominique's arms and trotted toward the television, swinging a doll by its arm.

"Come on, let's have us some *café con leche*," Mimi suggested. Once she had served herself and Dominique, she settled into a chair. "Mr. del Castillo is going to have some problems with pneumonia unless you can convince him to breathe deeply and to cough, no matter how painful it is."

"Is this coming from your nursing home experience?" Dominique didn't really need to ask. Mimi was forever quoting something that the physicians at the local nursing home had told her.

"You'd better believe it. Old people get pneumonia all the time. Have them breathe deep and cough; that's what the doctor would always tell us," Mimi said forcefully. "Well now, what about you? How are you doing?"

"I'm tired, Mimi."

"Why don't you lie down for a while, and let me fix lunch. I'll wake you when it's ready."

"I don't mean that kind of tired." Dominique sighed. "I'm emotionally frazzled. My husband's dead. Friends have died. Rolf was almost killed." The volume of her voice increased with each word, and tiredness gave way to anger. "I'm damned sick and tired of this freak having the power of life and death. The guy's either nutty as a fruitcake or just plain evil. Frankly, I don't give a damn which. He's got to be stopped. He should be locked up and the key thrown away, or he needs to be dead."

She paced the kitchen and spoke at a fast clip, "I'm going to get cleaned up, eat lunch and go back to the hospital to check on Rolf. Call Patti and tell her to be over here with her laptop when I get back." She stared into space and frowned. "That bastard isn't going to kill anyone else if I can help it."

\* \* \*

In Rolf's room at the hospital, Dominique found Papa Cisco sitting in the recliner reading *The Citizen.*

He gave her a quick kiss and excused himself to grab a cup of coffee. As he walked out the door, Francisco turned back toward Dominique. "If you know what's good for you, young woman, you'd better wake him up. If my son finds out you came, and he didn't have the chance to see your beautiful face, he'll be agitated and won't rest tonight. Believe me, I know. Like father, like son." He smiled and left.

Dominique lowered the bed railing. She noticed Rolf's lips had regained their normal color and smiled happily before bending to give him a kiss. "It's always Prince Charming who wakes Sleeping Beauty with a kiss. Do you suppose it works the other way around?" she whispered.

Rolf opened his eyes, and his hand reached for hers.

"How are you feeling?" she asked.

"Like shit."

"Such ugly language. If you're this grumpy, you must be on your way to getting better."

"Princess–"

"I know what you're going to say."

"You don't know. Please stop trying to second guess me."

"Okay, I'm sorry. What were you about to say?"

"I want you to know how much it means to me that you stayed, that as tired as you must be, you're back. I just had to say thank you, that's all."

"See. I told you I knew what you were going to say."

"You're crazy, and you lie." He began to laugh, and immediately, his hand flew to his chest. "Shit. That hurt."

"That does it. I'm leaving. You don't need to over-exert yourself. I'll come by tonight and make sure you're behaving."

"Don't go, please." He grinned. "If you stay, I'll give you some details I remember."

"You do know how to manipulate me. Okay, but only if you'll cough for me."

\* \* \*

Dominique sat by the pool with Linda and Tiny, a drink in hand. She talked, bounced ideas around and dictated to Linda who was working on her laptop. It was dark, and they had been at it for hours, stopping only for dinner. Things would be moving faster if Patti was doing the typing, but she had gone to a sporting event with one of her kids. Dominique had coerced Linda to fill in.

"All right, you guys. Let's re-hash. For starters, we know that Regina was five foot ten. According to the medical examiner, the killer was somewhat taller. It's a pretty safe assumption we're looking for someone who's taller than six feet. Agreed?"

Linda and Tiny nodded.

"Two. We've determined the individual is left-handed. Three. Rolf and I believe that neither Regina nor Judge Sanchez would have turned their backs on a stranger. We think the killer was some-one they knew. Four. Although whoever called Rolf tried to dis-guise his voice, it was obvious to Rolf that it was a man. Five. He's killed with a knife, a garrote, a bomb and shot Rolf with a rifle. Obviously, he has specialized knowledge you don't gain on the street. He's either been affiliated with a paramilitary unit of some sort, or more likely, he was with one of the Special Forces in Viet-nam."

"Wow, that really narrows it down. I don't know a single man in our age bracket who didn't serve in Vietnam," Linda quipped.

Dominique ignored her attempt at humor. "Six. He knows I have a butterfly on my cheek."

"Excuse me?" Linda piped in. "You have a what, where?"

"A little winged insect tattooed near my butt. Is that clear enough?"

"How come you never told me?"

"Maybe because I didn't think it was anybody's business. You do understand the concept of privacy, don't you," she chided. "It's not as if it's any place obvious."

"I thought there weren't supposed to be any secrets between us. Hell, I even told you about my boob job."

"It's not as if you could have kept it a secret. One minute you're flat as a board and the next you're practically poking out of your tee shirts. You had to tell me."

Tiny squirmed in his chair. "I'm going in for a glass of iced tea. I'll be right back." He beat a hasty retreat.

"Did you have to embarrass the poor guy? His face was beet red," Dominique scolded, while trying not to laugh.

"You're the one who referred to your butt and my boobs. I still can't believe you went and got a tattoo and never told me," Linda shot back.

"I'm sorry, okay? I had it done while I was in law school. Now, could we please drop the subject except for whatever importance we need to attach to the fact that this guy was aware of something even you didn't know about?"

Tiny returned, his face still flushed, and Dominique picked up where she had left off, "Seven. He dripped blood when he ran from the scene after shooting me. Whether or not he sought medical attention, whether or not the wound was bad enough to still be bothering him, we don't know. Eight. He's killed a pregnant woman and a judge; he intended to kill me when he blew up the hangar; he murdered an unknown young woman visiting from out of town, and he tried to kill the State's Attorney. Nine. . . ." She glanced at her watch. "Damn. It's after ten. I've got to run over to the hospital." She looked toward Tiny. "I guess you'll stick with me like glue?"

"You got that right."

* * *

Reina sat in the darkened hospital room, very much awake. Dominique whispered to her, "How's he doing?"

"All things considered, pretty good, but it's going to be a few days before the pain lets him concentrate for long on anything outside that depressing room. As you can see, the drugs are helping him sleep." Reina scrutinized her face. "What's the matter, *hija*?"

"I don't know." Dominique lowered her head, unable to look Reina in the eye.

"Yes, you do. Come sit." Reina walked her out of the room and motioned to chairs lined up next to the candy machine. "Tell Mama what's going on." Dominique remained silent, unsure of how to start. "Just say it, child."

That was all it took. The words spilled from Dominique's mouth, "Whatever it is that's happening to me, it's getting stronger, and there's nothing I can do about it, Mama. It used to be mostly dreams. Now, scenes pop into my head when I'm awake." She spoke faster, as if speed might help convey her emotions. "Sometimes, I'm part of those visions, and sometimes, I'm not. Mostly, I just see bits and pieces of other people's lives—people I know and people I don't." She looked up, trying to gauge Reina's reaction. She saw no condemnation in the older woman's eyes. "When I least expect it, I'll feel a cold so intense it goes into my bones. Forget the fact that it's ninety degrees outside; I can't get warm." Without thinking, she wrapped her arms tightly around herself. "It gives me a sense of foreboding, and more often than not, I have no idea why." Reina reached out for Dominique's hand, but she didn't interrupt her. "Sometimes, I hear things. It's almost as if—just for an instant—a static-filled radio station inside my head unexpectedly transmits a clear signal." Dominique hesitated. "I'm not crazy, am I, Mama?"

"Of course not, *hija*. You and I both know that."

"There are times when the surface of my skin feels like it's vibrating at a high frequency, as if I'm full of electricity, and if someone touched me, they'd get a shock. Usually, that means something is about to happen." Dominique hung her head. "I don't want this."

Reina grabbed her by the shoulders and looked at her sternly. "Listen to me, Dominique. I had a vision about Rodolfo at around the same time you did. I saw my son shot. I didn't know where he was, and I couldn't do anything about it. Tell me this; is it a curse that enabled you to save him?"

"You know I don't think that." Dominique shook her head. "I'm sorry if it seemed that way. It's just that it's terrifying not to know what's happening to me or how to control it."

Reina scooted her chair around until she sat, knee to knee, with Dominique and spoke quietly but firmly, "I've never comprehended the ability that you and I have been given. In the beginning, I prayed that you would be spared from a gift that can sometimes be terrifying. But, and it's a big but, if it causes no evil and sometimes helps us do good, then it must come from God. When our Lord bestows a blessing, you don't refuse, and you don't control. You take what He gives, and you do the best you can with it. You understand?"

"I understand what you're saying. I truly do. I just wish I didn't have a knowing that things are going to get worse. What frightens me most is that I can't sense the outcome."

"You will be all right in the end. You know that; the image of the phoenix told you so."

"And, my children? What about them, Mama?" Dominique's voice filled with anxiety.

"I can't tell you that, dear one. Hopefully, you will feel reassurance soon. Even if the doctors hadn't told us, there came a point when I knew Rodolfo would survive," Reina said. "In my mind's eye I saw him coming out of the hospital wearing his lucky trial suit."

Dominique kissed Reina's cheek and, hugging her, held on tight. "I'm sorry. I have no right to feel sorry for myself."

"You know I'm always here to listen when you need me. And Dominique," Reina said, smiling, and pushing her away so that Dominique was forced to look her in the eyes, "I want you to know I am very proud of you."

"You shouldn't be. I was petrified I would be killed and even more frightened that I would lose Rolf forever."

"That's the whole point, *hija*. You went right ahead and did what had to be done. Facing your fear, and conquering it, that's what courage is all about. That's what you did, so don't tell me not to be proud. I am very proud."

"Thank you."

Reina squeezed her hand. "Now, go see my boy."

* * *

"Rolf?" Dominique ran an index finger over his bottom lip and felt a kiss in response. "I can't stay long, babe. I've got a hearing in the morning, and I'm worn out. I need sleep. I just had to come back for a look at that handsome face of yours before I hit the sack."

Rolf nodded and, drowsy-eyed, smiled at her. "So, you think I'm good looking, do you?"

"Nawh. I'm just lying because you've been injured. I thought it would make you feel better."

"I feel better any time you walk into a room."

"And I really do think you're one gorgeous hunk. So then, is this a mutual admiration society?" She laughed.

Rolf didn't smile. "Papa told me everything. I owe you my life."

He held her gaze, and suddenly, she couldn't catch her breath. She feigned a cough, trying to regain her composure and think of something humorous to say. "Yes, well, this was a little more difficult than getting you out of a tree. Kindly don't scare me like that again." She kissed his hand, and unable to return to the earlier banter, said, "I thought I'd lost you, Rolf. I couldn't have stood that." Tears brimmed in her eyes.

"Believe me, I don't intend to depart this earth any time soon if I can help it," he told her solemnly. "But you can make it through anything. You're strong, princess. I want you to remember that in case something does happen to me."

"Nothing's going to happen to you," she replied firmly.

He grimaced with pain and squeezed her hand. "Nothing is certain except how I feel about you. I was close to dying. I know that. My children and you, that's why I had to make it." He raised his hand to the wound, and she knew he was hurting badly. "I'm told I was unconscious the entire time, but somehow, I knew you were there. I could feel you."

"I *was* there. All the way to surgery. They made me let go at the entrance to the OR." Tears streamed down her face.

Rolf's breathing was becoming labored with the exertion of talking. "Dominique–"

She put her finger across his lips and stopped him. "Stay quiet. I'll sit here and hold your hand. You rest, and we'll talk some more tomorrow. I promise. I won't leave until you've fallen asleep."

"Princess–"

"I know. Me too."

Within minutes the drugs dripping into his veins regained their hold, and he was sound asleep again.

When Reina returned, Dominique rose to let her sit. She couldn't help herself; the question slipped out. "Has Sarah been here today?" she asked quietly.

Reina's mouth tightened and her whispered words were said with a venom that was unusual for her, "Rodolfo's wife spent maybe ten minutes. She said the smell of the hospital made her nauseous."

Dominique frowned, more in annoyance at her own delight than at Sarah's lack of concern.

"I shouldn't be ugly, but it's my son's wellbeing I'm concerned with." Reina went on, making an obvious effort to keep her voice low, "She may be his wife, but it's you he needs right now, Dominique. Come back, and don't worry. No one will say anything publicly to hurt our family."

Rolf moaned in his sleep.

"You couldn't keep me away, Mama."

\* \* \*

She sat in front of the mirror, brushing her hair and focused on the details that had been a part of the afternoon discussion around the pool. How the hell could he have known about her tattoo? She showered, dried herself and stepped into a robe. Looking out the French doors toward the pool, the answer came to her. *Oh my God. Somehow he can see me.* Her first inclination was to close the blinds, but she restrained herself, instead turning her back to the window and flicking off the lights as if preparing for bed. If she was right, she didn't want him to know she had figured it out.

She needed to review a file for tomorrow's motion docket, yet couldn't bear the thought of turning the lights back on. She was suddenly frightened and distracted by the thought that he might be hidden nearby, staring at her, watching her every more. In the dark, she felt for her briefcase and, slowly, running her finger along the wall to distinguish where she was, made her way to the guest bathroom under the stairwell. It had no outside window and would keep her safe from hateful, prying eyes. She closed the door, turned on the light and sat on the floor, strewing the legal papers in front of her. For the moment, Rolf and murder were out of the picture.

\* \* \*

When Dominique stopped by the hospital early in the morning, Rolf was out of bed. The drainage tube had been removed from his chest. Jaw clenched, pushing an IV stand, he shuffled down the hallway toward her. A smiling Francisco walked close by his side.

"Hi," she called from a distance. When they caught up to her, she asked, "Did the doctor say you could be up and about?"

Francisco smiled. "Not only did he say it was okay, Dr. Ahern told us the more Rodolfo walks, the quicker he can leave the hospital. I have a feeling there will be a marathon going on around here for the next few days."

"I'm glad you're doing so well." She took hold of the IV stand and helped Rolf guide it in a straight path down the hall. "I don't suppose you would want to cough for me?" she asked.

Rolf merely glared.

"I didn't think so." She laughed. "Please try. If you don't, you're liable to wind up with pneumonia, and you'll be here longer." She heard him grunt a response she wasn't sure was agreement. "Any problem if I stop by at lunch time?"

"No problem at all," Rolf replied, cheerfully this time.

"No problem at all," Francisco echoed sarcastically. "You're the only beautiful woman he'll see today. Sarita isn't able to come. She has things to do." Francisco's face reddened.

"Don't worry about it, Papa," Rolf said. "It's okay."

Dominique offered a distraction. "How about a piece of *flan* from Jose's Cantina?" She cocked her head and twirled a strand of loose hair around an index finger.

"It's not fair to tease about something like that unless you mean it," Rolf said, scowling.

"Are you allowed to eat anything you want?"

"Anything my heart desires." He winked.

"Well, I guess you'll just have to wait and see what I have in store for you. After you're finished, you can let me know if it was good." She smiled coyly and strolled off down the hall.

\* \* \*

Francisco looked at his son. "Was that conversation about food or sex?"

"Papa!"

"I may be old, but I'm not dead, *hijo*. Why do you think your mother and I still lock our bedroom door once in a while? You never get too old for such things."

"That's more than I needed to know." Rolf smiled, lightly jabbed his father's jaw and then became serious. "I'm tired, Papa. Let's go back to the room."

Francisco looked at his son's face and frowned but said nothing.

They slowly returned to the hospital's best private suite. When Francisco saw Rolf sit on the side of the bed and grip the mattress until the veins on his hands popped out, he finally voiced his concern. "What's wrong, son? Are you feeling worse? Do I need to call the nurse?" Francisco asked anxiously.

"I'm all right, *viejo*," Rolf answered, referring to him as "old man," a term of affection in Hispanic culture. "But . . . He hesitated.

"But what?" Francisco prompted. "Come on; tell your father what's eating you."

Rolf spoke without looking at him. "Dominique and I are happy right now. I'm content to know she was never in danger. She's happy I'm alive. She does what she can to keep up my spirits and to make sure I get out of this place as fast as possible."

"Your mother and I feel blessed that she's returned to our lives," Francisco interjected.

Rolf turned to face the window. "She saved my life and spent every possible minute here. I'll always remember that. She goes beyond words, Papa. She acts on what she feels."

"And you're not happy about that? I thought she was the love of your life, *hijo*."

"She is. Always has been and always will be. That's the problem." He patted his father's knee. "As soon as I'm able to walk out of here, everything will be as before. Dominique will be out of my life again. She's free. I'm not. The Church says I can't have her, and we've agreed to abide by that." Rolf finally turned to look at his father. "She's a beautiful, intelligent, good woman. I'm not the only one who sees that, Papa. It's inevitable that I'll lose her to someone who can give her what I can't. That hurts worse than being shot." Rolf looked away. "I've told you because you asked. If you understand, please don't speak to me about it again."

Francisco frowned. He wanted to put his arm around Rodolfo but thought better of it. His son was affectionate by nature, but he would interpret such an act as pity, something from which he would recoil.

He said simply, "Si, *hijo*, I do understand."

The French doors leading from Dominique's
bedroom to the garden and pool.

# 19

Although life, despite numerous posted guards, had a semblance of normalcy, the killer was never far from Dominique's thoughts. She tried not to vary her routine, tried not to give any indication she suspected he was watching her. To protect the plan incubating in her mind she continued to drop her robe and swim in the nude. It was her custom, and if she failed to follow it, he would catch on. The only concession to her sanity was to cut the swimming of laps to three times a week. When she did enter the pool, she forced her imagination to transport her to a place and time where evil people and events didn't exist.

Together with Tiny, she searched the shrubs outside the del Castillo estate and found what appeared to be dried spots of blood. They scraped evidence, bagged samples and sent them off for testing. She assumed the police had done the same, but she wanted an analysis by a lab of her choosing.

Rolf had told her that he had called twice before going to the beach, and she hadn't answered. The killer must have known Rolf would attempt to find out if she was home before rushing off to a possible ambush. That meant she had been watched long enough to predict when she would, and wouldn't, hear the phone ring– when the children wouldn't answer and alert her to a call. With that information, the killer had been able to set his trap. But why? Why did he want Rolf dead?

Dominique worked, spent time with the children, and three times a day visited Rolf at the hospital. During the noon hour, she appeared in his room with some edible goodie or another, courtesy of Jose's Cantina. When she couldn't sleep, Tiny drove her to the hospital for middle-of-the-night talks. It wasn't a problem; Sarah was never there. Reina and Francisco left the room or faded into the woodwork when she showed up. Rolf had improved rapidly but still felt weak. Although they discussed the killings and traded theories, she didn't let him in on her plan.

\* \* \*

"Ms. Olivet? Dominique?"

"Yes?"

"This is Ben Silvas." After a short pause, he repated, "Ms. Olivet?"

"Dr. Silvas, of course. How are you? I'm sorry. I was momentarily stumped. I don't think we've ever spoken on the phone. My brain just short circuited."

"That's all right," the Medical Examiner replied cheerfully. "It's not as if I'm the most known person in town. Outside my small circle of family and friends, the people I associate with are all dead."

Dominique quipped, "Well, you know, that might not be such a bad thing. In your line of work, the deceased speak volumes without opening their mouths, and if you get tired of listening, you can walk off without hurting anyone's feelings."

The pathologist laughed appreciatively. "I was wondering whether you might have some time to come to my office, tomorrow."

"Of course, any time you say. What's going on?"

"I'm not precisely sure, but it has to do with our recent rash of killings, and I think it's something we should discuss."

\* \* \*

Dr. Silvas answered the door on the first knock. Books, articles, newspapers and periodicals were strewn and piled everywhere. Dominique followed on his heels as he walked a well-worn path from door to massive desk. He indicated she should stop short at two small chairs. One was piled high; the other—though the arms still retained a gray covering of dust—had obviously been cleared of its scholarly whatnots in honor of her visit. She did her best to keep her arms, and thus the sleeves of her white linen suit, in her lap. It was clear that this place was off limits to the hospital's cleaning crew.

"I suppose you're in a hurry. Most people who visit my corner of the hospital are." Dr. Silvas smiled apologetically.

"Not at all. I'm at your disposal. What is it you wanted to talk about?"

"I won't beat about the bush. The fact of the matter is that I don't know whether the man you're looking for has what he perceives as a logical motive for the murders he's committed, or for at least some of the murders, but I'm sure we're dealing with a really sick puppy."

"What makes you say that?" *I knew that. Didn't take a genius to figure it out.*

"For starters, whoever killed Regina DeWalt—and I don't for one minute think it's the young man who's sitting over there on Stock Island—didn't rape her. Actually, no one raped her."

"Oh?"

"Ms. DeWalt had sexual intercourse, but all the signs are that it was consensual. She had no tears, no bruising of her genital area whatsoever. Moreover, we've got the sperm motility test results back on the swabs from her vagina and cervix. The motility, or lack of it to be more accurate, indicates to me that sexual relations took place at least twenty-four hours prior to her death, maybe longer than that."

Dominique had dealt with several rape cases in the past and was familiar with the terminology. Sperm deposited in a woman's vagina only live, and are capable of moving toward their objective, for a limited time. After that, they begin to slow down and die. The fewer live motile sperm found in a sample, the longer the length of time since the sexual encounter.

"I understand what you're telling me, but what does that have to do with–"

"Bear with me, Ms. Olivet, and I think you'll see where I'm headed."

"Sorry. Please go on."

"What I've just told you doesn't mean too much in and of itself—except to say that the killer, whoever he is, didn't rape her. What caught my attention is that the investigators found evidence of other sperm of more recent origin on the victim's clothing and on the carpet next to the body—sperm that didn't match that in the victim's vagina."

"Huh?"

"That's really funny. That was my reaction, my exact word, if that's really a word." The doctor smiled jovially. "I don't know that I could have made anything of it except for the fact that some of the same evidence raised its ugly head at the judge's murder scene."

"What do you mean?" Dominique was becoming more puzzled by the minute.

"Among the samples collected from the judge's robe and the carpet next to his body we found evidence of sperm that didn't belong to the victim."

"Do you mean to tell me that someone jacked off at the scene of Judge Sanchez' murder?"

"I believe that's the common terminology," Ben Silvas replied. This time he didn't smile.

"What are we dealing with here? A necrophiliac, who's bi-sexual?"

"I don't think so. The creepy stuff is just about to begin. Hold on for a minute."

The doctor followed a narrow, but clear, trail to a cabinet. He rifled through several files and came out waving a piece of paper. He handed it to Dominique.

She looked it over and then glanced up. "I don't understand."

"The amount of blood remaining in Juan Sanchez, together with what soaked into the carpet, doesn't total up to fourteen pints, the average content of a human body. Some blood disappeared somewhere, Ms. Olivet."

"What do you mean, 'disappeared'?"

"I imagine you have more than a few questions, but wait until I fill you in on the details. That might cut the number greatly."

Dominique looked sheepish. "I apologize. Patience isn't one of my virtues."

"The murder of your husband—and I want to say how very sorry I am about your loss, my dear—didn't tell me anything. I think what happened there is that the killer wanted you dead; he had killed twice using the same MO. He wanted to do away with you cleanly, quickly and in a different manner. For me, there was nothing more to look at. I presume, since you're reputed to be a quick study, that you've already deduced the killer must have specialized knowledge. I understand it was one hell of a compact and powerful explosive device."

Dominique nodded.

"Then, there was Tiffany Hopper, the young lady found dead next to our prosecutor. Because of the effect of the sand and water, there was no way to determine how much, if any, of the victim's blood vanished from the scene. The investigators did, however, find the killer's clothing buried not too far from the water's edge. All the tags had been cut off. It wasn't particularly expensive fabric nor was there anything distinctive about the clothing, but, microscopically, it had, at some point, been soaked in the victim's blood. Most interesting of all, there was detectible semen on the underwear and the pants."

Dominique couldn't contain herself. "So, what are you saying? That, on top of everything else, this person has a vampire complex?"

"What I'm saying, Ms. Olivet is that I think this man is sick—very sick—and probably getting sicker. He's a sicko with a blood fetish of some sort. The blood of his victims turns him on, so much so that it brings him to climax without the need of physical contact. He doesn't need to penetrate the victim. From the way the semen was distributed on the clothing buried on the beach, I don't think he really even needs to touch himself. Something about the blood itself is enough to make him climax."

Dominique frowned, and her skin rose in goose bumps. "It's obvious I'm way beyond my field of expertise here. This guy is nothing if not scary. What you're describing is a monster, not a human being." She folded her arms on the doctor's desk. "Any idea where I might turn for help in understanding that kind of warped mind?"

Almost two hours after she had walked into Dr. Silvas' office, Dominique followed the same path out. In her hand she carried Dr. Silvas' professional card. On the reverse side, he had written the name of Leonard Bruce, M.D., Ph.D., a forensic psychiatrist at the University of Miami School of Medicine.

She looked at her watch. There was just enough time to pick up a lunch treat for Rolf and then head north to Miami. She called the airport and asked to have Dragon Lady on the ramp, gassed up and ready to go.

*  *  *

"Hey, good looking. Whatcha got cooking?" She asked, smiling as she closed the door behind her.

Rolf sat in the chair next to the bed reading the newspaper. "I'm going home tomorrow," he responded.

He caught her unprepared, and she did her best to sound excited for him. "That's wonderful, Rolf. I'm so happy."

"Are you really? Isn't that odd. I'm not happy about it at all, though I'll be glad to see my girls."

Though a guard was maintained outside Rolf's room, it was no longer necessary for anyone to sit with him. He was alone, and there was no reason not to be honest. They couldn't act on their feelings, couldn't build a life together, but there could be truth between them. She sighed. "No, I'm not really glad. It was a stupid thing to say. You know how much I want you to regain your health, but I wasn't prepared to hear that I won't be seeing you every day." She walked to him, positioning herself at the front of his chair, gently drawing his head to rest against her body. She ran her fingers through the silky, black hair—through her clothes, feeling the warmth of his lips on her belly.

It was Rolf who broke the silence, speaking so softly, she barely heard. "I need you, princess."

She didn't respond, but lowered herself to gently kiss him. When she found the strength to break away, she turned her back and looked out the window, trying to regain her composure. The world seemed a blur. "I'll always love you. You know that," she murmured.

"Is this it, then? A life of duty, trying to find some happiness in my children until they leave home? Hoping, and dreading, you'll find someone else to love?"

Her eyes burned. She had to leave or she would help him make a decision they'd later not be able to live with. "I need to go." She handed him the cup of mango ice cream she'd brought with her. "It's probably soupy by now." Her voice shook. "I've got to meet a cab at Kendall-Tamiami Airport."

"Of course." His eyes were empty. "Fly safe."

She pushed the door open and then turned. "I'll be back when I return from Miami. I want to spend this last night with you." She didn't wait for his answer.

\* \* \*

Dominique found herself looking up at a very large man with a bulbous red nose whose ears stuck out at a slightly odd angle from his head. He wore half-glasses which weren't properly adjusted. As he looked down at her, they slid on his nose until stopped by the artichoke-like shape of his nostrils. He pushed them back up with the tip of an index finger. Auburn hair, long and stringy, which she readily determined was neither dirty nor greasy, topped his head. There was something in his ingenuous smile and handshake that made the strange-looking man immediately likeable.

"Hello, Dr. Bruce. Thank you for taking the time to see me on such short notice."

"Don't think anything of it," he said, stepping aside to let her in. "Ben Silvas was one of my professors in med school. I owe him a lot, and to tell the truth, I was interested when he explained to me what was going on in your sea-lovers' paradise." He showed Dominique to a seat and, to her surprise, offered a cup of hot tea. "My wife is from the outskirts of London. She brought the habit with her," he explained.

Dominique declined; it was too hot to drink anything that didn't have ice cubes floating in it. "Would you like for me to give you a rundown on what's been going on?" she asked.

"I think a better approach would be for me to outline what Silvas and I discussed, and  you can fill in whatever gaps there might be."

She let him talk and when he was finished, asked, "So, Dr. Bruce, with whom, or with what, are we dealing here?"

"May I ask you several questions to lay some groundwork?"

Dominique nodded.

"Can we agree that it's possible for an insane person to act with purpose and intelligence?"

"Certainly.  I think that's the first unfortunate thing you learn if you practice divorce law."

Dr. Bruce laughed appreciatively and smiled. "Do you believe it's possible for a sane person to do acts which to the vast majority of humanity seem so disgusting and foul that they could only have been committed by a crazy person?"

"I believe it's possible for a sane, but evil, person to do as you say."

"We have a good foundation then." He leafed through sheets of lined yellow papers. "Without necessity of looking at these notes, I can tell you that your killer is, in a manner of speaking, a double-edged sword."

Dominique let out a breath and settled back in the overstuffed visitor's chair. "Sir, I don't mean to be impolite or ungrateful, but I'm extremely tired and this would be less time consuming for both of us if you'd forget the figurative stuff."

"I like you, Ms. Olivet. You say exactly what you mean. Because I'm a sane person, I admire that trait. It makes you honest, understandable and predictable. It also makes you easy prey. Remember that, my dear. It may stand you in good stead one day. In the meantime, I'll do my best not to play with the English language. So, let's begin, shall we?"

"Let's."

"Up to this point, as far as we know anyway, this individual has four murders and two botched attempts under his belt. Three times—when you were shot at, in the case of your husband, in which I was informed you were the intended victim and the attempt on the life of the state's attorney down there—the methodology was to stay at a distance. The other three individuals were confronted at close range. In each of the cases where the killer had contact with his victim, there was an obvious sexual response on his part. If it won't insult your intelligence, I would like to give you a short primer on criminal psychology. It will make it easier for you to understand my theory of what's going on."

"Please. It won't hurt my feelings in the least. I'm here because I don't understand what makes this man tick."

"Getting down to the nitty gritty, Ms. Olivet, the unlawful taking of a human life has many purposes: personal gain, satisfaction of jealous rage, power struggles, a battered wife who's finally been hit one too many times. The common denominator is that there's an understandable reason why the killer commits the deed. God's commandment not to kill is broken only once by most criminals. There are a select few, however, who do it once and keep right on going."

"I'm with you so far. Go on."

"The FBI considers someone a serial killer if he or she—they're mostly males, by the way—has murdered more than three people *and* there's been a cooling off period between the killings, a fact that indicates premeditation.

"At any rate, within the category of serial killers, there are different types. Three as a matter of fact. Since you're in a hurry, however, I won't give you a lecture on all of them. Let's talk about the category your man fits."

"I gather it's not important for me to understand the first two?"

"The only thing you need to know about the first two types is that the first has a reason for killing but can be stopped in his tracks by the fear of being caught and going to prison. The second is mentally ill as most people understand that term. If caught and treated with anti-psychotic drugs, he'll never kill again.

"It's only the third kind—your man, the sexual, serial killer—who won't stop. He has illusions and desires the rest of us can't comprehend." He peered over his glass at Dominique and then continued, "For example, you and I might fantasize about making love with a gorgeous movie star. The sexual serial killer's fantasy will begin like ours, but after that, it turns sick. He'll envision himself screwing as he disembowels with a hook or maybe pokes the jugular with an ice pick and watches the blood spew. He usually kills up close and personal, confronting his victims and knifing or strangling them to death. Motivation is nothing less than the sexual high he's unable to achieve any other way. Are you with me?" He didn't wait for Dominique to answer. "Many of these sexual serial killers are actually impotent without the aggressive aspect of their fantasies. Sadly, it's a situation where the sexual and aggressive natures of the male animal become one and inseparable. We call that kind of killer a paraphiliac sadist. The ultimate turn-on for him is total domination and humiliation. He will often torture his victims. He doesn't lose touch with reality, and he understands the difference between right and wrong. He can control his impulses, but he usually chooses not to. The gratification of brutal sex is too enticing. It's worth almost any risk. If you can't catch him or if you turn him loose, there's no question about it. He will kill again."

Dominique shook her head. "Good Lord. Is someone like that sick or just plain evil?"

"I'm not sure I can tell you. They don't become sexual serial killers overnight. Some of us believe they're born with the inclination. Whether we're right or not, it's generally accepted that they're on a collision course with those brutal tendencies from the time they're five or six years old. It's true they have no say in whether they experience the violent sex urges, but they definitely understand the difference between right and wrong and choose not to control those urges. Does that make them evil? In my book, it does."

"Are they psychopaths?"

"It depends."

"On what?"

"Basically, on whether they're sorry or not. Psychopaths—the professional community now refers to it as having an antisocial personality disorder; personally, I think the word *psychopath* says it best—are amoral and antisocial. They lack the ability to love, and they're extremely egocentric. Although they're usually charming, even charismatic, it's impossible for them to have meaningful personal relationships. Other people are important to the psychopath only insofar as they're able to meet a need. Once the need is met or the other person becomes boring, he or she is discarded in much the same way you'd dispose of your garbage. There's no remorse and no conscience to restrain a psychopath's actions. What keeps most of them from being killers is that their goals are mostly attainable by manipulating people and situations. They inflict emotional hurt, but they don't usually need to kill.

"After the fact, the paraphiliac sadist may be sorry for what he's done until the sexual urge becomes so urgent that he gives in and does it again. But then, because he does have a conscience of sorts, he may rationalize to himself what he does rather than admit he is controlled by perverted sexual drives. Perhaps he kills only prostitutes, justifying his crimes as an effort to rid the Christian world of sinful harlots.

"It's the combination of paraphiliac sadist and psychopath that's the most lethal. There's no remorse and no desire to curb the appetite. Two examples of paraphiliac sadists who were also pyschopaths are Ted Bundy and John Wayne Gacy. You probably saw them on television, and they looked no different than we do. About Ted Bundy, you might have even thought to yourself, 'My God, he doesn't look like a freak. He's young and handsome. He had a good career. He could have had any girl he wanted. Why this?' Am I right?"

Again, Dominique nodded.

"I'm about to educate you as to what makes many of these men so lethal." Dr. Bruce cleared his throat as if in preparation for a class lecture. "For all practical purposes, they're prime examples of Dr. Jekyll and Mr. Hyde, although unlike the fictional character, Mr. Hyde is always in control. Dr. Jekyll is simply the persona they use to lead ordinary lives right along with the rest of us. After all, they've got to eat; pay bills and taxes; buy clothing, cars and insurance. To outward appearances, they're just like you and me, and that inspires trust. Because they're often very bright, it's not easy to flush out what's inside. They look completely normal, and they're anything but.

"As Mr. Hyde, John Wayne Gacy tortured and inflicted sexual horrors upon the thirty or so young men he's known to have killed. The Dr. Jekyll face he showed the world ran a successful construction business, married, was active in civic activities; he even played the role of Pogo the Clown and visited sick children in hospitals. He was the 1967 local Jaycee of the year. Meanwhile, the Hyde in him buried victims in the basement of the home he shared with his second wife.

"Ted Bundy's mother considered him a model son, one of whom she was extremely proud. Bundy's Hyde persona killed, mutilated, decapitated and inflicted unimaginable terror upon scores of young women he raped and killed. As Jekyll, he was an attorney, swam in political circles and was acknowledged as a possibility for a stint in the governor's mansion. He dated widely, was engaged to be married at one point and lived with a lover for a short period of time. Women considered him wonderful husband material. He was extremely romantic, sent flowers and wrote love poetry.

"A woman, meeting either of these two men for the first time, might think herself the luckiest woman on earth. She certainly wouldn't be on her guard. Scary, isn't it?"

"It literally makes me sick to my stomach."

"Well, Ms. Olivet, I do believe your Key West killer could be well on his way to joining the ranks of these monsters."

"What makes you say that?" she asked, silently hoping he was wrong; instinctively knowing he was right.

"Years of practice give you a certain ability to predict what a person with a particular mind set is going to do or, for that matter, why he or she might have done something in the past. I suppose I've worked with these people for so long that I get a feel for their day-to-day mind processes. It's not pleasant. Sometimes, I wonder if the ability to get inside their heads means that, buried deep, I'm as dark as they. Fortunately, I go home to my wife and kids and forget all about it. I become just another semi-normal human being with a loving family."

Dominique was moved by his openness. "I believe we all have a dark side, Dr. Bruce. Parents and religion teach us to control it. Many of us just try to ignore it. You're more courageous than most. You dare to step inside your own darkness to help others, and you manage to come back out unscathed. Your family must be proud."

Dr. Bruce stammered, "Thank you." He cleared his throat. "Now, for the important issue." He smiled shyly and quickly added. "I don't handle compliments well."

Dominique laughed. "Thank you worked just fine." She leaned in towards his desk. "Okay. Tell me what you think about my nemesis."

Dr. Bruce spoke quickly and without hesitation. "I believe your first victim was murdered for a reason. I don't pretend to understand the motivation, but at least initially, it had nothing to do with a desire for perverted jollies."

"And you say that based on what?"

"I'm basing it on the fact that there didn't appear to be any appreciable amount of the victim's blood unaccounted for. The killer reached orgasm, an indication that he became sexually excited by the killing, or something associated with it, yet the semen outside the victim's body was the only early discernable calling card so to speak."

"I've heard that term. Isn't a calling card something a serial killer leaves behind to indicate he was the one who did it?"

"Yes and no. It's a sign of sorts, but it's not something done on purpose, unless you run into the kind of looney who also likes to play mind games with the cops. Usually, it's not an ego thing. It's just that a paraphiliac almost always dwells on one particular type of brutal fantasy. In acting it out, he inevitably leaves some mark on the victim's body that is characteristic of the sexual play in which he's the star. After several times, you see and recognize it."

"Got it."

"The second murder was that of the judge, and in retrospect, here's where the calling cards—I want you to notice that I'm speaking in the plural—become apparent for the first time. There was blood missing, semen at the scene and teeth marks on the bottom portion of the victim's exposed throat."

Dominique's stomach began to churn. She thought she understood, and the idea nauseated her. "So, what does that tell you?"

"It tells me that he may have begun with a motive, may still have a motive for that matter, but in the process, he's discovered that blood turns him on, that it brings him to climax. By the time he killed the judge, he was trying to drink as much as he could. Bingo. There you have the reason for the teeth marks and the missing body fluid."

"That's disgusting."

"That's life in the annals of perverts," the doctor said simply. "Get used to it. You'll see more if you don't get him soon."

"It makes him sound like a vampire. Are you sure?"

"Sure as I can be. It's not all that unusual. I can think of two right off the bat. There was one in Germany who got his kicks catching the victim's blood in his mouth and drinking it as it spurt from the body. In California, they had 'The Vampire of Sacramento.' Of course, he was psychotic. He killed six people and drank their blood. He did it to replace his own, which delusions made him believe was turning to powder."

"I give up. I thought I'd heard it all."

"There's always something new in my line of work, Ms. Olivet. By the way, the girl on the beach had the same teeth marks on her neck."

"Can you summarize?"

Dr. Bruce smiled fleetingly. "There are three important points to remember. One is that your killer will stop only if he dies or is nabbed by the cops. Numbers two and three: he's probably sadistic and intelligent. My guess is that the only way to catch him is to use bait; then hope and pray she's smart enough not to become another victim. If law enforcement goes that route, the female officer must never permit this monster to have the upper hand. Psychologically speaking, she has to be the initiator, has to grab control and never let it go. She can never let him see her fear, and most crucial, she must never bore him. If she's not a good actress, she'll lose her head." He squinted at Dominique over his glasses. "His criteria for selecting victims isn't obvious. That's going to make it hard to know what kind of lure will attract him."

He took off his glasses and folded his hands in front of him on the desk. He stared at Dominique intently. "You, young woman, are the only person we know he wants."

* * *

Rolf heard Dominique's soft greeting. She sounded nervous and unsettled and walked slowly into the darkened hospital room, stopping for a few seconds to acclimate her eyes to the lack of light.

"Hello, yourself," he responded. His voice resonated somber and without a trace of humor. He remembered their conversation of earlier in the day and didn't want to do, or say, anything that might scare her away. The television was off, the room illuminated only by moonlight shining through the window.

When she found the bedside chair, she sat down and curled her legs under her. Neither spoke a word after the initial greeting, and she fell asleep under his constant gaze. At midnight, they were awakened by a nurse coming in to check vitals.

The young LPN's shift had started only an hour earlier; night was day to her, she said. She was wide-eyed and full of cheer. "Everything looks good, Mr. del Castillo. You'll be out of here as soon as Dr. Ahern makes morning rounds and gives the discharge order. It'll probably be just after breakfast." She left, quietly closing the door behind her.

Still, they remained silent. What was there to say? He stared at her in the moonlight. Without a sound, she rose slowly and slipped in bed beside him. They lay facing each other. For a long time they remained in that position, hands clasped tightly. Rolf closed his eyes and brought his hands to her face, running his fingers lightly over her forehead, her eyes, her nose, her lips; in self-imposed blindness exploring every millimeter of skin, imprinting forever in his mind the feel and texture of her face. "You're so beautiful," he murmured.

His fingers felt wetness, and he opened his eyes. Gently, he brushed away her tears. There were no words for what he felt. He tried not to think about morning. Moments, or hours later, she turned and fell asleep again, her back nestled snugly against the warmth of his body. He buried his face in her hair. If the pressure of her body caused any physical pain, he didn't feel it. He felt nothing except the comfort of holding her.

Reina's voice awakened them. Francisco and Sarita would be up shortly Mama told them. Her long hair tousled and damp with sweat, Dominique sat up. She quickly slipped on her shoes, hugged Mama and left the room without once looking in his direction.

He didn't trust himself to speak.

# 20

Lydia Burns was filled with excitement. Her ex-husband, also a hair stylist, was on vacation. They were on good terms, and he had suggested to an elegant and rich client that he utilize Lydia's services until his return. Her ex had told her that this particular gentleman was willing to pay whatever it took for his hair to look good; however, he was extremely particular about every aspect of grooming, from the cut, to the glitzing, to the occasional perm which made it appear as if he had a head of beautifully wavy hair when, in fact, it was straight as a board. She needed to do exactly as the man told her, no arguments and no suggestions on her part. She should charge double her normal fee, and there wouldn't be a complaint. Lydia couldn't believe her good fortune. She desperately needed the extra money for the college classes she planned to take in the fall.

Her schedule was filled with standing appointments on the day he wanted his hair done. She wasn't about to lose a marvelous opportunity, so she told him to come in after she closed at seven. On the dot, she looked at the clock on the wall, and he walked through the door. She gave him her biggest smile. "You're right on time."

"It's one of those parental conditioning things. My mother has always been a punctuality freak; she taught me to be on time, or five minutes early, but never late," he replied cordially.

They discussed what should be done; a new perm was absolutely necessary. He explained, in detail, the procedure he and her ex had worked out—no perm rods, only the old-fashioned, long clippies women utilized in the early nineteen hundreds to mold waves into short hair. He handed her a small leather case. The man carried his own supply. They were his mother's, he explained, but they worked wonders to produce a natural look. He was right, she thought. His hair was the kind most women would love to run their fingers through.

Lydia was fascinated. If she hadn't known who he was and they'd had this conversation, she would've assumed he was gay despite his ruggedly handsome looks. But, she knew of him, of his reputation and his wife and his kids. There was no doubt in her mind he was straight, quite a stud she had heard. He must simply have an obsessive compulsive sort of thing about his hair.

He wanted the perm first and then a slight trim, only a smidge, to cut off ends frizzed by the perm solution. She worked slowly and with great care. She didn't want to steal her ex-husband's client, but she had a feeling that if she did a good job, the tip would be an extravagant one. She played a soft music CD, lit her best scented candles, handed him a glass of wine and placed the clips exactly where he indicated. They chatted continuously. He usually preferred women with long dark hair, he said, but he found her short, blonde, tousled curls quite charming.

It was difficult to trim the very small amount of hair he wanted. Using the fingers of her left hand as a guide, she cut with her right. Thankfully, she'd had her shears sharpened just the day before. As they chatted about the new band at Virgilio's, her concentration broke, and her hand slipped. The scissors nipped the side of the middle finger on her left hand. "Ouch!" She was extremely glad she had hurt herself and not him. The cut was neither deep nor serious; however, it bled profusely, staining his shirt before she could grab a towel. Damn, she had probably ruined an expensive shirt, and she would never get a good tip now. "I'm so sorry," she stammered, her face lined with regret. "I have some spray that might get that out. It's in the storage room. I'll get it and be right back."

His hand reached out and held her in place. "Don't be upset. It could happen to anyone. Your finger is more important than this old shirt. Let's take a look at that." He unwrapped the towel. Blood had ceased to flow from the small cut. He squeezed her finger, and immediately, red droplets popped to the surface. He stared intently. "You always need to squeeze blood out of a cut like this. It helps to clean the wound and stop infection from setting in." He brought her finger to his lips and gently sucked the blood. He stared at her almost reverently. "You're a healthy and strong woman. Your blood is rich, delicious in fact."

No man had ever looked into her face with such desire. She felt like a goddess—beautiful, worshiped and admired.

He lightly kissed her finger. "There. A magic kiss and all's well." He smiled. "I hope my comment didn't offend you."

"Oh, no. Not at all. On the contrary. I found it flattering, definitely different but flattering."

A small bandage later, the haircut complete, he held her wounded hand between both of his own and slipped her two, fresh, one-hundred-dollar bills. "Here's a tip for you, for your good work and your charming company."

Her knees almost gave way. Often she worked an entire week and didn't make that much in tips.

"Do you suppose I could interest you in dinner and drinks tomorrow evening?" he asked in a light-hearted tone of voice. "We could walk the beach and talk, get to know each other and then head out for a late supper and some drinks."

"But . . ." she hesitated, "You're–"

His smile was enticing. "Married? Yes, I am, but my wife and I are separated. I'm only living in the house until we get the details of the divorce worked out. So, what's your answer?"

His explanation was all she needed. "I'd love to. I'd very much like to go out with you."

"I'm glad. You can't imagine how anxiously I'll be waiting for tomorrow evening. I'll pick you up on the Whitehead side of the lighthouse at ten on the nose."

She thought that a bit odd. "You can just come by my place if you'd like."

He responded in an apologetic tone. "Ordinarily, I would. It's not very polite to ask you to meet me on the street, but I have some business a block from there. It'll only take a minute to round you up that way." Again, he smiled seductively. "I don't want one single moment lost searching for an address when I could be spending it with you." He took her hand and gently kissed the bandage that covered the small cut. He kissed her on the cheek and walked out into the night.

She floated on cloud nine as she blew out candles and turned off the music. This guy was rich, and she had him hook, line and sinker. If she played her cards right, she might land him in no time.

That night she fell asleep and dreamed of being the next, and last, wife in his life, of a huge diamond ring, gorgeous clothes, living in the big old house and belonging to Key West high society.

Three days later, some teenage girls found her disembodied head near the water's edge in Merry Christmas Park. The police located her body, piled high with seaweed, just around the bend, near the site of Tiffany Holler's death. Unidentifiable bloody clothes were buried in the sand, and teeth marks were easily distinguishable on the stump of her neck.

*  *  *

After Rolf's shooting, Dominique had called the travel agent and canceled her hurriedly planned vacation out of the country. Once he was discharged from the hospital, she had put her law practice on hold. She hoped to relax and concentrate exclusively on Jordan and Daniella. Chez agreed to cover any client emergencies that might arise during her absence. Still, she had felt a need to be close enough that she could return quickly to prepare the house in the event Elvira, the fifth hurricane of the season, turned her eye on the island. Europe was out of the question. Key Biscayne, a winter haven separated by bridges from the City of Miami, was a compromise.

She swam and sunbathed with the children while Mimi and Tiny, dressed in clothes that provided protection from the sun, relaxed in the shade. Together, they all visited the numerous tourist attractions in the area. Rolf's men were keeping an eye on her house. It was a restful time; she managed eight hours of sleep every night, and the dark circles disappeared from under her eyes. It was impossible to keep Rolf from her thoughts and out of her dreams, but her frame of mind improved.

On Saturday, a week after their arrival, minus Tiny who had elected to sleep late, they sat at the hotel's seaside restaurant eating breakfast. They were almost finished, when Tiny, huffing and puffing, caught up to them and took his place at the round, umbrella-covered table. He handed Dominique a folded newspaper. "Sorry, little lady."

Puzzled, she spread open *The Miami Herald.* On the front page, along with news of Elvira's progress and increase in intensity, was a picture of her hairdresser, accompanied by the story of Lydia's grisly murder. Dominique carefully refolded the newspaper and announced she was taking a walk down the beach. They would leave for Key West right after lunch. She saw the look of shock on the children's faces and knew they said nothing only because they were afraid. Her tone of voice had been too grim. She tried to lighten the atmosphere. "Listen, guys, if you finish packing early, Tiny can take you down to the beach for one last swim, and you'll be allowed to order pizza when we get home."

She tucked the newspaper under her arm and headed down the shoreline, kicking at the sand.

* * *

"What's going on?" Mimi asked as they emptied drawers in the suite they and the children had shared. "I thought you wanted to stay two weeks."

"There's been another murder. Lydia Burns is dead." She handed the newspaper to her housekeeper. "Time for another funeral," she added sarcastically.

The trip south was uneventful. Jordan and Daniella fell into sun-induced naps before they left the city limits. Once awake, they kept themselves busy counting bridges, "Key-Deer Crossing" signs and mangrove islands. Dominique dozed fitfully. She could tell how close they were to home by the disturbing feelings and images that filled that netherworld that lay somewhere between sleep and wakefulness.

As soon as they arrived, she telephoned Chez "Hey, it's Dominique. I read the paper and came home."

"I'm sorry. I know she was a friend of yours," he said, concern in his voice.

"Thanks." Her stomach still churned. "Do you know when the services are scheduled?"

"I'm pretty sure it's Monday at ten. I can check the announcement in the paper."

"No. That's okay. Linda's been saving the newspapers. I'm sure she'll know. Anything happen I should be aware of?"

"Not really. Law business was slow. Nothing I couldn't handle."

"Thanks, friend. I appreciate your covering for me. The kids and I needed that time."

"You deserved it, and I was glad to help."

"Chez, could you do one more thing for me?"

"Certainly."

"I'd like for you to stop by my office Monday afternoon. There's some work I want you to do, assuming you don't give me any static about paying. If you insist on doing it for free, I'll have to find someone else."

"What do you need?"

"I want to make up a new will. The one I had jointly with Bill is no longer appropriate. I'm going to nominate Linda as guardian of Daniella and Jordan in the event something should happen to me. I want them to live with her, and I want Rolf to be guardian of their property. They'll have to live with my parents, and Mimi will continue to care for them. Of course, there should be financial provisions for her for the remainder of her life. I have other matters— where certain belongings should go, that sort of thing, but I'll have it all written out for you so there won't be much to do except type it up in legal form."

"Are you all right?" Chez asked.

"Of course. I'm just being pragmatic. My husband is dead. I have two young children to worry about. I should have taken care of this right away, but I didn't, so this is the time. Will you do it for me?"

"You know I will."

"Thank you." She didn't want to talk about Rolf, but she knew Chez would notice if she didn't ask. "How's our prosecutor doing?"

"Surprisingly well. You know how he is. He's tried to do everything ahead of schedule, or at least on his own schedule rather than the doctor's. Nevertheless, I've got to admit his recovery has been remarkable. He says he intends to be in the office on Monday."

"That's awfully fast," she said, frowning.

"I agree. I sincerely hope he's only planning a couple of hours a day for a while. If he has any ideas of going at it full-time, he's going to be surprised at how worn out he'll be."

"I'm so glad to hear he's doing well, but I'm like you; I hope he doesn't overdo."

"By the way, there's a vase of white roses waiting for you. Your secretary said they've been coming in one a day."

"Who sent them, do you know?" Dominique asked.

"Nope. Your gal says they're from an unknown admirer."

Dominique heard the implied, *It's kind of soon, isn't it?* in his voice and remembered Alicia's warning of the rumors that were floating around town. She wasn't going to act guilty. "It's probably Rolf's way of saying thank you."

"That's right. You always did like white roses."

\* \* \*

Mimi and Linda were on their second set of Mimosas, and definitely relaxed, by the time Dominique joined them on the patio. Mimi excused herself, Mimosa in hand, to start dinner. Dominique poured herself a drink and fell into the nearest chair. Each time she returned home after being away, she marveled at the peace and beauty of the garden oasis she had created. Here, the real world could sometimes feel far away. "Why didn't you call and tell me about Lydia?" she asked.

"Because there wasn't anything you could do. You needed the time with the kids, and I figured you'd eventually read about it in the paper. If you hadn't, I wouldn't have let you miss the funeral; you know that."

Dominique reached over and squeezed Linda's hand. "As usual, you did the right thing." She added offhandedly, "By the way, if you don't mind, I'd like to go to church early tomorrow morning."

"Is it your turn to do the readings?"

"No. I just want to go to confession."

"I was eavesdropping on part of your conversation with Chez." Linda looked a little sheepish. "You want to draw up your will, and you're going to confession first thing in the morning. What's this all about?"

"Nothing concrete, I've just had bad feelings for a while. Real bad feelings that come in waves. I want to be ready, that's all. I need to have things lined up for the kids, and I want things right with God."

Linda looked at her askance. "You're scaring me, kiddo."

* * *

"Bless me Father, for I have sinned. It has been a month since my last confession."

Dominique scanned her notes. She couldn't remember when the nuns had taught her to do an examination of conscience prior to entering the confessional. She must have been very young because she did have a vivid recollection of nervously printing her childish sins on a piece of paper so she wouldn't forget to confess them. She had not yet learned cursive.

Her hand shook now, as it had then. She decided to get the big ones out of the way first, and she began by detailing the night when Rolf had come to her bed. She went on to confess their admission of feelings and the kisses they had shared at the hospital. She stressed her determination that nothing more would come of the emotional attachment. She continued, nit-picking the last month of her life and confessing anything that even remotely approximated a sin.

"Don't you think you're obsessing a little, my child?"

"I know I am, Father." She sighed. "I'm worried I might be our killer's next target. I don't intend to let him succeed, but you never know. I want to be prepared with a clean slate, just in case."

From the moment she answered her pastor's question, she sensed something different in his demeanor. She couldn't quite put her finger on it. A slight hesitation maybe. A quiver in his voice, or a subtle hurrying of her time in the confessional. The sacrament had been completed, and she had risen to leave. Something stopped her. She kneeled again and whispered through the grid-like screen. "You know who he is, don't you, Father?" She held her breath and waited for his response. There was none. She stood, made the sign of the cross and smiled pleasantly at the next person waiting in line. She walked straight to the priest's cubicle and deliberately, without knocking, pulled open the door. It was empty.

A stunned parishioner stammered, "Father came out a second ago. I'm sure he'll be right back."

Dominique knew better.

\* \* \*

On Monday, Dominique attended Lydia's memorial service and arrived at her office shortly after one. "Rotten day. I have a souvenir for you buried in my briefcase somewhere," she mumbled as she passed Patti's desk.

She opened the door to her office and gasped. She had never seen so many telephone messages. Her desk appeared to be completely covered. "What the hell is going on?" she yelled down the hall.

"I'm coming your way if you promise not to throw anything!" Patti screamed back without showing her face.

Again she yelled. "I promise. Just get in here and tell me what's going on!" Only after the fact did it occur to her that she could have used the intercom and spoken in a normal tone of voice. Thankfully, there were no clients to hear her outburst.

Within seconds, Patti peeked around the door. Somewhat meekly, a deviation from her usual approach to things, she said, "I'm sorry. Maybe I should have warned you."

Despite herself, Dominique laughed. "And I'm sorry if I snapped at you. The world is turning upside-down these days." Sitting at her desk, she motioned at the piles of paper. "Now— what, or from whom, are all these hundreds of messages?"

"Well, I'd say about thirty or so are from clients who wanted to talk to you when you got back or from prospective clients. The remainder are from a bunch of kooks who think you can read the future. Read palms. Find lost children. Communicate with the dead. Name it, and they think you can do it. They all wanted appointments, which I wouldn't give them, so then they insisted on leaving messages. They want to talk to you personally. Some of the calls are even long distance."

"Oh, Good Lord, no." Dominique banged her head against the computer screen.

"Oh, yeah. Have you got any idea what a pain in the ass this has been? I'm trying to work, and I have to stop every thirty seconds to talk to someone who thinks this is a fortune telling establishment. Maybe I should answer the phone, Dominique's Den of Delusionals?"

"That's not funny."

Patti laughed half-heartedly. "How are we going to stop this mess?"

"Run a notice in the paper that I'm neither a medium nor a spiritualist and that I won't speak to anyone who calls the office on anything other than legal matters. All calls will be screened before being put through, something to that effect. Word it to suit yourself."

"Sounds good, Anything to stop this madness."

For the remainder of the day, Dominique hibernated and prepared a list of assets for her Last Will and Testament. Chez arrived late in the afternoon. They discussed her wishes and concluded their meeting quickly.

Before heading home, she stopped to visit Lydia's mother. She didn't learn much. Lydia had confided in her mother only to the extent of saying she had a date with a new man who was great marriage material. She had refused to name him. He was still married, though in the process of a divorce. She didn't want word spreading just yet. It was obvious to Dominique that if Lydia didn't want to tell her mother, it was either because her mother knew the man or would have recognized his name.

By Friday, the estate documents had been completed to Dominique's satisfaction. They were signed, witnessed and notarized as required, and she rested easier. As the days went by and the newspaper ads ran several times, the calls for help with the supernatural dwindled to a minimum.

\* \* \*

The week following Halloween, Elvira stalled and gathered strength. Within days, she was a category three hurricane, her winds ranging from 111 to 130 miles per hour. Key West sweltered. It was the kind of weather old-timers said always preceded a vicious storm. Not even the central air could successfully keep the house cool despite the fact the wooden shutters were closed. Pulling in the shutters during spells of extreme heat was a long-standing, local practice that now protected Dominique's bedroom activities from view without alerting the killer that she had caught on to his surveillance. He had been watching her every move since their return from Key Biscayne; of that, she was certain. She could feel it in her bones.

In the twilight created by the closed shutters, she pulled up the zipper on her dress and surveyed the effect in the mirror. It was time to leave for the Mary Immaculate fund raiser and talent show, a festive, annual event attended by all segments of moneyed Key Westers, Catholic or not. Dominique hadn't planned on going, feeling it was too soon after Bill's death, but Sister Margaret had called and insisted. She wouldn't be with a date, and it was, after all, a benefit; one which brought in a generous amount of money. Those proceeds made it possible for the school to maintain a level of scholarships it couldn't otherwise afford. Having benefited from one of those scholarships years earlier, Dominique considered the fund raiser a worthy event. It was the talent competition which provided the bulk of the night's profits, and she had participated every year since returning to the Keys. Her Flamenco dance always yielded several thousand dollars for the school; big bucks that came from guests who drank a little too much and were loose with their money when it came to bidding on favorite performers. In all honesty, her ego hadn't been ready to let the trophy go to someone new. She had changed her mind and agreed to attend.

The dress for this occasion was the same every year. Black, low-cut, sleeveless and backless, it followed the curves of her body until it arrived at the knees. There it split, one side exposing leg, the other continuing to the ankle. The bottom quarter of the dress was of a light, but tightly pleated fabric so that when she twirled, kicked and stomped her heels, the flounce would flair right along with the hair that she let cascade in loose waves down her back. The most difficult part of getting ready had been finding a tuxedo for Tiny. There wasn't one large enough on the island, and it had to be shipped from Miami.

*  *  *

Dominique walked in on Tiny's arm. There was much ado about the arrival of the jolly, not-so-green giant and his miniature ward, and they were quickly led to a table where a newly released Ben Hargrave and his smiling father waited. Ben's mother stayed away, not wanting anything more to do with Key West.

Alicia was seated only a table away and moments later walked over to join them. Publicity about the subsequent murders, as well as the media reports following the bail hearing, had made it obvious to the public at large that Ben wasn't Regina's killer. Alicia had been one of the first to advocate Ben's release.

Dominique was generally well-pleased with herself. She had managed to gain Ben's freedom while still maintaining Alicia's secret. As icing on the cake, her curiosity had been satisfied when Jenna admitted to writing the anonymous note Tiny had found. The hint as to the blood type had been her way of calling attention to Regina's biological father, a man she had feared was responsible for her adopted daughter's death.

The Hargraves thanked Dominique repeatedly, describing what they termed as her brilliant cross-examination of the medical examiner to anyone willing to listen. The elder Hargrave had insisted she keep what remained of the retainer, which was most of it, and Dominique hadn't argued. A steady stream of congratulations flowed her way, and it promised to be a very good evening.

Dominique relaxed and scanned the room, trying to determine if the crowd was sufficiently large to insure another good year of much-needed, outside money for the school. Almost immediately, she spotted Rolf, Sarah's arm linked through his, and her heart sank. Wearing a simple, form-fitting, gold and white brocade gown, Sarah del Castillo was the portrait of a porcelain beauty queen. Dominique was forced to acknowledge that together, Sarah and Rolf presented to the world a magnificent pairing of universal opposites. Dominique managed to carry on lively polite conversation, while inwardly lecturing herself that Rolf was doing what he should; he was concentrating on his wife. It was the moral and politically expedient thing to do. She just didn't want to watch it going on. She wished she hadn't come, that she could walk out the door and go home, but of course, she couldn't do any such thing. Instead, each time the del Castillos moved toward her, she did her best to migrate to another part of the room. Thankfully, they weren't seated at the same table.

* * *

When it came time for Dominique to perform, she rose and walked to the platform. Men's eyes riveted themselves to her. She was well aware that she was no golden beauty, but she felt sexy in a gypsy sort of way, and knowing Rolf was there filled her with electricity. With an air of haughtiness, and undulating her hips, she sauntered to center stage. There was some anticipatory applause, and then a hush fell over the crowd.

She arched her back, thrust out a leg and raised both arms high. With a resounding clap of the hands and a throw of her head, she signaled the guitarist. The dance began, and magically, she lost herself in sound and movement. Body stretched tight, she thundered her heels on the wooden floor, maneuvering the black frill of her costume as she clapped powerfully in time to the passionate rhythm of the Andalusian music. When it was over, she bowed, straightened and tossed sweat-dampened hair from her face. Uproarious applause and raucous wolf whistles broke through the spell, and she beamed happily. The trophy would be hers for another year.

Briefly, she rode a wave of adrenalin. She was enjoying life, and then, she felt it. She felt him. His evil. He was watching her moment of community triumph. Oddly, though she sensed his presence, she caught no hint of the usual hatred he exuded. The effect, however, was the same. The smile left her face, and she quickly walked off the stage. On her table waited a bouquet of white roses. There was no card, but she knew, and ordinarily, it would have made her happy.

Throughout the remainder of the talent show, she sat between her client and his father, laughing and clapping at the other contestants, doing her best not to permit the evening to be ruined by the perceived presence of someone who exerted ominous power only because of his anonymity.

When the competition part of the evening was over, the orchestra began to play, and couples rose to dance. Well-wishers and admirers, both of her legal work and her dance, dropped by the table. It soon became apparent that the parade of locals would go on as long as she remained seated.

Harrison Hargrave came to the rescue by extending his hand. "Ms. Olivet, may I have the pleasure of dancing with the best, and most beautiful, lawyer I've ever had the good fortune to know?"

"Of course," she replied, smiling. "The pleasure will be all mine."

Ben's father was an accomplished ballroom dancer. Leading with a slight pressure on the small of her back, he smiled and talked. Though Dominique heard his words, they didn't register. The best she could do was to make polite noises at the appropriate times. She was intent on the vile feelings that intensified with each passing minute. He was closer now and again full of anger. Her eyes searched the sea of couples who moved to the music. She enticed Ben's father to maneuver through, and around, the dance floor, as she played the age-old, child's game. Was she getting hotter or colder? At one point, the feelings raged with a fury so intense she thought surely he had to be within touching distance. But, there were multitudes of men on the dance floor, and it was impossible for her to distinguish one from another. The feelings could be originating from any of them.  When the music stopped, the feelings ebbed.

She danced next with Ben. Again, he thanked her profusely, would not stop until, cupping his chin with her hand, she smiled and chided, "Ben, listen to me. I know you're happy with my services, and you appreciate me, and you're happy to be free. I'm happy you're happy. Now, please, shut up and dance."

The young man threw his head back and laughed. "Yes, ma'am. Anything you say, ma'am."

"And, don't call me ma'am. I told you that early on."

\* \* \*

He arrived late. As usual, his wife hadn't been ready on time. She was always fussing in front of the mirror about something— her dress, her hair, her make-up. As was also usual, he had told her she looked beautiful, to hurry up or they would be late. And, of course, they were more than fashionably late. They missed dinner, but he arrived in time to watch the bitch walk to the stage. His wife wanted to immediately search for a table, but he quickly put a stop to that. "Remember your breeding, my dear.  It's impolite to wander while someone is performing."

As he watched her body whirl, long, dark hair flowing, he was perplexed by his emotions. He had completely and inexorably hated her and then his feelings had subtly begun to evolve.  He had watched her fight him, the unknown force, with courage and tenacity, refusing to give up, and his admiration had grown. She definitely wasn't like the others. She wasn't the picture of one thing and the essence of another as Regina had been. She was the real thing—a woman truly worthy of him—a gem with which to adorn himself. If he could have her, he would make her his queen. He would be the envy of his peers. He would never hurt her. But that could never be, and he knew it. He was married with a family. A divorce would be messy, would interfere with too many aspects of his life. His mother was satisfied with her daughter-in-law, would be furious and unforgiving if he divorced her for someone else. He could bear many things but not the rejection of his mother. She was the one constant in his life, the one who would never abandon him; the one he worshiped. Anyway, the slut was in love with someone else.

Dancing with his wife, he spotted her on the dance floor. She was with a man he didn't recognize. He remembered the scene he had watched through night vision glasses, pictured the bitch clutching del Castillo's body to her own. His anger grew, and he hated her again. He had to keep those times in his mind. He had to remind himself of her sinful ways. He had to remember to hate her.

* * *

Father Madera tapped the young man on the shoulder. "May I break in, son?"

"Yes, sir," Ben stuttered.

Dominique couldn't help laughing. Ben wasn't Catholic and apparently not at all sure how one should address a member of the clergy of Christianity's oldest official religion. He hurried off the dance floor.

"I'm sorry, Dominique," her pastor offered immediately.

"You should be," she retorted. "That was inexcusable. I've never heard of a priest walking out on a confession. You, of all people, I didn't expect that from."

"Technically, confession was over. Your question was an afterthought and had nothing to do with your reconciliation with God."

"Okay. In religious legalese, if that's the footing you want to take, I suppose you're correct. Nevertheless, I'm one of your parishioners, a member of the flock you tend for our Lord. You knew the killings touched me personally, and you walked out anyway. You didn't minister to me very well, and I'm angry about that, Father." Her tone of voice was hostile, and she was talking so fast, she had to take a breath before adding, "For your information, by walking out, you let me know precisely what your answer would have been." The music ended and Dominique turned to leave the dance floor.

"I'd like to talk to you privately. Will you forgive me and do that?" Father Madera asked.

Dominique looked at him and stomped her foot. Her lower lip protruded into what Mama Reina teasingly termed "the pout". It lasted only a few seconds before she laughed. "Of course I will, Father. You know me. I blow off steam and then I get over it. I couldn't hold a grudge against you anyway. You're disgustingly sweet." She smiled at his look of relief. "When would you like to talk?"

"How about tomorrow after dinner?"

"Better yet, why don't you come to my place for something to eat? I'll make sure we have privacy after the food's gone."

"Just give me a time. I'll be there with bells on my toes and a bone in my nose," he said, now jovial.

"See you then." The music started up again, and she strained to make herself heard above the din. "Six thirty. And, Father, I'm not giving up on badgering you to tell me what you know."

* * *

Harrison Hargrave had just pulled out a chair so Dominique could rejoin the group when Rolf approached the table. She held her breath.

"Dominique," he said, executing a small bow. "May I have the next dance with the lovely woman who saved my life?"

She was at a loss for words, wanted to say, "Just what the hell do you think you're doing? Leave me alone," but twelve people were at the table and others close enough to hear. She didn't want to create a scene and tried to ease out of the situation. "I appreciate the compliment and the offer, but I've been on the dance floor constantly. I need to rest my weary feet. Perhaps  later?" If she thought he would let the matter drop, she should have known better.

"Don't tell me. I've been shot and just released from the hospital and I can dance longer than you?"

Giving in was easier than arguing in front of everyone. She smiled. "Point well taken. Challenge accepted." She turned to the Hargraves. "Excuse me, gentlemen. I'll return shortly. If I don't, come get me. I'll have collapsed from exhaustion."

Rolf took her hand and led her through the crowd and onto the dance floor. Once there, his arm encircled her, forcefully pulling her body against his own.

Her mind urged her to pull away, but his arm was tight around her waist. Her body rebelled, of its own accord molding itself to him. "Damn you. Why are you doing this? It only makes matters worse," she lashed out, her words caustic but her body soft.

"Why did you leave town without telling me? Without even saying goodbye?" he whispered harshly in her ear, his arm tightening even further.

"I thought it best," she said simply.

"I've missed you." His voice was husky, and she felt his breath, soft and warm against her ear.

"I've missed you, too." She couldn't deny him the truth, but she had made up her mind. What she wanted was wrong, and it must not be. "Look Rolf, I don't want to talk like this. I don't want to talk about us, period." She tried to pull away without pushing on his chest.

"All right, just dance with me. I promise I won't say another personal word." He winked at her. "Besides, that is, telling you that your dance was exquisite. Just like you."

She couldn't help smiling. "One of these days you are going to be the death of me, or me of you. I don't know which."

He momentarily backed away, the cockamamie expression on his face that he had used on her numerous times as a pesky young boy. She laughed and relaxed in his arms.

When the music ended, he followed her off the floor. "I'll escort you back to your table. I am, after all, a gentleman."

At that moment, the orchestra began the first strains of the *Blue Danube Waltz*. It was an indication of intermission, a time for the benefit guests to indulge in drink and conversation and hopefully, more generous donations. Dominique and Rolf looked at each other. First they smiled, and then, they laughed.

In a split second, she had been transported to the sixth grade, to the cotillion dance they had practiced time and again until they'd been ready to perform to the wild applause of Dominique's parents, the del Castillos and the families of the other children who had danced their own endlessly-rehearsed numbers. They had both been thoroughly embarrassed. The very next morning, Dominique had convinced her mother and Mama Reina that she would try harder if they would just let her switch to ballet or Flamenco, to anything else, so long as she didn't have to do it in public with a boy.

Rolf, smiling in his tailed tuxedo, bowed now as then, and held out his upraised hand, palm down, wrist bent, as Mrs. Ramsey, the cotillion mistress, had taught. Dominique gingerly, as she had also learned on pain of Mrs. Ramsey's stinging stick, placed her own hand on his, and they walked to the center of the floor. The music stopped. The del Castillos, their friends, as well as the now adult children of those friends, stopped, stared and smiled. Dominique and Rolf took their positions, and as if on cue, the music began anew. Rolf looked down at her, tightened his hold, and they began to glide, graceful circles in three-quarter time. She was eleven and he was twelve, and there were no falters, no missteps. Sure of themselves, knowing every synchronized move, they flowed through the room.

When the waltz was over, hands joined, he bowed, and she curtsied. There was applause, and she heard Francisco, "Bravo! Bravo!"

They were still in the center of the dance floor when her eyes abruptly opened wide, and she stared up at Rolf. "He's gone," she said urgently.

"What are you talking about? Who's gone?"

"He was here, Rolf. The killer was here. I could sense him the minute he came in and every moment since. Sometimes more, sometimes less, but always there. Now, suddenly, I can't feel him anymore. He's left. I'm sure of it."

Rolf stared at her. "Why didn't you say something earlier?"

"Because I couldn't tell who he was in the crowd of people, and besides, what was I supposed to do? Walk over and, in front of your wife, tell you I wanted to talk with you privately or maybe that I wanted to dance with you? I don't think so. Neither of those would have gone over very well." She added more gently, "Just like this dance, I'm sure, didn't help matters. Please, get back to Sarah. For everyone's sake, do some damage control."

"You let me worry about that. Anything else I should know about this guy besides the fact that he was here tonight?" He took her arm, and they began to walk off the floor.

"Father Madera knows who he is."

He took a step back and looked into her face. "Are you sure? How do you know that?"

"I asked him, in the confessional several Sundays ago. I suddenly had this feeling. I just knew that he knew, so I asked him."

"What did he say?" Rolf looked incredulous.

"He didn't. He walked out of his cubicle and left me there like a stupid fool, waiting for an answer."

"Maybe he was speechless you would even ask such a question, and you just jumped to a conclusion."

"The only place I jumped was to open the door on his side of the confessional. He wasn't there."

"Good Lord, Dominique." Rolf laughed. "You haven't done that since the third grade when you wanted to know which of the priests had imposed a half dozen rosaries on you for penance. As I recall, the nuns made you go back and apologize and then you had to stand in the corner for a while." He laughed again. "Oh yes, and then you had to confess your little prank the next time around, which cost you more rosaries."

Dominique became aware of people staring. "Rolf, I loved this. You know that. It's another wonderful memory, but please go and do what you can to pacify Sarah."

Without another word, Rolf dropped her arm and walked across the dance floor to his wife's side. As he approached Sarah, his arm went around her waist, and he kissed her on the cheek. Sarah's mouth curled into a tight smile. The guests clapped.

Dominique, now surrounded by Tiny and the Hargrave men, watched. She noticed he hadn't kissed Sarah on the lips, and it was she, not Sarah, who had gotten the white roses. She didn't want to be, but she was pleased.

At midnight, the party still in full swing, Dominique was ready to leave. The time after the waltz spectacle had been spent in laughter, mindless conversation she couldn't remember and in furtive glances toward Rolf, who, she noticed, was searching the room for her as well.

Rolf's eyes followed, and burned into her, as she left the building on Tiny's arm.

\* \* \*

She was alone in the car, though Tiny followed close behind. It was a relief to have if only a few moments by herself. On a weekend night, there was no such thing as driving fast through Old Town streets, and she tried to clear her mind and enjoy the night breeze.

Halfway home, the feeling crept back, barely palpable at first, just a hint, but there nonetheless. The closer she came to her house, the more raging and turbulent the emotions. He was extremely angry. The feeling had a strength that physically nauseated her.

Construction of the Convent of Mary Immaculate, the oldest Catholic school in Florida, was completed in 1876 by the Sisters of the Holy Names of Jesus and Mary who were under orders from their Mother Superior to establish a convent and a school for girls. Built of native coral rock quarried on the property, it

was designed by William Kerr of Ireland in the Romanesque style. During the Spanish-American War, it served as a hospital where the nuns tended to the wounded and yellow fever victims. It stood on Truman Avenue between Simonton and Margaret Streets until it was demolished in the 1960's and replaced by a concrete structure.

# 21

An hour after arriving home from the gala, Dominique rested by the pool, the portable phone on her lap. She dreaded the call but wasn't surprised when it came. Her hair stood on end when she heard his voice for the first time, and a thread of fear trickled down her spine. She took a deep breath, reminding herself she had the advantage. She could feel what he was feeling; he had no idea of her emotional state. All of his feedback would come strictly from her words and her tone of voice. Hiding true feelings—not letting them show in your voice—was something every effective litigator did well. Her reputation was partially based on the fact that she had learned to do it exceedingly well. She was a good actress.

* * *

He was expecting her to answer with the standard hello.

She didn't. Instead, in an even monotone, she said, "Tell me why you're so angry with me tonight."

He was caught off-guard. How could she have possibly known he was the one calling? Maybe she thought she was talking to some-one else with whom she'd had a disagreement earlier in the evening. Perhaps del Castillo had been upset with her. Merely thinking of her with the prosecutor sent his blood pressure soaring, and the back of his head felt as though it would explode. Maybe he would just hang up without saying a word, but then he would never be sure. Did she really know it was him?

Before he could reach a decision she spoke again, this time in a soothing tone of voice. "Please do calm down. You'll only make yourself ill, and there's absolutely nothing to be so upset about."

His voice was unrecognizable, disguised by a telephone synthesizer, but it seemed to make no difference to her. Somehow, she could read how he felt. He fought to bring his voice under control. "How did you know it was me?"

"You apparently find it necessary to watch me. I'm always aware when you're doing it," she said, an air of superiority in her voice. "I, on the other hand, am able to climb inside your head. There's no need for me to watch you. I know your thoughts."

"Bitch!" He was temporarily out of control. "You're dead meat! You hear me? Dead meat!"

The tone of her voice didn't change. "When this conversation is over, take a deep breath, settle down and go for a walk." She seemed to ignore, or not to have heard, his threat. "Think over what I'm about to tell you," she said calmly. "When you were watching me dance the Flamenco tonight, you weren't feeling particularly hostile. Then you saw me dance with Harrison Hargrave, and you became angry. After my waltz with Rolf del Castillo, you almost blew it. You knew it, and you left. You were jealous. You want me for yourself. That's why you're angry. That's why you called." She didn't wait for his reaction. "There's no reason to be jealous. You're brilliant, and I admire that. I've never been attracted to a man I could easily outwit. You're different, fascinating in fact."

Was she crazy? Did she have no fear of him? No fear of losing her life? His heart pounded, electricity leaping from one lobe of his brain to another. She knew he had been at the benefit, that he had seen her dance. Did she know who he was? Was she playing with him? Was he dealing with a beautiful woman or was there a witch—a Key West *bruja*—buried under the lovely exterior? Though he had never before come in contact with one, he had no doubt in his mind that witches existed, that they joined together in covens. Could she possibly attend Mass every Sunday and still be one of them? For the first time, he understood fear, yet he was also giddy with joy. She admired him, thought him brilliant and fascinating.

He was formulating a response when he heard the click, followed by a dial tone. Why had she cut the connection? He continued to watch her through military binoculars, excited to see what she would do next. He was frightened but sexually stimulated.

She rose slowly, dropped her robe and stood naked in the moonlight, turning a complete circle, letting him see all she was, tantalizing him as her fingers teased erect the nipples of olive breasts that hadn't sagged from childbirth and the suckling of infants.

He stared, eyes unblinking, mouth agape, panting like a dog gone rabid.

With an arresting, sadistic smile on her face, she inserted the middle finger of her right hand into her mouth and gracefully slid it in an s-shaped pattern between the valley of her breasts, down over her stomach and into that infinite warmth between her legs.

His arousal was uncontrollable, and frantically, he tried to hold the binoculars with one hand while undoing his belt and zipper with the other. He had to touch himself, to relieve the tension his genitals couldn't contain.

It was then she withdrew the slick finger—he could distinguish the musky scent of a woman wet with want—and brought it to her nostrils, sniffing, throwing back her head, exposing her throat. He no longer had the capacity to see. He dropped to the floor of the old widow's walk from which he had been observing her, grasped his dick hard, trying to stop the explosion that would propel him from his voyeur's perch. It was too late. The touch of his hand, hot with pulsing blood, succeeded only in igniting the sexual spasm— a convulsion that left him crumbled on the floor, wet with semen, panting, sobbing from the ecstasy of a high that neither heroin nor cocaine could hope to duplicate and from which he had no place left to go but down. Long minutes later, he was able to collect himself and again look through the night vision glasses.

She was gone.

Strangely moved, he did as she asked. He walked miles and miles of the Key West shoreline, thinking of her, of her perfection. Like a male dog scouting the bitch in heat, his want was beyond reason. He was determined to make her his own. His hands would roam every inch of hot skin, and he would sink deep, experiencing all she was, all they could be together. And what then? He didn't know. It would be a travesty to destroy such a jewel, a woman who could bring him to the knees of passion without having died to do so, without necessity on his part to visualize her bloody fate. Perhaps they were, after all, meant to be the perfect couple.

* * *

Feeling the need to purify with soap and water, Dominique went directly to the bathroom. It wasn't shame she needed to cleanse away. In her mind, she had done nothing degrading. No; it was the role she had played that was disgusting to her, that she wanted to wash down the drain. This was no beauty and the beast fairy tale. The man for whom she had acted out a semblance of masturbation had no princely alter ego. In any incarnation, he was a monster, full of hate and perversion. Dr. Bruce had educated her on what made him tick, and she had been able to mimic a woman he could not resist, one who was his spiritually grotesque equal, who could draw him like moth to flame. She would attract the demon, make him come after her and finish this once and for all. He should not be allowed to injure or destroy another human being. If it was necessary for her to do, or say, things personally and morally repugnant, then so be it. He would soon be behind bars, locked in a mental institution or  dead and buried—his unremorseful soul rotting in hell.

She climbed into bed, said her nightly prayers and tried to talk to God. In her heart, she felt she was doing the right thing. Sometimes, however, human ethics and God's Ten Commandments stood at odds. "Thou shalt not kill" sounded good on the surface; however, would it have been a sin against holy law to end the life of Adolf Hitler in order to stop his massacre of millions of Jews and other innocents? She didn't think so.

Two failed murder attempts, along with four lives terminated brutally and abruptly by a man who would continue to kill, was a situation someone had to bring to a halt. His identity remained a mystery, and except for his obvious desire to get to her, there was no way to predict his future movements. When, and how, he would attempt to violate and eliminate her, leaving her children orphans, was an unknown. And, how many others would he kill before finally reaching her? How many others would there be after her? No one, perhaps not even the killer, knew the answers. She certainly didn't.

Aside from the formula she had incubated during long nights, she could think of no other way to stop him. She said all of this out loud to God. Not that she knew what kind of reassurance she wanted from her Creator. Just a sign, any sign, that what she was undertaking was, if not enthusiastically approved, at least understood and condoned. Eventually giving up, she stared at the ceiling, making no attempt to sleep. Her mind spun, creating additional plans and discarding them. Soon, he would come after her, and she wanted Jordan and Daniella out of harm's way. How to accomplish that without arousing his suspicion was her chief concern at the moment.

"Mom! Mommy?"

Dominique heard the two voices simultaneously. She turned on the light and bolted up the stairs. "What's the matter, guys?"

"There's all sorts of spooky noises, Mommy," Daniella whined, tugging at the end of her long hair, badly tangled from apparent hours of uneasy sleep.

"It's just the wind blowing the shutters," Jordan proclaimed. "The house rattles more upstairs, that's all. I tried to tell Daniella." He yawned and muttered, "But she wants us to sleep with you."

Dominique made an effort not to smile. "Do you think you can tolerate sleeping in Mom's bed for your little sister's sake?" she asked solemnly.

"Oh, sure. No problem," he answered without hesitation. "I don't want her to be scared or anything."

They followed her down the stairs.

"Okay, you two, climb in. It's curl-up time."

Wrapped around her youngest child, while Jordan lay warm against her back, she quickly followed the children into a rare night of peaceful dreams. She awoke, refreshed and oddly certain the night of restful slumber had been God's answer.

* * *

At breakfast, Dominique chatted nonchalantly about the approaching hurricane and the preparations necessary to safeguard their house.

"Look, Mommy, the sun's shining, and it's raining at the same time." Daniella's voice was full of awe.

Her daughter's enthusiasm carried Dominique back to her own childhood, to a time when she had gazed out through panes of glass, transfixed by the same sight, while Mama Reina spun an elaborate tale of sun and rain occurring together only when Satan wed. Now, the memory raised goose bumps as she flashed on an image of the beast who would soon come seeking his mate.

"Looks pretty doesn't it, honey?" Dominique smiled and added, "Sometimes that happens, a couple of days before a storm hits." She seized the opportunity. "I've made up my mind, kiddos. You two and Mimi are going to leave day after tomorrow to visit Tata and Granddaddy. Your grandparents will be happy to see you, and you can stay for a few days until Elvira comes and goes or changes her mind and veers away. I'm going to fly you to Miami to catch a big jet, and then I'll get Dragon Lady into shelter before the bad weather hits."

"The hangar isn't very strong, Mom. Won't it blow over in the storm?" Jordan asked.

"You might be right, son. That's why I'm not keeping Dragon Lady at our hangar for the next few days. A friend of mine has a concrete block warehouse near the Kendall-Tamiami Airport. I'm going to fly there after I drop you off at Miami International. I'll hangar Dragon Lady there and ride home with Tiny. So, you guys need to decide what to pack up. Now listen to me," she continued, "I want you both to exercise some judgment. Don't try and take everything you own. You won't be gone long. Understood?"

"But, Mommy," Daniella whined, "I'll miss you. And will you be safe, too?"

"God will be with me, and I'll be extra careful. Now, get packing please."

Both children nodded miserably.

* * *

"That was a wonderful meal, Dominique. Thank you."

"I'm glad you enjoyed it, Father." She handed him a glass of Merlot. "Now that the polite chitchat is over, what exactly did you want to say?"

"You know, it's a very disconcerting trait you have there, child. No beating about the bush, just dead aim on the jugular." The priest paled as soon as he said the words. "Good Lord, what a terrible pun. I assume you know I didn't intend that." He was sweating despite the air conditioning. "Anyway, I'm not criticizing. I admire your directness." He stopped and took a big gulp of wine. "So, to get to the point, what I wanted to tell you is that I understand how unhappy you are that I wouldn't answer you. I'm unhappy with myself, Dominique. There's just nothing I can do about it. I-"

She interrupted. "First off, you're only half right. Yes, I was angry you wouldn't answer, but what angered me most was your walking out. I thought I made that clear. You could have suggested it wasn't an appropriate time for a discussion. You could have said we'd talk later. You could have done numerous other things that wouldn't have been nearly as hurtful as leaving me when I needed you most." The pout was back.

The old priest didn't argue against her chastisement. "You're right, and again, I apologize. I didn't intend to hurt you. I wouldn't ever want to hurt you, but you know, I'm only human, and it wasn't something I thought out. You caught me by surprise, and I didn't know what to do or what to say. I suppose walking out was a form of temporarily avoiding the issue."

The expression on her face eased. "Well, I still don't like it, but I can understand why you reacted the way you did. So now

what? We both know that you know who it is. I attended Catholic
school. I was taught that the priest has to keep secret the sins people
confess. I suppose no one would go to confession if they thought
their deepest and darkest faults would be spread around for everyone to hear." She wrinkled her forehead in thought. "But surely
there's some exception, Father. We are dealing with a man who's
killed four people and tried, but failed, on a fourth and a fifth.
According to the expert I consulted, he's not going to quit of his
own accord. It's me he wants now, but he'll want others.  If you
can find a way to tell me who it is, we can stop him."

The pastor frowned. "I wish it were that simple.  There are no
exceptions to the rule."

"You're kidding, right?"

"No.  I most certainly am not. I wish there was a way around
this." He fished in his pocket and brought out a folded paper.  "This
is for you to read. It's a copy of Canon Law."

Angrily, she ripped the sheet of paper from his hands and
scanned the short document.

> *Can. 983 § 1 The sacramental seal is inviolable. Accord-*
> *ingly, it is absolutely wrong  for a confessor in any way to*
> *betray the penitent, for any reason whatsoever, whether by word*
> *or in any other fashion.*
>
> *Can. 984 §1 The confessor is wholly forbidden to use*
> *knowledge acquired in confession to the detriment of the peni-*
> *tent, even when all danger of disclosure is excluded.*

She waved the piece of paper and shook her head sharply back
and forth. "Surely there must be an exception somewhere in church
law? Maybe you just missed it, or it's in another section of the
Canon."

"No."

"Are you positive?"

The old priest took several more swallows of wine before responding. "There's a section in the Catechism, 2491 I think, that
says certain secrets may be revealed where very grave harm can
only be avoided by divulging the truth, but that paragraph relates

to professionals, like doctors and lawyers, not to the clergy. I don't believe it in any way dilutes the absolute ban against a priest breaking the sacramental seal of confession."

"You mean to tell me that the Catholic Catechism condones a Catholic attorney or doctor breaking confidentiality if doing so is the only way to prevent grave harm, but a priest is supposed to let an innocent die rather than reveal the secret of a serial killer? Is that what you're telling me? Because if it is, Father, that's crazy, and I want you to ask the Archbishop for clarification." She paced the floor, wanted to hit someone or something. The fact that she didn't know who or what made her anger worse.

"It's not crazy, child. The Catechism of the Catholic Church says that when a priest celebrates the sacrament of penance, he is the sign and instrument of God's merciful love for the sinner. I— any priest hearing confession—we're not the masters of God's forgiveness, but its servants. We unite ourselves with the intention and charity of Christ."

"What the heck does being an instrument of forgiveness have to do with stopping someone from continuing to kill? Do you think Jesus would approve the murder of a good person to preserve the secret of an unrepentant killer?"

"And how would you know he wasn't truthful when he voiced his words of contrition?"

"It's really easy, Father. The man is a psychopath. Psychopaths have no love and no conscience, and that equals no remorse."

"Dominique, I promise you I'll discuss this dilemma with the Archbishop, but I don't believe he'll say anything other than what I've told you. If it's disclosed in the confessional, there can be no breaking of the sacramental seal."

She remained silent, suddenly exhausted. There was apparently nothing more to be said on the subject. All religions are composed of fallible human beings. If her pastor was right, the Catholic Church had blown it big time on this issue.

"I suppose that's the end of our discussion. I just hope my life never depends on your knowledge, because you'll let me die. And when he kills again, and then again, as I've been told he will, I pray you're able to live with the consequences of your silence."

* * *

Tiny was awakened, not by the alarm he had set for a too-early six in the morning but by Dominique banging loudly on his door. He squinted at the clock, noting it wasn't yet five. Once he had made himself decent, he opened the door and looked down. "Up awfully early, aren't you?" he managed to groan.

Dominique was definitely not cheerful. "Hurry up. Get dressed and join me in the kitchen for breakfast. We need to talk."

*This can't be good*, he thought, and by the time she had finished telling him what she had in mind, he knew he was right. He didn't think the lady understood just how dangerous the situation was into which she intended to place herself. He agreed to help only because there was no other conscionable choice. Elvira was bearing down. The head of the National Hurricane Center in Coral Gables was predicting that by noon Monday, gale force winds would batter the island city; the full brunt of the hurricane would make landfall sometime close to midnight or in the very early hours of Tuesday morning. In all likelihood, the off-duty officers who had been guarding Dominique's house would be pulled off sometime Monday to help in the evacuation of the city. Tourists would be ordered to leave. Residents would be given the choice of staying or leaving, and many would take the safest option and head for the mainland. U.S. Highway 1, the only route to and from Miami, would be clogged. Influence or no, there was nothing Rolf could do about it; there were certain procedures that had to be followed in the event of natural disasters in the Keys, and those protocols took precedence over everything else. With the departure of the posted sentinels, the little lady would be alone except for him. However unwise her agenda, he had to be there for her.

He was no coward, but he wished there was some kind of backup. He understood the reasoning she had for secrecy. If the prosecutor knew, or even got wind, of her intention to act as bait, he would make it impossible. There was no way Rolf del Castillo would permit her to put her life in graver danger than it already was.

He ate the huge breakfast cooked by a grim-faced Dominique, took a shower and left for Miami. His main thoughts during that drive were of his family. If the little lady's plan backfired, if something went terribly wrong, he hoped he hadn't left anything unsaid or undone.

* * *

Dominique did not leave until after lunch. It would take only fifty-five minutes or so to fly to Miami International and drop off Mimi and the children. Cruising to the north was delightful, and though she was flying on the Atlantic side of the island chain, it was difficult to believe that somewhere out there, now probably only three hundred miles or so to the southeast, a Category Three hurricane was bearing down on the Florida Keys. If you didn't listen to the news, you would have no earthly idea bad weather was on its way. It was easy to see why, in the days before accurate weather forecasting, a vicious hurricane could hit without warning, its winds, flying debris and tidal surge killing hundreds, and sometimes thousands, of unprepared humans standing in its path.

She had asked Tiny to pick her up at the general aviation center on the north side of the airport, telling him only that she needed to run an errand before storing Dragon Lady and heading home. Dominique spotted his waiting car as she taxied to the terminal area and smiled. Tiny disliked being late, so he had probably been sitting there for a while. Most likely, he was napping behind the wheel.

Her thoughts quickly returned to the plan. She would spend a good chunk of money on audio equipment today, and she had surfed the Web before settling on a particular Miami store. It was her intent to covertly record anything the killer had to say once inside her house, and there must be no possibility of technical failure. She had specific reasons for wanting an audio recording; it would help the state in obtaining a conviction, and protect herself from being sued in the event she had to kill the man. It was not unheard of for the family of a criminal to sue the victim who injured or killed the would-be assailant. If it came to his life or hers, she wanted it on the record that she'd had no other choice. Tiny had suggested she might be better off carrying a voice-activated recorder, but she had discarded the idea. The year before, such a machine had reached the end of its tape and whined loudly, alerting the person being recorded. Not only had it been embarrassing, it had led to a confrontation of sorts when the man grabbed her briefcase, found the recorder and stomped it to pieces. Obviously, she had gotten no useful information. In this instance, a malfunction could mean her life. Besides, she couldn't afford to have anything on her person in the event she was searched.

In less than two hours, she absorbed a salesman's advice for placing the state-of-the-art microphones to avoid detection and paid out six thousand dollars. Once the shopping foray was over, she ferried Dragon Lady to safety and returned to Key West with Tiny.

It was after nine o'clock when they reached the house. The answering machine was blinking. She retrieved her messages and found several from her male colleagues, as well as two from Rolf. All were offering to come to her home the next morning to move anything that might be blown about and to anchor storm shutters. It was one burden off her mind; she had serious doubts about Tiny's enormous frame on a two-story ladder. It was only Rolf's calls she failed to return.

# 22

Dominique had been up all night with Tiny, installing surveillance equipment, and it was six in morning before she fell into bed, exhausted. Fortunately, her crew of volunteers didn't appear until after lunch.

Several times during the day the telephone rang. Caller ID showed the calls originated from Rolf's home. She didn't answer, and he persistently left messages. Please, he asked, would she at least check in with Father Madera, and let him know she was safe. After the fourth call, she relented and telephoned the rectory. There was no answer. She left a message on the recorder saying she had help battening down the hatches and asking Father Madera to tell Rolf and his parents that she was fine.

She went over the hurricane checklist she kept taped to the back of her favorite cookbook. There was no question that she had an adequate supply of matches. Bill had collected matchbooks from hotels, restaurants and lounges. There were hundreds of them in a large fish bowl in a corner of the library. Candles she always had in over-abundance, whether she needed them or not; she loved candlelight. The use of candles by the Catholic Church was one of the many things—her present frustration aside—that delighted her about the religion in which she had been raised.

There were the more mundane matters: filling the generator that would run the fridge once electricity failed; checking batteries and radios; filling the bathtubs and sinks with water so you could bathe and flush the toilet; a last minute run to the grocery for bottled drinking water; taking the dog, who hated thunder and lightning, to the kennel to be medicated for the duration; making sure the cell phone battery was completely charged. The camping stove was brought out of hiding, attached to its propane tank and set up on the kitchen counter. From the dark recesses of a closet, she pulled out the glass hurricane lamps which had belonged to her parents when they lived in the Keys. She checked to see that the wicks were in good condition and filled them with oil. The lamps, though they gave out an odor she found disagreeable, were more reliable illumination than candles; they burned a high flame for hours before needing to be re-fueled and weren't subject to being blown out by a draft when you carried them from room to room.

By the time she finished what had to be done in advance of a hurricane, her friends had secured the main house and were working on Mimi's cottage. It was dark inside the shuttered house, and the lights, that most evenings seemed cheerful, did nothing to lighten her mood. She heard the wind howling and noticed it was picking up in steady intensity and in the frequency of the more powerful gusts. She made the sign of the cross and reminded herself that a really bad hurricane hadn't hit Key West since the building of the grotto in honor of the Virgin Mary. The stone alcove had been erected at the direction of the Mother Superior of Mary Immaculate in nineteen twenty-two. The nun's prayer had been that, so long as the grotto honoring the mother of Jesus stood, no devastating hurricane would wreak havoc on the island. It was many years later, and so far, so good.

* * *

Tiny's voice broke into Dominique's thoughts. "Mrs. Sanchez is here to see you. She's in the sunroom."

"Chez' wife or his mother?" she asked, a bit puzzled as to why anyone would be out and about when a storm was barreling toward the city.

"His mom. She's brought a big thermos of that weak beige stuff you drink and a plate of microscopic, triangle sandwiches. The entire lot wouldn't begin to make a dent in my appetite." The big man smirked. "I had a cup of so-called coffee, but I'll wait for your supper handout. It's bound to be bigger."

"You're all right, Tiny Bishop." Dominique laughed. "I promise I'll make dinner early this evening while everything's still functioning. There'll be lots, and it'll be just you and me to eat it."

Dominique was dressed for the inevitable power outage and lack of air conditioning. The choice was to face a lady of the white-glove generation wearing a bikini with its cover-up sarong skirt or change and soon be hot. She chose to stay as she was and went to greet her guest.

"Anna." She held out her hand, and shook that of the older woman. "I wasn't expecting anyone so I showered and got ready for the heat," she volunteered. "It's nice to see you, though I admit I'm a little surprised due to the weather." Goose bumps rapidly and inexplicably covered her arms and caused her to stammer. Hate was in the house. She looked around, seeing no one except Tiny and Anna. She fixed her eyes on the vase of white roses on the coffee table and steadied herself with images of Rolf.

"I hope I'm not intruding," the older woman offered.

"Of course not," Dominique responded graciously, trying to concentrate on her guest. "It's just that the winds are occasionally gusting up to seventy miles an hour. It will be worse before long. It's not safe to be out." Her thoughts spun between Rolf's flowers and the feeling of doom that engulfed her. Was the killer a lawyer? Someone she considered a friend? Was he out there now, on her home turf, filling himself with hatred, just as he had done the night of the benefit? Her mind reeled with possibilities.

Chez' mother shrugged. "I know Chezito and his friends are helping you. The daughter-in-law and grandchildren went to Miami to get away from the hurricane, and I really don't care to stay by myself in that old house, especially not after everything that's happened. It's better when everyone's home."

"Oh? I thought you lived alone."

Anna seated herself, poured a cup of *café con leche* and handed it to Dominique. "Son and his wife are in the process of selling their home. They're living with me now. I have plenty of space. We all get along, and it gives me company."

"I hadn't heard, but it sounds great." Dominique set the coffee cup down. She couldn't think of anything she wanted less right now than a hot drink.

Anna Sanchez continued, "I thought I'd check on the men's progress and visit for a while. We haven't seen each other since the funerals."

"That's true," Dominique murmured softly, at a loss for anything to say. She had previously expressed her condolences; she knew the Sanchez marriage had been a loveless one. What more was there to say? Her mind fixated on the powerful emotions she was receiving.

Her guest went on. "Chezito hitched a ride over. I'm driving the Hummer. Big thing. If we lived on one of Old Town's narrower streets, he would never get anywhere near the house with it."

"You're right," Dominique answered as she stared at the shuttered windows. At least no one could look in.

"He should've known better than to buy something like that for Key West, though I must admit I'm glad about it today. It'll take a lot more than a seventy-mile-an-hour wind to blow that tank away. Anyway, I thought I'd give him a ride home."

"Ladies, if you don't mind, I'm going to take a short nap before dinner," Tiny announced. "I'm so sleepy, my eyes are about to cross. We were making preparations for the hurricane and didn't get much sleep last night," he added, glancing at Anna.

"I'll wake you when dinner's ready," Dominique called after him as he lumbered down the hall. She turned to her guest. "I'd offer some cookies, but I see you brought all sorts of homemade goodies."

"It's nothing fancy, just a little *merienda*," Anna Sanchez responded politely.

Dominique was used to the custom of *merienda*, a Spanish version of English high tea. As a child, she had loved the treats

Reina set out in the afternoons; as a calorie conscious adult, she avoided the tradition.

"The way the weather's progressing," Chez' mother said, "tonight's meal is probably the last decent one we'll have for a while."

Dominique was having little or no success ignoring the feelings that reverberated through her consciousness. "Anna, if you'll excuse me for a moment, I'll round up some plates and napkins." Not waiting for a response, she rushed toward the kitchen. Once there, she opened the back door and spoke to the men. How were they doing? Was there anything they needed? They stared at her skimpy attire, but she sensed no hatred or loathing. *Thank God. It's not one of them.* He was somewhere watching, angry that she had men at the house. Where the hell was he?

She returned to the sunroom and the unmistakable electricity of loathing intensified. He was near. She set the dessert dishes and napkins on the wicker table and looking at Anna's food tray, out of politeness choose several of the filled triangles and a small pastry. Her stomach rebelled, and she struggled to politely swallow and keep it down. She eventually drank several cups of the heavily sugared coffee. It might help keep the solid food down, and it wouldn't hurt to have both sugar and caffeine in her system. Hurricanes usually kept residents of the stricken areas from bed until the winds did their damage and passed, and she had worries over and above what Mother Nature was about to send the island's way.

Though she felt prepared, her skin continued to crawl.

\* \* \*

"Dominique!" one of the local attorneys yelled cheerfully from the kitchen, "We're finished!"

She smiled politely. "I'm sorry, Anna, would you excuse me again? I'll see if I can spot Chez and let him know you're here."

"That's fine. You go right ahead, dear."

Four wet men, huddled in a puddle of water, stood inside the back door. All wore immense grins, probably, she thought, as much from the huge volume of beer they had consumed as from the good deed they had completed. It never dawned on her that they might also be enjoying her bikini-clad body.

"Thank you, guys. You're all knights in shining armor." She smiled at their bedraggled appearance. "You do look a bit the worse for wear, and I can't thank you enough. I owe you." She warmed blankets in the dryer and started handing them out. "These should keep you rainproof for about ten seconds after you go out the door." She handed one to Chez "Your mom's here. She's waiting to take you home."

"She came out in this mess?"

"And brought food and coffee with her. She's something else."

"Yeah, she is," he agreed, smiling. He poked his head out the door and yelled at the top of his voice. "Go on, Joe! Mom's here, and I'll hitch with her!"

Dominique watched Chez try to dry off with his blanket. "Listen, that blanket has fabric softener on it and isn't going to absorb water. If it wouldn't bother you, Bill was approximately your size. Why don't I round up some dry clothes; you can dry up and change in the guest bath. We'll have coffee and sandwiches before you head out in the storm."

\* \* \*

Dominique rummaged through her husband's closet looking for something appropriate. Without warning, a thought materialized that the telephone would ring, and she should answer it. Carrying clothing and fresh towels, she returned to the kitchen.

A short time later, a dry Chez joined the women in the sun room. Dominique was glad for the company. More people to talk to helped her ignore the bad feelings she was unable to shake on this side of the house. The weather was worsening rapidly. She urged Chez and his mother to spend the night and was happy when they agreed. She poured coffee for Chez, loaded a plate and was handing it to him when the phone rang. It startled her, and if Chez hadn't already had his hand on the dish, she would have dropped it on the tile floor. She walked to the far side of the solarium, now darkened by the closed shutters, and looked at Caller ID. It was Rolf. She hesitated and did not reach for the phone.

The thought was compelling. *Answer!*

She took a deep breath and picked up the receiver. "Hello, Rolf," she said softly, not sure whether she felt annoyance or relief at the lifeline he had established.

"Lucky guess?" His tone was jovial.

"No. Caller ID, actually." Her skin crawled, and she shivered.

"Are you all right? Is everything okay over there?" he asked.

"Everything is fine. I called Father. He didn't answer, so I left word on his recorder. Didn't he get the message to you?"

The venomous feeling in the normally sunny, cheerful room magnified and multiplied; she fought for each breath as the emotion became overwhelming. He knew to whom she was talking. All the phones had been checked for bugs. How could that be? She turned, bracing herself against the table on which the phone rested.

Anna and Chez stared at her.

As Dominique watched, Anna Sanchez rose and walked to the vase of white roses. She lifted one out of the vase and held it to her nose. "My son remembered that you loved white roses. He sent them to you when were on vacation and, again, saw that you got them at the benefit. You gave all the credit to the del Castillo boy." She handed the rose to Dominique. "You really should learn to say thank you to the right people," she whispered harshly, pulling on the thorny stem as Dominique's hand closed around it.

*Oh, shit.* Dominique dropped the flower and the phone, making an audible noise of surprise and hurt, instinctively bringing the injured hand to her mouth.

"What was that? Are you sure everything's okay over there?"

She vaguely heard Rolf's voice from a distance and wiping the blood on her skirt, she picked the phone up off the floor. She struggled to keep her voice even. If Rolf suspected anything, he would come out in the storm—straight into hell. He had almost died once. She wasn't about to let that happen again. "Everything's fine. I was working on the wick of one of the hurricane lamps and just cut myself with the scissors; that's all."

"How deep is the cut?" came the concerned question. "Do you need to have it looked at?"

She cut the conversation short. "It's no big deal, Rolf. I appreciate your call, but you don't need to worry. Chez and his mother are here, and they're going to ride out the storm with me."

"I love you, princess. Stay safe, will you?"

"Of course." She looked at her bleeding hand. "I need to get off the phone so I can fix dinner before the electricity goes off. You take care of yourself."

\* \* \*

This was the moment of truth. Of that, Dominique was certain. She had attributed Tiny's lethargy to the previous evening's long hours. She now realized she'd been wrong. Anna Sanchez loved the bad seed to whom she had given birth, and whatever Chez had in mind, his mother had probably aided by drugging Tiny. Dominique could only hope the gentle giant who had elected to stay with, and protect, her was sedated and not lying dead of an overdose. Whichever, the effect was the same for her. She was on her own.

Fighting to stay calm, she reminded herself to trust in God, but to also remember that God helps those who help themselves. The courtroom had taught her how to bluff; her quick thinking had made her outstanding at rebuttal, at listening to the other side's final argument and, on a moment's notice, responding logically and convincingly. You could win or lose a case on rebuttal. This time, if she didn't think fast enough, she would die.

One thing was on her side. Both mother and son were native Key Westers. Most Conchs believed in spiritualism, in *brujas,* as they referred to the Hispanic witches, and in communication with the dead. She possessed a gift they might fear, particularly if they weren't aware of its limitations.

She returned to her chair. To buy time, she sucked droplets of blood from her hand, glancing at Chez and silently playing to his obsession. Then, smiling, she wrapped her hand in a napkin and took a bite of a dainty sandwich. She fought the nausea and spoke in a cordial voice, "Anna, I completely understand how jealous Chez is whenever I'm around Rolf del Castillo, a man he knows I've been attracted to in the past. He and I can resolve that problem. Rolf can't hold a candle to your son. You, on the other hand, have been hostile toward me since you set foot in this house. Would you care to explain why?" She stared straight into the woman's eyes. "These sandwiches are delicious, by the way."

* * *

Anna Sanchez detested Dominique, but it was a loathing now tempered by fear. She hadn't believed her son when he said the lady lawyer possessed supernatural powers, but perhaps Chezito was right and she, the unbeliever, had allowed them both to be lured into a black widow's web. She tried to defuse the situation. "I'm sorry if I've sent you a wrong message, and I apologize for hurting your hand. I neither dislike, nor hate, you, Dominique. I assure you of that."

"You shouldn't lie to me."

The words were said in a clipped, clinical monotone, but Anna perceived the implied threat. She tried again to appease the witch. When she spoke, there was no sign of Conch aristocracy. "You're right, I shouldn't. I'll be right up front about this. I don't care if you sleep with my son; I just don't want you hurting him. I don't want you to disrupt our lives, and I don't want you to break up our family. Aside from those considerations, I have nothing personal against you." She made a show of digging through her purse for a tissue; perhaps she could slip her some of the pills. How could her son be fascinated by such a woman? There were plenty of other females in Key West who were more than willing to provide an hour or two of uncomplicated sexual diversion. Didn't he see this one was dangerous? She reached for the coffee pot and began to refill Dominique's cup.

"No, thank you." Dominique waved the pot away. "Incidentally, Anna, tell me what drug it was you put into Tiny Bishop's coffee. Please be truthful with me, I beg you. For your own good." There was a menacing edge to her voice.

Anna's fear came in rhythmic contractions. The *bruja* knew she had the upper hand.

* * *

Chez answered for Anna, "There's no need to worry, Dominique. I provided the pills. I had her deposit some powdered Rohypnol pills in his coffee. That's all."

"The date rape drug?"

"Precisely. You're quite well informed, my dear."

"Don't be condescending, Chez. I practice criminal defense, remember? I volunteer at the hospital, and I'm anything but stupid. Do we understand each other?"

"Yes. I think we do." His voice was sweet and sticky, yet had the same quality as that of a small child who has been reprimanded.

The bulge in his pants didn't escape Dominique's notice. "Now, let's try this again. Just how much Rohypnol do you mean by a few pills?"

"Two, one milligram pills. He's a very large man; that dosage doesn't put him in danger. It's just going to keep him knocked out for a good long while, probably until late tomorrow morning, and he won't remember much when he does come to."

"Why didn't you just kill him?"

Chez stared at her, desire evident in his eyes. "Because if I feel I can trust you, that we're meant to share the same bed, there's no reason for him to die. That would only create a problem I don't need. Doping him up avoids that issue and paves the way in the event you're trying to toy with me. If I can't trust you, you'll die and it'll look like Tiny did it." Chez smiled. "Poor overgrown idiot." Arrogance had crept into his voice as he spoke.

She felt the mother's hatred resurface, the fear receding as the return of her son's air of superiority bolstered her.

Dominique had to play the only hand she had. "Chez," she said, a forced lilt in her voice, "you and I need to talk, but what I have to say is none of your mother's business." The ferocity of the mother's ire escalated and reverberated in Dominique's chest. "I suggest Anna stay here." She deliberately dropped the tone of her voice, imitating the huskiness it sometimes possessed when she spoke to Rolf. "You and I can talk in my bedroom." She smiled sweetly at Anna Sanchez, who glowered malevolently but said nothing. Dominique held her breath and waited.

Chez spoke to his mother without once taking his eyes from Dominique. "Mother, I want you to move the Hummer into the garage. If it's too wide, drive the thing into the back yard. It shouldn't be seen from the street. When you've done that, come back and wait here," he instructed. "If someone comes to the door, which is doubtful considering how hard the wind is blowing, make up some excuse why Dominique can't see anyone and get rid of them. Understood?"

"Chezito, remember I love you, and you can trust me. This woman is trouble, son. She's a *bruja*. Be careful."

"I can take care of myself, Mother." Chez' tone of voice was hateful, and Dominique breathed a sigh of relief.

* * *

Taking Chez' hand, Dominique led him into the bedroom. Gently, she put her hand on his chest and pushed him backward until his legs bumped the bed, and he sat down. She walked to the door and closed it, trying to collect her thoughts. Finally, she stood in front of him. Her face showed neither the fear nor the disgust that could betray her.

"Chez," she murmured, slowly running a hand along his right cheek and through his hair, "just how did you have in mind for me to convince you that I'm attracted to you, that I want you and intend for you to be mine?" Her voice was low and seductive. Much as a mother would her child, she kissed him on the forehead. A second later, she let her tongue emerge, wet over his skin.

He groaned audibly before answering, eyes replete with adoration. "I don't know the answer, Dominique. I wish I did. I want badly for you to convince me."

She saw the desire on his face; it was there, intermingled with fear. She also felt the hate that lay waiting, a hate capable of destroying her if he suspected treachery or if she failed to satisfy the appetite that controlled him. He was a killer who thirsted for the blood that turned him on. That made him no more predictable than any beast of the jungle. Imprinted clearly in her consciousness were Leonard Bruce's words and the necessity of applying them to this warped scenario as it developed. Somehow, she had to gain the upper hand. Perhaps if she transformed into the mother who aided and abetted him; into an abuser and a lover, she might turn his head; she could become the dominatrix. It was a dangerous game to play, but if you were about to die, any game would yield better odds than pleading for mercy.

"I think I know how to convince you so there's no doubt in your mind." She smiled enticingly and then, ever so slowly, twisted her features into an ominous mask. She slapped him viciously, leaving the red imprint of her hand on his cheek. Before he could react, not waiting for him to collect his wits, her lips met his. The semblance of a deep, passionate kiss left him breathless. "I know who and what you are, Chez. I understand your cunning and just what you're capable of. It's those very qualities that draw me to you."

As her finger caressed his lips, his tongue flicked out to quickly taste skin.

She fought to hide revulsion. *I'll die before I let you fuck me, you bastard.* She tried to mimic the look of warm fondness she had felt for him before learning what was inside. "I don't want to play games, so let me be very clear." She tilted his chin with her finger, forcing him to look up at her. "You told me you came here intending to kill me if you were suspicious of my motives. You were truthful, and that was good. Let me be truthful with you—whatever conclusion you come to—and I don't believe that will be a problem—don't *even* fantasize about hurting me, because I'll know. And believe me, I'll kill you. I'll torture you, I'll maim you—and only then will I let you die."

* * *

Dominique was an enigma. He understood nothing about the woman except his want of her. His imagination ran wild. His brow was on fire, and it transmitted the heat to nerve endings directly connected to his already uncomfortably swollen penis. She appeared to know all that he thought, felt and needed. She flattered him, threatened him, abused him and then gave him her lips to taste. Everything she did only served to make him grit his teeth with desire. She was his goddess incarnate, and his unsatisfied obsession to possess her, to be possessed by her, was unbearable. Seated on the bed, looking up at her deliciously beautiful, cruel face, he felt the familiar oozing, the throbbing. He grabbed the bedspread between his fingers, squeezing hard. He needed to touch himself, to do something to release the incredible sexual tension she had generated, but he was ashamed for her to comprehend how little control he had over his body's reaction to her. It was possible, highly likely in fact, that he would lose her respect if she realized he was nothing more than her slave, to command as she saw fit.

Mutely, he watched her step back, undo her sarong and let it fall to the floor. Without taking her eyes from his, she undid the bikini top, paying it little heed as it slipped off her shoulders, exposing golden breasts and deep rose-hued nipples. What a joy to be a babe in arms, held close to her heart, suckling and lapping warm milk released from the beautiful fountains with which nature had endowed her.

"Chez."

She had said his name softly, but lost in imagination, he jumped at the sound of her voice.

"Show me that part of you that can't hide its desire, that's so uncomfortably restricted by the clothes you're wearing."

The words seemed to float on heat waves emanating from between her lips, and his breath came in short gasps as she untied one side of her string bikini bottom. He was mesmerized, unable to respond or to move. All he could do was to run his eyes slowly and boldly over her body. He had known she was glorious, had seen her naked body through the binoculars but never had he been close enough to visualize the silken smooth texture of her skin as it stretched tightly over high breasts and flat stomach.

"Take off your clothes," she said sharply.

Finally he moved, quickly shedding everything, his eyes never leaving her body. His dick, freed at last from its confinement, bounced against his lower abdomen, threatening to explode as lubrication seeped from the head and ran down the shaft.

"Give me your belt," she ordered.

He understood what she intended to do—what was about to happen to him for the first time in his adult life—and his blood-engorged organ involuntarily moved faster. He could no longer control himself. He grabbed his cock roughly, needing somehow to decrease the sensations that now exceeded what he thought himself capable of bearing.

"Don't touch yourself, and give me the belt."

He felt himself out of touch with reality. The physically painful and agonizing sexual arousal was unlike anything he had ever known. He did as he was told.

"Now, lie stomach-down on the bed," she commanded harshly.

He heard his own voice, meek, like that of a child, as he prostrated himself on the bed, "Yes, Mama."

The belt came down hard and sharp, stinging his ass like a million, angry nettles. The pain was exquisite. There was one overwhelming spasm after another. All that he was, ever had been, poured out through his dick. He convulsed and whimpered. If he could pick a time to die, it would be now, at this most perfect moment of his life, in the aftermath of that glorious explosion as he lay breathless, but safe and comforted, in the warmth of his life-giving fluids.

When reason returned, he felt her sit on the bed next to him. She ran her hand over his head in a slow, consoling rhythm. Perhaps he had died and gone to heaven, but no, that couldn't be. There yet remained a part of him that knew he belonged to Satan and to hell.

"Chezito, are you all right?" His mother's words filtered through the closed bedroom door.

He inhaled deeply, willing air into his lungs so he could speak despite the overwhelming exhaustion. "I'm fine, Mama. Go away. Wait in the sunroom like I told you."

"Dominique?" He reached for her, but she was already putting on her clothes.

\* \* \*

"How are things at Dominique's house?" the priest inquired.

"According to her, everything's just fine. The shutters are secure, and that's the most important thing. "

The two men were seated in the formal living room of the del Castillo home. On the table next to Rolf's chair was an open bottle of Scotch from which he was pouring himself shots. He had thought that talking to Dominique would relax him, but she had been detached and aloof, and he was worried about her. How bad was the cut, and did it really happen the way she said? After the call, he remained listless and was using the liquor as a narcotic.

"It must have taken Tiny a while to latch the storm shutters," the priest commented, sipping from his second goblet of wine. He smiled. "Hmmm. I can't imagine that man on a two-story ladder, but then Dominique's stubborn, and she would be on the ladder herself if he didn't go up."

"No, Father. Neither of them had to do a thing." He was having a difficult time not slurring his words. "Several of the bar association members let her know they'd be glad to get the outside of her house ready. She accepted all the offers except mine, didn't even have the courtesy to call and say, 'No, thank you.' I had to call her house four times before she bothered to answer the phone." He had ingested way too much alcohol to bother hiding the hurt of rejection.

"Rolf, you know why Dominique tries to stay away from you. It has nothing to do with not caring. It's because she cares too much that she has to avoid you. Try to give her credit for doing the right thing."

Rolf scrutinized the priest and wondered if the elderly man could understand what it was like to be separated from a woman you loved beyond reason. He leaned back in his chair and did his best to formulate a respectful answer. "I do, Father. I understand. It's just that. . . . Oh, never mind. It really doesn't help to talk about it."

"What you mean is that you can't talk to me because you don't think I know what it's like to love a woman and not be able to have her. Let me tell you something, young man. I may be a priest, but I'm also an *hombre* like you, and I wasn't always old." He paused for a moment, running his hand through his hair. "A long time ago, I was very much in love. She died. That's why I became a priest."

Rolf was taken aback. "I'm sorry. I didn't know. I certainly didn't mean to be unkind. You know that my family and I. . . ." His tongue didn't want to cooperate. "We consider you a friend. We value that friendship highly."

"It's all right. It was many years ago. The hurting stops after a while, son, and I know that someday, in heaven, wherever that might be, I'll see her again. I've given my earthly life to God since her passing, and I have no complaints. I told you only because, to this very day, I miss her, and I want you to know that I do understand what you're going through."

Rolf was touched by Father Madera's candor. It somehow brought the priest down from the pedestal of enforced aloofness on which parishioners had a tendency to place the man who offered Mass and heard their most personal and private confessions. "Father, it may be a sin, but I want to put my arms around her, hold her and protect her from the world. I can't do that, and it's driving me crazy." He laid his head against the back of the chair and closed his eyes.

"Try to concentrate on your wife and your family. Remember your vows."

Rolf's face flushed. "You say you understand love. If that's so, then how can you say that to me? You should know that I can take care of my wife, protect her, support her; do all the things that I'm honor bound to do, but I can't make myself love her. You either love someone or you don't. It's not an emotion you command or unplug when it doesn't suit you." He swallowed another shot. "I made a bad decision when I was young. Dominique was gone. I wasn't thinking with my heart or with the right head for that matter. I married the best body in town because she happened to satisfy my vanity and my hormones. Now, I've got to pay dearly for that mistake." He sighed. "At least I don't have to feel guilty about hurting Sarah; she doesn't love me any more than I love her." He tossed another shot of Scotch down his throat. Was it six or seven? He'd lost track, and he didn't really care.

"Getting drunk won't help, son. You'll just feel worse in the morning."

"I'm not your son, and I don't give a damn. After a while, I'll pass out, and I can forget that for the next few hours it'll be Chez, not me, who's with her, making sure she's safe."

"What? Chez is with Dominique?"

Rolf felt the effects of the eighty-six proof liquor, but it hadn't lessened the hurt, nor made him any less jealous. He didn't appreciate the excitement in the priest's voice. "Don't rub it in."

"Are you sure?"

"Hell, yes, I'm sure." His eyes threatened to close, and his head dropped. He wished Father Madera would just shut up. "She told me," he said softly, not bothering to lift his head. "She said she had to hang up so she could fix dinner–"

The priest cut him short. "Good Lord, man. We have to get over there—right now."

"Huh?" Rolf's head came up, eyes only half open.

Father Madera shook him by the shoulders and called out loudly, "Francisco!"

Rolf's father appeared in the doorway, his eyes wide with alarm..

"Help me sober up your son. There's trouble, and I need him. Now."

* * *

Once again clothed, Dominique sat at the skirted dressing table across the room from her bed, mechanically brushing her hair, eyes focused on the brass crucifix that hung on the wall. Her lips moved silently in prayer.

She had no idea whether Tiny had activated the recording master switch and its backup generator before falling into a drug-induced sleep. Furthermore, there was no way for her to determine that without giving away the presence of the system. Alone, she might be able to handle Chez, but what about his mother? There was no doubt in her mind that the woman would be willing to kill in defense of the demon she had spawned.

The plan had been for Gertie to call Tiny shortly after dinner. The records custodian would pretend to be an employee of the Stock Island facility, ordering Tiny back on an emergency basis. The charade would be carried out on the off-chance the killer had bugged Dominique's phone and would be enticed by thinking she was alone. Tiny would leave, park a safe distance away, backtrack and sneak into the house. With Tiny hiding, ready to come to her aid, she could confront the killer and, hopefully, obtain his confession on tape. It had never crossed her mind that the madman was a friend, that there would be two of them to contend with, and that they would be inside her house before she understood what it was that she was up against. Her head was splitting.

She had no choice but to convince Chez of her loyalty and passion. If she could make him believe he was safe in trusting her, that he could have an affair that would sexually satisfy him without disrupting his domestic and professional worlds, he would let her live; he would leave and take his mother with him. She couldn't think ahead any further than that. After he was gone, or more correctly, if he left and if she remained alive, she would decide what to do next. Right now, her main objective was to come out of this breathing and with her head still attached.

"Dominique?" Chez' voice quivered and glazed eyes looked at her in wonderment.

It was more than just a headache. She didn't feel well overall. Perhaps it was the tension making her feverish. She turned to him. "Yes, my love?"

"That was the most wonderful sexual experience I've ever had. I thought I had reached the heights before, but this was the ecstasy of dying without death itself. I love you, Dominique, I truly do. I want us to go on forever. I want you to make me feel that way over and over again."

Reflected in the mirror she saw the unnatural appetite in his eyes, and chills raced down her spine. "It pleases me greatly to have pleasured you," she said with an air of confidence she didn't feel. "But, my darling blood-thirsty killer, both of us know I've not yet earned your trust. I make you feel good, but that doesn't mean you can have faith in me, now does it?"

Chez cleaned himself with a towel she had dropped on the bed and dressed. He came up behind her and kissed her on the neck. "You think of me as a vampire, my sweet?" he asked, kissing her again, this time near the artery that pulsed on the side of her neck.

"Ah, darling Chez, I told you I wouldn't play games with you; don't play them with me. I know what happened when you killed Regina. The bloodbath turned you on. It was a sexual high like you'd never known. You thought you couldn't experience that in any other way. Now, you know better." She smiled and turned to kiss his lips.

\* \* \*

Dominique's tongue danced inside the warm folds of his mouth, expressive, affectionate, yet not particularly erotic. He found it disappointingly mundane. Nothing distinguished this kiss from those of his wife when, having indulged in a high quality joint, her body demanded immediate climax irrespective of his own lukewarm response. His mind drifted irritably and then she bit—hard enough to make him gasp and his bottom lip to bleed. Eyes open wide, staring directly into his own, she licked and sucked the blood away. Once more, to his surprise, his dick hardened. He had never recovered the urge so quickly.

"Damn. That hurt good." He reveled in the sting that remained as a reminder of her unpredictable nature, basked in the thought of residual swelling and pain he would enjoy in the hours to come.

Her hand curved around the back of his neck. Again looking squarely into his eyes, candlelight flames dancing in her own, she brought her mouth closer to his. He felt her begin to nibble on the edges of the laceration she had inflicted, simultaneously exerting suction—drawing out more of the bright, rich-red fluid, making the hurt more intense. His entire genital area was hot and engorged, and his thoughts and feelings concentrated on the world between his legs. When she backed away, he saw his blood covering her lips, smeared on her chin, and he groaned. Her tongue emerged. Like a thirsty snake seeking moisture, it licked the crimson fluid from the rim of its cavern home and slowly retreated. An electric shock ran through his cock. He inhaled sharply. His eyes fixed on a point beyond reality, and then his pants were wet.

While he drifted somewhere within the embryonic cocoon of his imagination, she gathered and held his face between her hands. "Chez, listen carefully to me."

He closed and opened his eyes slowly, acknowledging that her words were trickling in through the mist of sexual desire that still held his exhausted body in its grip.

"I'm about to do something that will prove my love. It will be a permanent sign of our bond. If it satisfies you, I want something in return." He leaned forward to kiss her, but she avoided his mouth. "Is that a yes?"

Still in a daze, he nodded.

"Say it," she demanded.

"Yes. Anything you want, Dominique, anything."

"Very well, then. Sit on the chair over there. I want you far enough away that you'll know I mean you no harm."

At the foreboding sound of her words, he was shocked into alertness, instantly on guard. He worshiped this female, didn't want her to ruin everything by betrayal, and he didn't want to have to destroy the only woman who had ever pushed him over the edge of sexual desire. He walked to the chair and sat, every cell vigilant. The electricity was gone, but he could see well enough by the candlelight in the room.

From nowhere, a Swiss Army knife appeared in her hand. With a pale, manicured thumbnail she easily lifted open its shortest blade. She couldn't possibly hurt him with the miniature version of the weapon. Having no idea what to expect, he watched in fascination.

With lightning speed, she slashed diagonally above her eyebrow. Instantly, blood was everywhere, and he whispered her name in a panic.

She threw the knife to the floor and doing nothing to stem the flow of blood, she spoke to him, "I've marred my face, branded myself yours and given you what you thirst for, what excites you above everything else. Does that satisfy you, Chez? Have I earned your trust?"

Tears ran down his face, but she sat quietly, blood covered and composed. Every fiber of his being crackled with the energy of raw shock, with sadness at the marring of her perfect features, with admiration for the rare courage she possessed and with gratitude, an emotion he rarely experienced, for her unique insight into his craving. As with everything else that involved her, those emotions transformed into a blazing sexual desire. He didn't move instantly to her side only because, watching the scene she had created, without so much as touching himself, he had ejaculated in his pants. He couldn't catch his breath—wanted, and badly needed, to retreat into restful, restorative sleep. No longer fearful of her, he refused to sleep not out of a need for vigilance but rather from a desire to come to the aid of the one who was now his mother, his lover, his queen—his everything.

She crossed over to him and stood at the foot of the bed.

He rose then, gathering her into his arms. "Oh, Mama, Mamacita, I love you. I love you so much. Don't leave me. Please don't ever leave me," he sobbed.

She returned his embrace and, instinctively, whispered softly, "Drink your fill, Chezito. I want you to understand the depth of my love for you."

It was her blood she offered, the ultimate elixir. He pressed his lips to her forehead, to the cut she had inflicted on herself, the image of that shocking scene replaying in his mind. Instantly, he was hard again, groaning with want, tasting and drinking the intoxicating crimson fluid. It was sweet, portions of it sticky now, all of it still warm, kept from cooling by the extraordinary heat of her skin. His mouth ignited the red fluid and sent it, fiery and electrified, directly to his crotch. He screamed in pain as spasm after spasm hit him without emission. His well was dry, and his dick, for the first time ever, experienced dry heaves. In agony, he fell to the floor at her feet.

She dropped down beside him. "I'm sorry, sweet baby. I never intended to cause you pain."

He managed to smile. "For those kinds of feelings, I would gladly die." Still hurting and short of breath, he admonished her, "You'd better apply some pressure to your cut and hold ice to it.

I'll wait for you here. I need a few minutes before I can move around."

She smiled at him, pressed some tissues to her forehead and left the room. To reach help she would willingly brave the hurricane, but from the kitchen door peephole, through sheets of rain, she saw the Hummer parked in front of the garage. It blocked access to her car and effectively imprisoned her.

When the bleeding ceased, she cleaned the red smears off her face. She took a deep breath and steadied herself, knowing there was no way to avoid returning to the bedroom.

* * *

Anna Sanchez took one look at the blood that was eerily illuminated by the hurricane lamp Dominique carried toward the kitchen and screamed a mother's anguish. She raced toward the master bedroom in dread of whatever atrocity the *bruja* might have perpetrated upon her son. She found him sprawled on the floor and ran to his side. His eyes were closed, his clothing blood-smeared, but he was alive. "Chezito? Son, are you all right?" She smelled the acrid odor of semen, and her stomach lurched.

Bracing himself on the side of the bed, he stood in front of her. "I have someone else to look after me now, Mama. She'll do anything and everything for me. She can make me whole." His look was one of loathing. "She can make me experience sexual feelings you couldn't arouse even when you were young and beautiful— which, by the way, you are no longer."

She shrank from him. She had not expected his response or the tone of his voice. He had toyed with other women, but his heart had always been hers. Did he have no recollection of having viewed her as beautiful only the night before? Of having desired her maternal arms over those of his wife even as he awoke early on this very day?

He continued, his voice harsh and cold, "I want you to know I see you all too clearly." Taking her by the shoulders, he forced her to look in the mirror. "Now, if you don't want to lose what little affection I have left for you, go back to the solarium. Don't let me see or hear from you again until I come for you."

Understanding turned her skin cold. She had lost the most important element that bound her son to her. He lowered himself to the bed and turned on his side, his back to her, to the one who had given him life, who had loved him in every way imaginable. She had resisted her husband for the touch of her son, and now he was rejecting her for that bitch.

"Of course, Chezito." She walked away. *Maybe not tonight, but the bruja will die, and it won't be at Chezito's hands. He's mine, and she's not going to take him away from me. No woman will ever take him from me.*

\* \* \*

Chez embraced Dominique gingerly, but she slipped away from him.

"Not yet," she said flatly, no trace of emotion in her words. "It's time for reciprocity. It's I who now want concrete proof of your feelings. You either show me, or leave now and never come near me again."

"Just tell me what it is you want, my darling. I won't fail you. I promise."

"I want your mother out of this house," she responded, not lowering her eyes but looking directly into his. "She's the one who can't be trusted. She's jealous, and she hates me; I knew it as soon as she entered the house. If your mother finds the slightest opportunity, she'll try to do away with me. I can read her as I do you, and I want her gone."

Chez approached her, his arm encircling her waist again. He marveled at the warmth she radiated. This time she didn't pull away. He exulted in his domination, tempered only by the knowledge that it was his by permission that could be withdrawn at any time. She was his so long as he was worthy, so long as he could prove that worthiness and, in so doing, remain pleasing in her eyes. "You've done so much, brought elation to me, filled me with ecstasy, and you ask for so little." He moved her along with him. "Come. I'll grant your wish and then we can sleep."

\* \* \*

His mother waited in the solarium. He no longer felt the emotion toward her that he had once viewed as love, but he had no feeling of animosity either. She had been useful to him. She smiled sullenly when he entered, his arm around Dominique. He could read the displeasure in her eyes at the transfer of affection he was flaunting.

"Are you two all right? I was worried when I saw so much blood," she said.

He stepped away from Dominique and toward his mother. "We're fine, Mama." He took her face in his hands. "I'm sorry I spoke to you harshly," he said gently. "You interrupted a very intimate, private moment, and it upset me."

"I'm sorry, too, Chezito. Can I make it up to you?"

"Of course, Mama," he responded, kissing her gently on the forehead. Her mouth curled into the sweet smile with which she had graced him as far back into childhood as he could remember. He knew how happy it made her for him to show her affection in front of the *bruja*. He kissed her again and brought forth an expression of pure gratitude, a look he had seen many times before when he had shared her bed.

In one skillful move his powerful hands twisted counterclockwise. There was an audible snap of spinal vertebrae, and Anna Sanchez dropped to the tile floor.

* * *

Dominique gasped, instinctively making the sign of the cross. *Oh God, forgive me. I never meant for this to happen.*

Chez looked at Dominique as he spoke. "You needn't worry any longer, my love. Was that sufficient to reassure you how important you are to me, to prove to you that I love you above everyone and everything else in my life?"

She was speechless, struck dumb. Never before had she witnessed the death of one human being at the hands of another. This killing had taken place without warning, following an offspring's tender kiss. She was cognizant of the look of shock on her face, but willpower failed her; she was unable to disguise the horror reflected there. She blinked and, for a micro-second, saw not a human being but a bestial image beyond description—the possessor of Chez' soul.

"What's the matter, Dominique? Wasn't that enough?" His eyes held hers.

Perhaps he could not read her mind, but he had caught her reaction. She took a breath and spoke, her voice smooth and foreign to her own ears, "I already trusted you. It was only a matter of what you would do to prove your feelings. I let my guard down and didn't expect this. I wasn't invading your mind, and when I don't, I'm like anyone else–"

Chez interrupted. "You could never be like anyone else."

She continued. "What you did shocked the hell out of me, Chez. I hadn't anticipated you would go this far. Yes, I'm convinced of your love and very appreciative that I no longer have to worry about your mother."

Silently, Dominique said a prayer for the repose of the soul of Anna Sanchez, a woman she had disliked and feared. She did so because she believed that one must forgive before expecting forgiveness. It was what she had been taught to pray each morning and night—*And forgive us our trespasses as we forgive those who trespass against us.* It was a hard lesson, one with which she continued to struggle, but it seemed particularly important at this moment.

Chez hesitated only a second before taking her by the shoulders and kissing her lightly. He winced as his lips met hers, yet when he backed away, there was a smile on his face. "You know, with the sexual energy temporarily exhausted, I'm surprised and pleased to find that I have a basic affection for you."

Though his touch disgusted her, she was grateful to be safe. Perhaps safe wasn't the right word. Perhaps it was more correct to think that, at this moment, she had no need to fight, and she could dismiss rape from her mind. Even perverts had their physical limitations, and this one had reached his. Chez' wife continued to survive because she had no inkling what he had become and because she was necessary to the portrait of normalcy he painted for the world. Anyone else was dispensable. Dominique's realistic hopes hinged on the sexual appetite she had whetted but not satisfied. He continued to desire her, and that was keeping her alive.

"Thank you, sir," she replied lightheartedly. Her voice became serious as she addressed an issue he had ignored. "I hate to ask a tedious question, but just what do you plan to do about your mother's body?" She wasn't able to awaken from this living nightmare, but she might be able to convince him to move the wretched soul's corpse out of her house.

"Don't worry. Tomorrow morning, when the storm's over and before Tiny comes around, I'll take the Hummer and park it between here and our house. I'll sneak back to your place, and you can drive me to the car rental agency."

"What about the body?" she persisted.

"I'll load her up after I've leased a car. The Piper's at Kendall-Tamiami. I'll drive there, transfer her to the plane, return the rental car, fly over water and dump the body before landing at Miami International. The sharks will insure there's nothing left to find. I'll pick up the family in Miami, and no one will be the wiser."

She was astounded at his easy verbalization of a macabre mental checklist. He could have been discussing the disposal of refuse. Hopefully, his words were being recorded for the police and the court.

"All the guys who worked on the house know she was here. This'll surely be the first place they ask questions when it becomes apparent she's missing. What do you want me to say?"

"I'll report her missing as soon as I return. When they question you, just tell them my mother became upset because she thought I was coming on to you. During the worst part of the hurricane, against our objections, she insisted on taking the Hummer and going home. The next morning, you drove me to a car rental place. I told you I wanted something I could drop off at the airport when I picked up the plane at Kendall-Tamiami. You took a different route back home and saw the Hummer on the side of the road. You stopped; the keys were still in the ignition, but there was no sign of my mother. You called the house to check on her, but she didn't answer. You were worried and left a message on the answering machine telling me what had happened. That's all you know." He patted her playfully on the shoulder. "Don't forget to call and actually leave that message. They'll check out the facts you give them."

Her insides twisted painfully. She couldn't, and didn't want to, comprehend the amoral fiber of which this man was made. Steeling herself, she stared at him with the look she had rehearsed years earlier for law school moot court competition. It was a mask she sometimes used with opposing counsel but, wisely, never on a panel of jurors, a relaxation of the facial muscles into a bland veil that gave no indication of what she was thinking or feeling.

If he noticed her lack of expression, he gave no indication. "I'll be upset when I report her disappearance. No one will suspect me; they'll remember how hard I took the judge's death and go out of their way to help the grieving son bear this second tragedy." He smiled, pronounced dimples painting a sweet expression that belied the malignant, inner essence. Juxtaposing his words with the innocence of the facial portrait was akin to hearing "no mercy" from a saintly apparition of Mother Teresa. It was disconcerting and bizarre. "To most people's way of thinking, it's truly devastating to lose both parents in rapid succession." Almost as an afterthought, he added, "If they ask you about us, deny it. We're friends, and that's all. Mother walked in and saw me with my arms around you. I was simply comforting you after a close lightning strike. We tried to explain, but she wouldn't listen."

After convincing himself that they had their stories straight, he told her he was going to shower and inquired what there was to eat. Dominique said she would scavenge through the refrigerator. She closed the solarium door behind them. She didn't want to see Anna Sanchez again.

* * *

Chez disappeared into the master bathroom, and Dominique found leftovers she could arrange into an acceptable meal using the emergency kitchen equipment set up earlier in the day. She had promised Tiny a big dinner and now choked back tears of worry.

The faintest, most innocuous, food odors made her nauseous. Her skin was hot while, inwardly, she shivered from a bitter cold that permeated her bones. Either she was ill, or nerves could do things to the human body she had never imagined. She ignored the symptoms and set an elegant table sure to pleasure Chez. He had impeccable taste, and she did not want to do anything that might cause him to look at her with a critical eye. Outside, the storm raged and battered the house with ever-increasing strength.

In the midst of her meal preparations, she thought of the guns she had started keeping in each of her night stands. She considered going for the one closest to the hall if she could tell that Chez was in the shower. Stepping lightly, she hurried to the bedroom, holding the hurricane lamp in front of her. She couldn't hear the water running, but the door of the dressing room that led to the shower was closed. She was about to walk in when her eyes settled on the night table nearest the bathroom. Laid out on top, in a neat row, were the rounds that had filled the clip of her .25 semi-automatic. Obviously, he knew about one of the guns, perhaps both. If she entered the room, there was a good chance he would hear the wood floor creak; if the other gun wasn't there, he would kill her on the spot for her betrayal. Her earlier relief gave way to despair. If he didn't trust her now, there was no way he would permit her to live. Sooner or later, in his eyes, it would be time for her to die.

* * *

He appeared, dressed in a tuxedo, obviously having rummaged through Bill's closet and drawers until he found something that suited him.

"You're quite handsome," she said, forcing the corners of her mouth into the semblance of a smile. "Those clothes do you justice." She couldn't—didn't try to—stop the feelings of hatred from overflowing. *Son of a bitch. Give me half a chance, and I'll kill you.*

"Thank you," he replied. "Dominique, do me the honor, please, of dressing for dinner. I would like to see you in the beaded, white dress you wore the night of your garden party last summer. It will be even more beautiful by candlelight."

There was nothing to lose, and angrily, she lashed out. "Tell me, why should I bother to please you, Chez? You lied to me. You don't trust me at all, and you have no intention of letting me go. Just why the hell should I dress up for dinner? So they can find a beautiful, white, blood-stained dress on a headless corpse?"

He appeared genuinely surprised. "What are you talking about? Of course, I trust you. You say you can sense what I'm thanking. Well then, I'm yours; I'm open. Look inside," he pleaded.

She tried to quiet herself inwardly so she could feel what he was feeling. Slowly, an element of relief crept in. "Did you unload the gun I keep in my night stand and leave the bullets out for me to see?" she quizzed, careful not to speak about weapons in the plural.

The lines in his forehead deepened into furrows. "No. I swear to you. I did no such thing. I saw them when I walked through to the bathroom. I thought you had laid them out, but maybe, my mother put them there."

She gazed intently at the fiend she had once considered a friend. He wasn't lying. It confused her—sensing no danger from him, yet simultaneously perceiving hatred, buried deep, of a magnitude such as she had never known. She didn't want to comprehend what lay concealed from her or what it was she might confront at any moment. "I believe you. I'll dress as you wish," she said simply.

The grotto, containing statues of Our Lady of
Lourdes and Bernadette, stands on the
grounds of St. Mary's. Erected by Sister
Louis Gabriel, Mother Superior of the convent,
it was dedicated on May 25, 1922.

Tradition says that Sister Louis Gabriel
prayed on that day that so long as the grotto
stood, "Key West would never experience
the full brunt of a hurricane." So far, so good.

# 23

His head hurt, and the pain became more excruciating with each passing moment. His only relief was in knowing that the crisis with Dominique had passed.

She returned, a walking vision in crystal beads that caught and reflected the flickering candlelight. Her long mane was pulled into a loose chignon from which dangled occasional curls and stray wisps of hair. She wore diamond earrings and on her forehead, a steady hand had transformed the cut above her right eye into a henna-hued tree. Her appearance was at once ethereal and indomitable. He was struck by her overwhelming beauty and felt a sudden, and unfamiliar, sadness. He stood, felt unsteady, and leaned on his chair for support. Something was taking place he could not comprehend, something in which he was passive observer rather than active participant.

"Sit down, Chez. You must be feeling weak." She smiled at him. "Love is debilitating."

He didn't respond but slowly lowered himself into the chair situated at the head of the long dining table. With the ease of a skillful hostess, she poured him a glass of wine, twirling the bottle at the last moment, deftly avoiding the spilling of even a drop on what he recognized as an antique cloth. Serving herself, she took the hostess seat at the opposite end of the cherry wood table.

\* \* \*

Dominique brought the crystal goblet to her lips and swallowed long, ignoring the formality of raising her glass in the absence of a verbal toast and downing half the contents of the glass. Long moments passed in silence, and she closed her eyes and savored the alcoholic warmth that permeated her body and allowed a measure of relaxation amidst the night's horror.

"So beautiful and so rude. You've forgotten your manners, my dear."

The words, cold and cutting, instantly brought her back from the numbing mist of alcohol. She opened her eyes, then closed and reopened them. She told herself that what she saw sitting across from her wasn't real, all the while knowing better. *Oh, God. Please.*

Whether the image was macabre reality or lurid imagination made no difference. It was the antithesis of good, an effigy of evil whose nostrils released the putrid, dank air of that which has been ousted from God's light. In one clarifying instant dread encompassed her, a dread tempered by recognition that anticipation of death is not the ultimate fear. Rather, it is the possibility of losing the infinite spark that transcends life—the immaterial and eternal part of oneself—which elicits an unbridled fight or flee response. With that understanding, she resigned herself to physical death, if that was necessary, yet determined to acknowledge and face the vision—whatever it was—and to emerge with her immortal soul intact. She drank again without toasting, lowered the glass to the table and speared a piece of meat onto her fork. Enunciating each word clearly and precisely, she responded, "I have forgotten nothing. I do not knowingly honor iniquity." She slowly raised the fork to her mouth and removed the bit of steak.

Across the table, eyes that held her own darkened with rage. They smoldered, at first faintly, escalating in depth and degree until it was the crimson fire of hell that blazed unhidden. The deceitfully attractive face of a human killer had dissolved and melted into the features of another being—grotesque not in disfigurement but in its composite image of dark abomination.

Panoramic scenes rushed across her consciousness, forcing her to bear witness to man's inhumanity to others of its kind: nameless victims of merciless Crusades and Inquisitions; African slaves, dead and dying, in the holds of sea-crossing ships; Jews, gypsies, Catholics and gays forcibly marched into the gas chambers of Hitler's Third Reich; people at war, killing for the sake of one religion or another—always in the name of God or Allah or Jehovah.

A voice, at once alluring and repulsive, human yet bestial, spoke through the mouth of Juan Sanchez, Jr. "You needn't fear Chez, Dominique. He is mine to command." The smile was unmistakable. "I might add that you are extremely beautiful this evening, except of course, for that abhorrent tattoo." A long, pointed finger motioned in the direction of her forehead, at the tree of life she had carefully drawn for a reason even its human artist did not comprehend.

From beneath her unused napkin, where she had concealed it earlier, Dominique withdrew a silver and diamond cross bearing the corpus of the Christ. It was what she needed, a tangible something that represented God and her faith in the Supreme Being. She grasped the crucifix tightly. "And to whom do I speak?" she asked, fearing the answer before it was given.

"My name is whatever you choose it to be. It makes no difference to me at all. If it pleases you, Rolf del Castillo would be perfectly acceptable."

Immediately, it was Rolf who sat across from her, attired in formal wear, smiling, holding out his hand.

She stared in disgust. "Do not flatter yourself. You bear no resemblance to the man."

The words left her mouth, and Chez instantaneously re-appeared. "There now." The indescribable voice reverberated in her ears. "Do you find yourself more comfortable in the company of my servant with whom you've spent so many hours this day?" Chez smiled. It was not the smile she had seen earlier. This was a sneer of palpable animosity.

Dominique lifted the silver chain over her neck, settling the delicate crucifix between her breasts.

"Am I given to believe you suppose me to be a vampire? A creature who will grovel and melt at the sight of the man on the cross?" The metamorphic Chez laughed, filling the room with a howl of contemptuous malevolence.

The unbearable weight of infinity pressed against her chest, making it difficult to breathe. She knew herself to be in the presence of something not human. With effort, she responded, "I do not suppose you to be anything other than what you are. The crucifix has nothing to do with you. It is meant to remind me of a power higher than your own." *The Lord is my strength and my shield.* Over and over, she silently repeated the phrase to herself. It did not matter that in her present state it was the only part of the twenty-eighth Psalm she could remember. The words gave her solace, strength and continued sanity.

"And just who am I, my lovely?" His words mocked her.

"As you yourself said, the name makes no difference."

Whoever, whatever, it was that sat across from her continued to speak. "You are a unique woman, Dominique. There is much I can offer you. All that your heart desires is yours if you but choose to stand by my side." The voice was persuasive and melodic.

She felt warm, and her eyes closed. It was Rolf who spoke to her of eternal feelings, of a bond which could never to be severed. The effect was hypnotic and enticing. It would be so easy—too easy.

She forced her eyes open, fingered the cross around her neck and sadly eyed the illusory figure. "Why would anyone wish to be the companion of evil? As for myself, I find the thought repulsive." She uttered the words with disdain and, in trepidation, awaited the results of its wrath. What would happen to her she had no idea. Would there be pain, uncontrollable levitation, mutilation, or deformity at a wave of its hand? Something to punish her insolence? Could she stand firm in its grip?

Seconds passed, and nothing happened. The voice, however, turned harsh, "I have many brides, men as well as women. You would do well to reconsider."

She was sure of a barely audible hiss. Perhaps it was remnants of a childhood fantasy—the Book of Genesis and its serpent seen through the imagination of a child—that caused her to visualize eyes hooded with lazy, reptilian torpor, opening wide with hatred.

*The Lord is my strength and my shield.* A thought, crystal clear, materialized. It had no possible origin outside of the One to whom she prayed, and for the first time, she felt an air of confidence. "You have a problem, don't you?" It was a statement on her part, not a question. "You have tremendous ability to create discord, to bring about separation from God, but you can't carry it out except through humans, human beings who must freely choose to sell out to you. Otherwise, you're powerless. That's right, isn't it?"

"It is dangerous to underestimate what you're dealing with, Dominique Olivet. You should never play with high voltage."

Again she heard the low hiss. *The Lord is my strength and my shield.* "You want Chez to hurt me right now, but he won't do it. He's not completely under your control. Oh, he's done much to please you, but your possession isn't complete, is it? There's still a part of his soul that's not yours." Her words flowed on the energy of prayer and a faith that sometimes wavered but never left her.

It was Chez who spoke next, "Dominique, this is a wonderful dinner. The table is beautiful. You're beautiful. I love you as I have never loved another."

Whatever hidden part of his nature had revealed itself to her was now concealed. She had no illusions of having exorcized the demon that controlled Chez. It would lie in wait, to act again through the human steward of its evil.

She felt light-headed, and though the blood flowed hot in her veins, chills ran down her spine and raised the hairs on her arms. She eyed the contents of her goblet with suspicion. If she was ill, or if the wine had been drugged, much of what she thought transpired was probably a  hallucination, a figment of fever or drug-induced paranoia.

Trying hard to shake the cobwebs from her mind, she responded to Chez' compliment. "Thank you. We are a perfect match, you and I."

"Shall we toast to that, my darling?" His words held a tone of gentleness she had not heard before.

Her head spun, and she was fearful of finishing the wine that remained in her glass. Further and more horrific visions might be in store. If she wasn't thinking straight, she could lose control over the lethal game she had instigated. Chez might try conventional sex and find it unsatisfying. That would mean her death. If she had lived this long, surely she was meant to survive, to live out a natural life. Morbid possibilities floated on a disconcerting sea of fog. She had the wine bottle in one hand, was about to purposefully let it drop to the floor, when loud and insistent knocking sounded over the storm.

"Chez?" She was surprised and genuinely dismayed. A new person added to the mix might jeopardize her plan and her chances of survival.

* * *

Chez was not pleased. After Dominique's late-afternoon conversation with del Castillo, he'd insured she would have no further communication with the outside world. He had instructed his mother to cut the telephone lines and remove the cell phone battery. He was certain Dominique could not have called for help. Furthermore, he believed she didn't want help. She loved him. She had proved it. She belonged to him.

It had to be del Castillo; Dominique had told the bastard that he and his mother were there for the duration of the storm. The jackass was probably jealous. The wind had not slackened. Power lines were down. Coconuts and other flying missiles hit the house at intervals. Absent an emergency, only an idiot would attempt to travel the streets. No, it had to be the covetous lover out to assure a beautiful prize wasn't snatched from under his nose.

Irritation gave way to glee as he envisioned the prosecutor's distress at the scene that would unfold before him. He relished the anguish del Castillo would feel when he realized that Dominique now belonged, body and soul, to him, Juan Sanchez, Jr. "Answer the door, my dear. It will be all right."

Dominique approached the front entry and hesitated. He was right behind her. The eye of the hurricane had passed, changing the wind's direction; it was blowing against the door, and she needed his help to let in the adversary.

He was surprised to see not only del Castillo but Father Madera being blown through the doorway along with rain and debris. Neither man wore rain gear.

Dominique left the room, quickly returning with towels and robes. "Why are you out in this storm? What are you doing here?" she asked curtly.

He noticed she didn't invite the two men farther into the house. That pleased him. All of her actions tonight only served to convince him of her love, and he smiled to himself.

"The regular phone lines are down, and your cell isn't working either," the prosecutor responded.

Chez watched del Castillo's facial expression intently, amused at how disconcerted the man was by Dominique's less than enthusiastic reception.

"When we couldn't get through, Father and I became worried. We wanted to make sure everything was all right. You didn't tell me whether or not your cut was bad. You just hung up." Del Castillo's words trailed off, and he sounded apologetic.

"As you can see," Dominique replied, "we're doing just fine. Please go home. You know the back side of the hurricane is the most dangerous. At his age, your father has no business trying to look after the family and that big house all by himself."

* * *

Rolf took in the surreal scene—Chez in a tuxedo, Dominique, beautiful in evening dress, her forehead decorated with a vivid design sketched on and around what was an obviously fresh laceration. That she was nervous, and didn't want them there, was obvious. What the hell was going on?

"Nonsense, darling," Chez responded to Dominique's demand that they leave. "We need to be appreciative that our friends were concerned about you and willing to brave the storm to check on your safety. They're soaking wet, and it's dangerous out there. Francisco and Reina can handle things just fine until the wind calms."

Chez stepped up and slid his arm around Dominique's waist, plainly implying a relationship Rolf knew didn't exist. "Come in Rolf, Father," Chez said, directing them toward the main part of the house.

Dominique did not move away from Chez nor did she contradict him. "I'm sorry if I appeared rude or ungrateful. Please, come on in," she said, following Chez' lead.

Rolf stared hard at Chez. Did the man have no conception that this theatrical production was ludicrous? Akin to hanging out a sign that read, "Danger, Proceed With Caution"

Chez led the way to the dining room where the table, illuminated by candelabra, was elaborately set for two. "Dominique, do we have enough to invite our guests to dine with us?"

"I'm sure there's plenty, my love. I'm never short of food. You should know that."

"Wonderful." Chez smiled at her. "Please, sit down, won't you?" he said, pulling out a chair for Father Madera. "Perhaps, after we've eaten, Dominique can find some clothes for you among Bill's things." Again showing possessiveness, he stepped to her side and wiped hair away from the cut on her forehead.

Father's earlier demeanor had alarmed Rolf into sobriety, and he had grabbed the shoulder harness that held his .38; it was concealed under his jacket. From the look of Dominique's brow, this so-called friend of theirs had dared to hurt her. She had to be scared, or she wouldn't be so obviously trying to placate the man. Hot, Hispanic blood egged him on, demanded he avenge the injury to this woman. He breathed deeply, reminding himself that reason had to take precedence over impulse. Self-control was most important. If someone had to be hurt, it must be Chez and no one else.

He tried to assess the situation. Chez had a tendency to drink to excess; that was true. But, no matter how much he'd had, it was no excuse for what had apparently happened and was going on still. Moreover, he didn't believe Chez was drunk. He smelled only a mild odor of wine and had seen no evidence of hard booze. The man just appeared out of touch with reality. That made him extremely dangerous, and Rolf had no idea whether he was armed.

* * *

There was silence at the dinner table while all but one picked at their food. Only Chez ate with relish, enjoying each of the foods Dominique had laid out. .

It was Father who broke the silence. "Where is your mother, Chez? I thought Dominique said she was here."

Chez laid down his fork and wiped first one corner of his mouth and then the other with the embroidered linen napkin. He carefully re-folded the cloth along its original creases. Only then did he smile at Father Madera and acknowledge the question. "Mother's resting in the sunroom. Would you care to say hello, Father?"

"That might not be such a good idea," Dominique interjected in a panic. "Your mother's been very nervous about the hurricane, Chez. She was sleeping when we were last in there. I think it's better to let her remain oblivious until this thing has blown over."

She wasn't able to sway him. From across the table, he leveled his gaze at her, and once again, she was buffeted by a violent hatred. It was an emotion Chez didn't presently harbor toward her. This was not the man over whom she had managed to gain some semblance of influence. The other had reappeared.

"Heaven's no, Dominique. Father must indeed grace Mother with his presence. She would be completely distressed if she learned our pastor had been here, and we hadn't awakened her."

Dominique felt an urge to scream well up inside of her but kept silent, hoping Father, out of politeness, would elect not to go into the solarium.

The priest, however, pushed his arthritic body away from the table and rose. "Well then, I'll just have to talk to her and soothe away any fears she might have. God will, after all, protect us. He always does."

"Amen to that," Chez said, his eyes glowing as he made the sign of the cross.

The color washed from Dominique's face. He had performed the traditional sign of reverence to the Holy Trinity in a backward, mirror image. *Lord, please don't let me hallucinate now.* No one else seemed to notice the act of desecration.

Almost languidly Chez got up and followed the old priest.

* * *

Father Roberto Madera was as leery of the mother as he was fearful of the son. He understood this mother and son team well. He wished he did not. He was certain Rolf could protect Dominique as long as there was no dangerous interference from Anna Sanchez. His aim was to be sure of the woman's whereabouts and to do whatever he could to even the odds.

In his peripheral vision, as he entered the solarium, he caught sight of a pair of women's shoes, toes up on the floor. The vision made him choke on his own saliva, but it was too late to pretend he hadn't seen. He rushed to check on Anna Sanchez. There was no doubt in his mind that she would be dead.

He knelt by the side of Chez' mother, his mind jumbled, feeling for a non-existent pulse. This was the great love and master influence in the man's life. Why would Chez have done this? He scrutinized the body. During the early fifties he had served as an army chaplain and had seen horrific injuries during the Korean War. His eyes traveled to her head, and he knew instantly that her neck was broken. Chez had confessed first to the murder of Regina and then to that of his own father. Now, the death of his mother was on his soul.

"It seems she's resting quite well, Father. I don't believe there's any way of waking her, do you? After all, she is not Lazarus, and you are not the great man himself." The tone of Chez' voice was conversational, if not jovial.

"Dearest son, what have you done now? Your own mother? Why?" Tears of pity ran down his face. Dominique had been right, of course. The killer in Chez had no remorse, but, there was also the man who occasionally came to confession—the one who cried over deeds he had committed, who questioned what it was that took him over and who wondered whether it wouldn't be better to kill himself and rid the earth of his presence. That was the Chez who understood the evil of his acts and offered true contrition. That was the soul to whom absolution had been granted. That was not the man who was speaking to him.

"It's simple, old man. She was a threat to Dominique. I killed her to protect what is mine and to prove to Dominique that no one is more important than she is."

As he buried his face in his hands, weeping for the loss of a soul he had hoped was salvageable, he felt Chez' breath on the back of his neck.

\* \* \*

Chez reached into his pants pocket and withdrew the garrote. He lightly tapped Father Madera on the shoulder. He did not want this to be a surprise. This time he wanted his victim to see what was coming, to breathe the fear, to experience the anguish of knowing he was about to die. He wanted the priest to understand that the fate of John the Baptist would be his—minus, of course, the head's presentation on a silver platter. He could feel the pleasure welling, was disappointed the physical reaction was nowhere close to what Dominique could arouse with just her voice. He raised the wire.

Dominique screamed, "No!"

Immediately, there was a shot, and he turned. Dominique stood between him and an ashen-faced del Castillo. Chez saw her sway and knew she had been hit. He wanted to go to her, to help her, but she was conscious, not dead, and his instinct for survival prevailed. He ran toward the door leading to the garden. Del Castillo was in love. Even knowing that Dominique had thrown herself in front of him to block his shot, the idiot would stop and take care of her. That would provide precious seconds to make it out. Del Castillo was armed, and Chez had to save himself. Later, he could return for Dominique and reward her for this second demonstration of love and loyalty.

The boarded-up glass door to the back yard was going with, not against, the strength of Elvira's winds. The protective plywood was heavy, but one small push and the hurricane did the rest, slamming the door against the side of the house. The unprotected inside panes of glass exploded on impact and became deadly shooting knives. One skimmed through his hair, cutting skin and sending blood into his eyes. Adrenalin pumping, he ignored the cut. Blood was no aphrodisiac now.

He made it to the hedge that separated Dominique's property from the sidewalk and tried to crawl through to the open space beyond. It was physically impossible. The trunks of the old Bougainvilleas had grown fat, intertwined with age and formed a barrier denser than any he had penetrated in the underbrush of Vietnam.

He changed direction, keeping low to avoid the power of the cyclonic wind that made standing and using his legs impossible. Even if he could fight the wind and stand, he would succeed only in becoming a target for debris spiraling through the air. He clung to the bases of the bushes and trees, striving to reach the side gate.

He didn't look back; he didn't need to. Years of jungle warfare had honed his instincts, and he prided himself on his ability to smell the enemy stalking. He kicked his feet constantly, anticipating an attack, protecting himself from the rabid prosecutor who probably trailed not far behind. Out here, he didn't worry about being shot. There was no way del Castillo could aim and fire during this exhibition of nature's fury.

When, at last, he made it to the gate, it took every bit of strength he possessed to pull himself upright. He reached for the latch that held the wrought iron gate closed and cursed when he found it was locked. He would have to climb over. Unwinding a foot from the gate's upright bars, he lifted his leg. One vicious gust, and suddenly, he was no more than a human banner blowing in the wind, attached to the gate by the vise-like grip of his hands.

\* \* \*

There had been no time for Rolf to aim carefully and no choice but to shoot. His thought had been that if he didn't bring Chez down, or at least manage to distract him, the wire would cut, and it would be too late to save Father Madera. To his horror, it was Dominique, already unsteady on her feet and shifting her stance, who had been the recipient of his bullet.

Frozen in horror, he had watched the scene as it unfolded in front of him—Dominique bracing herself against the wall, Chez pushing open the solarium door and rushing into the storm. Breathless, heart pounding, Rolf had forced himself to move, to run to her side and confront what he had done. Her knees had buckled, but she hadn't fallen.

"It's all right!" She had screamed, trying to reassure him over the din of the hurricane that had now infiltrated the house through the open door. "I'm okay!"

\* \* \*

Convincing himself that Dominque wasn't seriously wounded, Rolf worked his way outside. He dragged himself across the ground, much as a paraplegic might do, using upper body strength to pull himself along and stay on Chez' heels—gritting his teeth against the pain of intense exertion too soon after surgery. The full force of Elvira's previously sustained winds was no longer battering the island, but she continued to play a violent game of darts, and airborne debris hurled itself indiscriminately at targets. He winced as shards from a broken terra cotta pot sliced through his shirt sleeve. Amazingly, it inflicted only a surface cut. The propelling gust was the hurricane's final, brutal blast at Key West. From that moment forward, the island city merited only vestiges of Elvira's most passionate winds. Much as a human being discards a lover, she began a slow withdrawal, continuing her travel into the Gulf of Mexico.

As the last hard gust dissipated, Chez' lower body abruptly dropped to the ground. Immediately, he went into defensive mode, moving his body forward toward escape while striking out with his feet at anyone who pursued. Rolf lunged, grabbed Chez' ankle and inhaled sharply as the diminished force of a kick caught him in the ribs. His chest throbbed, and he wondered if the incision had ruptured. He fell hard, pulling Chez with him face first into the mud.

"Rodolfo!" Over his labored breathing, Rolf heard Father Madera's scream. The wind garbled what the priest was saying, but Rolf recognized urgency in his voice. He turned his head trying to make out the words, unwittingly giving Chez the opportunity he needed to pull his leg free. Before Rolf realized what was happening, Chez' fist slammed against the side of his head, momentarily stunning him.

Chez leaped toward the gate.

"Rodolfo! Come back!" Father Madera was bent low, partially out of the house, trying to fight his way closer. It was still dangerous to be outside, and the elderly man was no match for the slackened remains of the storm winds. There had to be something gravely wrong.

"Go back, Father! I'm coming!" Rolf yelped and grabbed his chest as the exertion of filling his lungs with air after Chez' kick caused another sharp pain to run the length of the incision. He tentatively moved his finger over the area. Everything appeared to be holding together.

Anger momentarily replaced the hurt, and he shook a fist at a retreating Chez, "Go ahead! Get out of here if you can! They'll find you! If they don't, I will!"

He applied pressure to his chest in an effort to ease the latest stabbing sensations and steadily made his way back to Father Madera. Though he could no longer see Chez and did not expect a response, he heard it clearly as the wind blew the words his way. "She's mine, del Castillo! Mine forever! Take that and stick it up your ass! Everything she did, she did for me! Do you understand? For me! She would die for me! You're a loser, Rolf! You always were!"

Rolf spoke under his breath, the words intended more for himself than anyone else. "You're sick. Really sick, man. You need to be locked up."

\* \* \*

Dominique lay crumpled on the floor.

"Oh, God, No!" Rolf raced to her side and gently lifted her to a sitting position.

She was alive, but her body shook, and she attempted to curl into the fetal position. "You didn't do this," she said, her eyes glazed. She moaned, and her teeth chattered. "I've been sick all night, and I'm so cold. Get me a blanket, please. I'm freezing."

Rolf spoke, more in control of his emotions. "Father, look for a thermometer." He held Dominique close, trying to warm her with his own body heat.

Father Madera returned quickly and held out a plastic container. "I've seen her stick this thing in Jordan's ear."

Rolf grabbed the thermometer from his hand. With one arm, he held Dominique; with the free hand he maneuvered the instrument into her ear. He looked at the readout, cleared the thermometer and tried again. It still read 104.7. She continued to moan and shiver in his arms, a sure sign of a rising fever.

"Where's there a tub?" he asked the priest. "I've got to get her fever down."

"There's a spa in the downstairs bathroom, but that's hot water, and it's probably not cooled off. There are two tubs upstairs, I think. She would have filled them with water." He wrinkled his forehead. "Rodolfo, don't panic. I'm no doctor, but I've never heard of an adult having a seizure because of a fever. I think that just happens to children. Why don't we put her to bed, give her some aspirin and force some fluids?"

Rolf did not respond to the suggestion, instead speaking directly to Dominique. "Princess, listen to me. When we were kids and got that horrible flu, you ran a high fever. I don't know if you remember, but you had a seizure. Father's probably right, and that doesn't happen to adults, but I don't know enough to take a chance. We've got to bring this fever down." Without waiting for an answer, he lifted in his arms.

"Rolf, let me take her," Father Madera said. "You shouldn't be doing that after your surgery."

"Don't worry about it, Father. If the incision hasn't ruptured at this point, it isn't going to." He climbed the stairs, the old priest leading the way with a hurricane lamp. For the first time, he noticed how much the pain was directly related to the expansion of his lungs, so he avoided breathing deeply.

"Second door to the left," Father volunteered when they reached the second floor hallway.

Rolf pushed the door open with his foot, sat Dominique on the toilet seat, with one hand holding her steady, while he unzipped and removed her gown with the other.

"Please don't hate me for this," he mumbled as he lowered her into the cool water. Instantly, she began to kick and scream; water went everywhere as she struggled to get out. Fully clothed, he stepped into the tub, wrapped his arms around her and held her down.

"Father, give me a mouthwash cup." He motioned in the direction of the sink. "And see if you can find aspirin or anything else that will bring the fever down."

Father Madera fished a bottle from the medicine chest and held it out to him.

Rolf shook his head trying to clear his eyes of the water Dominique was splashing. "Fill the cup from the tub and give me four of those." After some effort, he placed the pills in Dominique's mouth and coaxed her to swallow. She continued to whimper as he held her tightly.

An hour later her temperature had dropped to just under 100.2, and she was quiet. He lifted her, limp and exhausted, from the tub and dried her off. Once she was settled in bed, he fashioned a dressing for her surface wound, then wrapped his ribs tightly with an Ace Bandage he found in the medicine chest. The fact that it lessened his pain considerably probably meant that Chez' kick had cracked one or more ribs.

He needed to know what had taken place before he arrived, but that would have to wait until Dominique felt well enough to discuss what must have been a terrible experience. Foremost in his mind was that he had no idea what had caused such a high fever; she should be seen by a doctor as soon as possible.

He sat, holding her hand, until she fell asleep.

* * *

Rolf checked the French doors as well as the windows of Dominique's bedroom to insure they were securely locked and motioned to Father Madera. "We need to do something about the body. We can't just leave it there. In this heat and humidity, she'll begin to reek, and the odor will permeate everything. There's no way to get rid of that kind of stench."

"Isn't there a law or something that says you can't move a corpse until the police show up?" the priest asked hesitantly.

"We can't notify the P.D. until the phones work, and even then, they'll figure a dead body's not going to go anywhere. They'll take care of emergencies first," Rolf responded testily. "I don't see that we have much choice. I'll just have to outline the body and go from there." He found pronouns disconcerting when referring to the body; he presumed "it" was grammatically correct, but wasn't comfortable dehumanizing someone who had been alive only hours earlier. That, together with a constantly aching chest, made him extremely irritable.

Father Madera helped him wrap the body in garbage bags. It was early morning before it was safe to venture out, and Rolf, with Father Madera's help, hoisted the body over his shoulder and carried it to the patio. He set the plastic-wrapped corpse down and, despite the pain, breathed deeply of the wet clean air. As soon as the clouds parted, warmth would become intense heat and Key West, a veritable steam bath. When that happened, to simply fill your lungs with air would be a chore.

* * *

He wasn't prepared to see Chez step into view. Without warning, the man stood less than ten feet in front of him, a look of pure hatred imprinted on his face.

"You stupid fool," Chez hissed. "Did you really think I'd leave Dominique here for you?"

Chez held an axe in his hand, and Rolf was unarmed. His .38 lay on the floor by the side of Dominique's bed. "Chez, listen to me, man.  You're sick." He stalled, trying to give himself time to think. "You need to go someplace where they can help you."

"What you mean is, you think I'm crazy.  You can't accept that I was *hombre* enough to take Dominique away from you.  Sure, just lock me up, and throw away the key.  That would solve everything for you, wouldn't it?" Chez was screaming, his face red and contorted. He laughed and lifted his arms high, holding the axe directly overhead—taking aim.

There was no doubt in Rolf's mind that he was about to die. Chez had been with Special Forces in Viet Nam. He had the ability and the strength to land the axe. There would be no recovery from that.

As Rolf stared, immobile, a sudden look of panic crossed Chez' features, and he screamed. "Careful!"

The noise was intense, like the sonic boom of a military jet directly overhead.  Chez' body stiffened, and the axe dropped from his hands. There was another deafening roar, and he fell backward into the pool.

Rolf turned to look behind him. Dominique stood by the open door, braced against the remaining gusts of wind, wet hair thrashing her face and the still brightly emblazoned Tree of Life. In her hands, she clenched his .38. No less frozen in place than an albino-white, street mime, she remained perfectly still, the .38 aimed directly at the spot where Chez had stood only a moment earlier.

He walked to her, took the gun and laid it down. His arms went around her, and he buried his face in her hair. "I told you not to get out of bed."

She leaned on him, and he supported her as they walked to the edge of the pool. Together, they peered through floating rubble into the black water.  It was the most bizarre sight he had ever seen.

Eyes open wide and bulging, Chez stared up, his mouth opening and closing rhythmically like a fish, sending bubbles of air to the surface. Very much alive, his feet kicked and his arms thrashed; yet, he seemed unable to do anything but move in place. The look on his face was one of horror. He was drowning, and he knew it.

Reason told Rolf to jump in and pull the lunatic out, save him for the justice of the courts. Instead, he turned to look at Dominique. She continued to stare into the water, a cold and detached look on her face. There was no doubt she had to be seeing what he was seeing, but she seemed oddly unsurprised by the scene playing itself out before them. He said nothing, knew that something was happening he wasn't a part of. Fascination kept him from action, and he continued to watch her. She slowly closed her eyes; her face softened. She made no sound as tears followed one another slowly down her cheeks.

Seconds later, she signed herself with the cross. "In the name of the Father, the Son and the Holy Spirit."

Chez stopped his frantic flailing and floated slowly to the surface.

Built in 1847 to guide ships attempting to
navigate dangerous reefs, the 46 feet tall lighthouse
was extended to 86 feet in 1894. It is located
at 938 Whitehead Street.

You can climb 88 iron steps to see spectacular
views of the city and the ocean beyond.

# 24

Rolf fished a gasping and bleeding Chez from the water's surface. There was no need for CPR, and neither shot appeared to be lethal. Rolf tied up the man who had once been his friend. He wanted to beat him to a pulp but, instead, threw him into a chair in the solarium, secured him to it and did what was necessary to stem the flow of blood.

He walked with Dominique to her bedroom, left her there—this time under Father's watchful eyes—and went to check on the jailor. Tiny proved difficult to arouse, but four strong cups of coffee later, he was coherent and able to function. He agreed to sit with Sanchez until the police could be notified and were able to respond. Rolf had no fear of Tiny falling asleep again; the man's head was smarting too badly.

When he again went into the solarium to let Tiny know he had contacted the police, Chez looked directly at him and spoke without visible emotion. "She's mine. You remember that, del Castillo."

Rolf walked out without responding.

\* \* \*

Although she had remained in her room, Dominique wasn't in bed; he found her up, sitting in a chair. She had opened the French doors and was staring at the quieting scene outside.

"The hurricane didn't do any irreparable damage to the garden," were her first words when she acknowledged his presence.

He knelt at her side and whispered softly, "How about you, princess? Did he do you any irreparable damage?"

She didn't hesitate. "No. The emotional baggage will heal. I have children who need me. I can't dwell on the past."

"Are you up to telling me what happened before I got here?"

"If I can have something to drink first."

"How about a cup of coffee? I made some for Tiny on the camp stove."

"I'd prefer a glass of Absinthe."

His eyes widened, and he grinned. She was going to be all right. "That stuff's illegal; it's loaded with oil of wormwood. It drove Van Gogh insane, you know."

"Nevertheless, I smuggled a couple of bottles into the country. They're in the wet bar."

"Don't tell me how you managed that. It's none of my business."

She smiled wearily at him. "I'm very tired, Rolf. Give me a couple of hours to sort this all out in my head, and then we'll talk.

* * *

It was much later when the officers arrived. They wanted to interview Dominique. Rolf lied and said she was sleeping. He gave the police his statement and told them she would come to the station, or they could come back after her surface wound had been seen and treated and the doctor had determined that whatever had caused her high fever no longer posed a threat. The cops didn't push and busied themselves with arrangements to process and remove the body.

As soon as they were gone, Rolf returned to her bedroom. He had many questions, but urging him on was a powerful need to know what it was that had transpired at the pool. Had her perceptions been the same as his? When the time came, however, he couldn't bring himself to ask. Perhaps she didn't know the answer, and if she did, maybe it wasn't something he was ready to hear, not yet.

He handed her a small glass of the translucent, green liquid and fished for the details that would later help make the prosecution's case. Several drinks of the ancient liqueur warmed her and loosened her tongue. She told him the basics of what he wanted to know; it nauseated him. It was an effort not to sound shocked, but for her sake, he tried. "You did what you had to do to survive. It was foolish to set yourself up like that, but it took a great deal of courage." She looked away, staring toward the garden, and he laid his hand on her knee. "If your children were old enough to understand, they would be angry but proud. They are fortunate to have you for a mother, princess."

Tears streamed down her face.

He took her in his arms and held her close.

\* \* \*

Dominique didn't want to close the French doors. "I want to see him go," she said. "I want him to see me watching. I want him to know I tried to kill him. And, I did, you know. At that moment, I wanted him dead." Together, she and Rolf watched as Chez was led away in handcuffs.

Chez did not go easily, thrashing and screaming despite his injuries. "She loves me, del Castillo! One of these days you'll realize that! Right before she kills you!"

Dominique looked at Rolf in disbelief. "Good Lord, how can he still believe I love him?"

"You have to remember, he's delusional. He believes in the reality of what it is that he wants to be true. In his mind, you weren't accidentally hit. You took that bullet to save him; he as much as told me so. He said you would die for him. He believes that, so it must have been an easy step to convince himself that you were aiming at me when you wounded him."

Chez' eyes remained glued on Dominique as he kicked and cursed the officers restraining him. His last words were directed at her, and she knew, without a doubt, that it was not Chez who crossed in front of her doors. This time, she couldn't blame what she saw and heard on a fever. Her eyes were held by those of a grotesque being, growling words and uttering garbled sounds she had no trouble comprehending. She crossed herself and looked away.

The last sound was that of the patrol car pulling away with the Key West killer and the men who guarded him.

"Could you understand any of that mumbo-jumbo?" Rolf asked.

"Yes." she said with contempt. "He was telling me that it isn't over—that I shouldn't play with high voltage."

Rolf frowned. "In his warped way, he loves you. Why the hell would he threaten you?"

"Because he isn't himself. There's something inside that takes over and controls him. I don't know if he's insane, if he has a split personality or if he's possessed. If he's evil, is he all evil? Maybe there's a shred of his soul that deserves mercy and is sorry for the horrible things he does. Only God can judge."

She paused, looked up at him and added softly, "I had to make myself remember that. Otherwise, I would have let him die." She was giving him an opening to ask about the unexplainable. He didn't take it.

* * *

The ordeal was over, and it was time for Rolf to leave.

"How about me?" he asked.

"What?" She knew what he meant, but she stalled momentarily, too tired to be able to think quickly and pursue the avenue down which he was traveling.

"I don't want to pressure you, princess, but I need to know. Am I a part of the past you can forget? Something you need to put behind you?" His eyes fixed on hers, unwavering, waiting for an answer.

She sighed and ran a finger over his lips. "Rolf, you have always been, and always will be, a part of my life. That's a problem I can't cope with right now."

"I understand. I can't ask for more, than that." He lowered his gaze.

She kissed him goodbye, wanting to hold on but knowing she would not. "Go Now. Your family needs you."

## To lighten the mood, read about these great old places a native conch still enjoys.

**El Siboney** - 900 Catherine Street - serves reasonably priced and delectable Cuban cuisine. A favorite is the Cuban chicken-fried steak.

**Fausto's** - at two locations - 1105 White Street and 522 Fleming Street - was first opened in 1926 by Faustino Castillo, who was born in Cuba in 1888 and came to Key West at the age of twelve. They carry many of the Cuban everyday foods and vegetables, as well as other Caribbean delicacies.

**Jose's Cantina** - a hole-in-the-wall restaurant on the corner of White and Petronia Streets, serves a mouth-watering Boliche and pressed-crisp, Cuban sandwiches.

**L. Valladares & Sons Newsstand** - 1200 Duval Street - has been in Key West for approximately 75 years, selling to the likes of President Harry S. Truman, Ernest Hemingway and Tennessee Williams. It is, and has always been, a family-owned Conch business. It carries approximately 3,000 titles, including softbound books.

**La Concha Hotel** - 430 Duval Street - in the heart of Old Town is a seven-story skyscraper (There aren't very many tall buildings in this island city) opened in January 1926. Among its guests have numbered royalty, presidents and Pulitzer Prize winners. There is a beautiful island view from the rooftop bar. Aside from elegance and history, another claim to fame is that several people have jumped to their deaths from the top of this highrise.

**The Five Brothers' Grocery & Sandwich Shop** - 930 Southard - at the corner of Southard and Grinnell - has been at this location for 26 years. They have the best Bollos (Cuban hushpuppies) and a great Cuban mix sandwich.

**Wyndham Casa Marina Resort** - 1500 Reynold Street - Built in 1920, by Henry Flagler of railroad fortune fame, it was used by the Navy as Officers' Quarters during World War II and later re-opened to the public. The Astors, the Vanderbilts, Al Jolson, Gregory Peck, Rita Rayworth, Ethel Mermen and many other notables all stayed here.

The following are excerpts from The Key West Citizen Newspaper. They were taken from the Crime Report, Citizens' Voice, Today In Keys History & general articles.

A shoplifter snatched a life-sized inflatable doll of a woman with a built-in vibrator. The man ran down the street and ducked into an alley. The police report said the doll's name was Terry.

Pirate-Loving candidate eyes city treasures - Dressing the cops up like pirates - is the city ready for it? If so, then Sloan Young has a shot at becoming the next mayor. We need to enhance our history, playing on the pirate, said Young, 61. We came here because it's a seedy place. We have clothing optional bars and brothels, and I don't want to change that. This is a very mystical place.

Key West's museum of the bizarre is missing a three-legged chicken. The stuffed attraction disappeared from Ripley's Believe It or Not! The museum hosted a liquor promotion party and about 300 people were in and out. Despite security checkpoints, the chicken slipped through.

Using a stolen credit card makes you a criminal. Using it to buy jewelry in the place you work makes you an unemployed criminal. Such may be the plight of a Key West cashier who is now wanted for grand theft.

1953 - The crew filming the movie Beneath the 12 Mile Reef arrived and took over the Casa Marina Hotel.

## Excerpts Continued.....

1982 - The Florida Keys seceded from the Union in a ceremony to protest the Border Patrol establishing a road block at Florida City to check the citizenship of everyone leaving Monroe County. Traffic delays at the roadblock caused a dramatic drop in tourist traffic to the Keys. Prime Minister Dennis Wardlow then announced the establishment of the Conch Republic.

Marriage, like tattooing, can also be regrettable...waiting period or not! You (who I assume have no tattoos) are putting way too much energy into worrying about a tattoo on a body that one wishes they no longer had. I didn't even put that much thought into the marriage that I once had that I wish I hadn't.

Officers responding to a fire alarm encountered two naked swimmers. According to reports, they left their belongings by the pool. A man started to watch them around 3:30 a.m. They said he was smiling as he sprinted off. Shortly thereafter, they exited the pool and had a better idea what the man had found so funny. He ran off with approximately $1,063 of their clothing and other belongings, including a cell phone. They pulled the fire alarm to call for help.

A woman seemed surprised when the homeless man she let sleep in her home disappeared with $429 she kept in the refrigerator. She received a case number and the suspect probably received a case of beer.

Gotta love the Weather Channel. One of their talking heads actually said that Dennis will strike Key West early Saturday and then hit U.S. soil around the Florida panhandle on Sunday. Either they need geography lessons up in Atlanta, or else they take this Conch Republic concept really seriously.

Excuse me, where should I park? I don't know and I don't care. I ride my bike everywhere. Excuse me, how much is gas? I don't know, all I know is, the gas I pass is free. Get a bike.